REGULAR SHOW™

NOIR MEANS NOIR, BUDDY

REGULAR SHOW: NOIR MEANS NOIR, BUDDY, August 2015. Published by KaBOOM!, a division of Boom Entertainment, Inc. REGULAR SHOW, CARTOON NETWORK, the logos, and all related characters and elements are trademarks of and © Cartoon Network. (S15) All rights reserved. KaBOOM!™ and the KaBOOM! logo are trademarks of Boom Entertainment, Inc., registered in various countries and categories. All characters, events, and institutions depicted herein are fictional. Any similarity between any of the names, characters, persons, events, and/or institutions in this publication to actual names, characters, and persons, whether living or dead, events, and/or institutions is unintended and purely coincidental. KaBOOM! does not read or accept unsolicited submissions of ideas, stories, or artwork.

For information regarding the CPSIA on this printed material, call: (203) 595-3636 and provide reference #RICH – 619782. A catalog record of this book is available from OCLC and from the KaBOOM! website, www.kaboom-studios.com, on the Librarians Page.

BOOM! Studios, 5670 Wilshire Boulevard, Suite 450, Los Angeles, CA 90036-5679. Printed in USA. First Printing.

ISBN: 978-1-60886-712-7, eISBN: 978-1-61398-383-6

REGULAR SHOW™

NOIR MEANS NOIR, BUDDY

CREATED BY JG QUINTEL

WRITTEN BY
RACHEL CONNOR
& ROBERT LUCKETT

ILLUSTRATED BY
WOOK JIN CLARK

COLORS BY
FRED STRESING

LETTERS BY
SHAWN ALDRIDGE

COVER BY
ANDY HIRSCH

DESIGNER
KARA LEOPARD

ASSISTANT EDITOR
MARY GUMPORT

EDITOR
SHANNON WATTERS

WITH SPECIAL THANKS TO MARISA MARIONAKIS, RICK BLANCO, NICOLE RIVERA, CONRAD MONTGOMERY,
MEGHAN BRADLEY, CURTIS LELASH, KELLY CREWS AND THE WONDERFUL FOLKS AT CARTOON NETWORK.

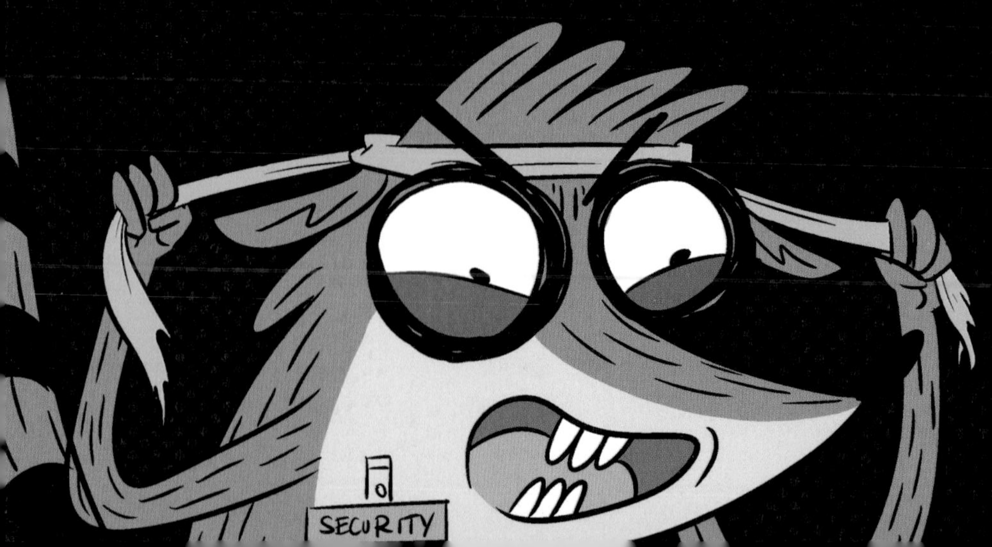
SECURITY

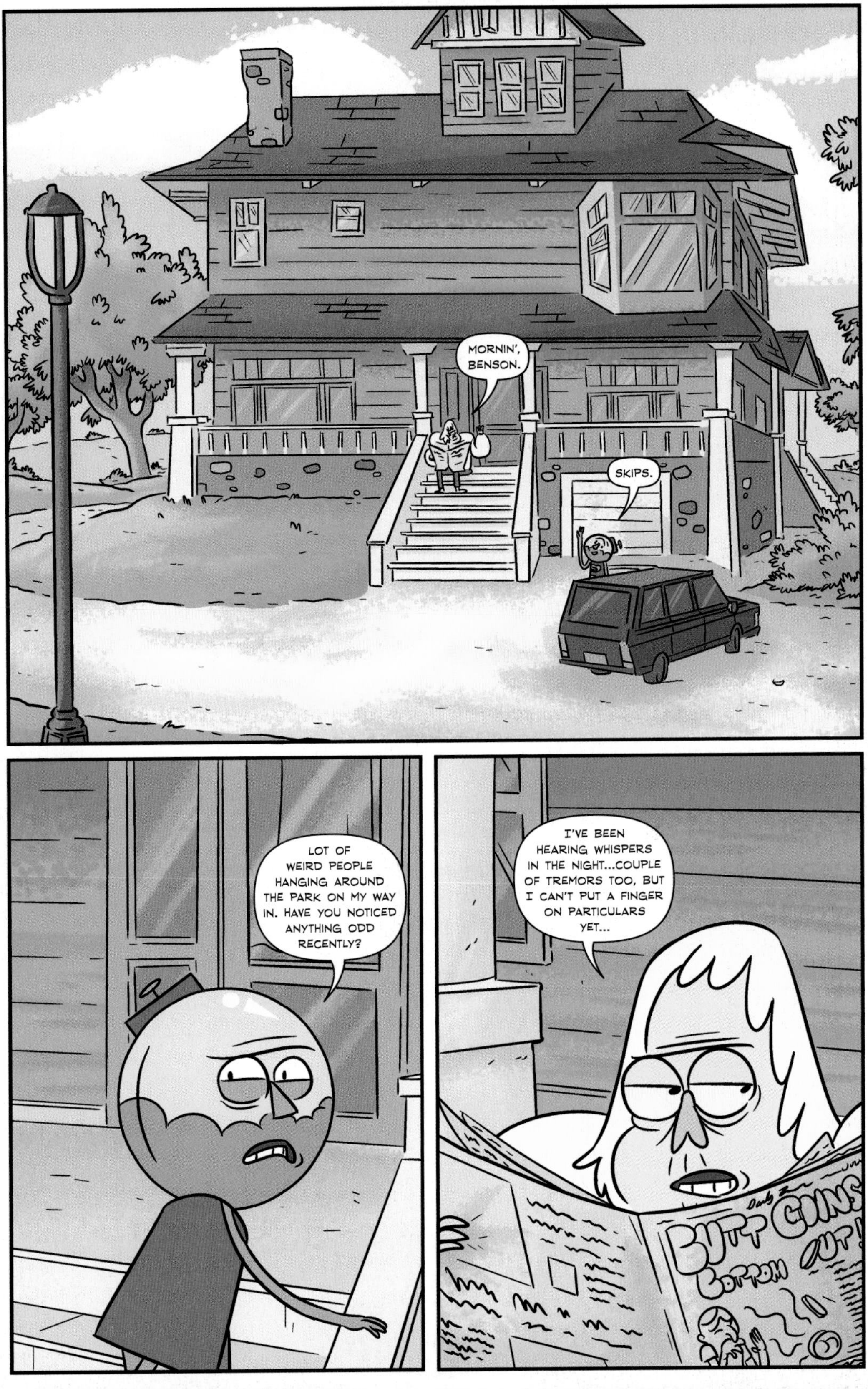
MORNIN', BENSON.
SKIPS.
LOT OF WEIRD PEOPLE HANGING AROUND THE PARK ON MY WAY IN. HAVE YOU NOTICED ANYTHING ODD RECENTLY?
I'VE BEEN HEARING WHISPERS IN THE NIGHT...COUPLE OF TREMORS TOO, BUT I CAN'T PUT A FINGER ON PARTICULARS YET...
BUTT COINS BOTTOM OUT!

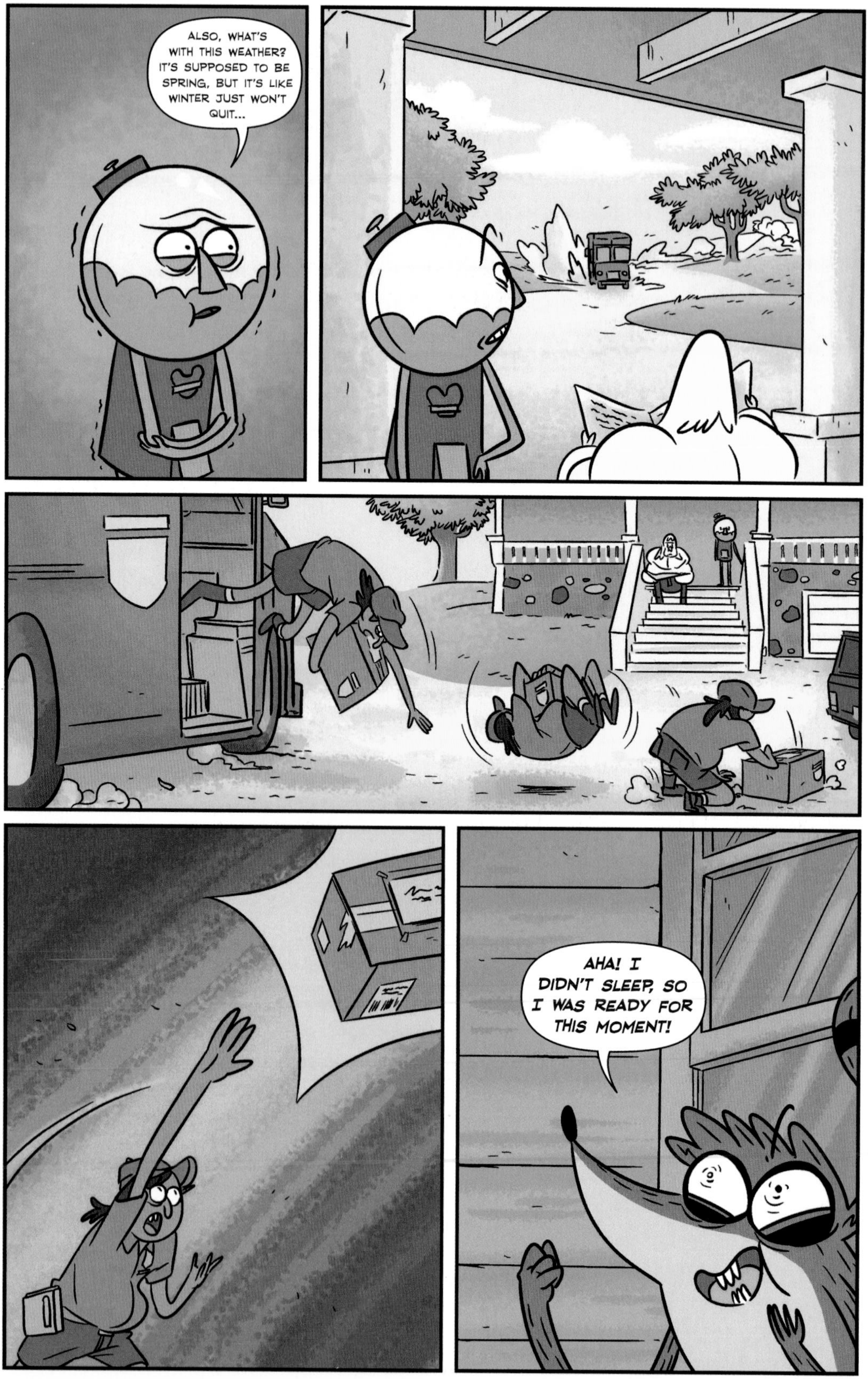
ALSO, WHAT'S WITH THIS WEATHER? IT'S SUPPOSED TO BE SPRING, BUT IT'S LIKE WINTER JUST WON'T QUIT...
AHA! I DIDN'T SLEEP, SO I WAS READY FOR THIS MOMENT!

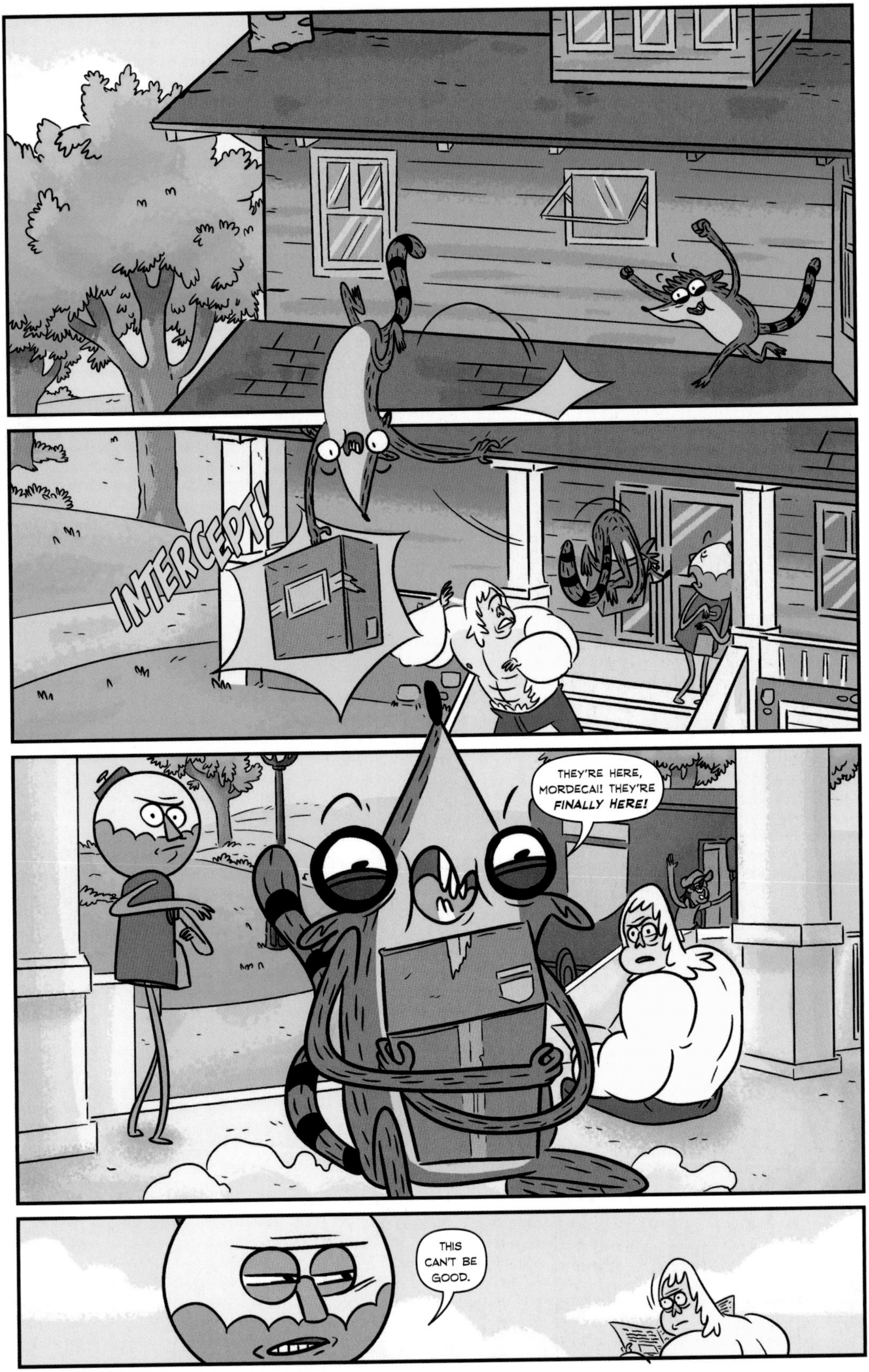
INTERCEPT!
THEY'RE HERE, MORDECAI! THEY'RE *FINALLY HERE!*
THIS CAN'T BE GOOD.

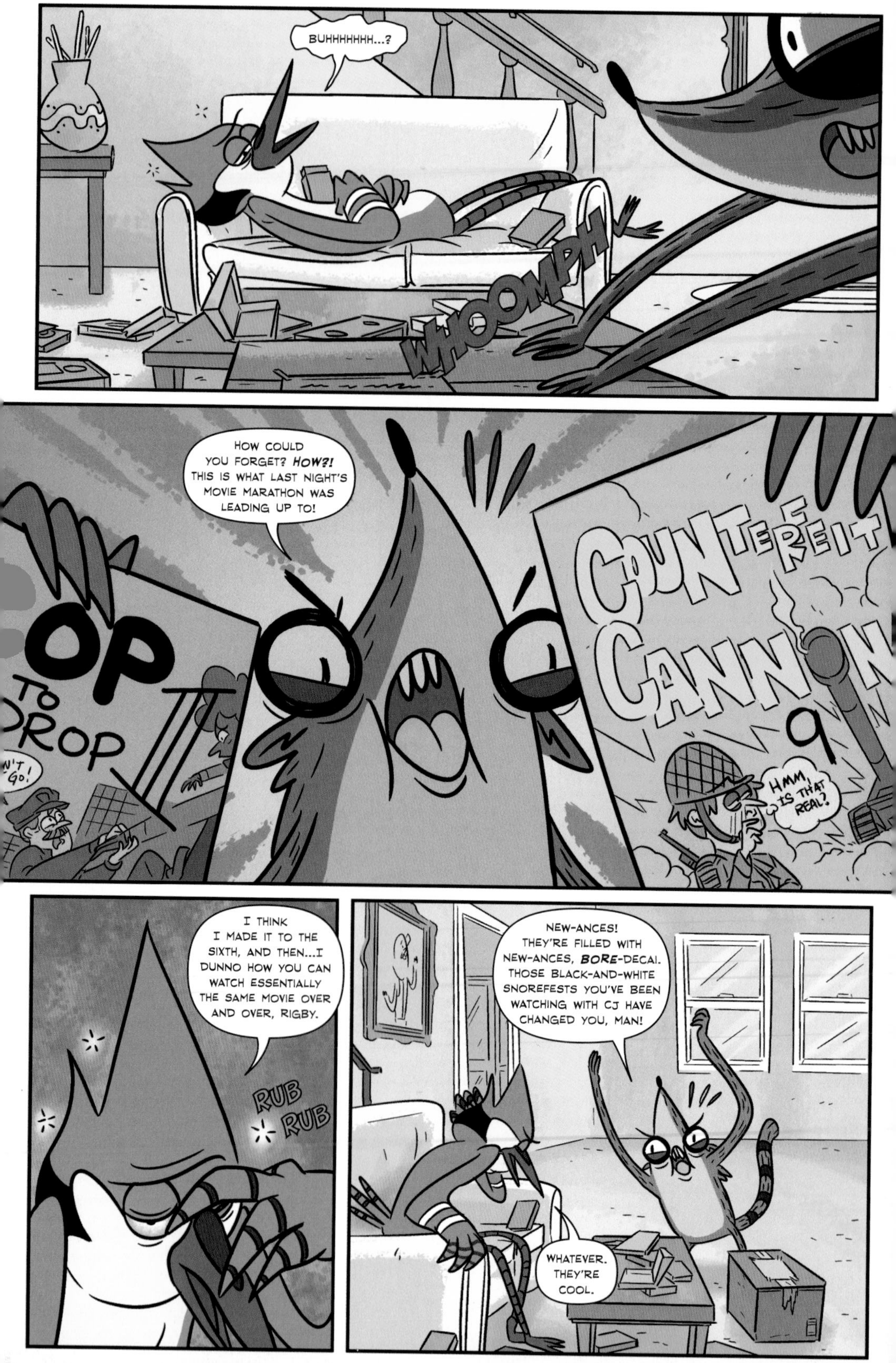

BUHHHHHHH...?
WHOOMPH
HOW COULD YOU FORGET? HOW?! THIS IS WHAT LAST NIGHT'S MOVIE MARATHON WAS LEADING UP TO!
OP
TO
ROP
COUNTERFEIT CANNON 9
HMM, IS THAT REAL?
I THINK I MADE IT TO THE SIXTH, AND THEN...I DUNNO HOW YOU CAN WATCH ESSENTIALLY THE SAME MOVIE OVER AND OVER, RIGBY.
RUB RUB
NEW-ANCES! THEY'RE FILLED WITH NEW-ANCES, BORE-DECAI. THOSE BLACK-AND-WHITE SNOREFESTS YOU'VE BEEN WATCHING WITH CJ HAVE CHANGED YOU, MAN!
WHATEVER. THEY'RE COOL.

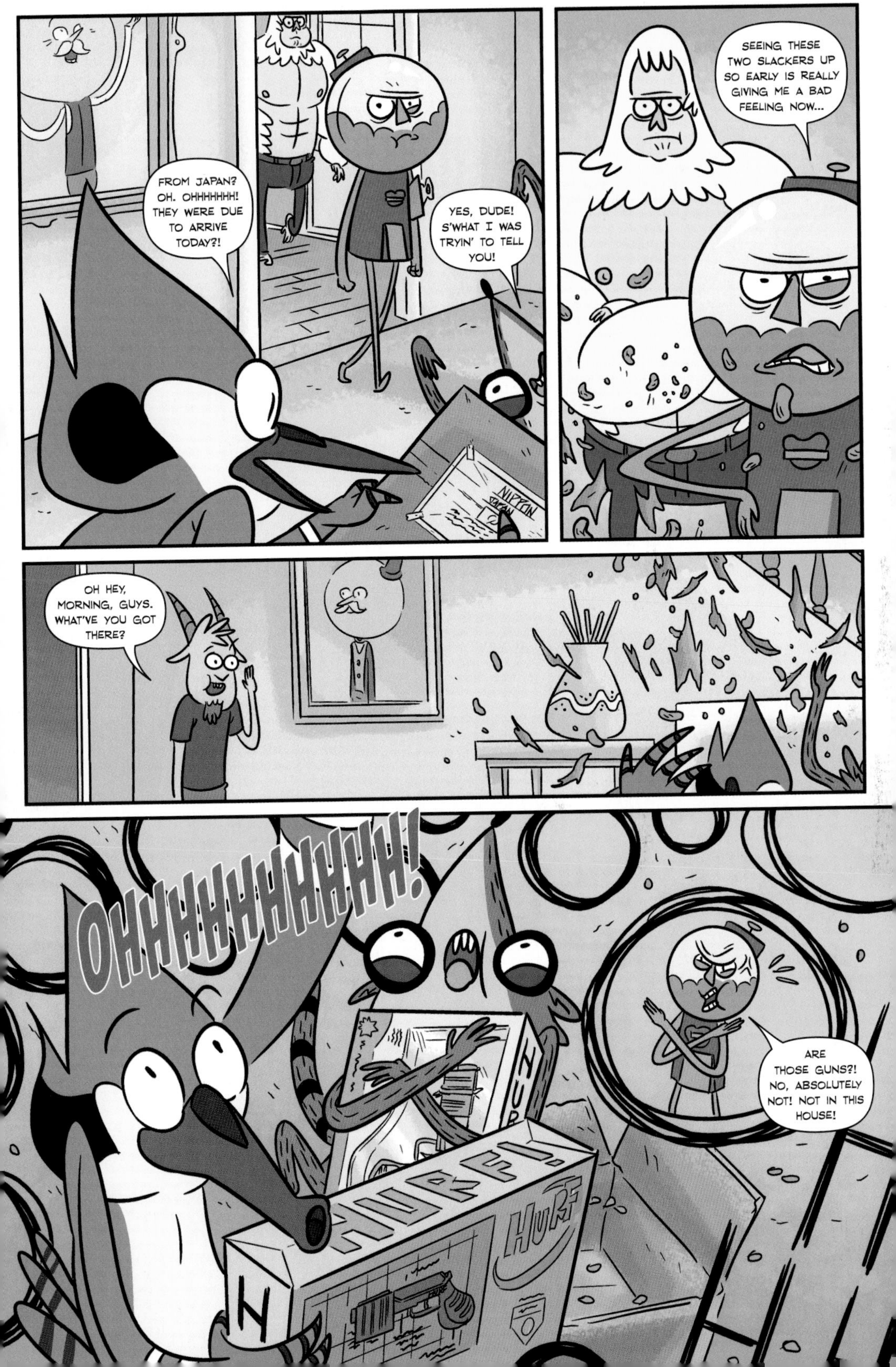
FROM JAPAN? OH. OHHHHHHH! THEY WERE DUE TO ARRIVE TODAY?!
YES, DUDE! S'WHAT I WAS TRYIN' TO TELL YOU!
NIPPON
SEEING THESE TWO SLACKERS UP SO EARLY IS REALLY GIVING ME A BAD FEELING NOW...
OH HEY, MORNING, GUYS. WHAT'VE YOU GOT THERE?
OHHHHHHHHHHHH!
ARE THOSE GUNS?! NO, ABSOLUTELY NOT! NOT IN THIS HOUSE!
HURF

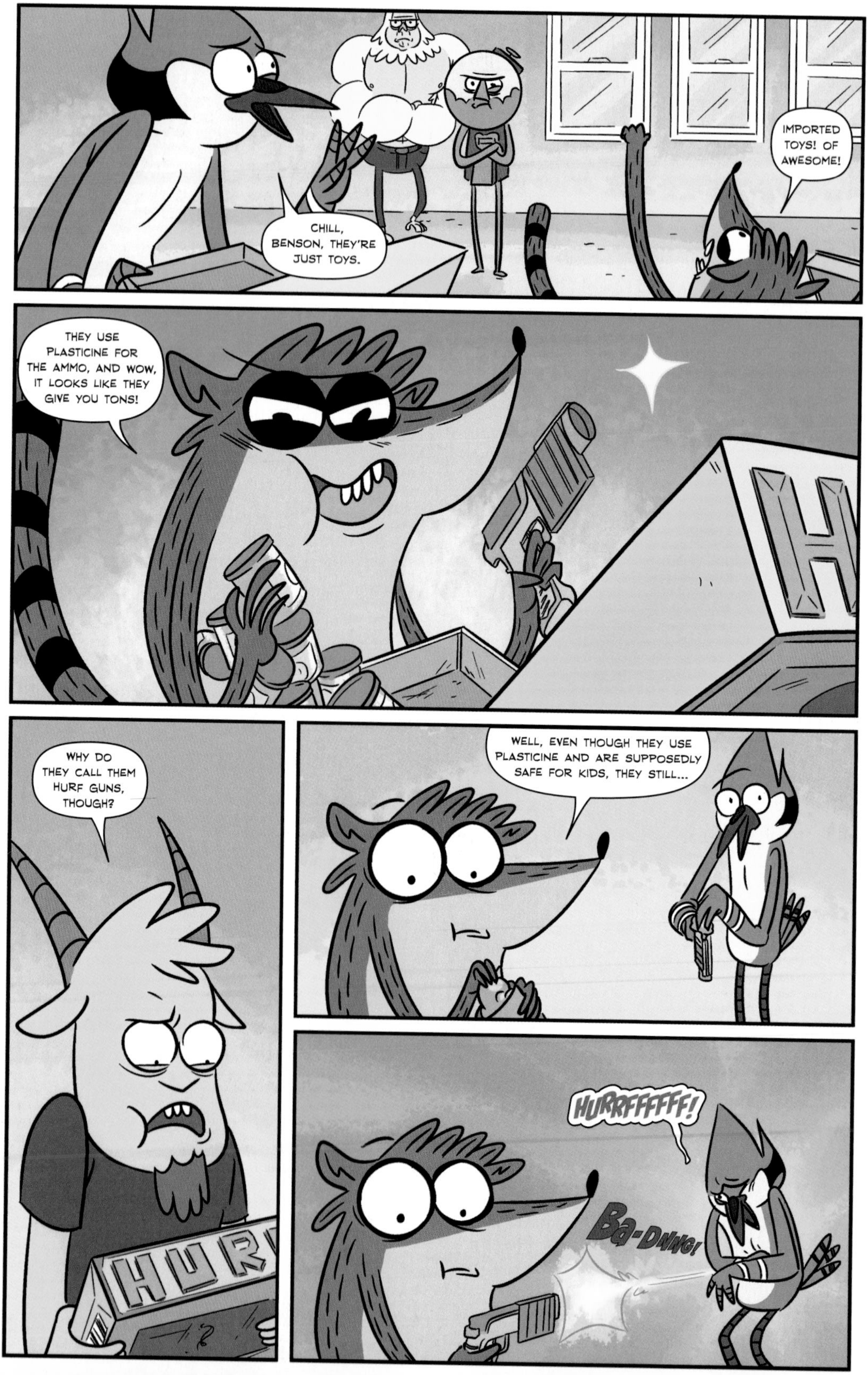
CHILL, BENSON, THEY'RE JUST TOYS.
IMPORTED TOYS! OF AWESOME!
THEY USE PLASTICINE FOR THE AMMO, AND WOW, IT LOOKS LIKE THEY GIVE YOU TONS!
WHY DO THEY CALL THEM HURF GUNS, THOUGH?
HUR
WELL, EVEN THOUGH THEY USE PLASTICINE AND ARE SUPPOSEDLY SAFE FOR KIDS, THEY STILL...
HURRFFFFFF!
Ba-DNNG!

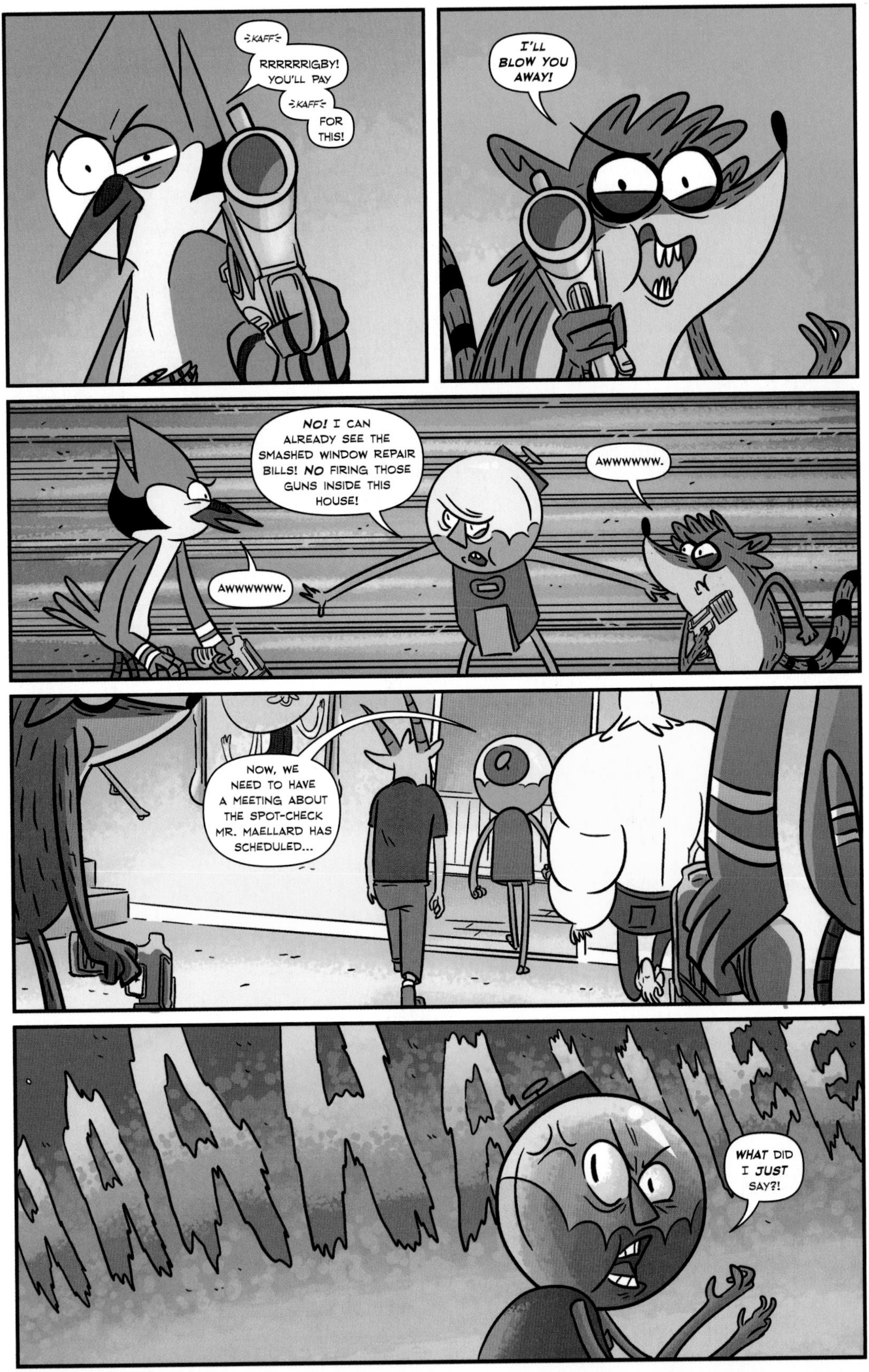

KAFF
RRRRRRIGBY! YOU'LL PAY
KAFF
FOR THIS!
I'LL BLOW YOU AWAY!
NO! I CAN ALREADY SEE THE SMASHED WINDOW REPAIR BILLS! NO FIRING THOSE GUNS INSIDE THIS HOUSE!
AWWWWWW.
AWWWWWW.
NOW, WE NEED TO HAVE A MEETING ABOUT THE SPOT-CHECK MR. MAELLARD HAS SCHEDULED...
WHAT DID I JUST SAY?!

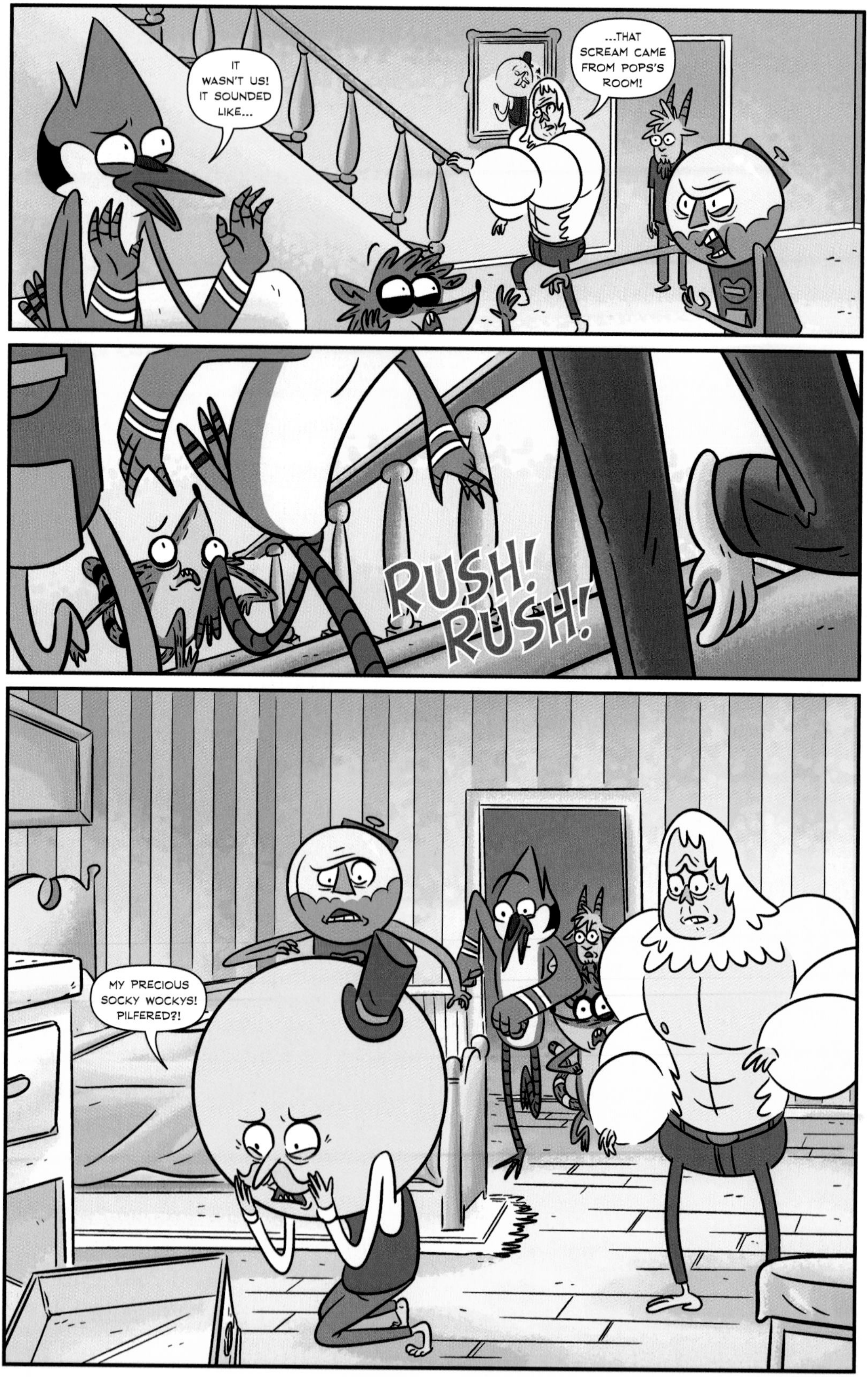
IT WASN'T US! IT SOUNDED LIKE...
...THAT SCREAM CAME FROM POPS'S ROOM!
RUSH! RUSH!
MY PRECIOUS SOCKY WOCKYS! PILFERED?!

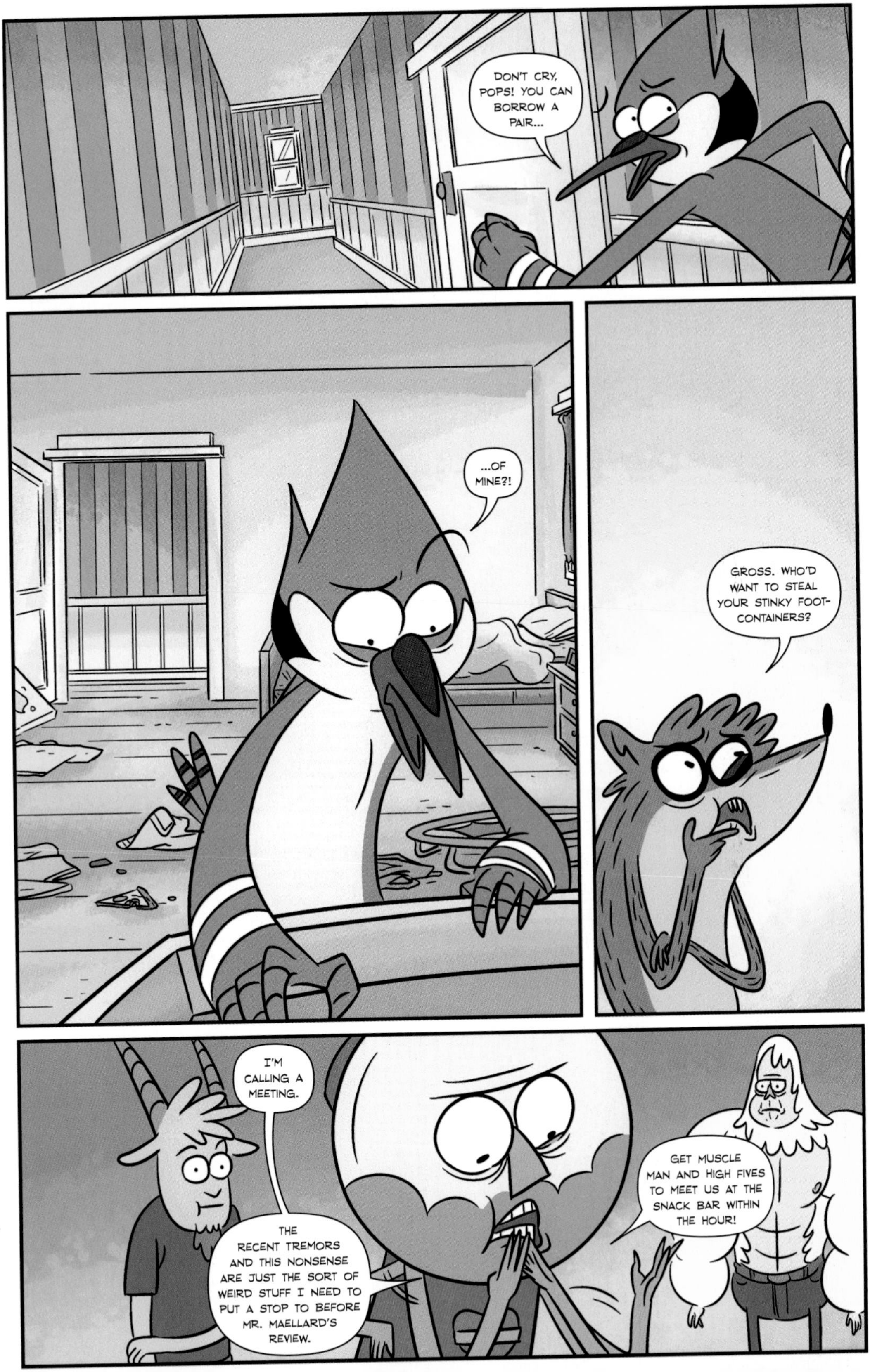
DON'T CRY, POPS! YOU CAN BORROW A PAIR...
...OF MINE?!
GROSS. WHO'D WANT TO STEAL YOUR STINKY FOOT-CONTAINERS?
I'M CALLING A MEETING.
THE RECENT TREMORS AND THIS NONSENSE ARE JUST THE SORT OF WEIRD STUFF I NEED TO PUT A STOP TO BEFORE MR. MAELLARD'S REVIEW.
GET MUSCLE MAN AND HIGH FIVES TO MEET US AT THE SNACK BAR WITHIN THE HOUR!

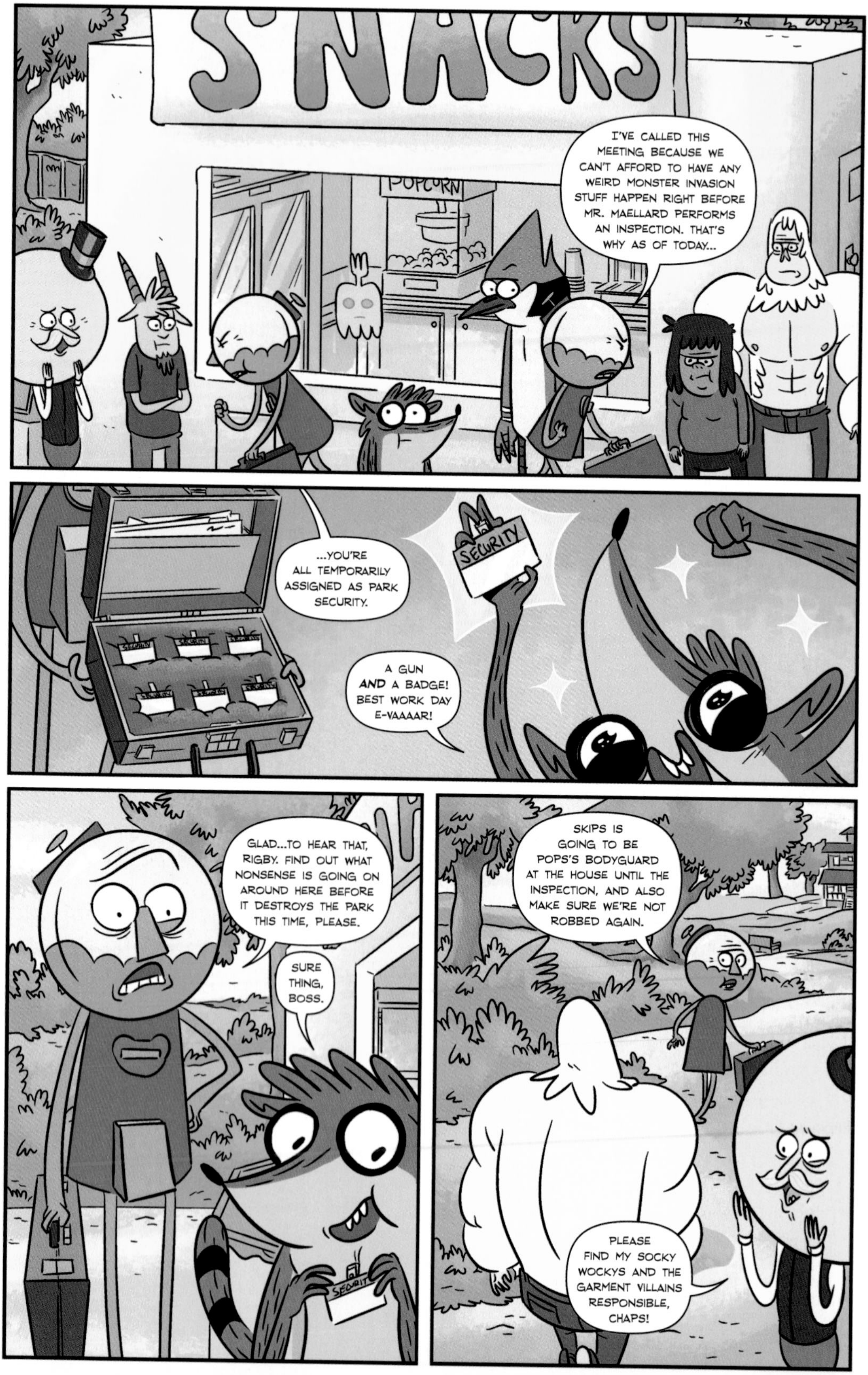
SNACKS
POPCORN
I'VE CALLED THIS MEETING BECAUSE WE CAN'T AFFORD TO HAVE ANY WEIRD MONSTER INVASION STUFF HAPPEN RIGHT BEFORE MR. MAELLARD PERFORMS AN INSPECTION. THAT'S WHY AS OF TODAY...
...YOU'RE ALL TEMPORARILY ASSIGNED AS PARK SECURITY.
SECURITY
A GUN **AND** A BADGE! BEST WORK DAY E-VAAAAR!
GLAD...TO HEAR THAT, RIGBY. FIND OUT WHAT NONSENSE IS GOING ON AROUND HERE BEFORE IT DESTROYS THE PARK THIS TIME, PLEASE.
SURE THING, BOSS.
SKIPS IS GOING TO BE POPS'S BODYGUARD AT THE HOUSE UNTIL THE INSPECTION, AND ALSO MAKE SURE WE'RE NOT ROBBED AGAIN.
PLEASE FIND MY SOCKY WOCKYS AND THE GARMENT VILLAINS RESPONSIBLE, CHAPS!

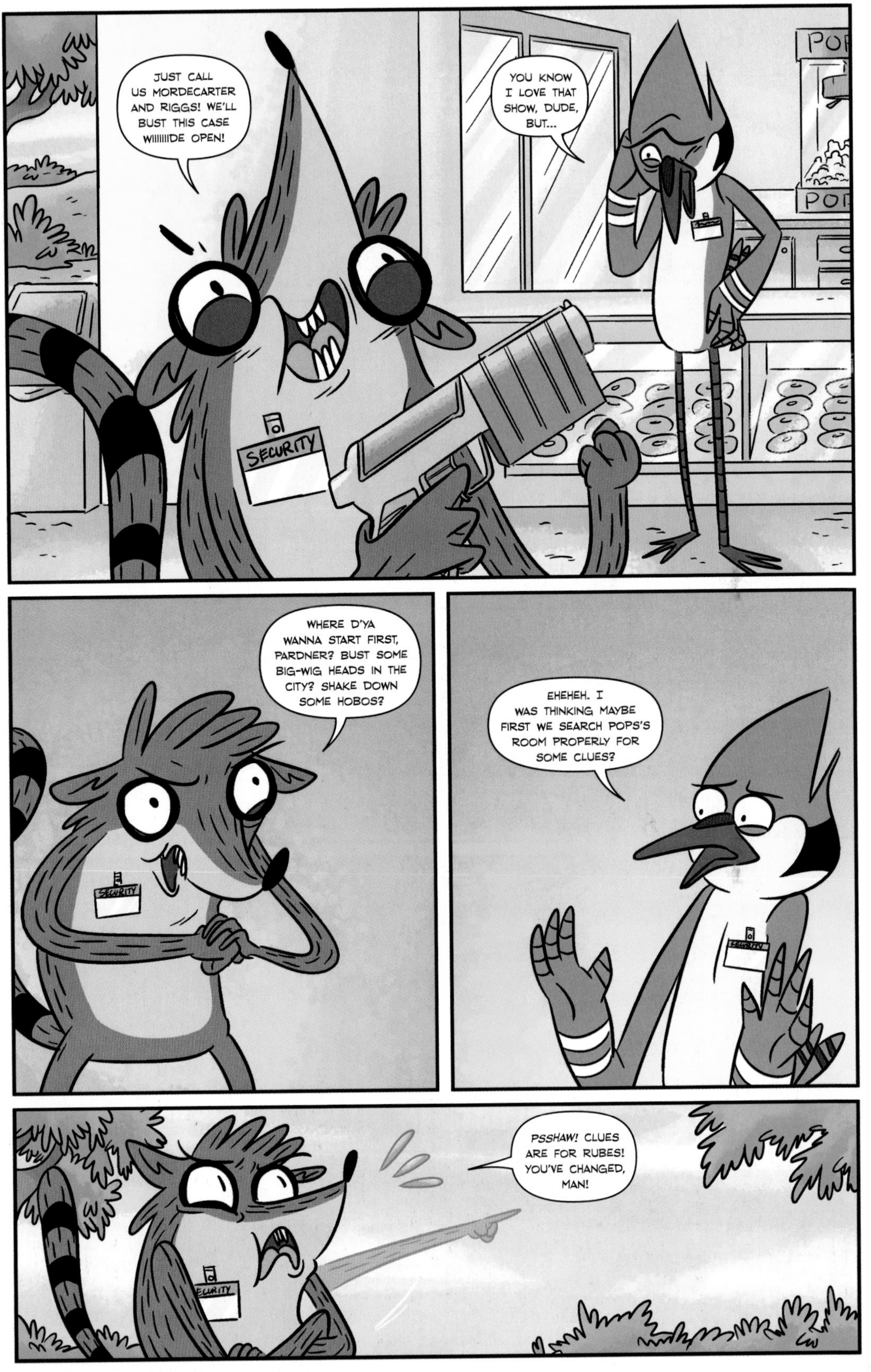
JUST CALL US MORDECARTER AND RIGGS! WE'LL BUST THIS CASE WIIIIIIDE OPEN!
SECURITY
YOU KNOW I LOVE THAT SHOW, DUDE, BUT...
WHERE D'YA WANNA START FIRST, PARDNER? BUST SOME BIG-WIG HEADS IN THE CITY? SHAKE DOWN SOME HOBOS?
SECURITY
EHEHEH. I WAS THINKING MAYBE FIRST WE SEARCH POPS'S ROOM PROPERLY FOR SOME CLUES?
SECURITY
PSSHAW! CLUES ARE FOR RUBES! YOU'VE CHANGED, MAN!
SECURITY

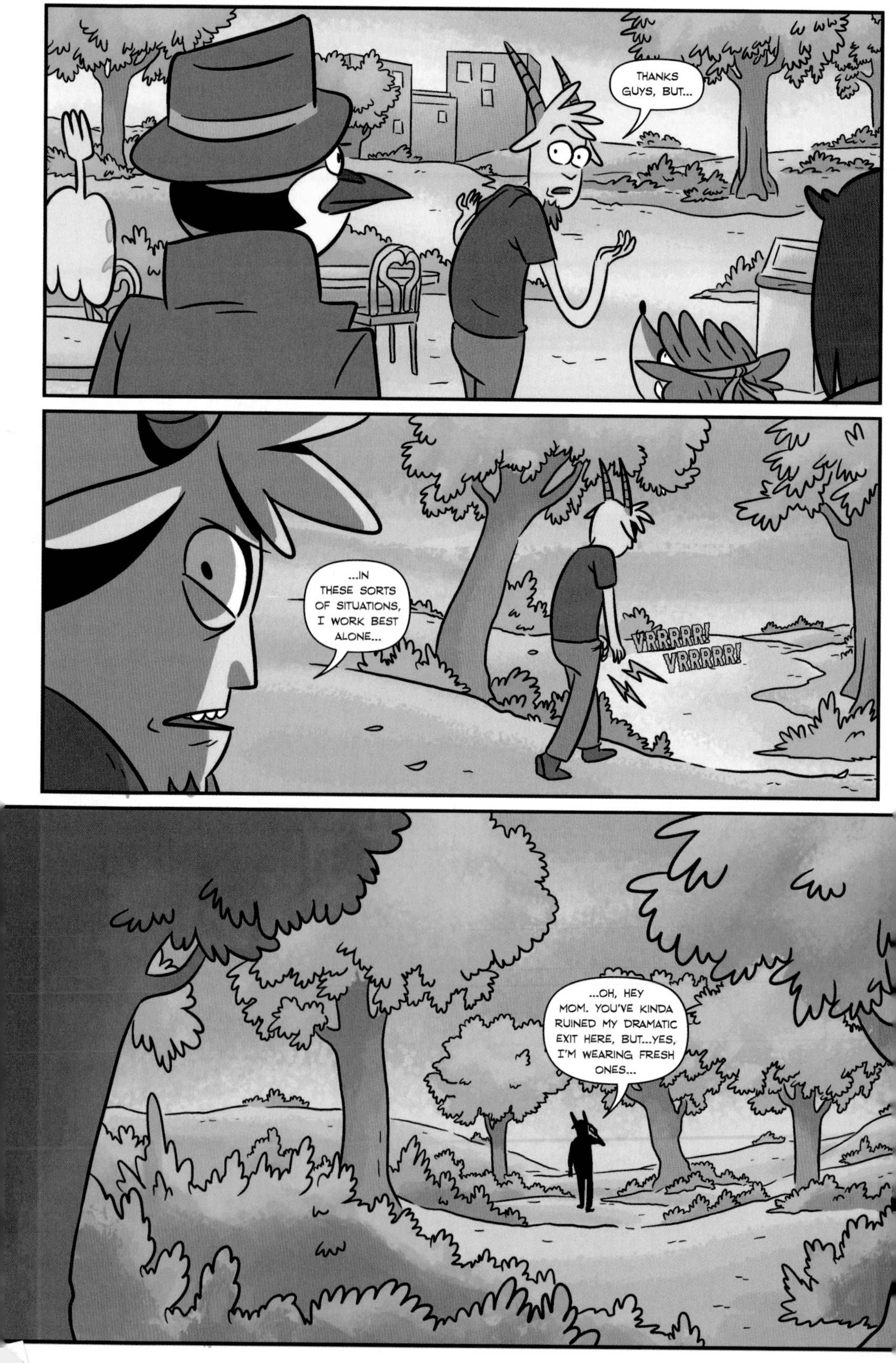
THANKS GUYS, BUT...
...IN THESE SORTS OF SITUATIONS, I WORK BEST ALONE...
VRRRRR! VRRRRR!
...OH, HEY MOM. YOU'VE KINDA RUINED MY DRAMATIC EXIT HERE, BUT...YES, I'M WEARING FRESH ONES...

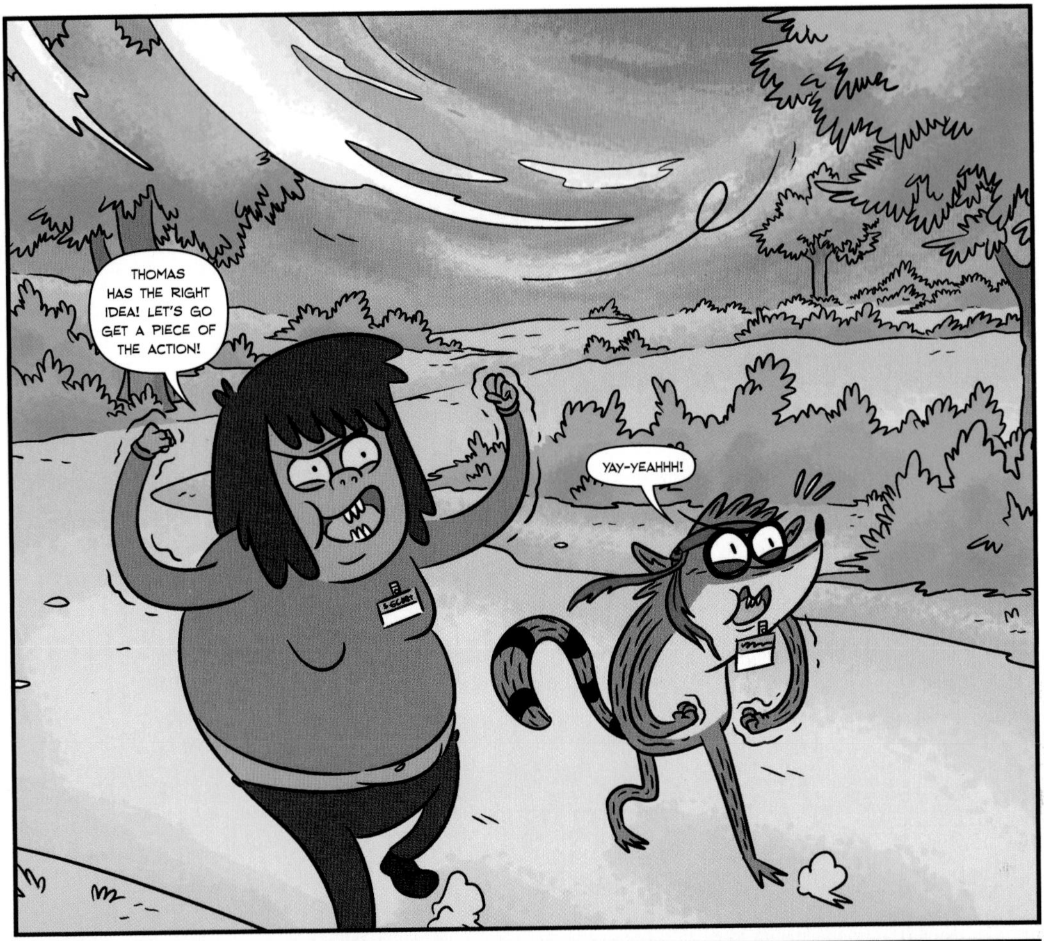
THOMAS HAS THE RIGHT IDEA! LET'S GO GET A PIECE OF THE ACTION!
YAY-YEAHHH!

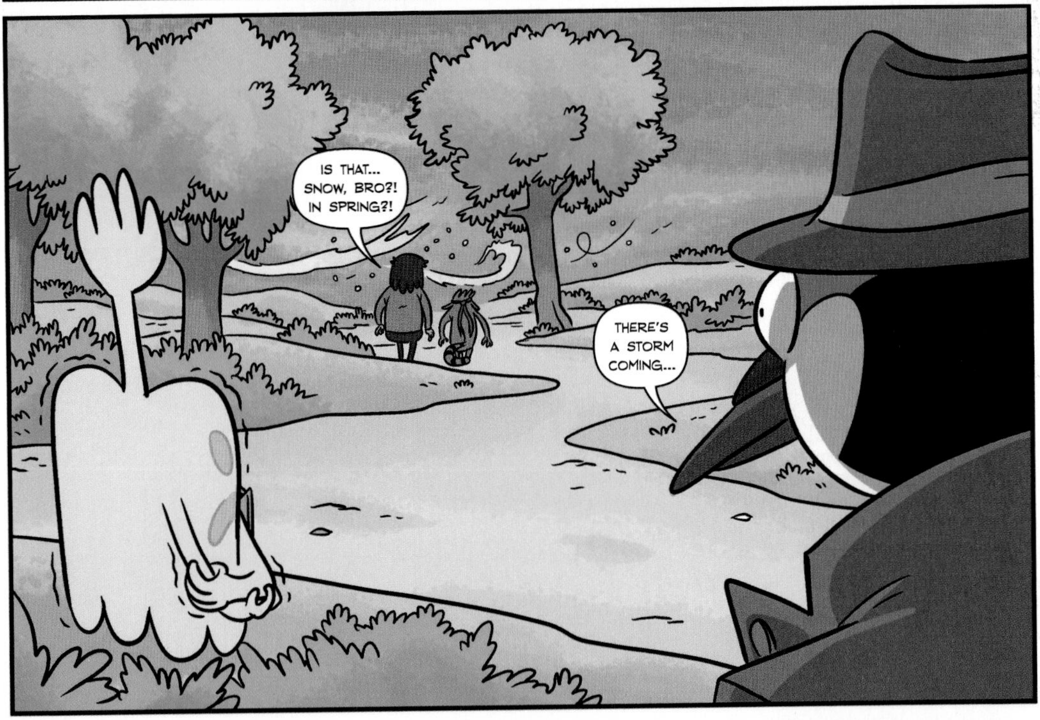
IS THAT... SNOW, BRO?! IN SPRING?!
THERE'S A STORM COMING...

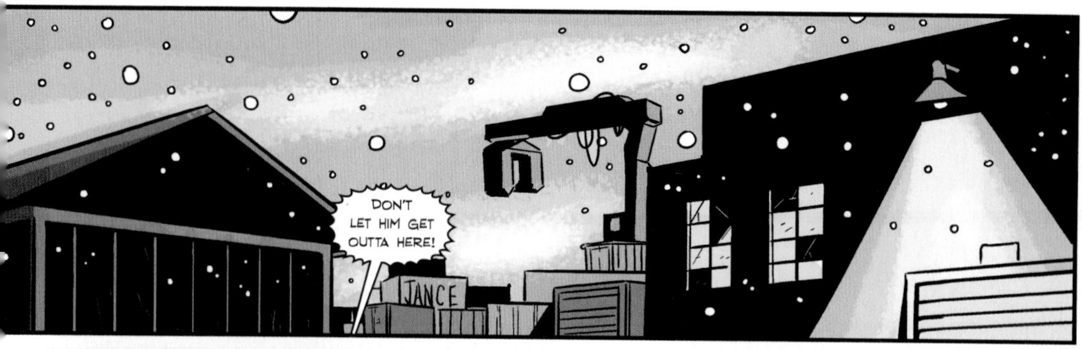
DON'T LET HIM GET OUTTA HERE!
JANCE

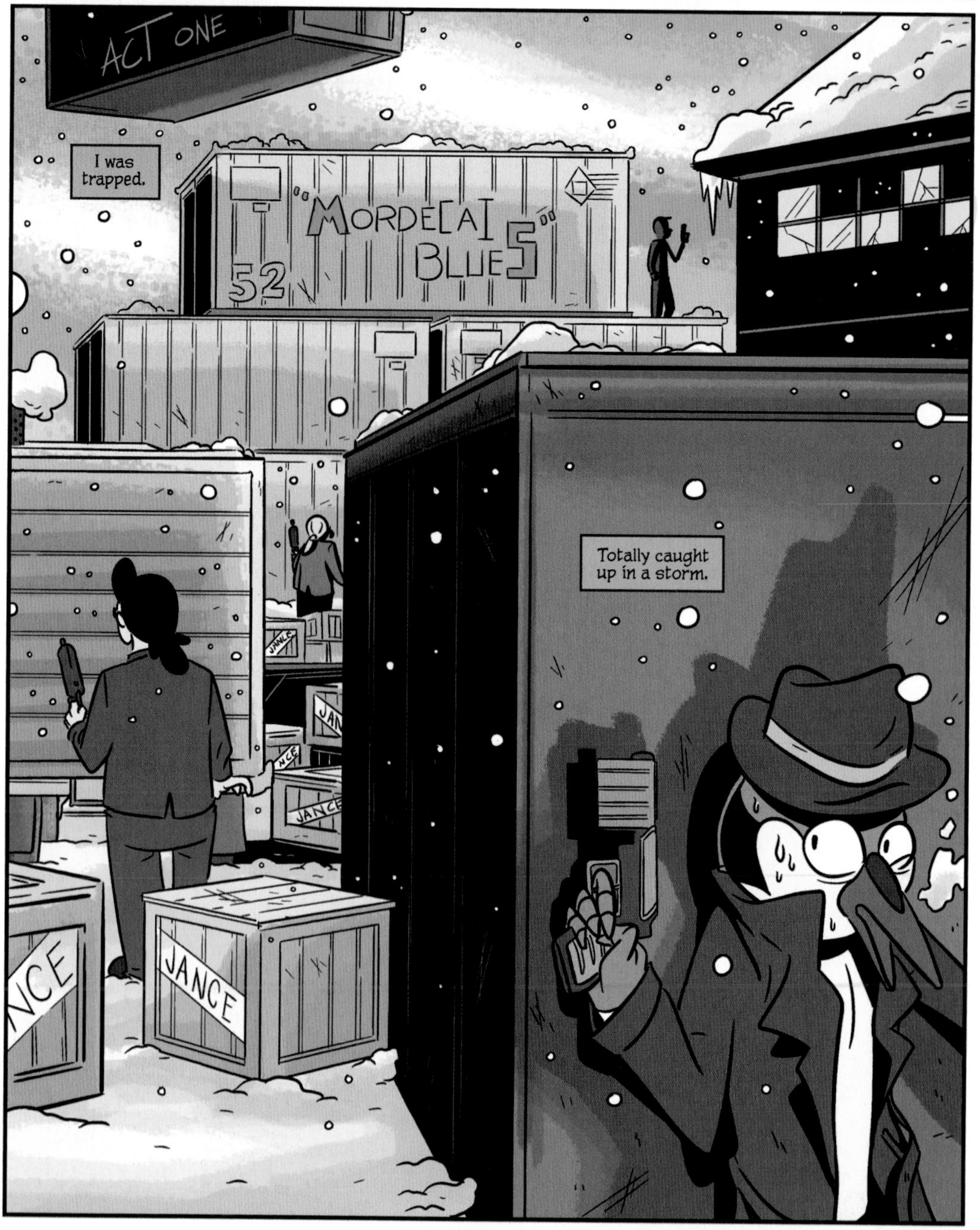
ACT ONE
I was trapped.
"MORDE[A] BLUE5"
52
Totally caught up in a storm.
JANCE
JANCE

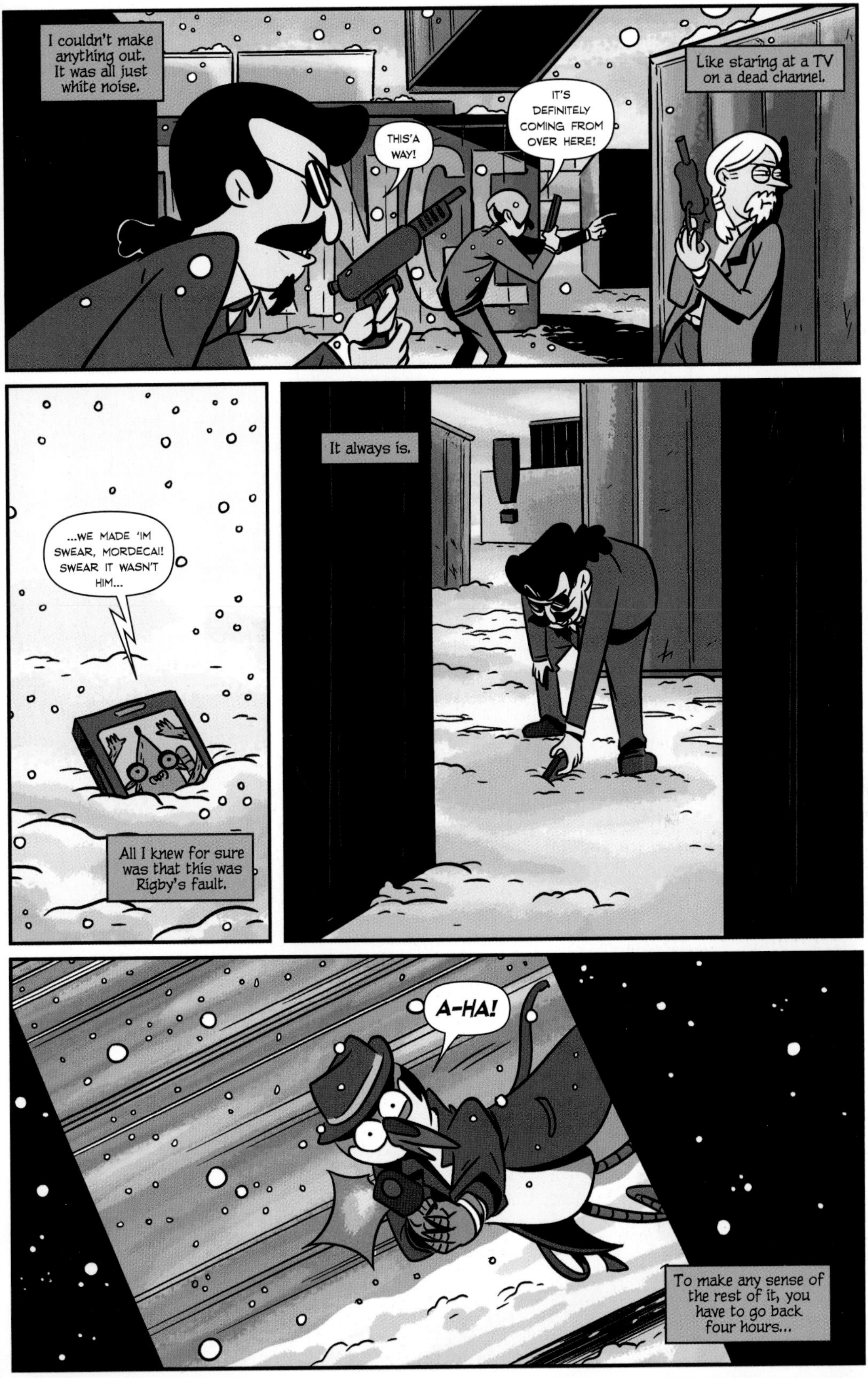
I couldn't make anything out. It was all just white noise.
THIS'A WAY!
IT'S DEFINITELY COMING FROM OVER HERE!
Like staring at a TV on a dead channel.
...WE MADE 'IM SWEAR, MORDECAI! SWEAR IT WASN'T HIM...
All I knew for sure was that this was Rigby's fault.
It always is.
A-HA!
To make any sense of the rest of it, you have to go back four hours...

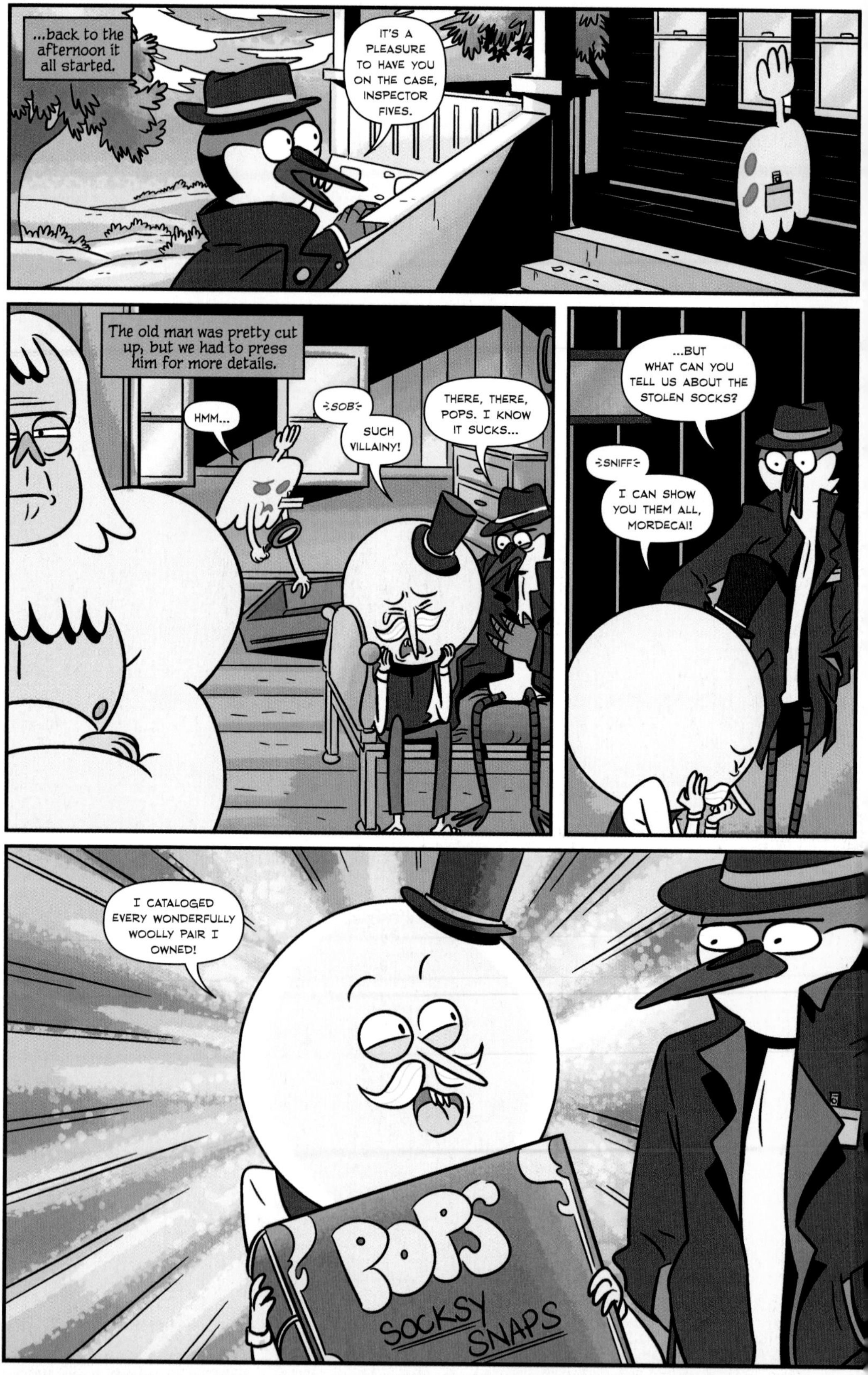

...back to the afternoon it all started.
IT'S A PLEASURE TO HAVE YOU ON THE CASE, INSPECTOR FIVES.
The old man was pretty cut up, but we had to press him for more details.
HMM...
SOB
SUCH VILLAINY!
THERE, THERE, POPS. I KNOW IT SUCKS...
...BUT WHAT CAN YOU TELL US ABOUT THE STOLEN SOCKS?
SNIFF
I CAN SHOW YOU THEM ALL, MORDECAI!
I CATALOGED EVERY WONDERFULLY WOOLLY PAIR I OWNED!
POPS'
SOCKSY SNAPS

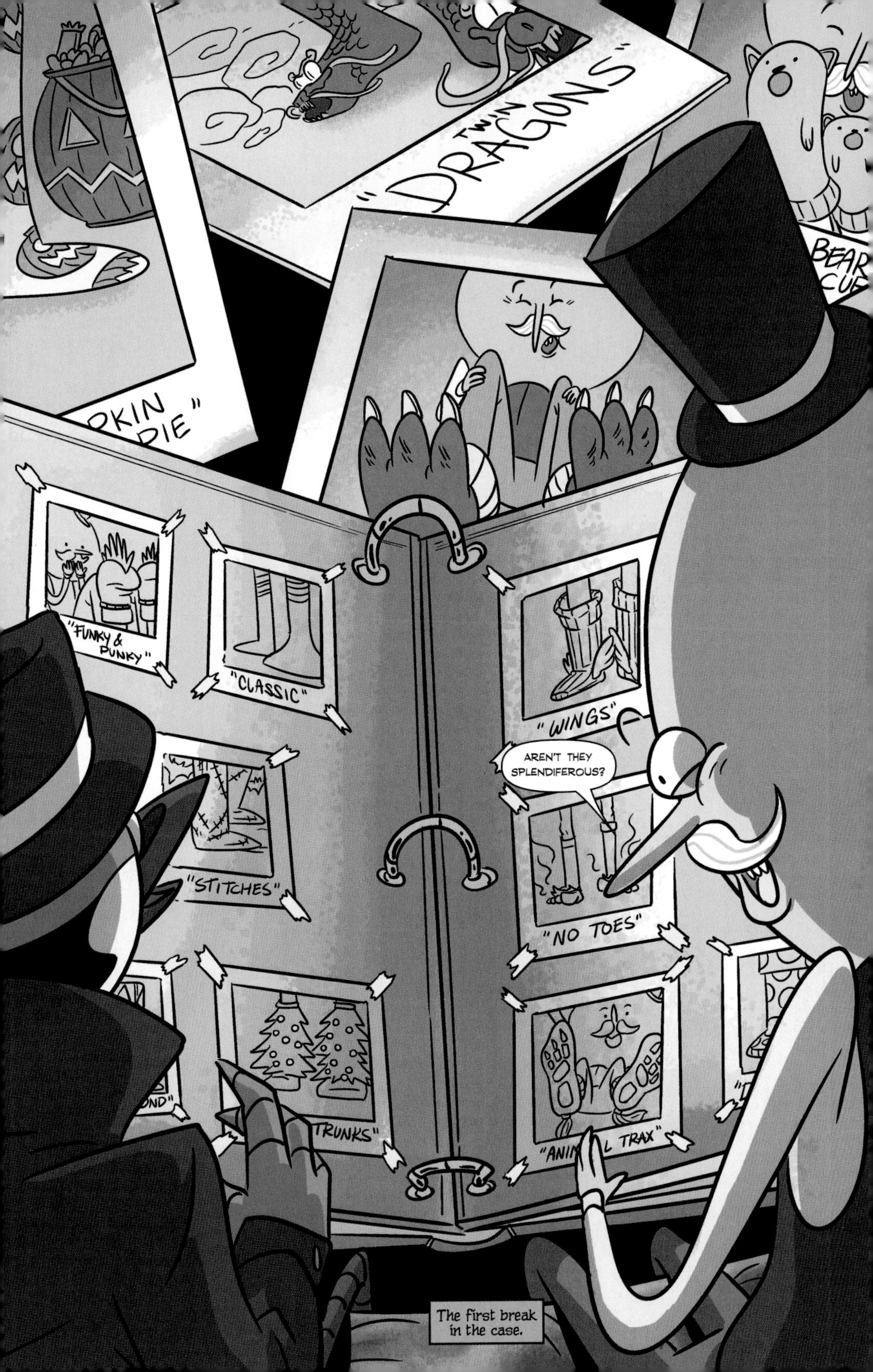

"TWIN DRAGONS"
"FUNKY & PUNKY"
"CLASSIC"
"WINGS"
ARE'NT THEY SPLENDIFEROUS?
"STITCHES"
"NO TOES"
"TRUNKS"
The first break in the case.

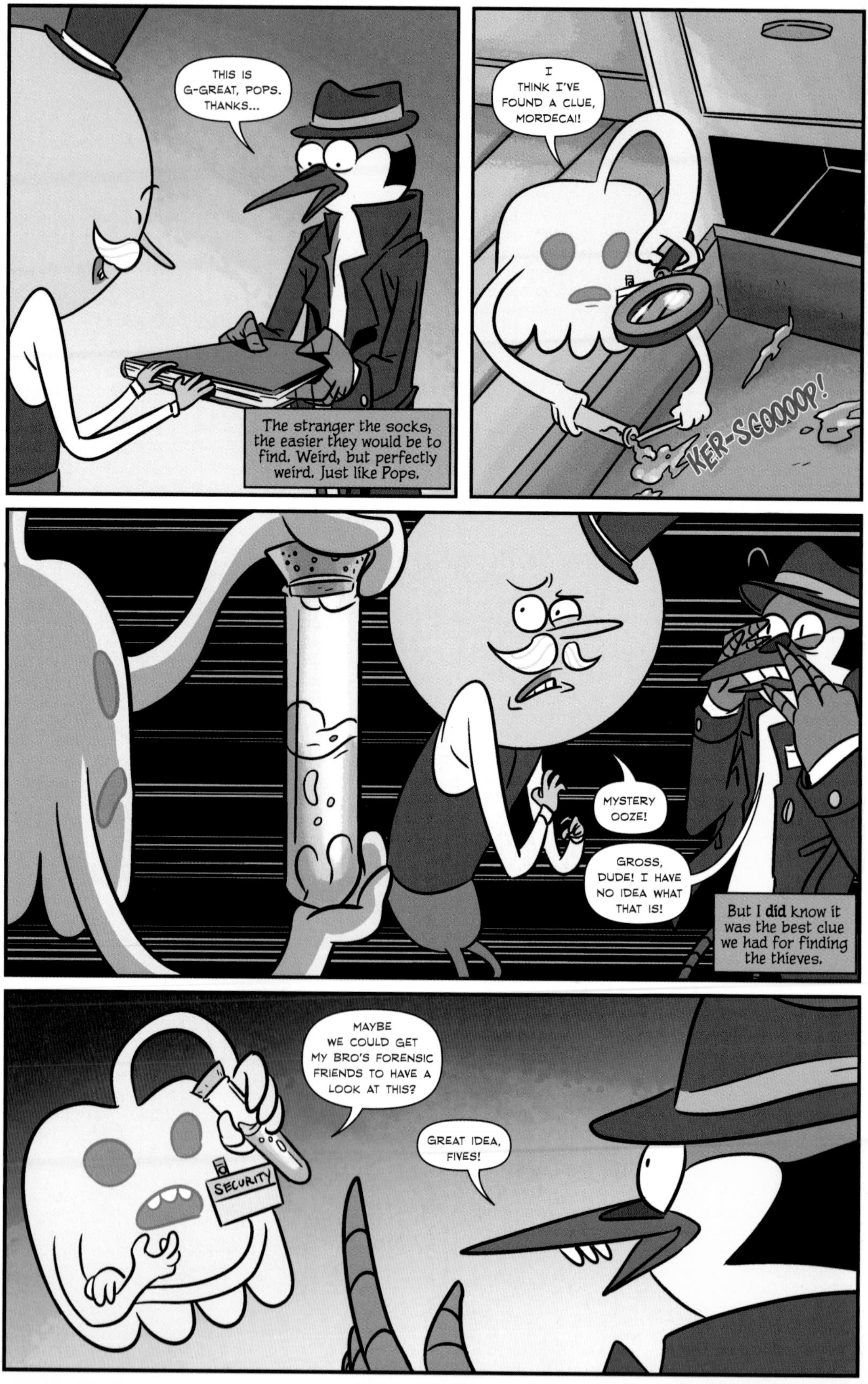
THIS IS G-GREAT, POPS. THANKS...
The stranger the socks, the easier they would be to find. Weird, but perfectly weird. Just like Pops.
I THINK I'VE FOUND A CLUE, MORDECAI!
KER-SCOOOOP!
MYSTERY OOZE!
GROSS, DUDE! I HAVE NO IDEA WHAT THAT IS!
But I **did** know it was the best clue we had for finding the thieves.
MAYBE WE COULD GET MY BRO'S FORENSIC FRIENDS TO HAVE A LOOK AT THIS?
GREAT IDEA, FIVES!
SECURITY

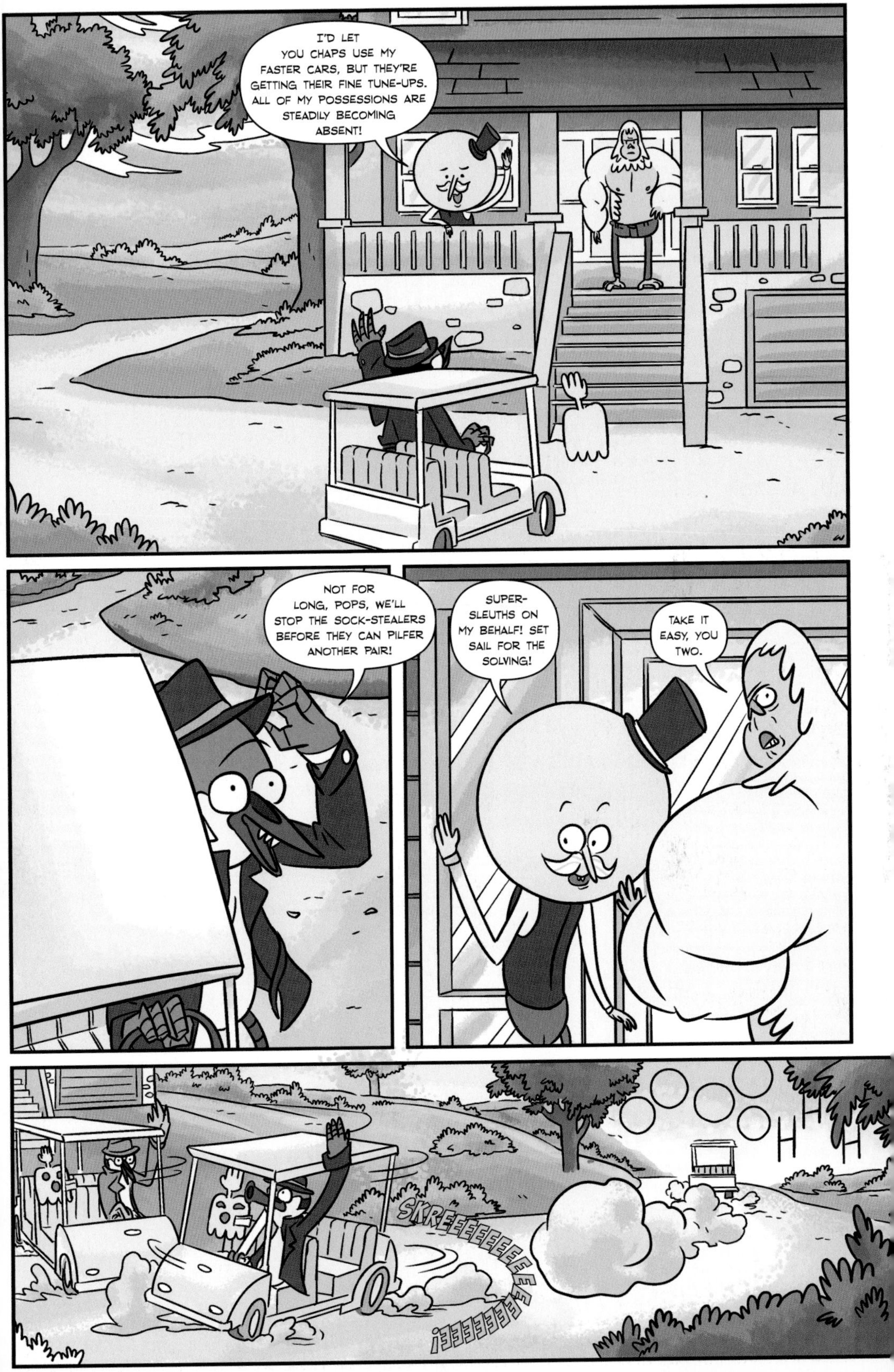
I'D LET YOU CHAPS USE MY FASTER CARS, BUT THEY'RE GETTING THEIR FINE TUNE-UPS. ALL OF MY POSSESSIONS ARE STEADILY BECOMING ABSENT!
NOT FOR LONG, POPS, WE'LL STOP THE SOCK-STEALERS BEFORE THEY CAN PILFER ANOTHER PAIR!
SUPER-SLEUTHS ON MY BEHALF! SET SAIL FOR THE SOLVING!
TAKE IT EASY, YOU TWO.
SKREEEEEEEEEEEEEEEEEEE!

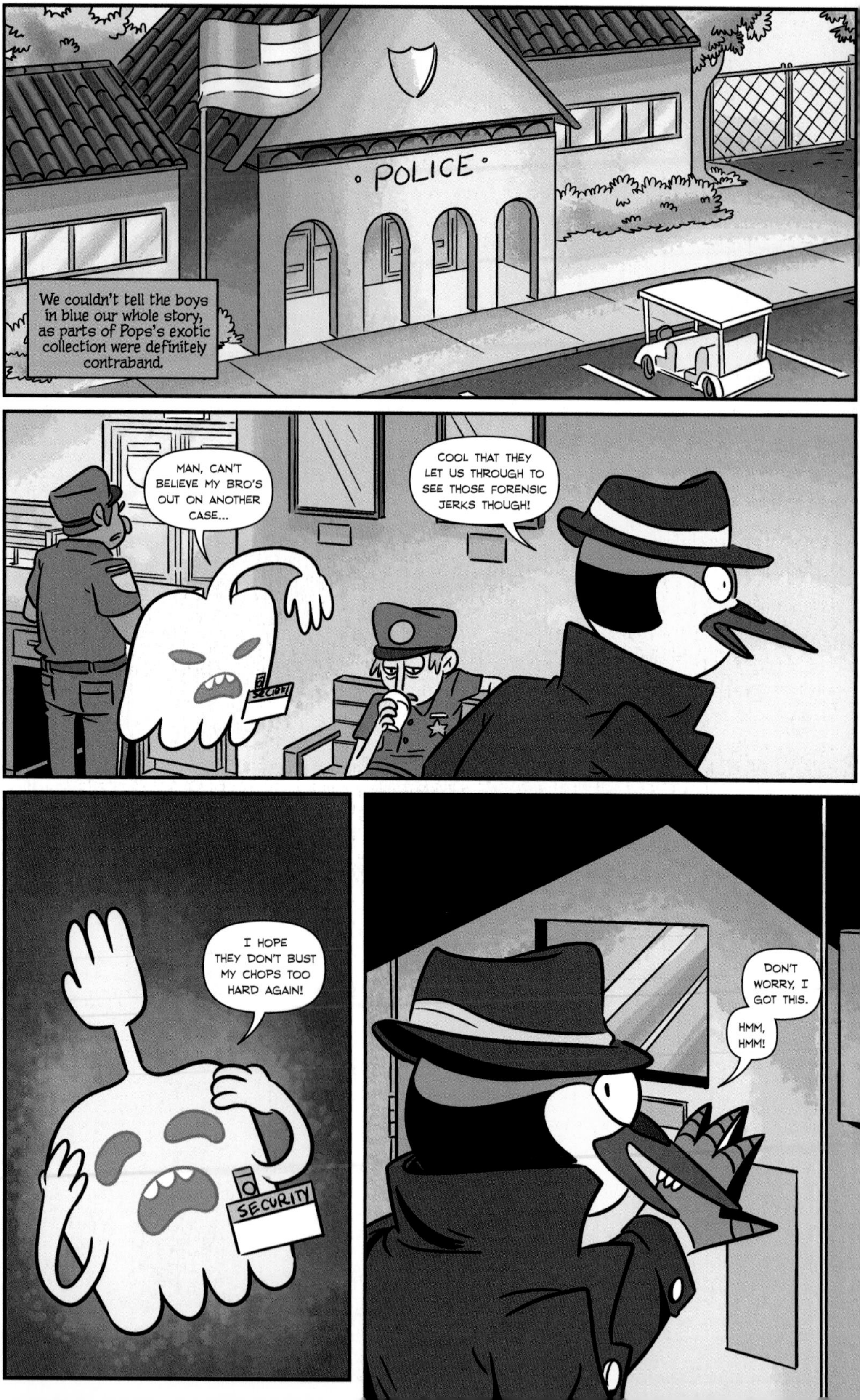

POLICE
We couldn't tell the boys in blue our whole story, as parts of Pops's exotic collection were definitely contraband.
MAN, CAN'T BELIEVE MY BRO'S OUT ON ANOTHER CASE...
COOL THAT THEY LET US THROUGH TO SEE THOSE FORENSIC JERKS THOUGH!
I HOPE THEY DON'T BUST MY CHOPS TOO HARD AGAIN!
SECURITY
DON'T WORRY, I GOT THIS.
HMM, HMM!

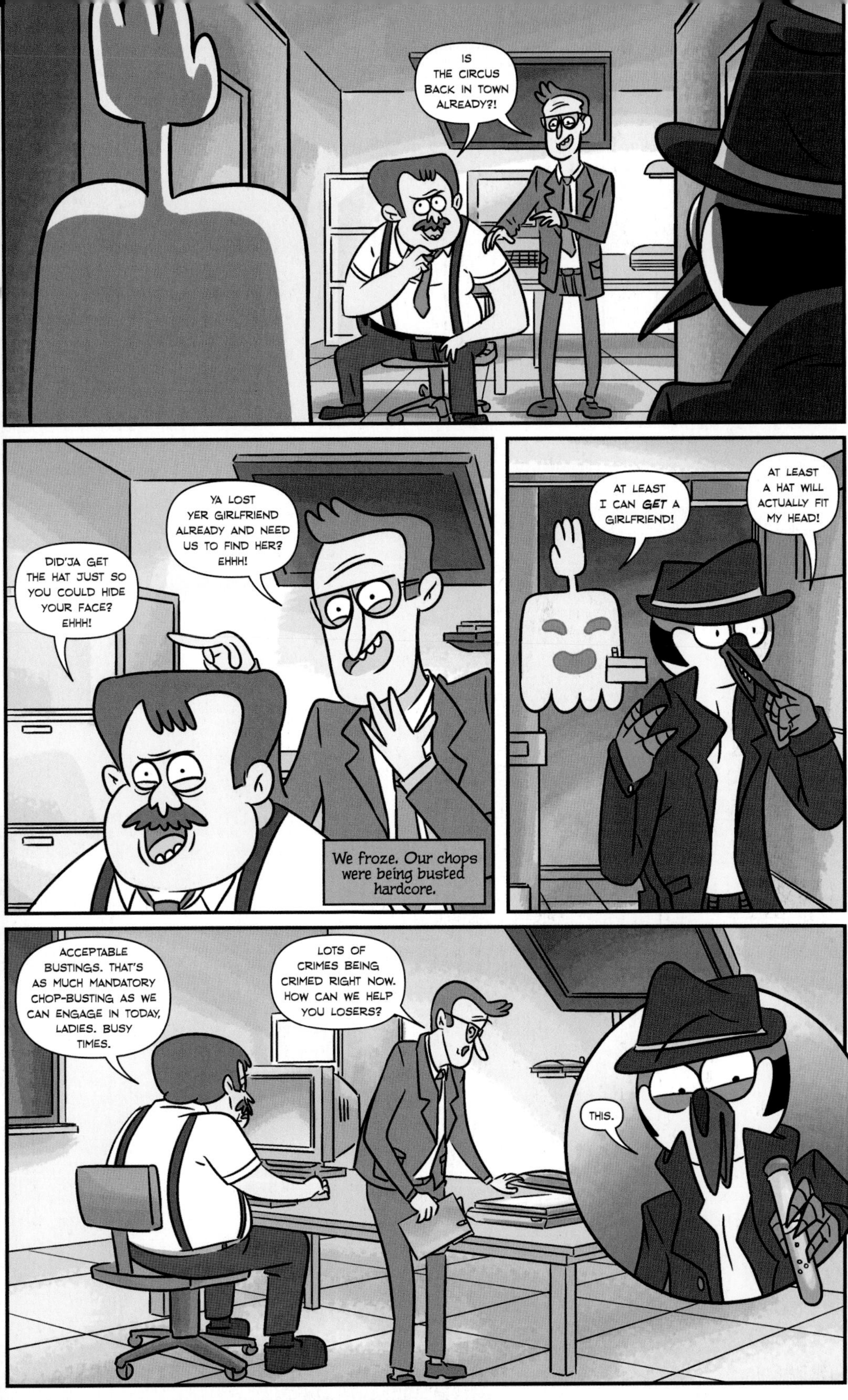
IS THE CIRCUS BACK IN TOWN ALREADY?!
YA LOST YER GIRLFRIEND ALREADY AND NEED US TO FIND HER? EHHH!
DID'JA GET THE HAT JUST SO YOU COULD HIDE YOUR FACE? EHHH!
We froze. Our chops were being busted hardcore.
AT LEAST I CAN GET A GIRLFRIEND!
AT LEAST A HAT WILL ACTUALLY FIT MY HEAD!
ACCEPTABLE BUSTINGS. THAT'S AS MUCH MANDATORY CHOP-BUSTING AS WE CAN ENGAGE IN TODAY, LADIES. BUSY TIMES.
LOTS OF CRIMES BEING CRIMED RIGHT NOW. HOW CAN WE HELP YOU LOSERS?
THIS.

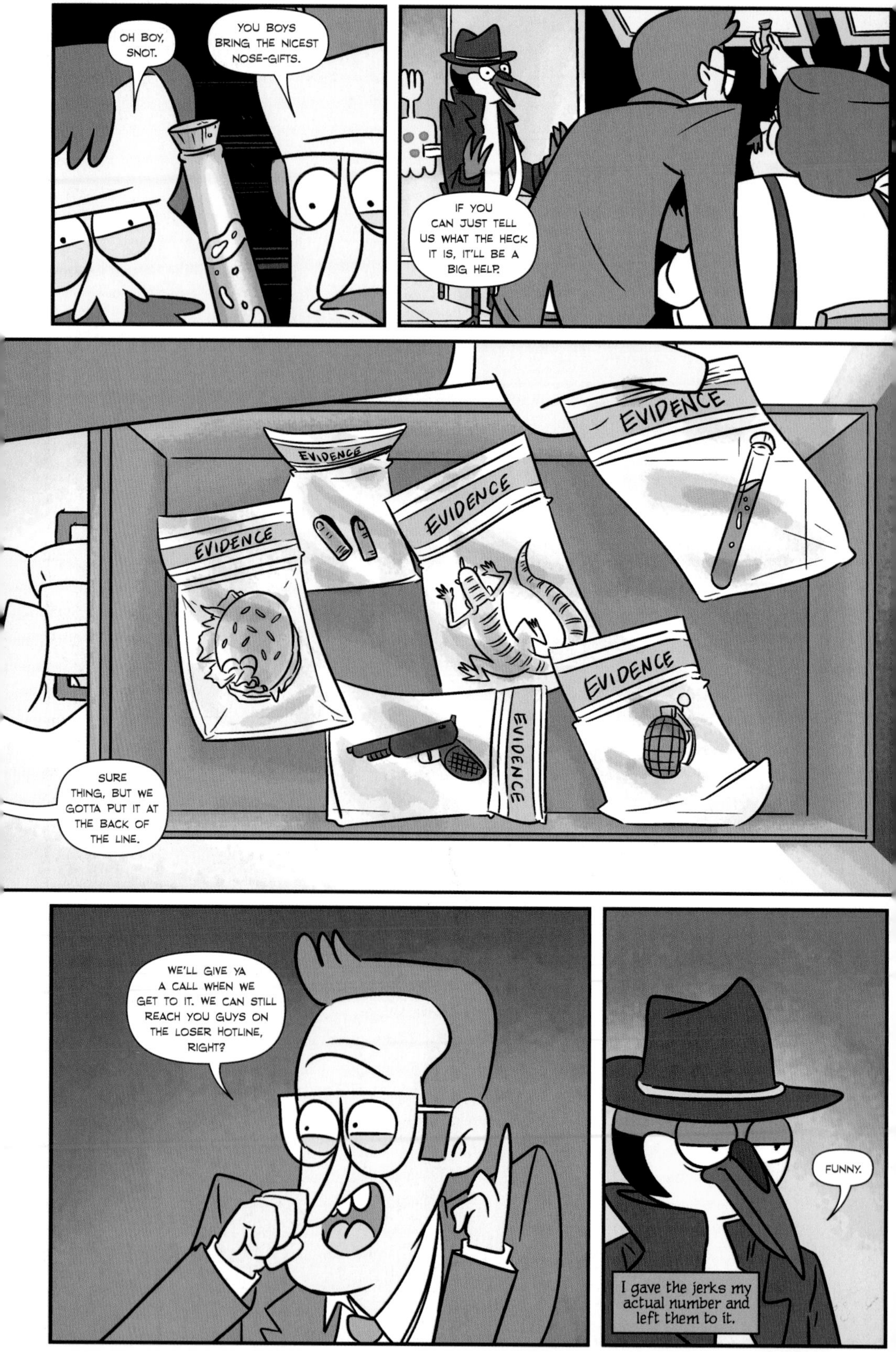
OH BOY, SNOT.
YOU BOYS BRING THE NICEST NOSE-GIFTS.
IF YOU CAN JUST TELL US WHAT THE HECK IT IS, IT'LL BE A BIG HELP.
EVIDENCE
EVIDENCE
EVIDENCE
EVIDENCE
EVIDENCE
EVIDENCE
SURE THING, BUT WE GOTTA PUT IT AT THE BACK OF THE LINE.
WE'LL GIVE YA A CALL WHEN WE GET TO IT. WE CAN STILL REACH YOU GUYS ON THE LOSER HOTLINE, RIGHT?
FUNNY.
I gave the jerks my actual number and left them to it.

We returned to the office while we waited for their all-important call.

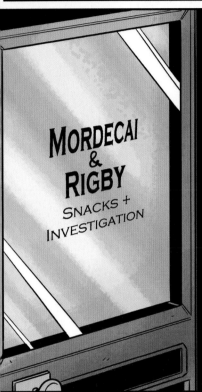

MORDECAI & RIGBY

SNACKS + INVESTIGATION

My usual partner was out cold from the stakeout he'd been at the night before.

WAKE *UP,* BRAH!

UGH. GO AHEAD, YOU BABIES CAN PLAY CLUEDO ALL DAY, BUT LET ME KNOW WHEN WE GET TO THE HEADBUTTING OF SKEEVY SUSPECTS.

THINK I MIGHT TAKE FIVE AS WELL, FIVES...

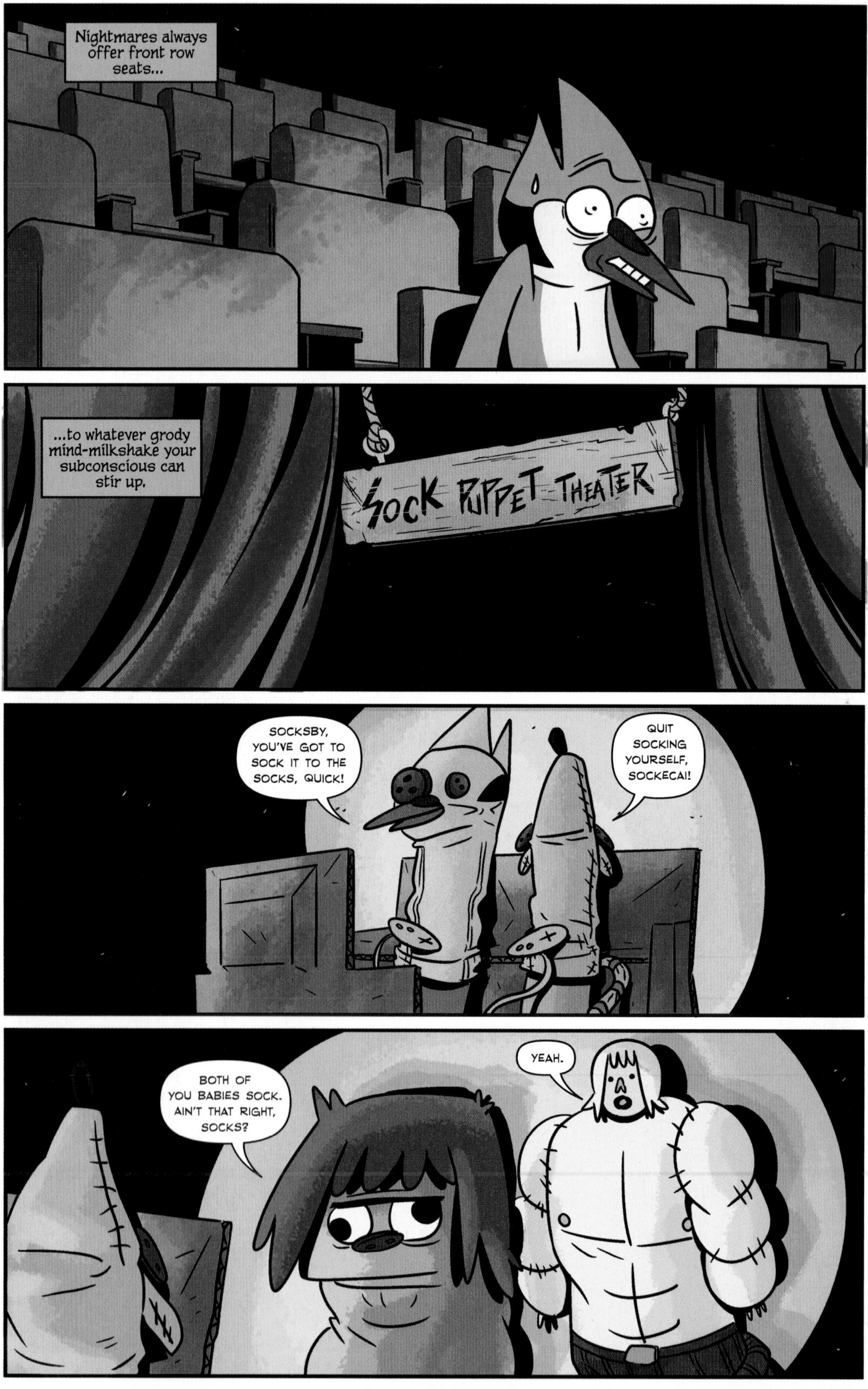

Nightmares always offer front row seats...
...to whatever grody mind-milkshake your subconscious can stir up.
SOCK PUPPET THEATER
SOCKSBY, YOU'VE GOT TO SOCK IT TO THE SOCKS, QUICK!
QUIT SOCKING YOURSELF, SOCKECAI!
BOTH OF YOU BABIES SOCK. AIN'T THAT RIGHT, SOCKS?
YEAH.

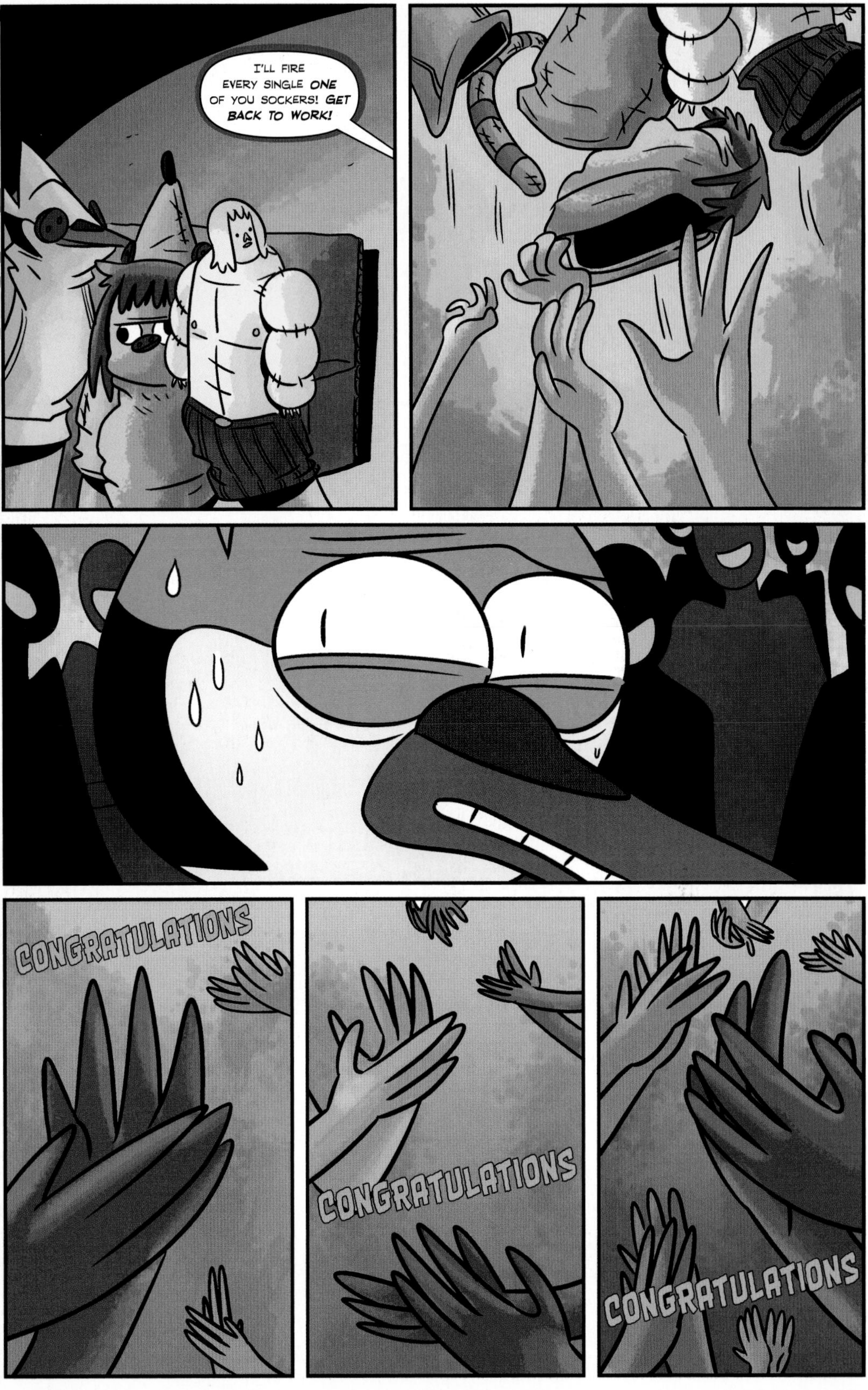
I'LL FIRE EVERY SINGLE ONE OF YOU SOCKERS! GET BACK TO WORK!
CONGRATULATIONS
CONGRATULATIONS
CONGRATULATIONS

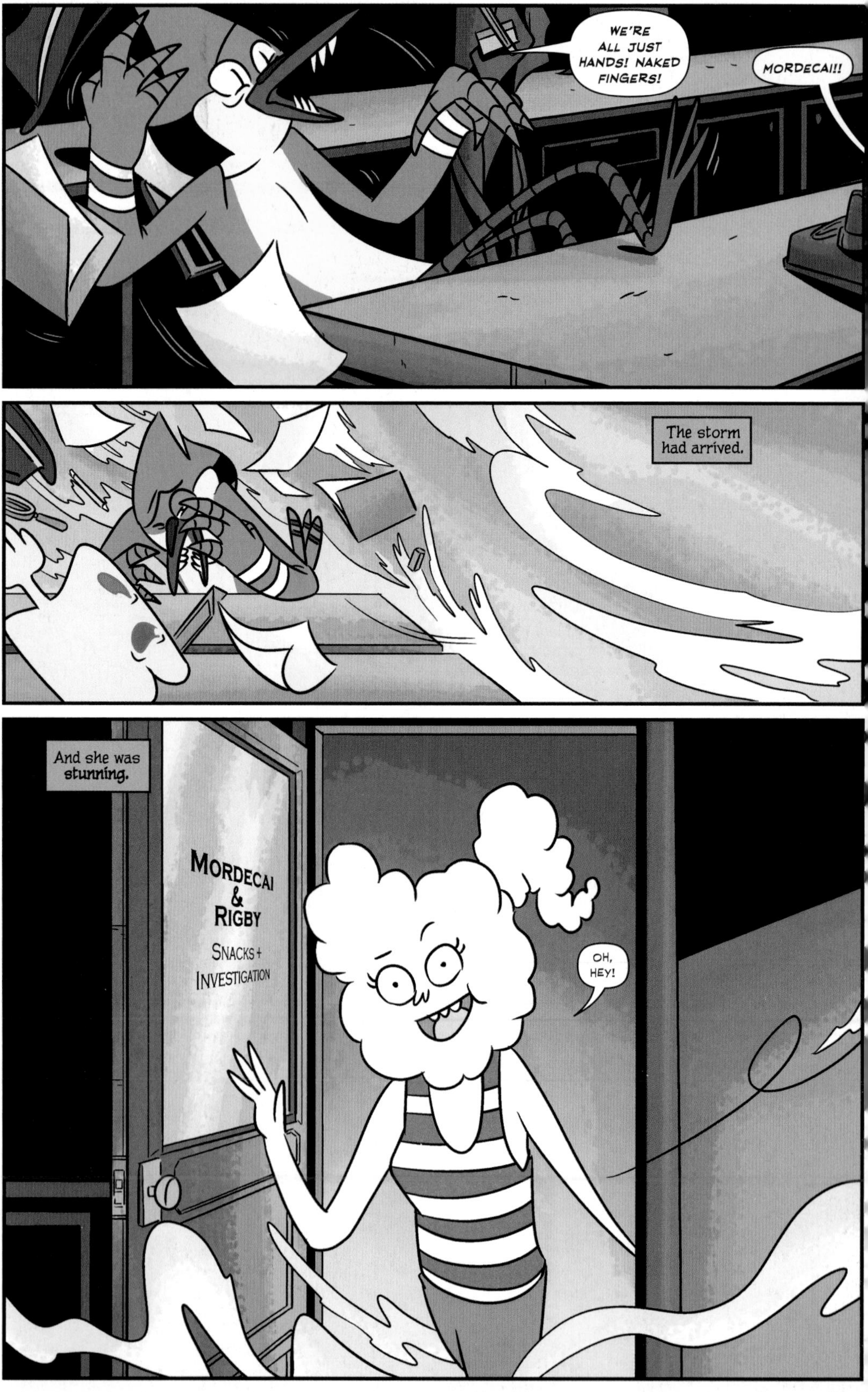
WE'RE ALL JUST HANDS! NAKED FINGERS!
MORDECAI!!
The storm had arrived.
And she was stunning.
MORDECAI & RIGBY
SNACKS + INVESTIGATION
OH, HEY!

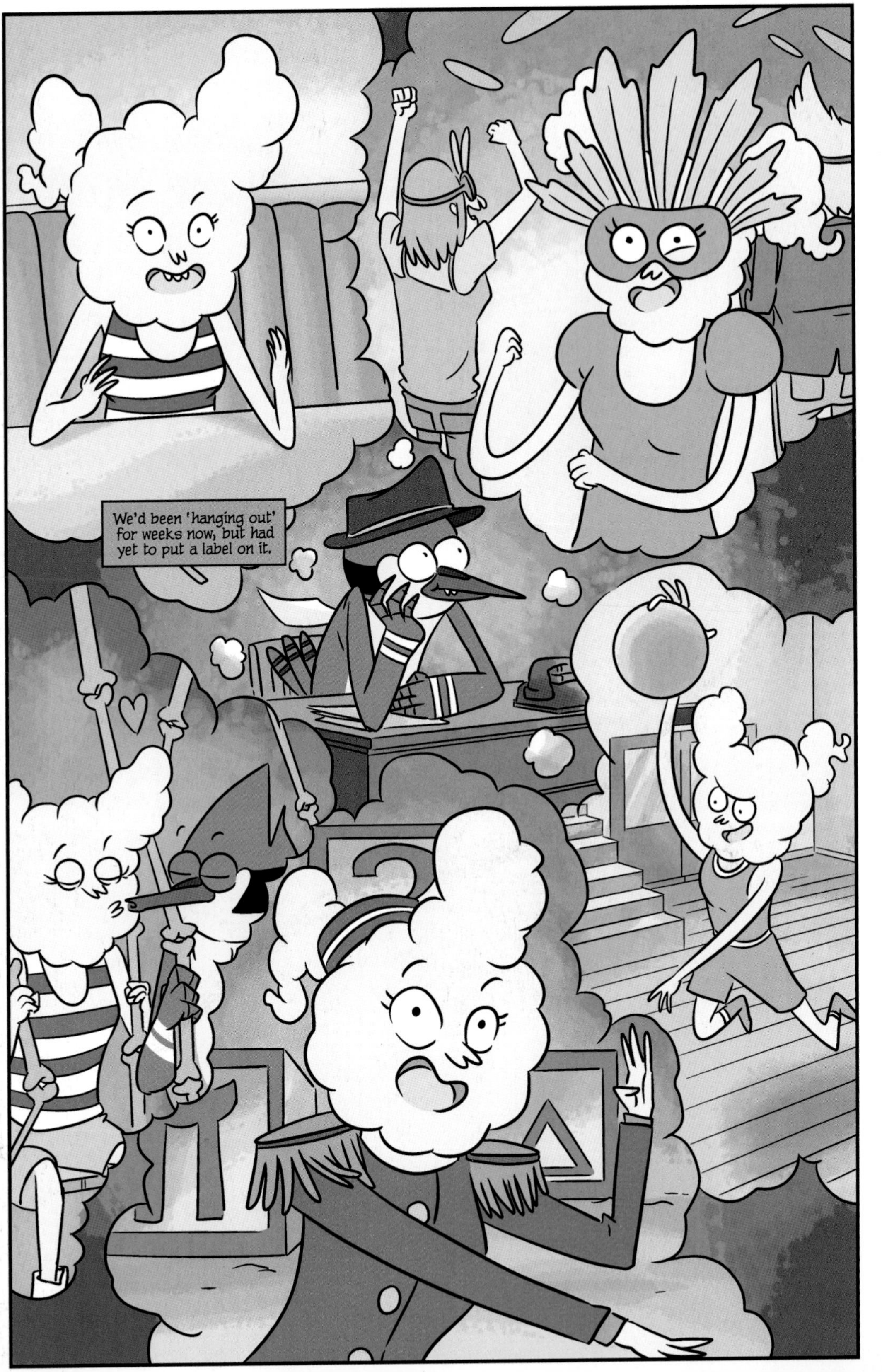
We'd been 'hanging out' for weeks now, but had yet to put a label on it.

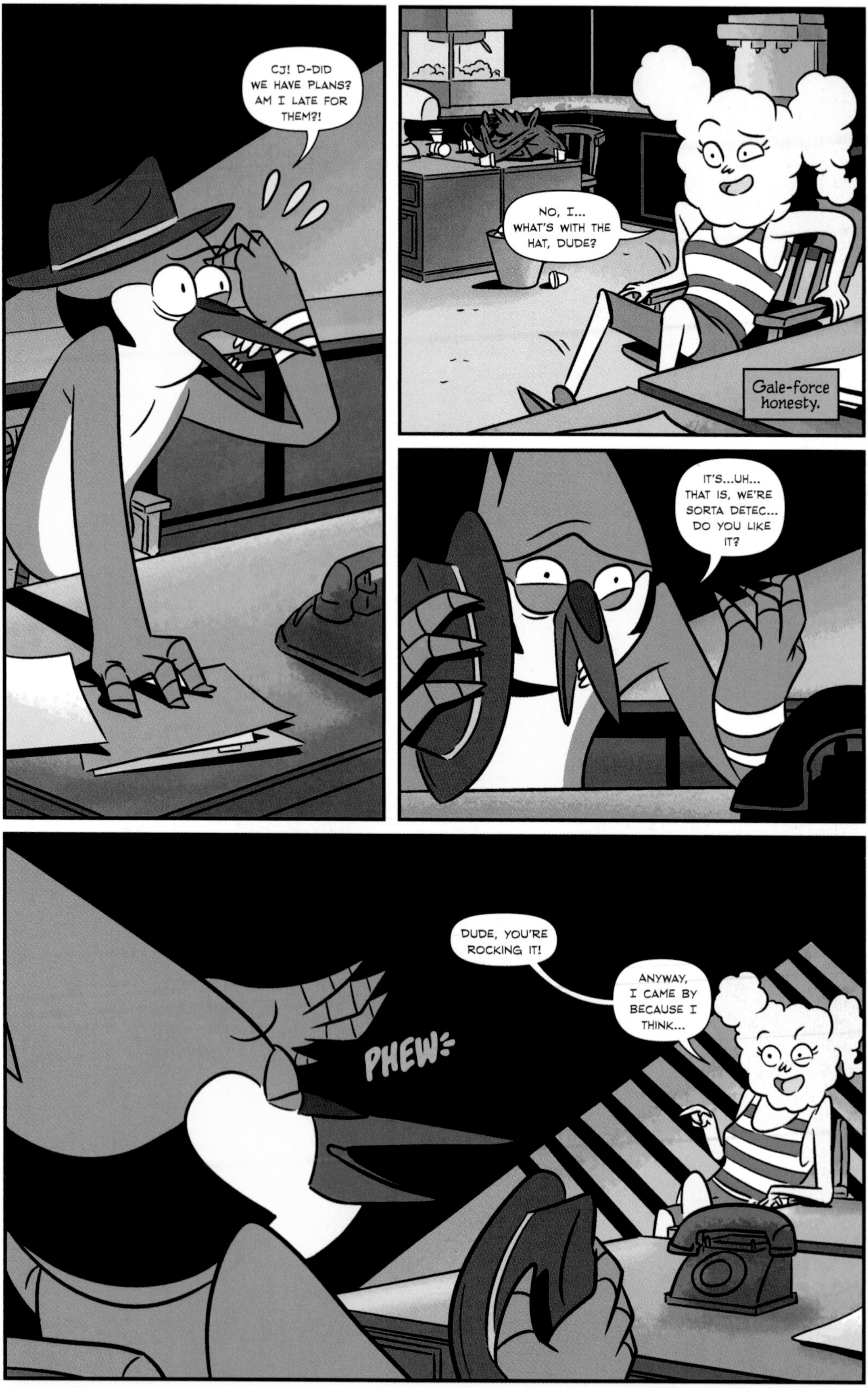
CJ! D-DID WE HAVE PLANS? AM I LATE FOR THEM?!
NO, I... WHAT'S WITH THE HAT, DUDE?
Gale-force honesty.
IT'S...UH... THAT IS, WE'RE SORTA DETEC... DO YOU LIKE IT?
PHEW
DUDE, YOU'RE ROCKING IT!
ANYWAY, I CAME BY BECAUSE I THINK...

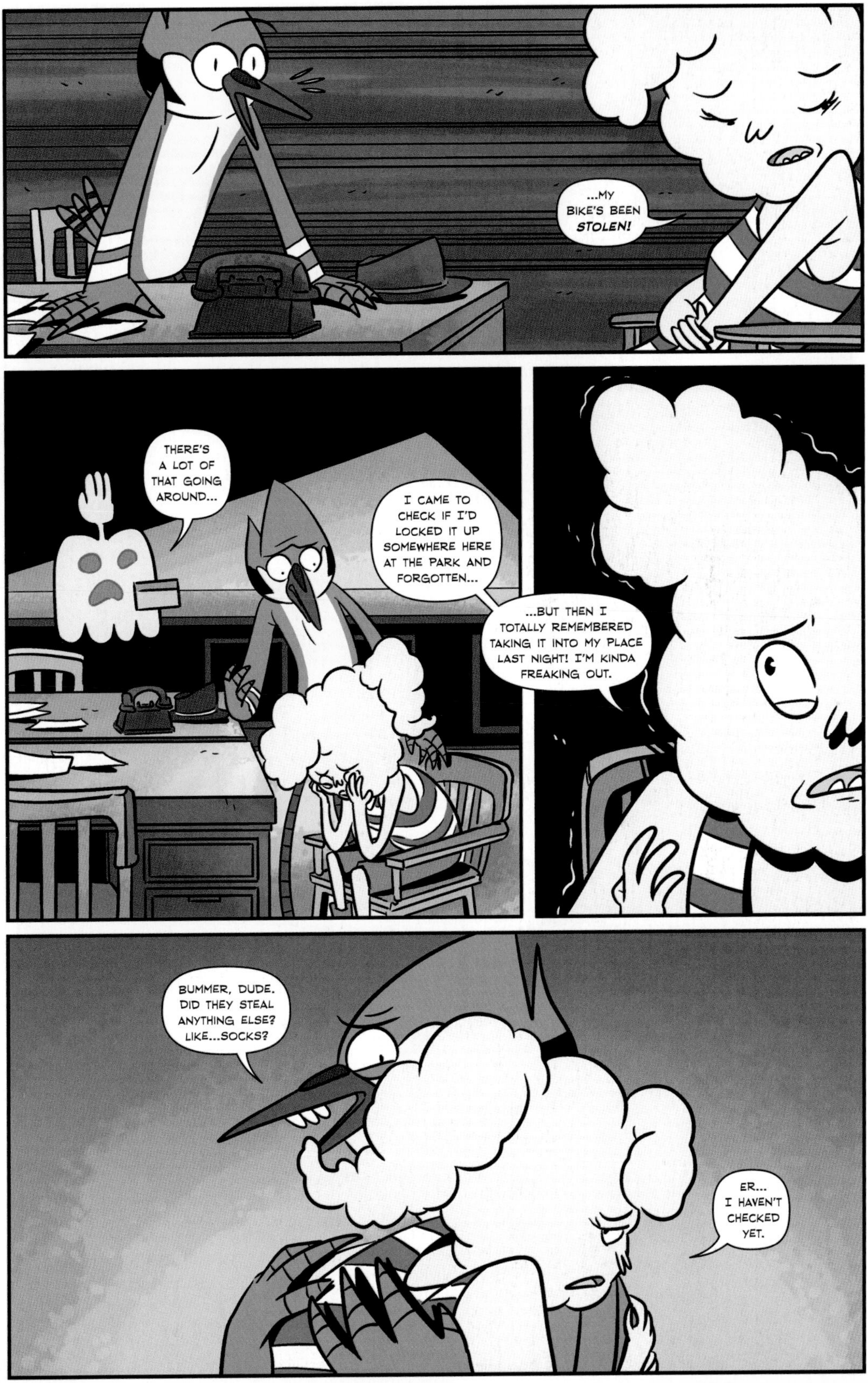
...MY BIKE'S BEEN *STOLEN!*
THERE'S A LOT OF THAT GOING AROUND...
I CAME TO CHECK IF I'D LOCKED IT UP SOMEWHERE HERE AT THE PARK AND FORGOTTEN...
...BUT THEN I TOTALLY REMEMBERED TAKING IT INTO MY PLACE LAST NIGHT! I'M KINDA FREAKING OUT.
BUMMER, DUDE. DID THEY STEAL ANYTHING ELSE? LIKE...SOCKS?
ER... I HAVEN'T CHECKED YET.

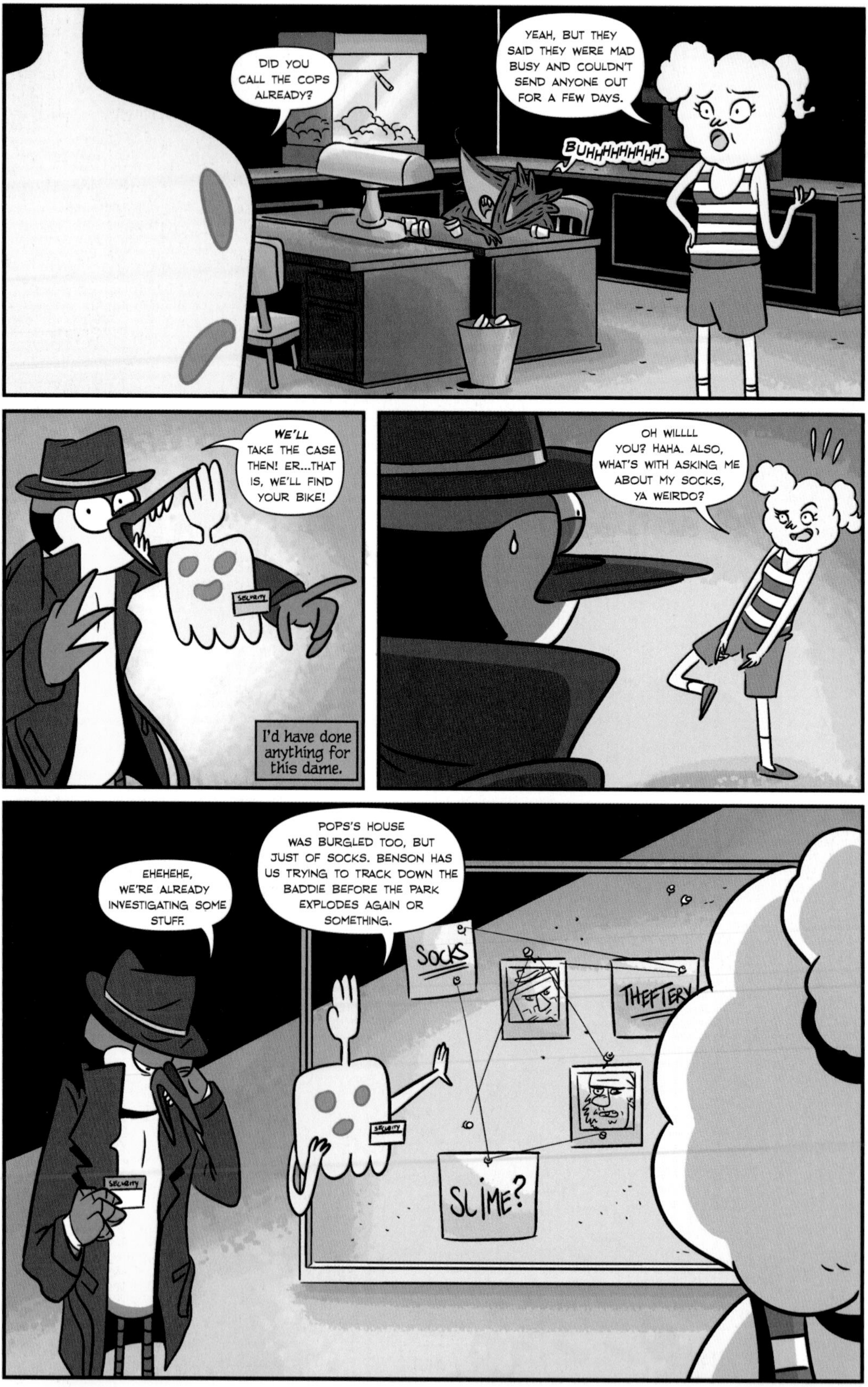

DID YOU CALL THE COPS ALREADY?
YEAH, BUT THEY SAID THEY WERE MAD BUSY AND COULDN'T SEND ANYONE OUT FOR A FEW DAYS.
BUHHHHHHHH.
WE'LL TAKE THE CASE THEN! ER...THAT IS, WE'LL FIND YOUR BIKE!
I'd have done anything for this dame.
OH WILLLL YOU? HAHA. ALSO, WHAT'S WITH ASKING ME ABOUT MY SOCKS, YA WEIRDO?
EHEHEHE, WE'RE ALREADY INVESTIGATING SOME STUFF.
POPS'S HOUSE WAS BURGLED TOO, BUT JUST OF SOCKS. BENSON HAS US TRYING TO TRACK DOWN THE BADDIE BEFORE THE PARK EXPLODES AGAIN OR SOMETHING.
SOCKS
THEFTERY
SLIME?

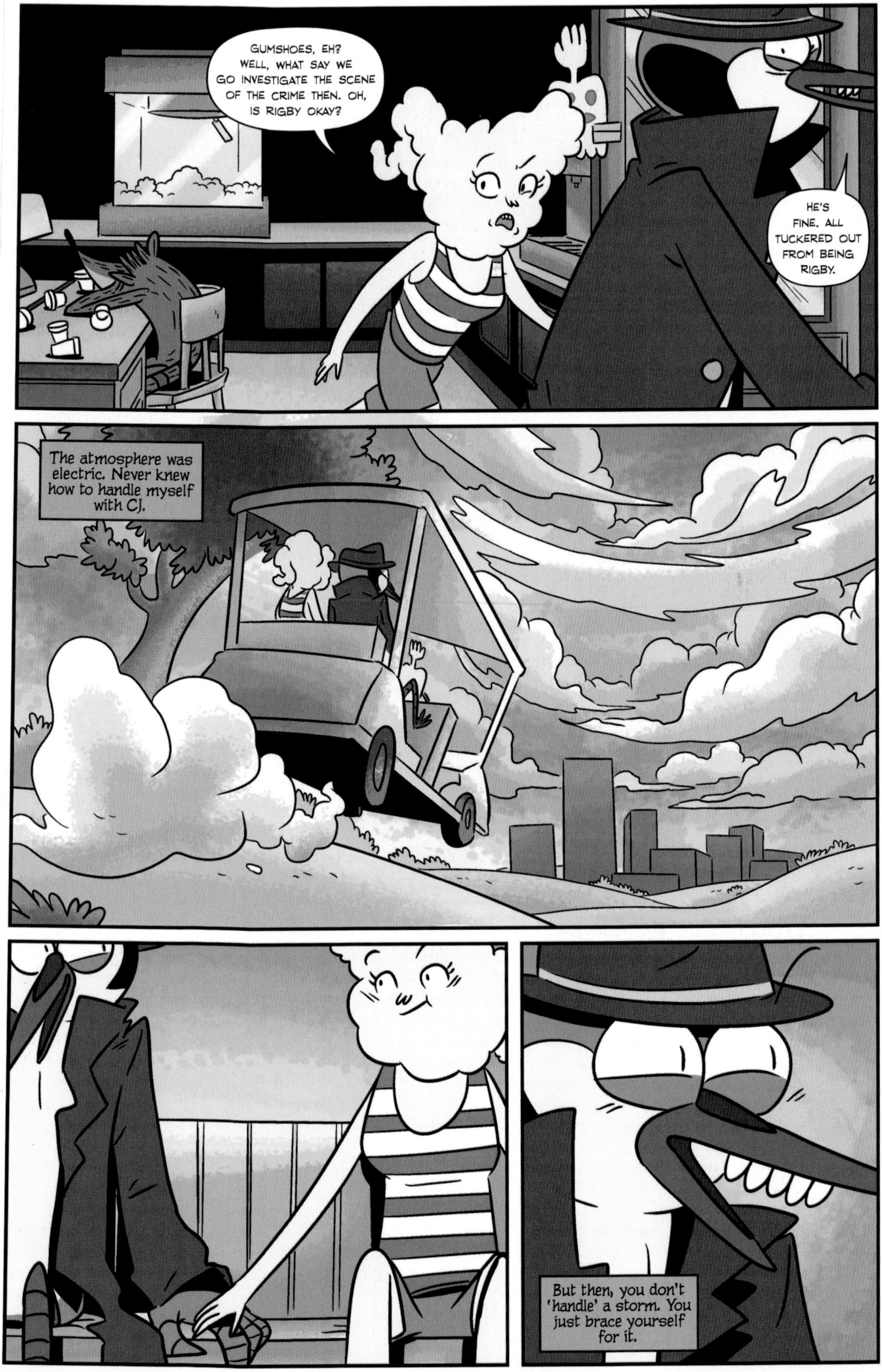

GUMSHOES, EH? WELL, WHAT SAY WE GO INVESTIGATE THE SCENE OF THE CRIME THEN. OH, IS RIGBY OKAY?
HE'S FINE. ALL TUCKERED OUT FROM BEING RIGBY.
The atmosphere was electric. Never knew how to handle myself with CJ.
But then, you don't 'handle' a storm. You just brace yourself for it.

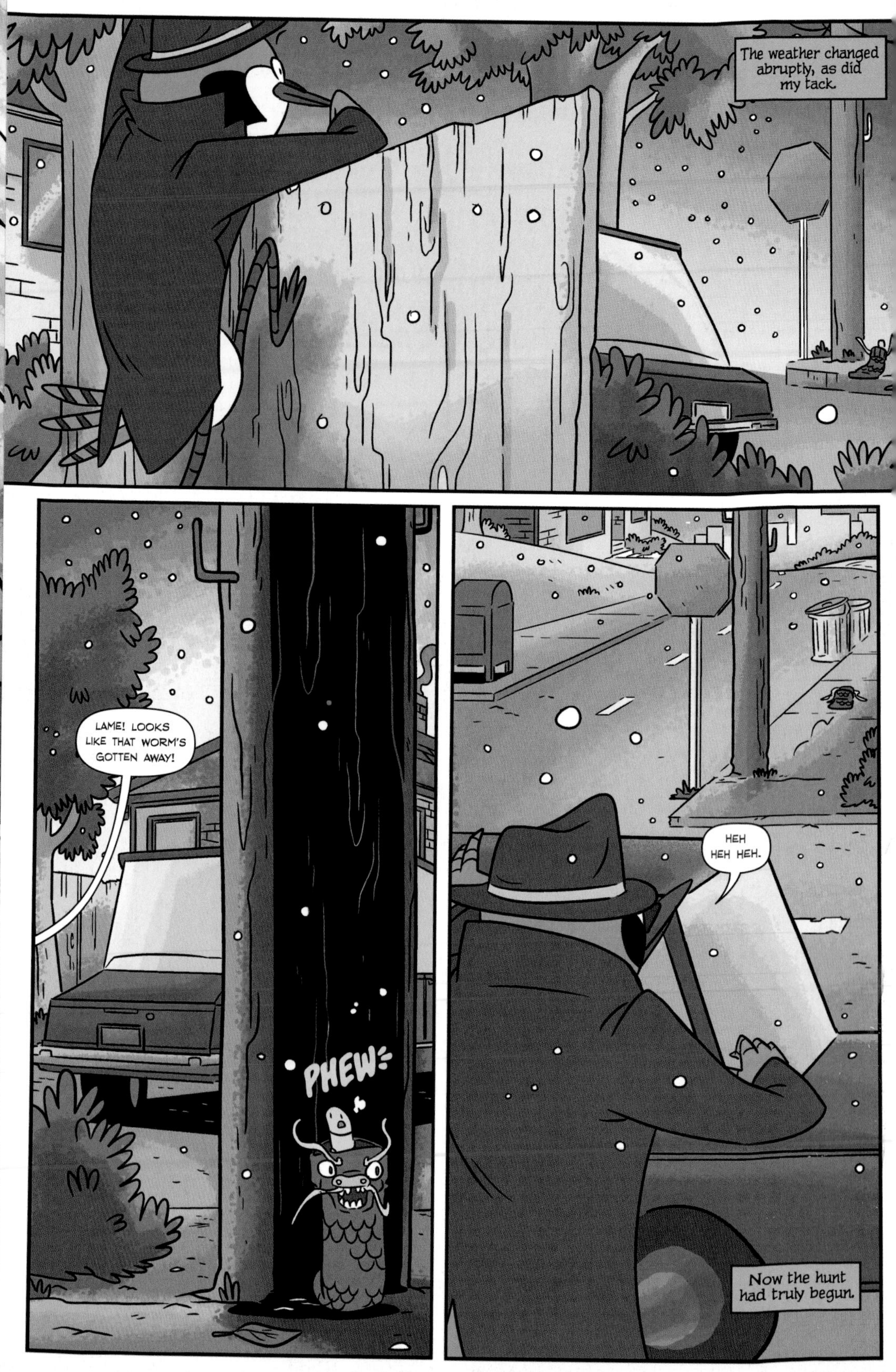
The weather changed abruptly, as did my tack.
LAME! LOOKS LIKE THAT WORM'S GOTTEN AWAY!
PHEW
HEH HEH HEH.
Now the hunt had truly begun.

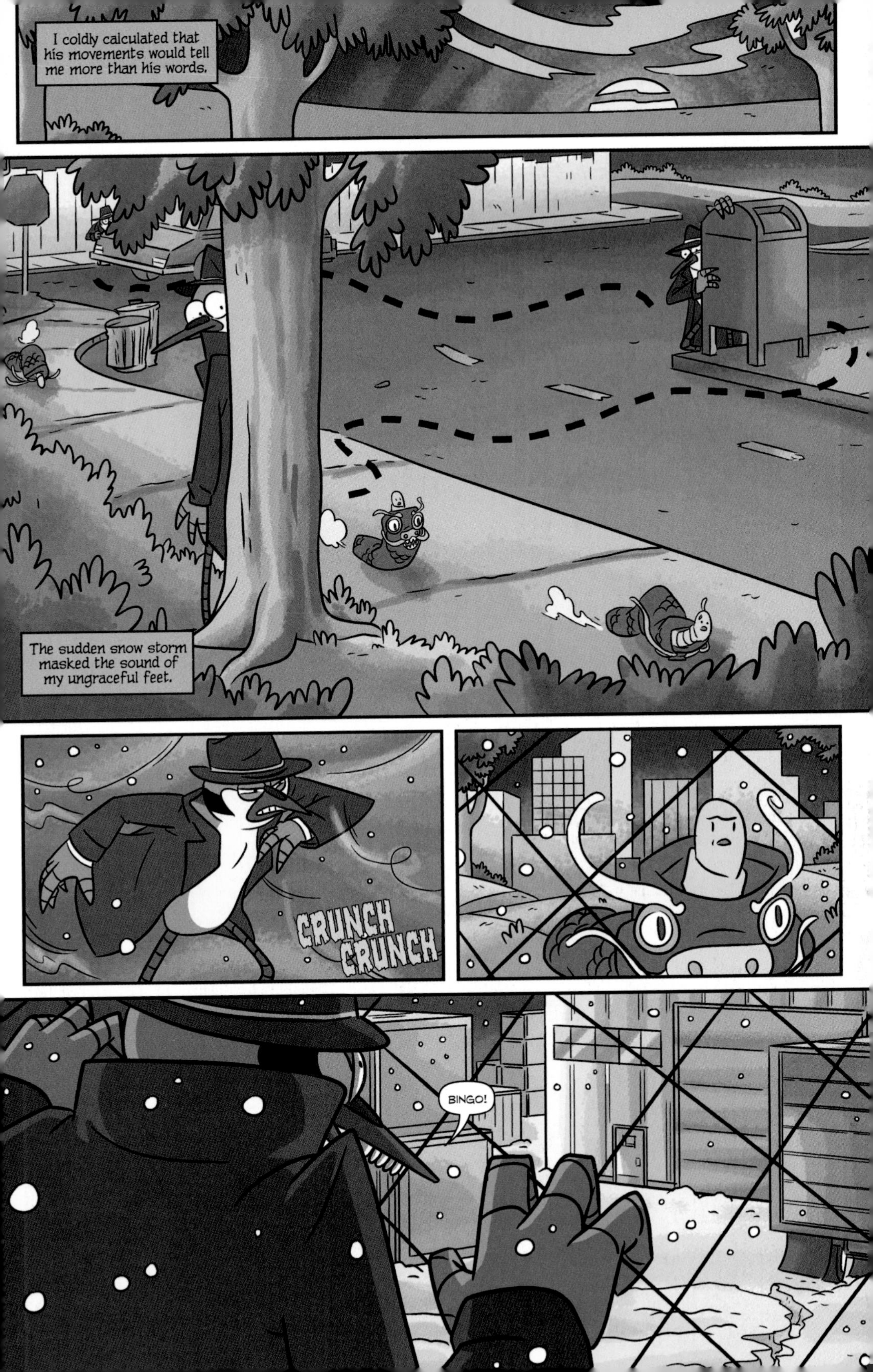
I coldly calculated that his movements would tell me more than his words.
The sudden snow storm masked the sound of my ungraceful feet.
CRUNCH CRUNCH
BINGO!

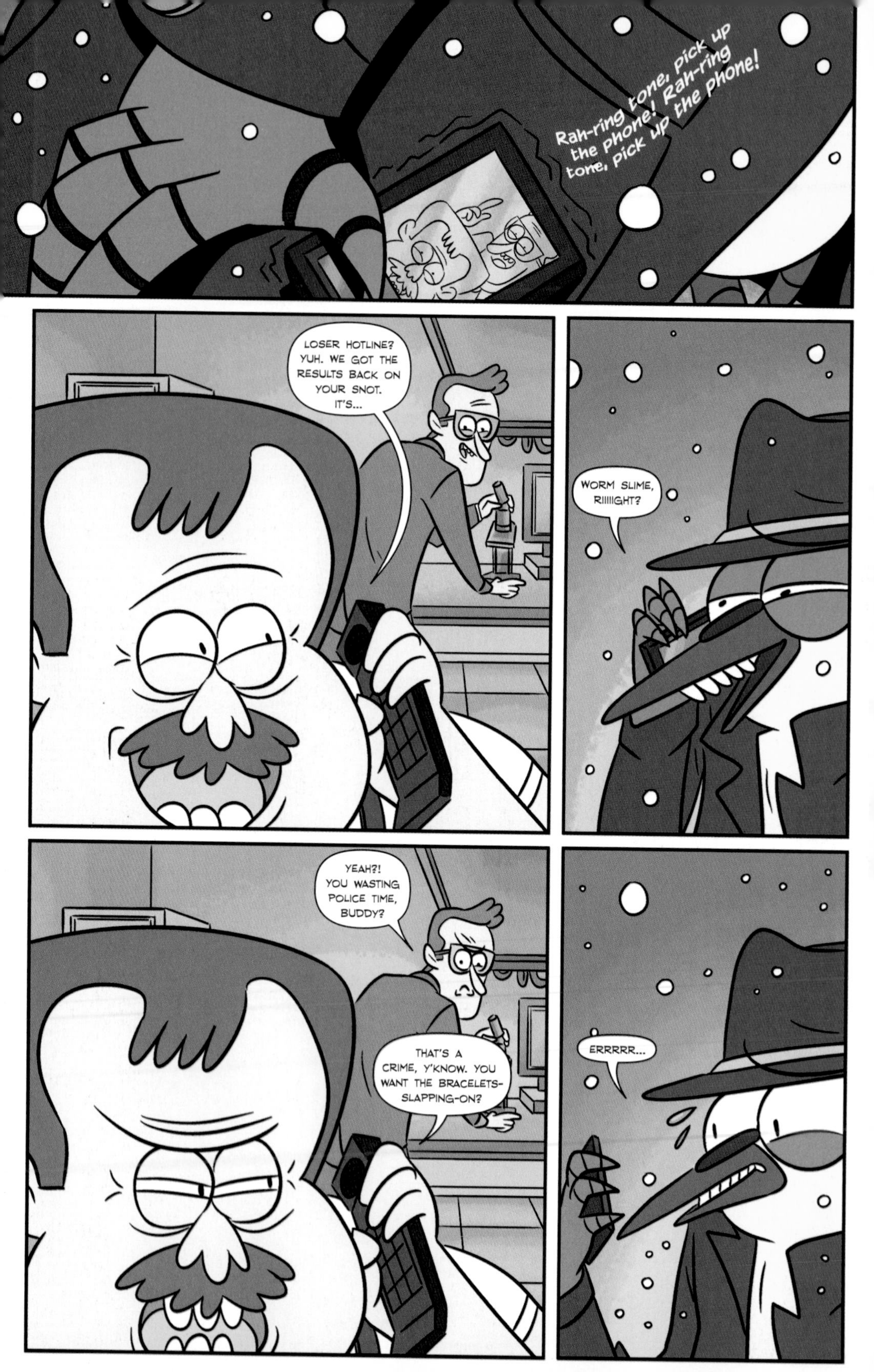
Rah-ring tone, pick up the phone! Rah-ring tone, pick up the phone!
LOSER HOTLINE? YUH. WE GOT THE RESULTS BACK ON YOUR SNOT. IT'S...
WORM SLIME, RIIIIGHT?
YEAH?! YOU WASTING POLICE TIME, BUDDY?
THAT'S A CRIME, Y'KNOW. YOU WANT THE BRACELETS-SLAPPING-ON?
ERRRRR...

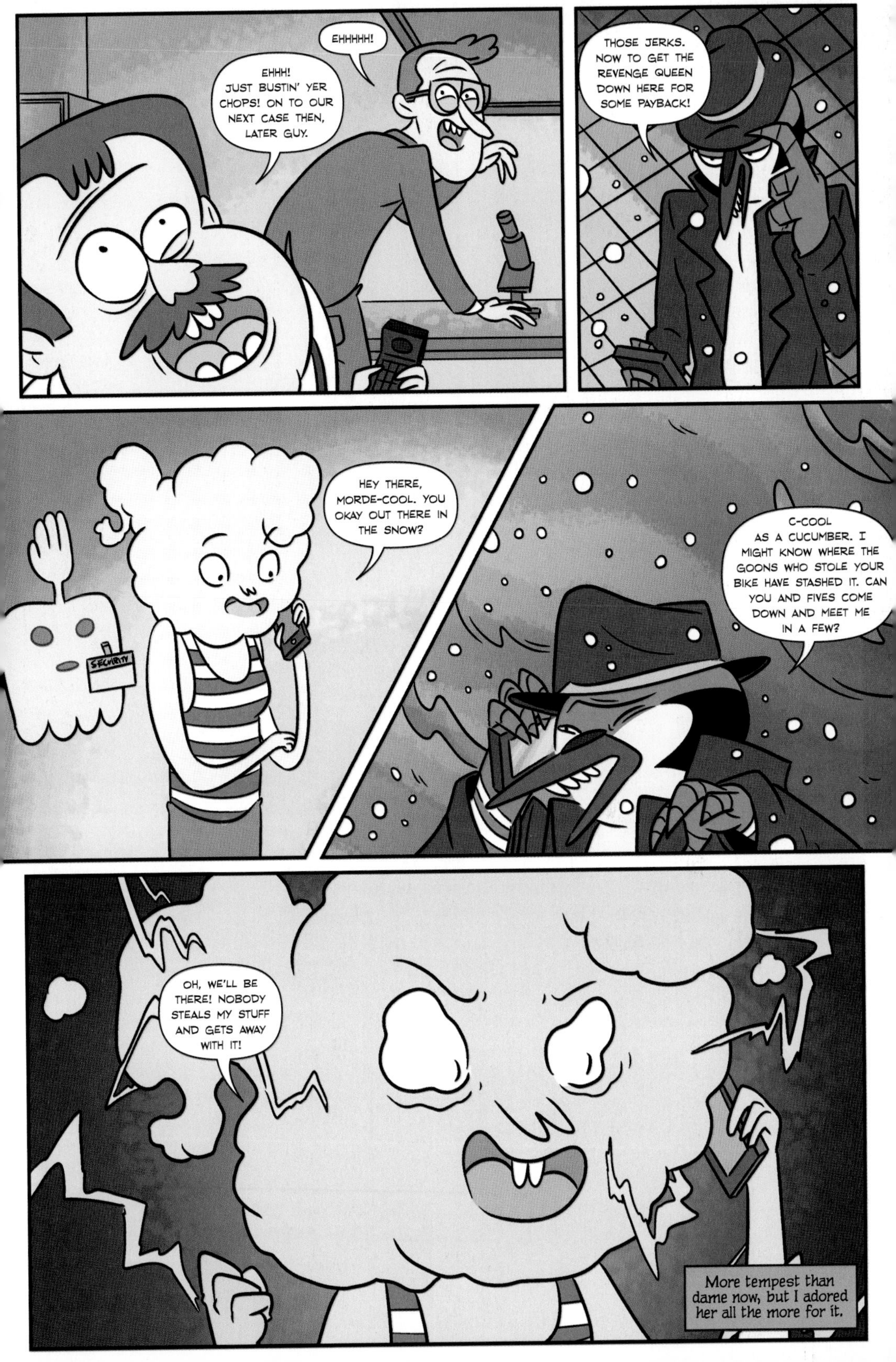
EHHHHH!
EHHH! JUST BUSTIN' YER CHOPS! ON TO OUR NEXT CASE THEN, LATER GUY.
THOSE JERKS. NOW TO GET THE REVENGE QUEEN DOWN HERE FOR SOME PAYBACK!
SECURITY
HEY THERE, MORDE-COOL. YOU OKAY OUT THERE IN THE SNOW?
C-COOL AS A CUCUMBER. I MIGHT KNOW WHERE THE GOONS WHO STOLE YOUR BIKE HAVE STASHED IT. CAN YOU AND FIVES COME DOWN AND MEET ME IN A FEW?
OH, WE'LL BE THERE! NOBODY STEALS MY STUFF AND GETS AWAY WITH IT!
More tempest than dame now, but I adored her all the more for it.

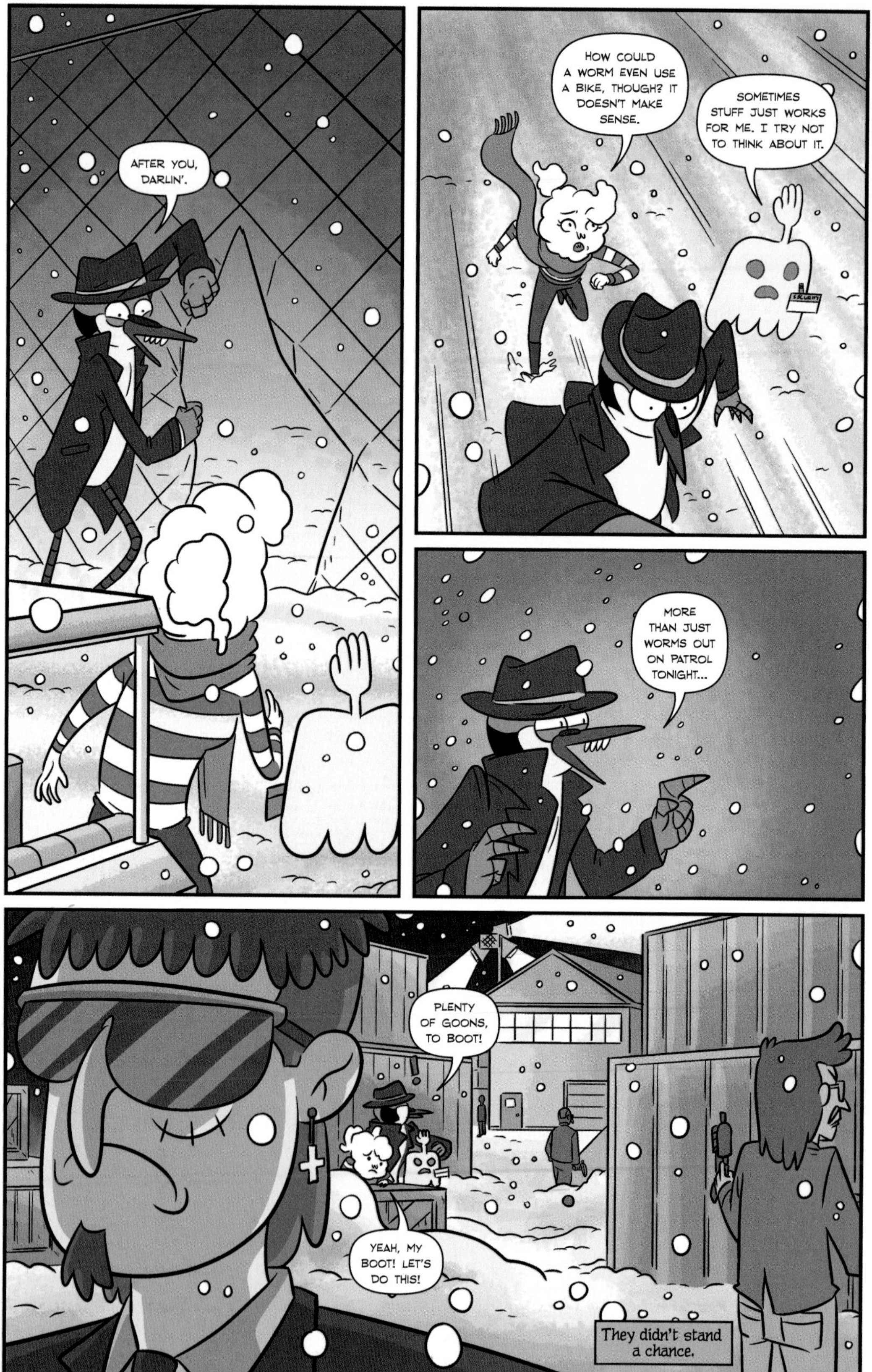
AFTER YOU, DARLIN'.
HOW COULD A WORM EVEN USE A BIKE, THOUGH? IT DOESN'T MAKE SENSE.
SOMETIMES STUFF JUST WORKS FOR ME. I TRY NOT TO THINK ABOUT IT.
MORE THAN JUST WORMS OUT ON PATROL TONIGHT...
PLENTY OF GOONS, TO BOOT!
YEAH, MY BOOT! LET'S DO THIS!
They didn't stand a chance.

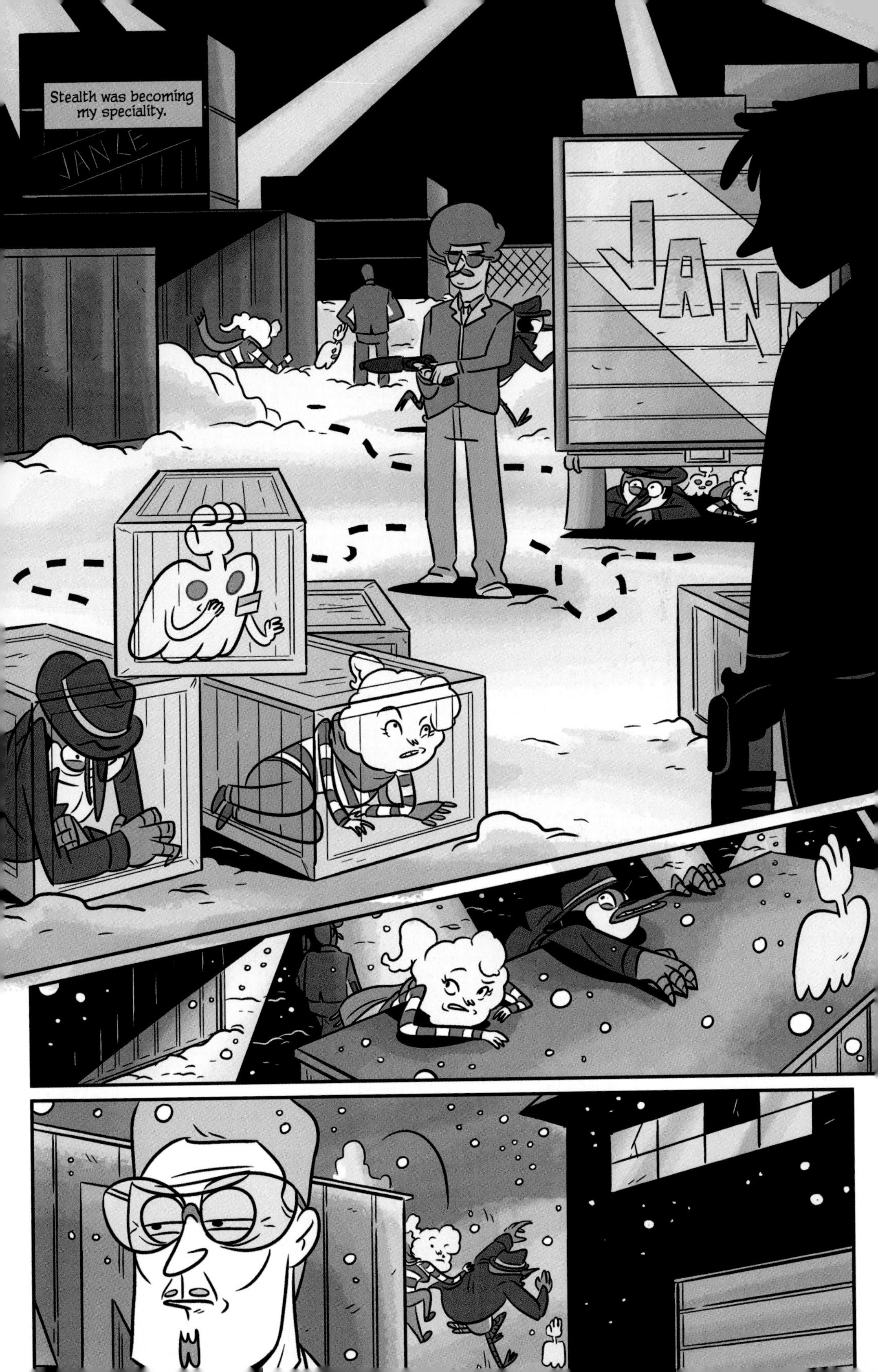
Stealth was becoming my speciality.
JANKE
JAN

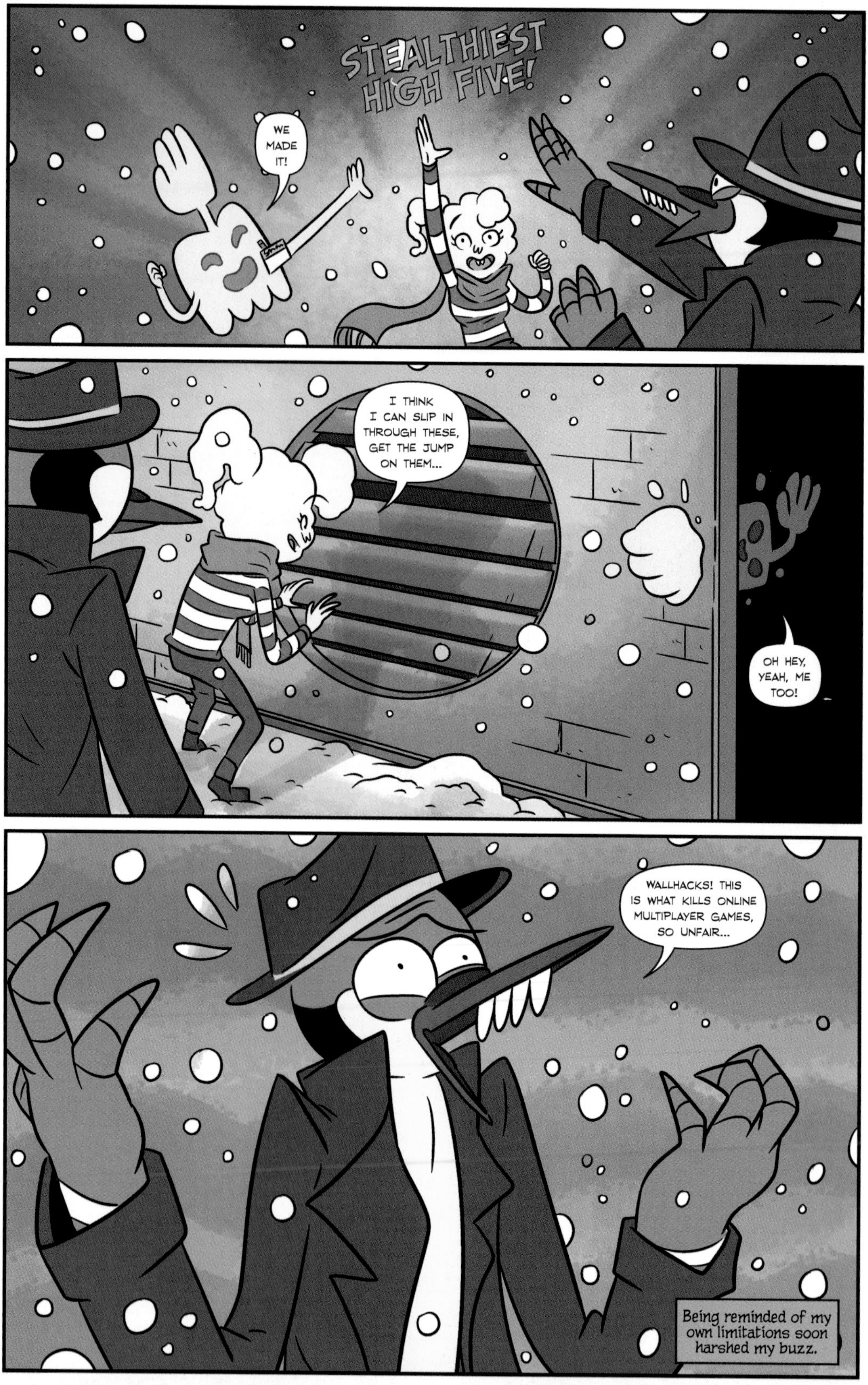
STEALTHIEST HIGH FIVE!
WE MADE IT!
I THINK I CAN SLIP IN THROUGH THESE, GET THE JUMP ON THEM...
OH HEY, YEAH, ME TOO!
WALLHACKS! THIS IS WHAT KILLS ONLINE MULTIPLAYER GAMES, SO UNFAIR...
Being reminded of my own limitations soon harshed my buzz.

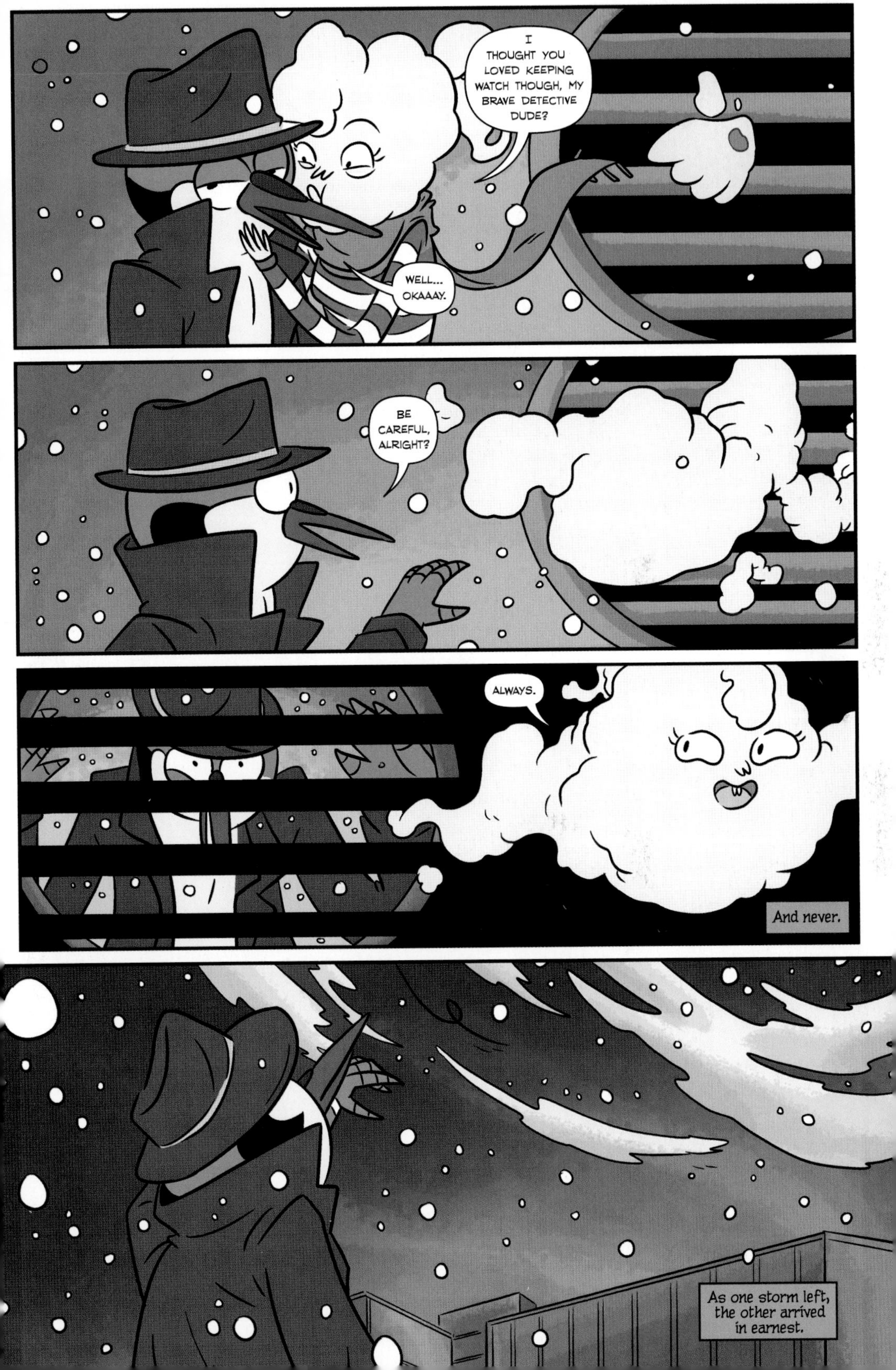
I THOUGHT YOU LOVED KEEPING WATCH THOUGH, MY BRAVE DETECTIVE DUDE?
WELL... OKAAAY.
BE CAREFUL, ALRIGHT?
ALWAYS.
And never.
As one storm left, the other arrived in earnest.

OH CRIPES!

There was more than one variety of storm headed my way, however.

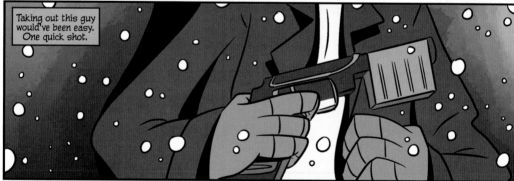

KER-DIVE!

Taking out this guy would've been easy. One quick shot.

But I knew how much hurt just one squeeze of that trigger could bring.

All too well.

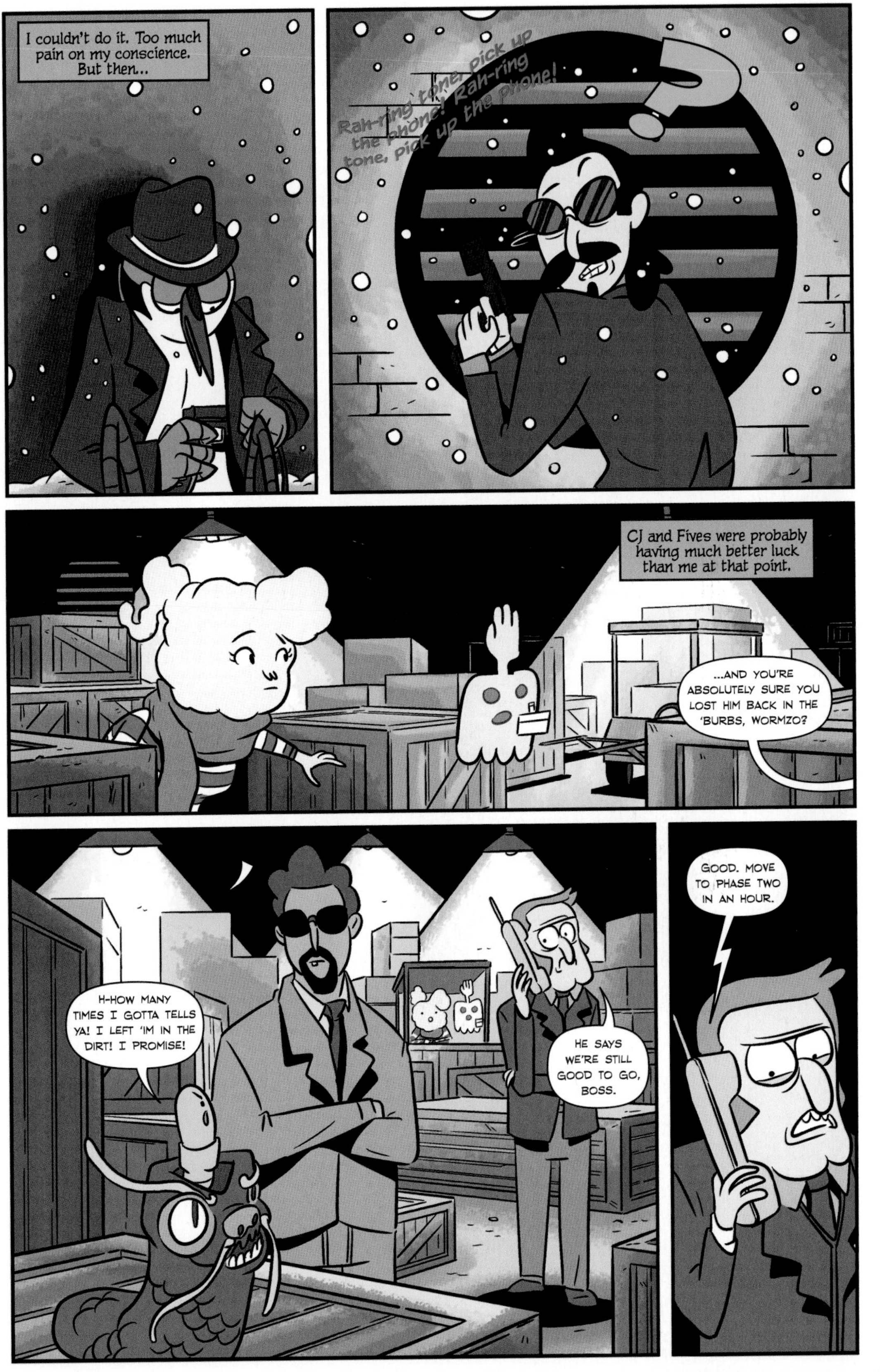
I couldn't do it. Too much pain on my conscience. But then...
Rah-ring tone, pick up the phone! Rah-ring tone, pick up the phone!
CJ and Fives were probably having much better luck than me at that point.
...AND YOU'RE ABSOLUTELY SURE YOU LOST HIM BACK IN THE 'BURBS, WORMZO?
H-HOW MANY TIMES I GOTTA TELLS YA! I LEFT 'IM IN THE DIRT! I PROMISE!
HE SAYS WE'RE STILL GOOD TO GO, BOSS.
GOOD. MOVE TO PHASE TWO IN AN HOUR.

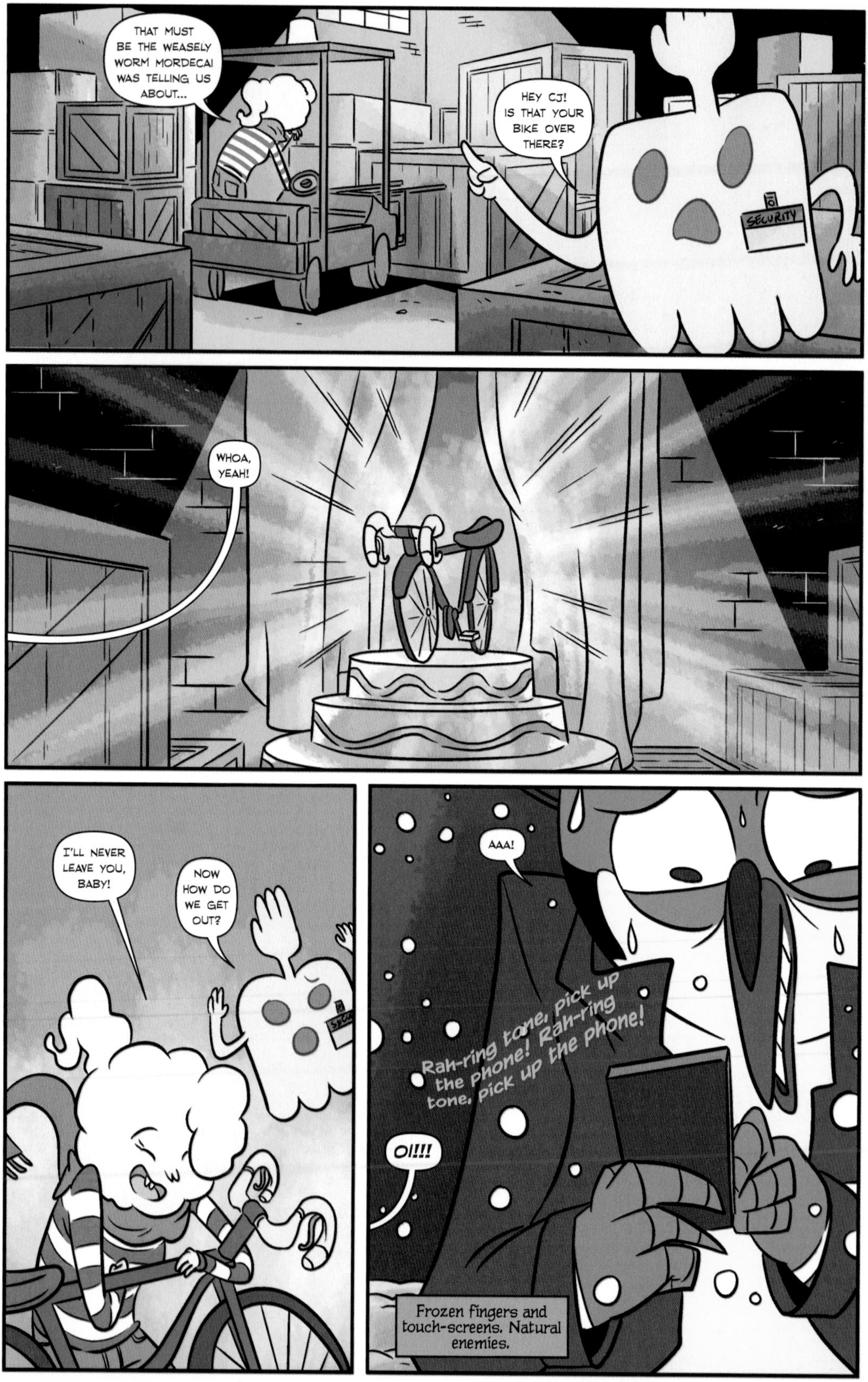
THAT MUST BE THE WEASELY WORM MORDECAI WAS TELLING US ABOUT...
HEY CJ! IS THAT YOUR BIKE OVER THERE?
SECURITY
WHOA, YEAH!
I'LL NEVER LEAVE YOU, BABY!
NOW HOW DO WE GET OUT?
AAA!
Rah-ring tone, pick up the phone! Rah-ring tone, pick up the phone!
OI!!!
Frozen fingers and touch-screens. Natural enemies.

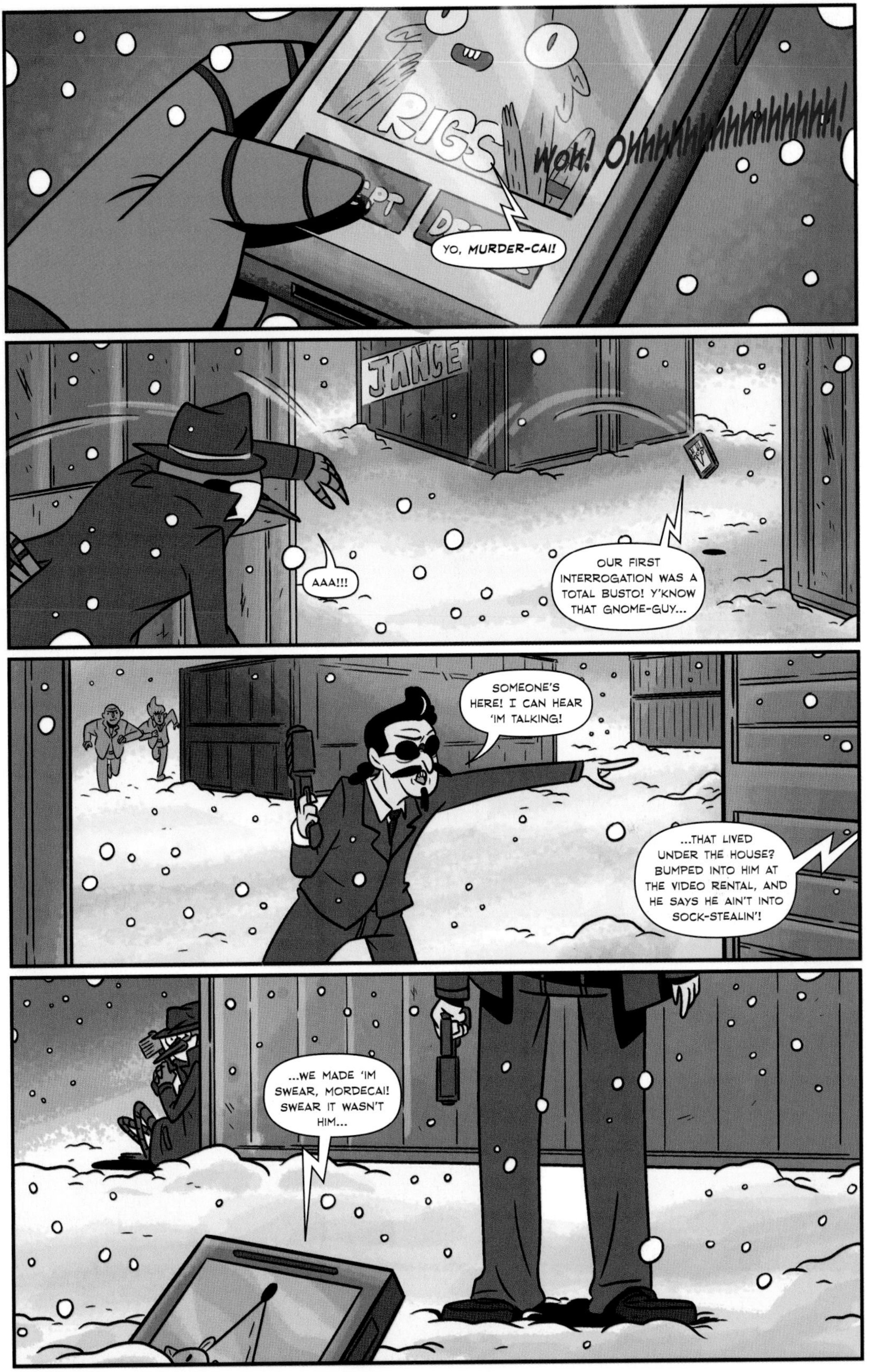
RIGS
Woh! Ohhhhhhhhhhhhhhh!
YO, MURDER-CAI!
JANCE
AAA!!!
OUR FIRST INTERROGATION WAS A TOTAL BUSTO! Y'KNOW THAT GNOME-GUY...
SOMEONE'S HERE! I CAN HEAR 'IM TALKING!
...THAT LIVED UNDER THE HOUSE? BUMPED INTO HIM AT THE VIDEO RENTAL, AND HE SAYS HE AIN'T INTO SOCK-STEALIN'!
...WE MADE 'IM SWEAR, MORDECAI! SWEAR IT WASN'T HIM...

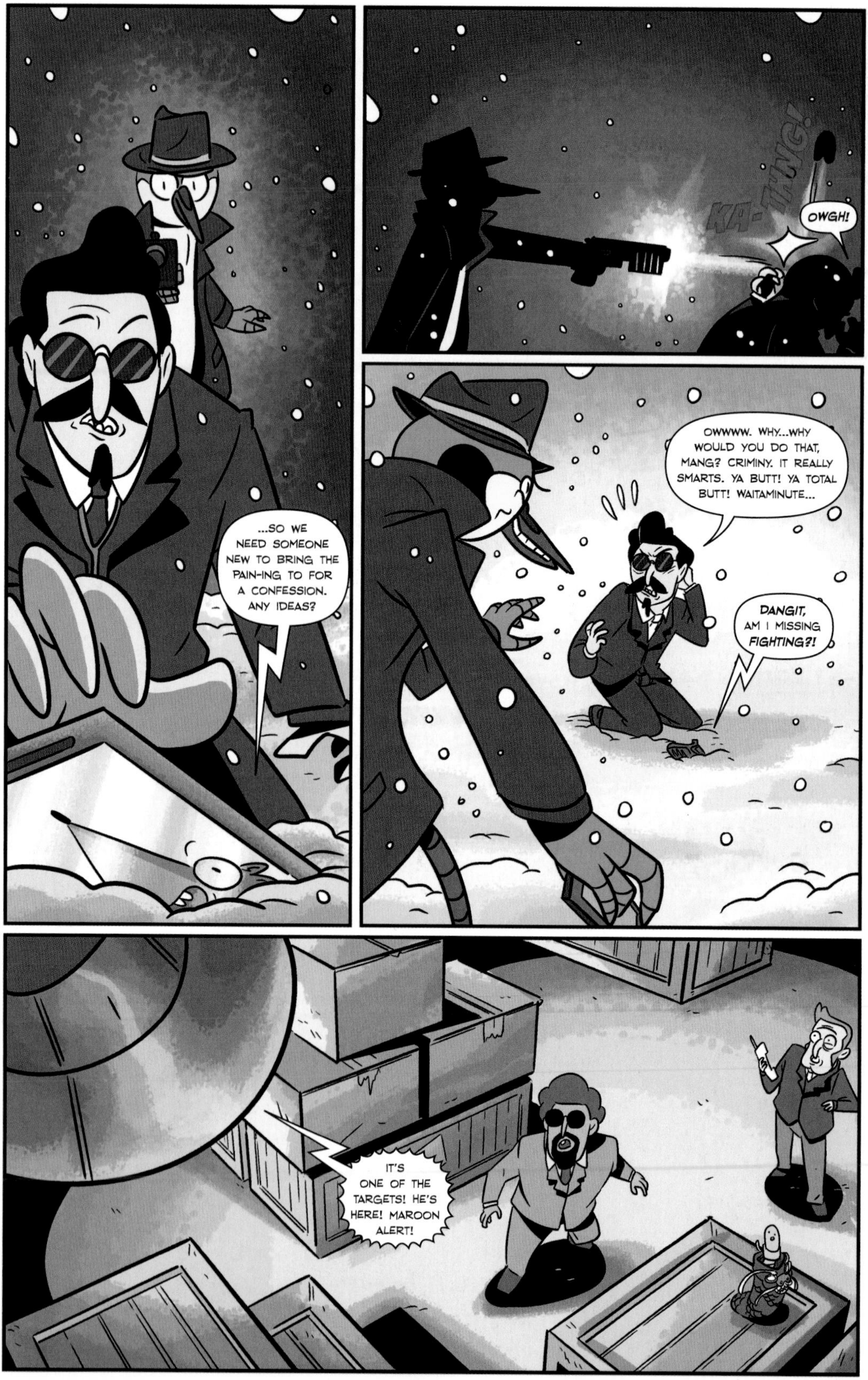
...SO WE NEED SOMEONE NEW TO BRING THE PAIN-ING TO FOR A CONFESSION. ANY IDEAS?
KA-TING!
OWGH!
OWWWW. WHY...WHY WOULD YOU DO THAT, MANG? CRIMINY. IT REALLY SMARTS. YA BUTT! YA TOTAL BUTT! WAITAMINUTE...
DANGIT, AM I MISSING FIGHTING?!
IT'S ONE OF THE TARGETS! HE'S HERE! MAROON ALERT!

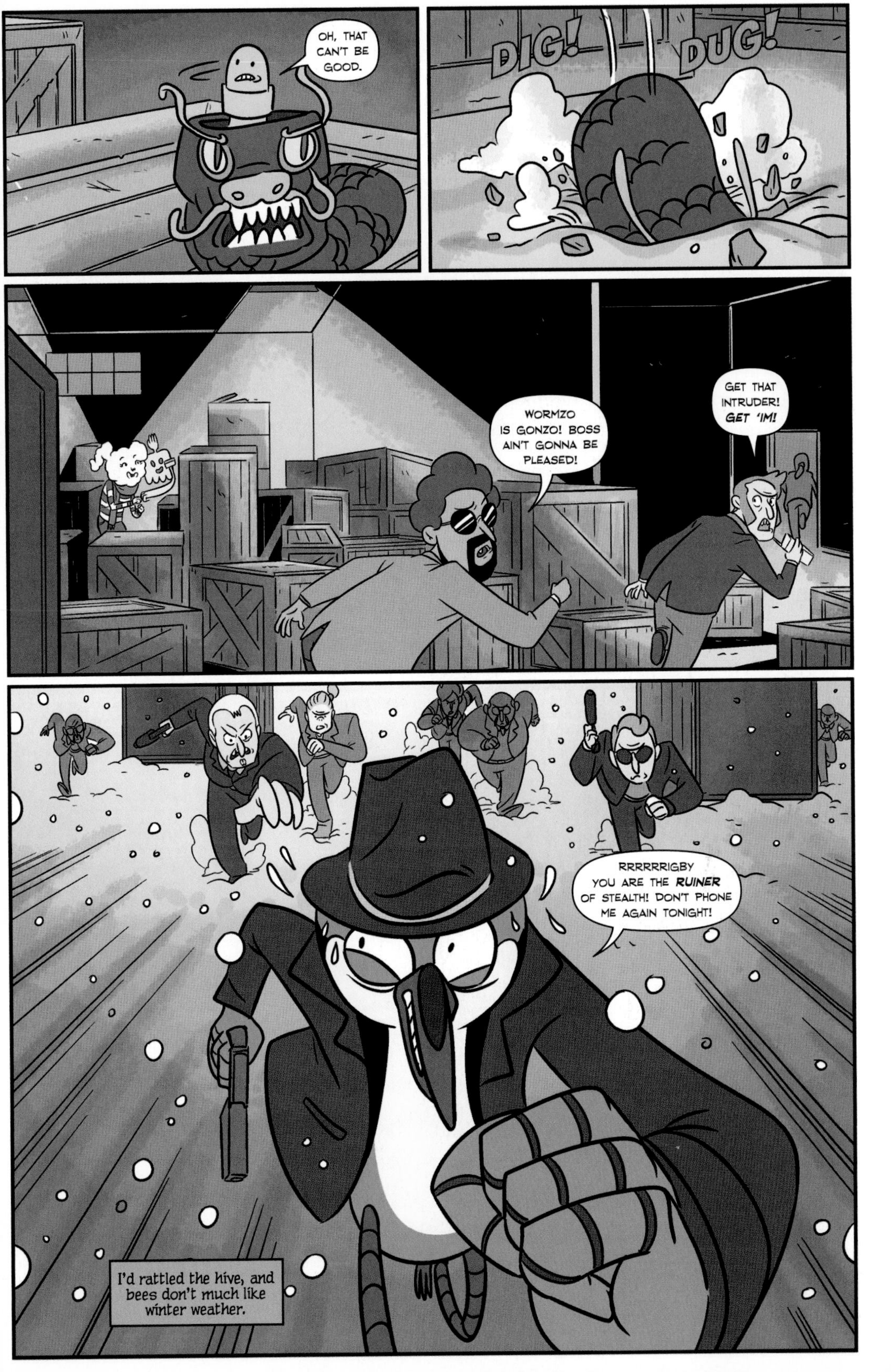
OH, THAT CAN'T BE GOOD.
DIG!
DUG!
WORMZO IS GONZO! BOSS AIN'T GONNA BE PLEASED!
GET THAT INTRUDER! GET 'IM!
RRRRRRIGBY YOU ARE THE RUINER OF STEALTH! DON'T PHONE ME AGAIN TONIGHT!
I'd rattled the hive, and bees don't much like winter weather.

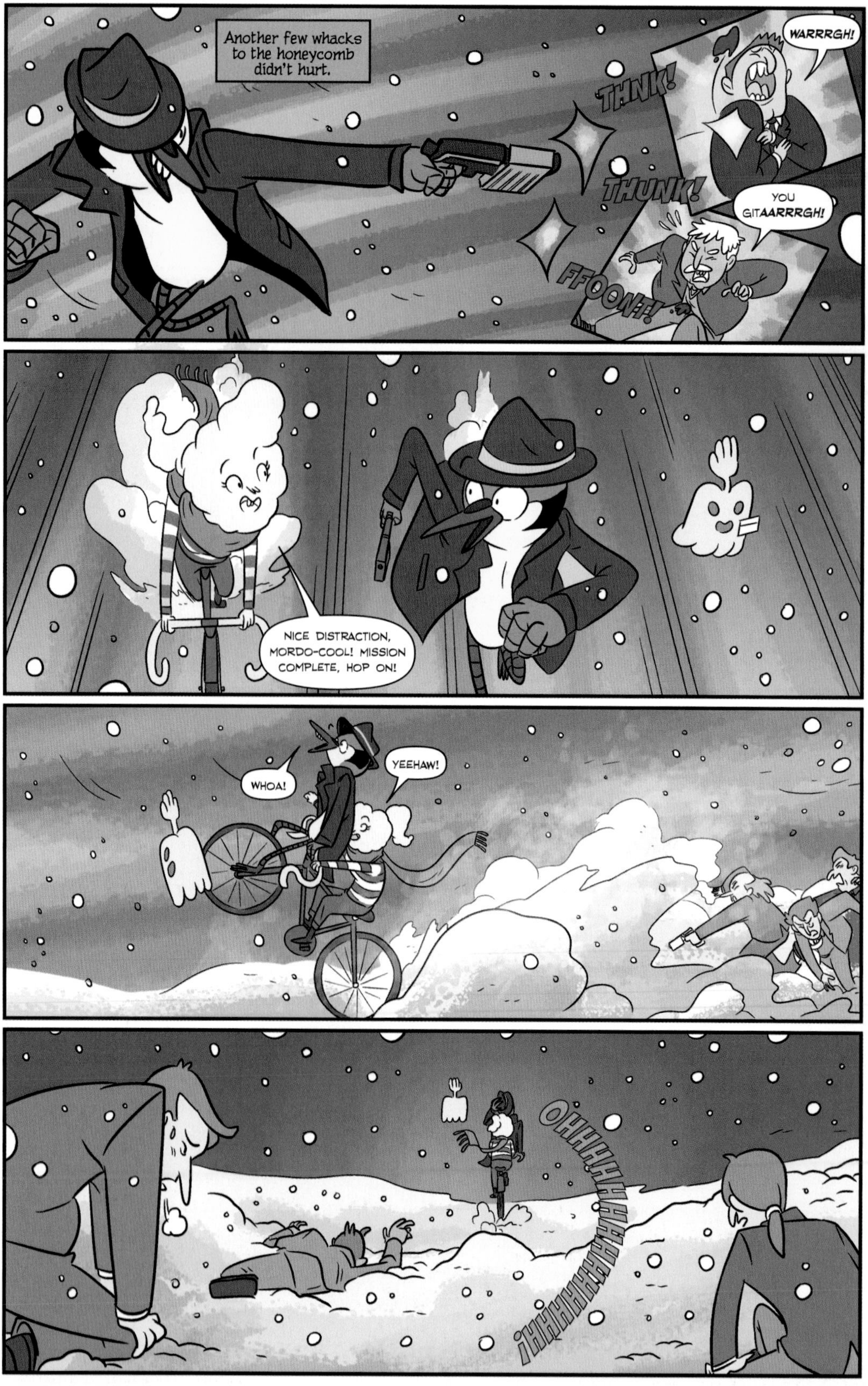
Another few whacks to the honeycomb didn't hurt.
THNK!
WARRRGH!
THUNK!
YOU GITAARRRGH!
FFOON!!
NICE DISTRACTION, MORDO-COOL! MISSION COMPLETE, HOP ON!
WHOA!
YEEHAW!
OHHHHHHHHHHHHHHHHH!

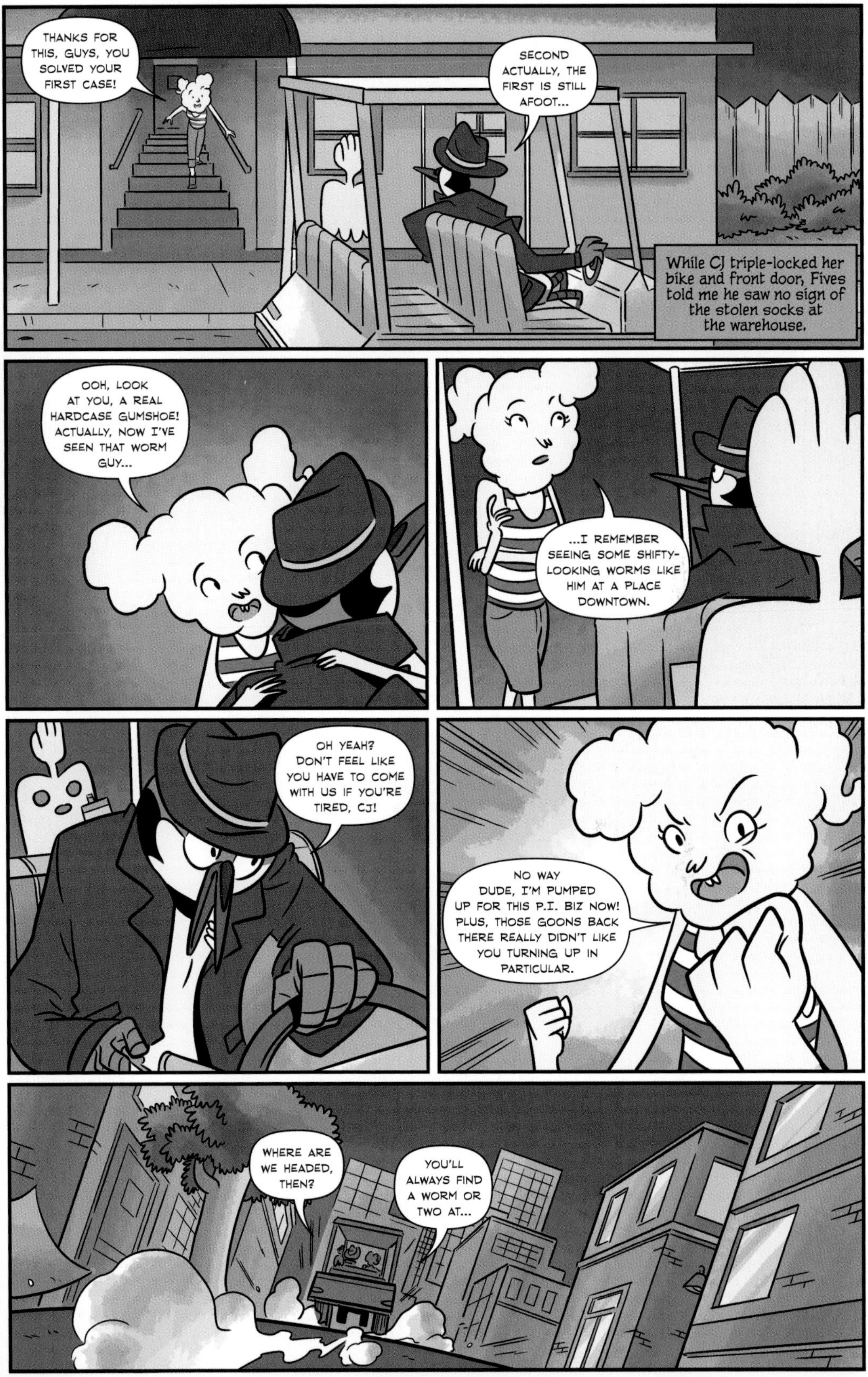
THANKS FOR THIS, GUYS, YOU SOLVED YOUR FIRST CASE!
SECOND ACTUALLY, THE FIRST IS STILL AFOOT...
While CJ triple-locked her bike and front door, Fives told me he saw no sign of the stolen socks at the warehouse.
OOH, LOOK AT YOU, A REAL HARDCASE GUMSHOE! ACTUALLY, NOW I'VE SEEN THAT WORM GUY...
...I REMEMBER SEEING SOME SHIFTY-LOOKING WORMS LIKE HIM AT A PLACE DOWNTOWN.
OH YEAH? DON'T FEEL LIKE YOU HAVE TO COME WITH US IF YOU'RE TIRED, CJ!
NO WAY DUDE, I'M PUMPED UP FOR THIS P.I. BIZ NOW! PLUS, THOSE GOONS BACK THERE REALLY DIDN'T LIKE YOU TURNING UP IN PARTICULAR.
WHERE ARE WE HEADED, THEN?
YOU'LL ALWAYS FIND A WORM OR TWO AT...

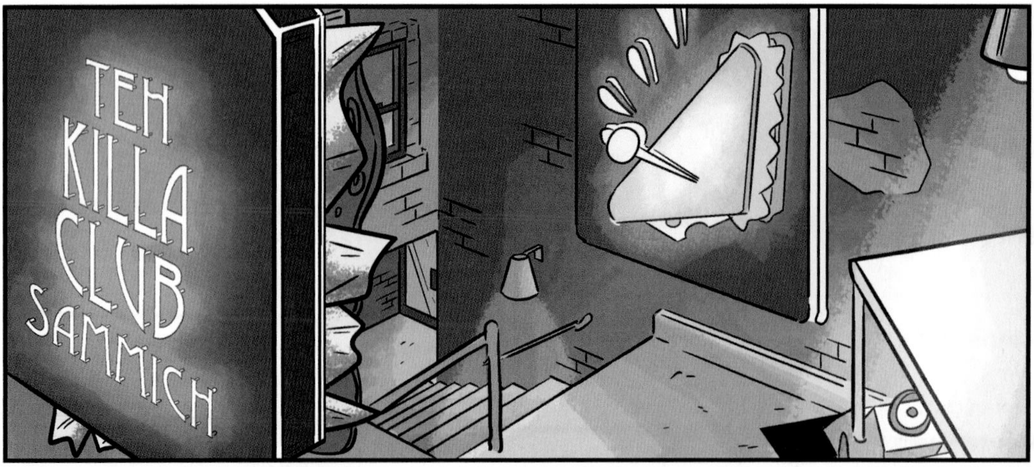
TEH KILLA CLUB SAMMICH

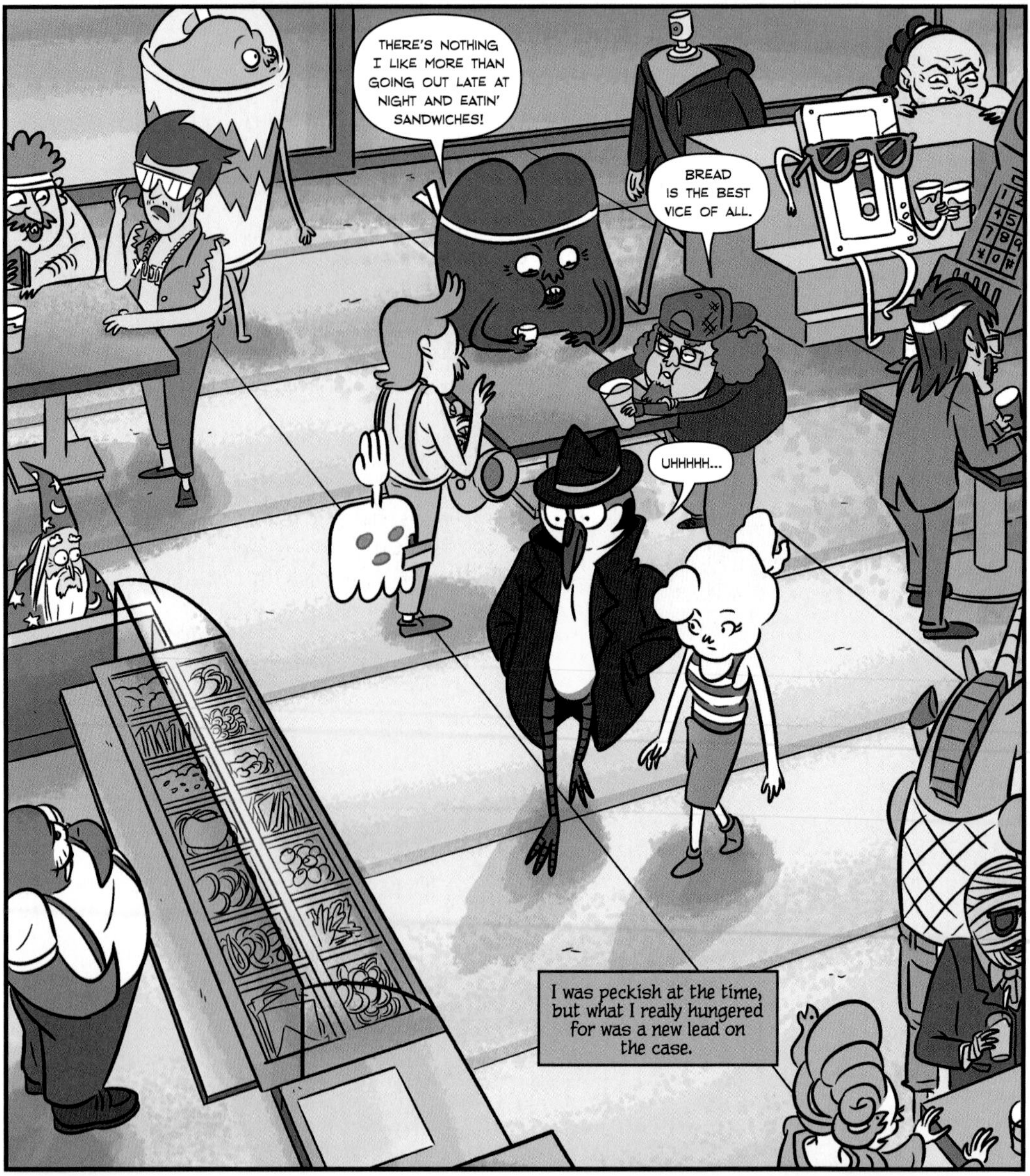
THERE'S NOTHING I LIKE MORE THAN GOING OUT LATE AT NIGHT AND EATIN' SANDWICHES!
BREAD IS THE BEST VICE OF ALL.
UHHHHH...
I was peckish at the time, but what I really hungered for was a new lead on the case.

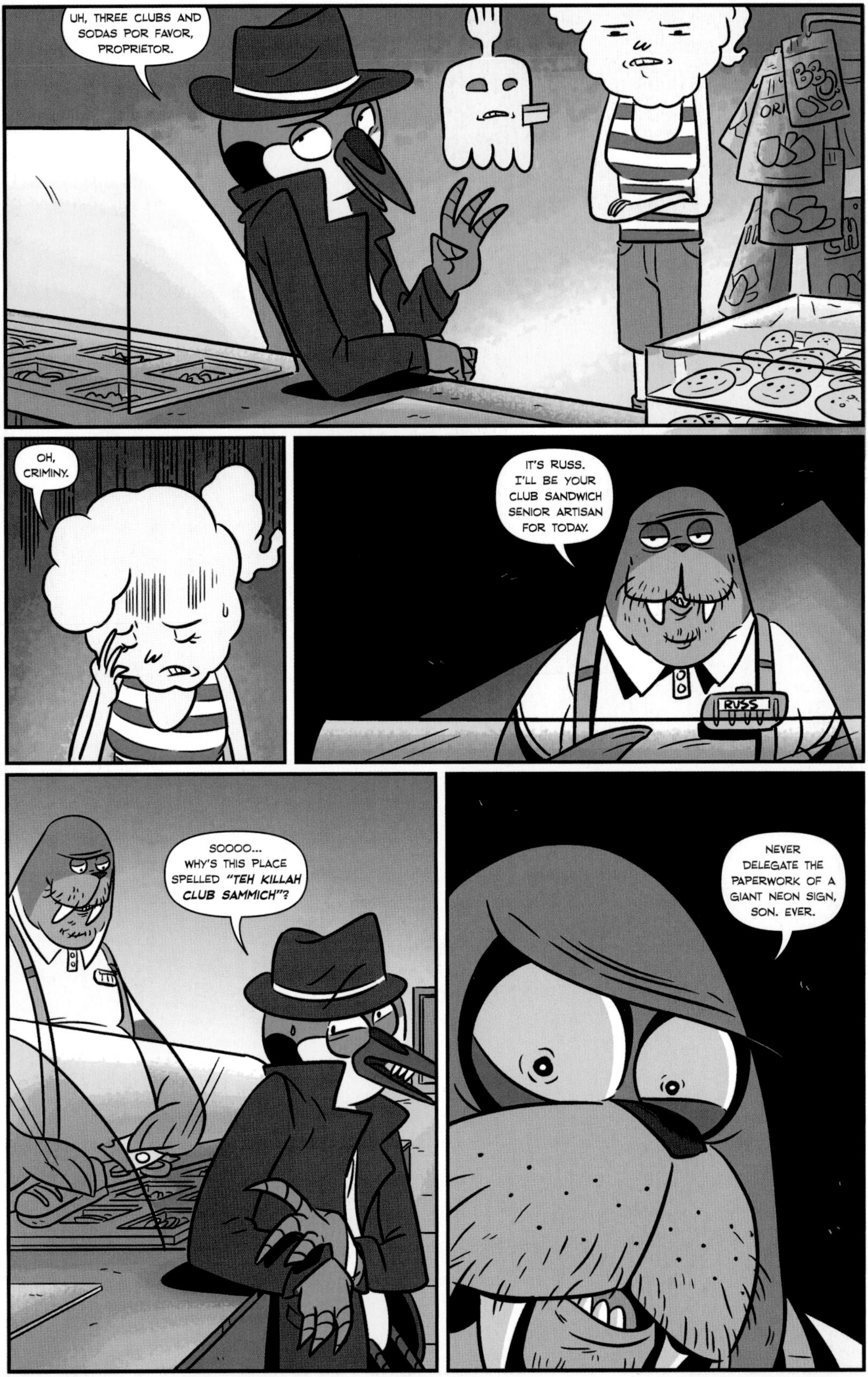
UH, THREE CLUBS AND SODAS POR FAVOR, PROPRIETOR.
OH, CRIMINY.
IT'S RUSS. I'LL BE YOUR CLUB SANDWICH SENIOR ARTISAN FOR TODAY.
RUSS
SOOOO... WHY'S THIS PLACE SPELLED "TEH KILLAH CLUB SAMMICH"?
NEVER DELEGATE THE PAPERWORK OF A GIANT NEON SIGN, SON. EVER.

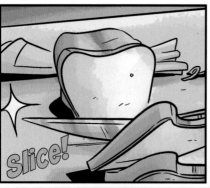

Slice!

Soda *Sppppsssshhhh!*

Ding!

OH MAN, THOUGHT RUSS WAS GOING TO CLOCK YOU ONE THERE!

EHEHEHE.

WOW, THIS IS LIKE A REAL STAKEOUT. WE COULD DO WITH SOME MUSCLE IF THOSE GOONS SHOW UP AGAIN, THOUGH. SOME MUSCLE... MAN...

SECURITY

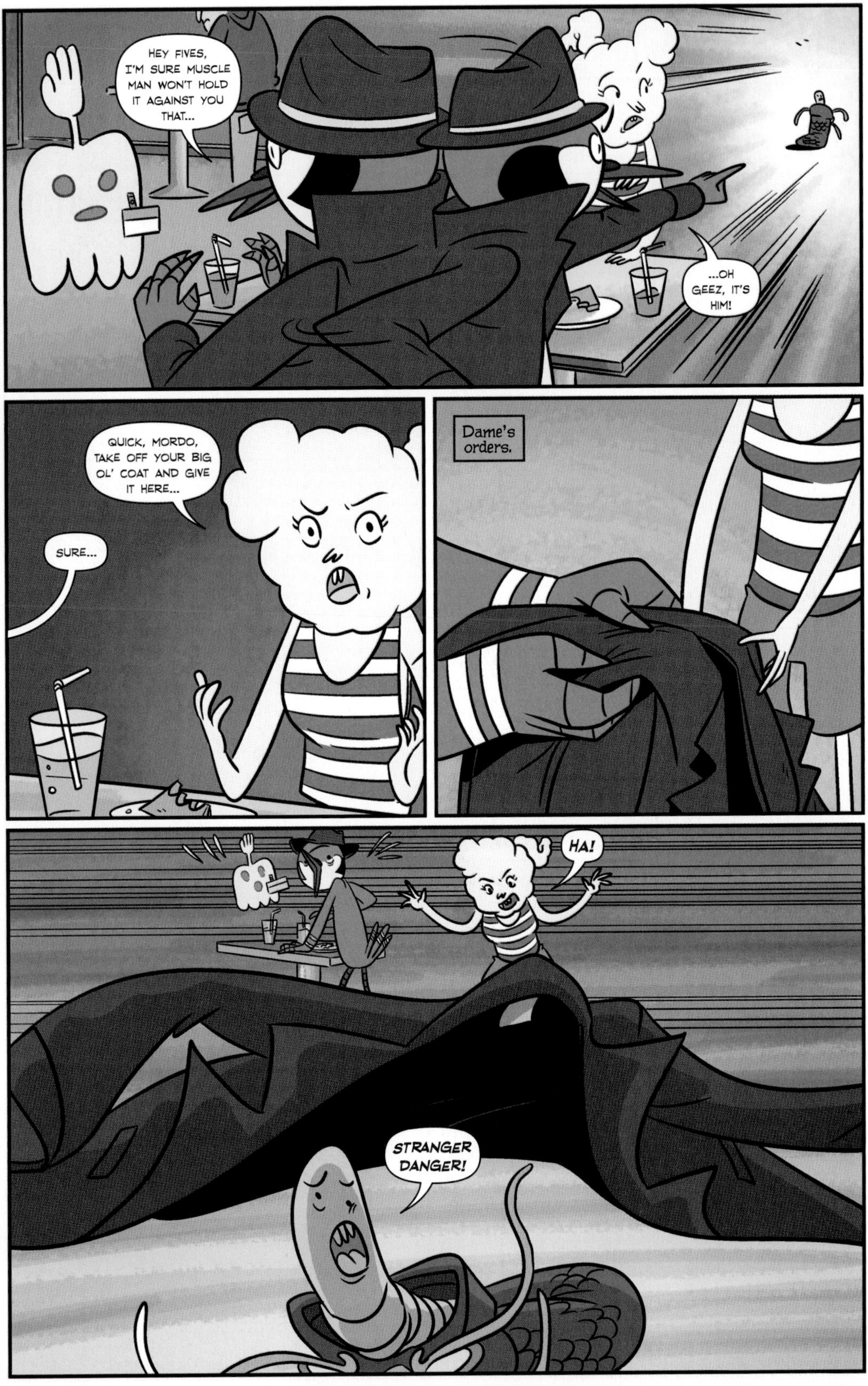
HEY FIVES, I'M SURE MUSCLE MAN WON'T HOLD IT AGAINST YOU THAT...
...OH GEEZ, IT'S HIM!
QUICK, MORDO, TAKE OFF YOUR BIG OL' COAT AND GIVE IT HERE...
SURE...
Dame's orders.
HA!
STRANGER DANGER!

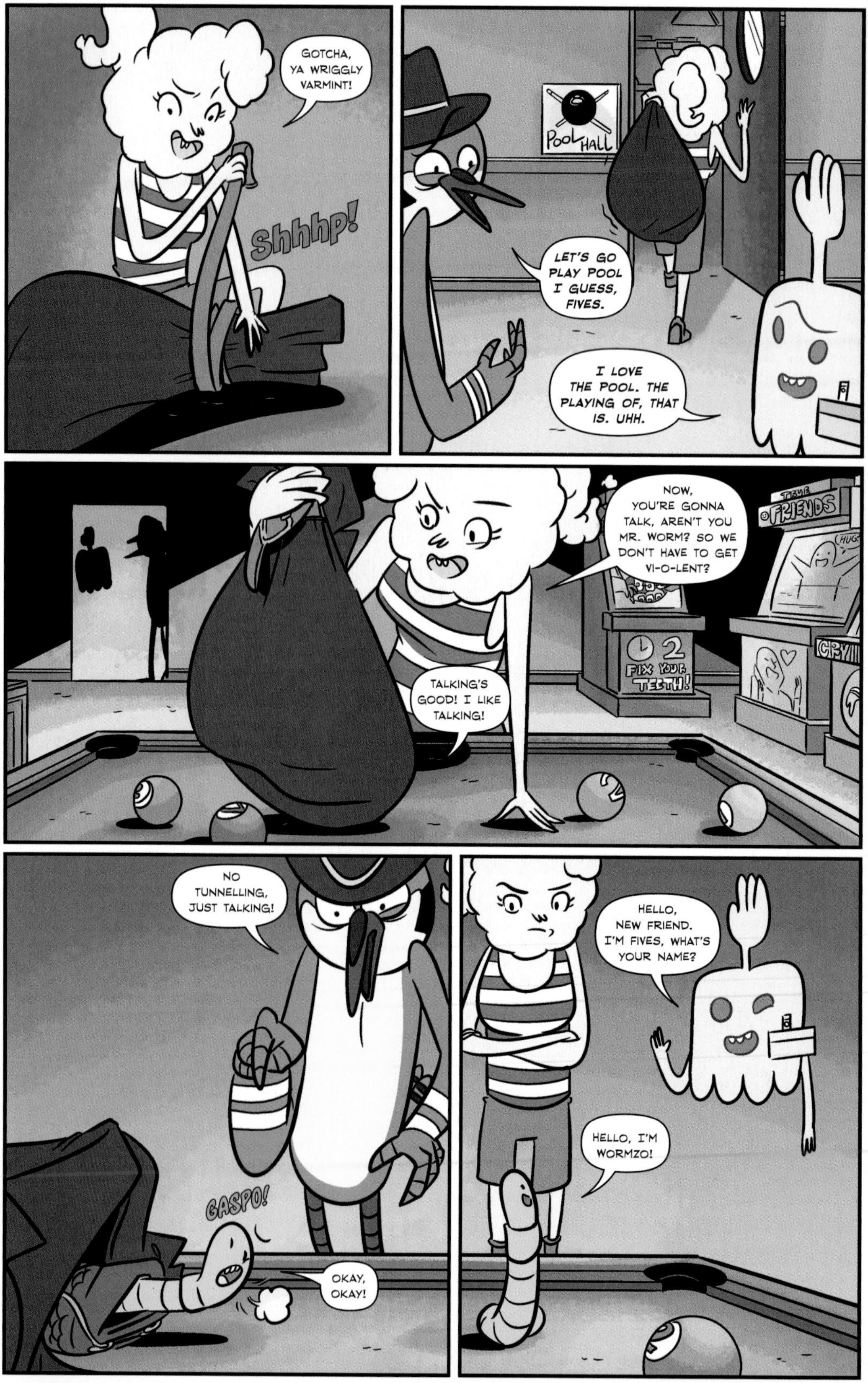
GOTCHA, YA WRIGGLY VARMINT!
Shhhp!
POOL HALL
LET'S GO PLAY POOL I GUESS, FIVES.
I LOVE THE POOL. THE PLAYING OF, THAT IS. UHH.
NOW, YOU'RE GONNA TALK, AREN'T YOU MR. WORM? SO WE DON'T HAVE TO GET VI-O-LENT?
TRUE FRIENDS
HUG
2 FIX YOUR TEETH!
TALKING'S GOOD! I LIKE TALKING!
NO TUNNELLING, JUST TALKING!
GASPO!
OKAY, OKAY!
HELLO, NEW FRIEND. I'M FIVES, WHAT'S YOUR NAME?
HELLO, I'M WORMZO!

THAT'S THE EASY ONE OUT OF THE WAY. NOW, WHY DID YOU STEAL ALL THE SOCKS FROM OUR HOUSE?!

Y-YOU...

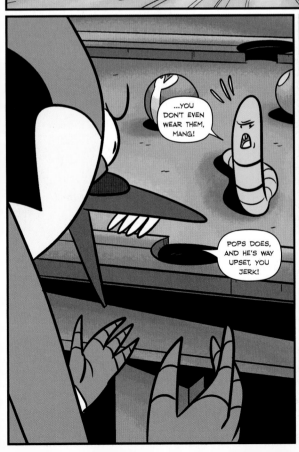

...YOU DON'T EVEN WEAR THEM, MANG!

POPS DOES, AND HE'S WAY UPSET, YOU JERK!

YOU DON'T KNOW WHAT IT'S LIKE OUT THERE...FOR A WORM. WHEN THERE'S EXTREME WEATHER, WE'RE TOTALLY EXPOSED TO THE ELEMENTS!

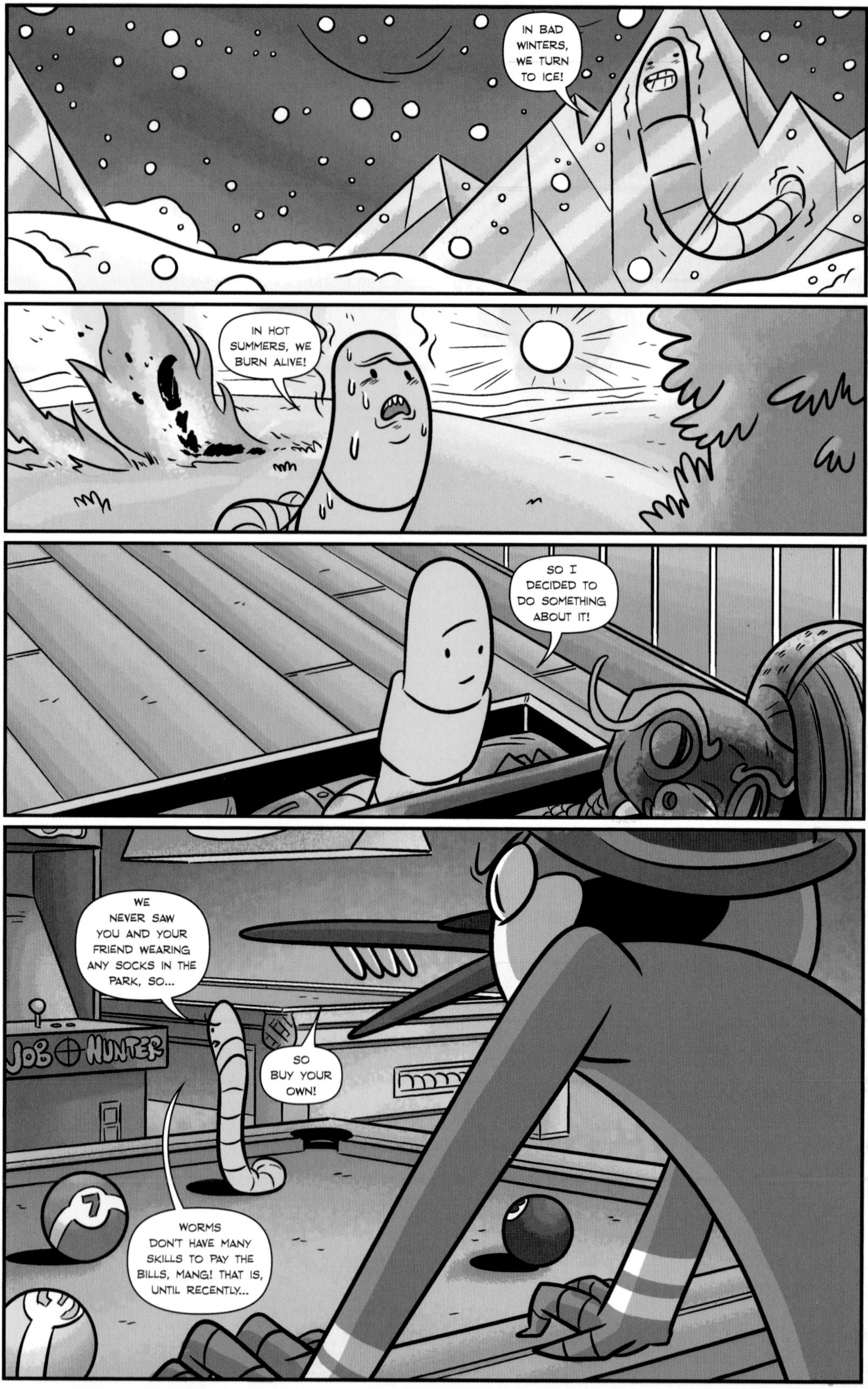
IN BAD WINTERS, WE TURN TO ICE!
IN HOT SUMMERS, WE BURN ALIVE!
SO I DECIDED TO DO SOMETHING ABOUT IT!
WE NEVER SAW YOU AND YOUR FRIEND WEARING ANY SOCKS IN THE PARK, SO...
SO BUY YOUR OWN!
JOB HUNTER
WORMS DON'T HAVE MANY SKILLS TO PAY THE BILLS, MANG! THAT IS, UNTIL RECENTLY...

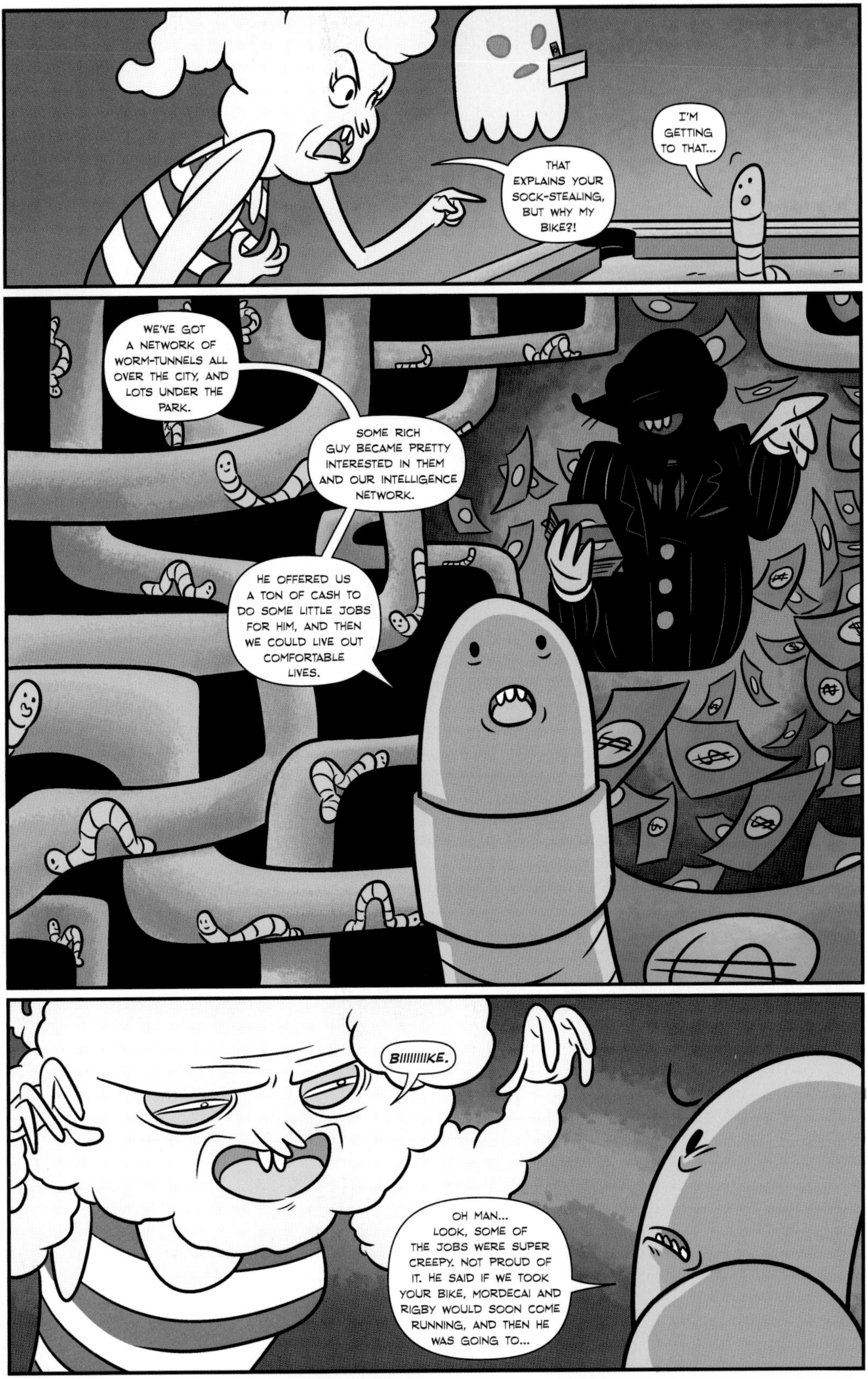
THAT EXPLAINS YOUR SOCK-STEALING, BUT WHY MY BIKE?!
I'M GETTING TO THAT...
WE'VE GOT A NETWORK OF WORM-TUNNELS ALL OVER THE CITY, AND LOTS UNDER THE PARK.
SOME RICH GUY BECAME PRETTY INTERESTED IN THEM AND OUR INTELLIGENCE NETWORK.
HE OFFERED US A TON OF CASH TO DO SOME LITTLE JOBS FOR HIM, AND THEN WE COULD LIVE OUT COMFORTABLE LIVES.
BIIIIIIIKE.
OH MAN... LOOK, SOME OF THE JOBS WERE SUPER CREEPY. NOT PROUD OF IT. HE SAID IF WE TOOK YOUR BIKE, MORDECAI AND RIGBY WOULD SOON COME RUNNING, AND THEN HE WAS GOING TO...

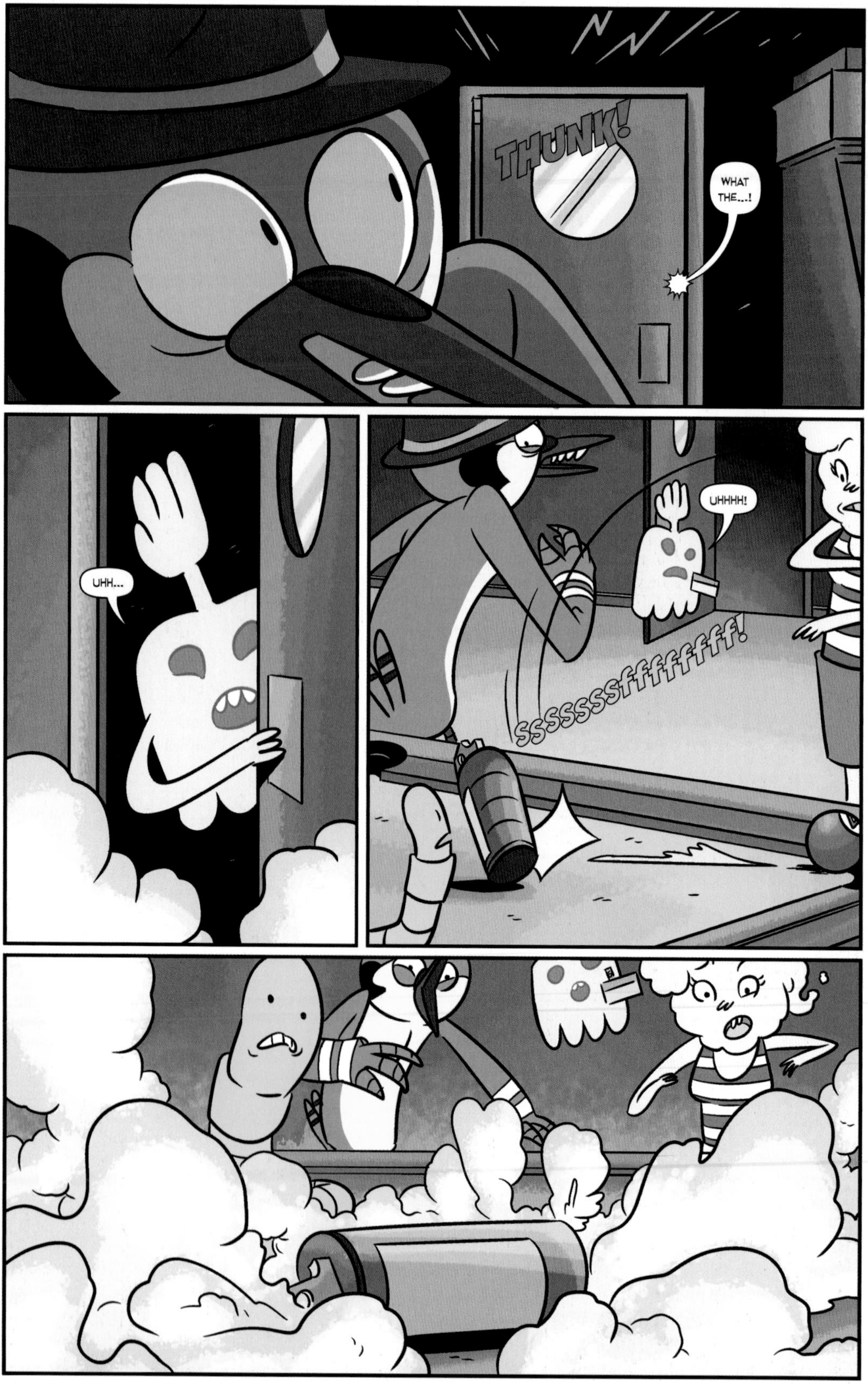

THUNK!
WHAT THE...!
UHH...
UHHHH!
SSSSSSSFFFFFFFF!

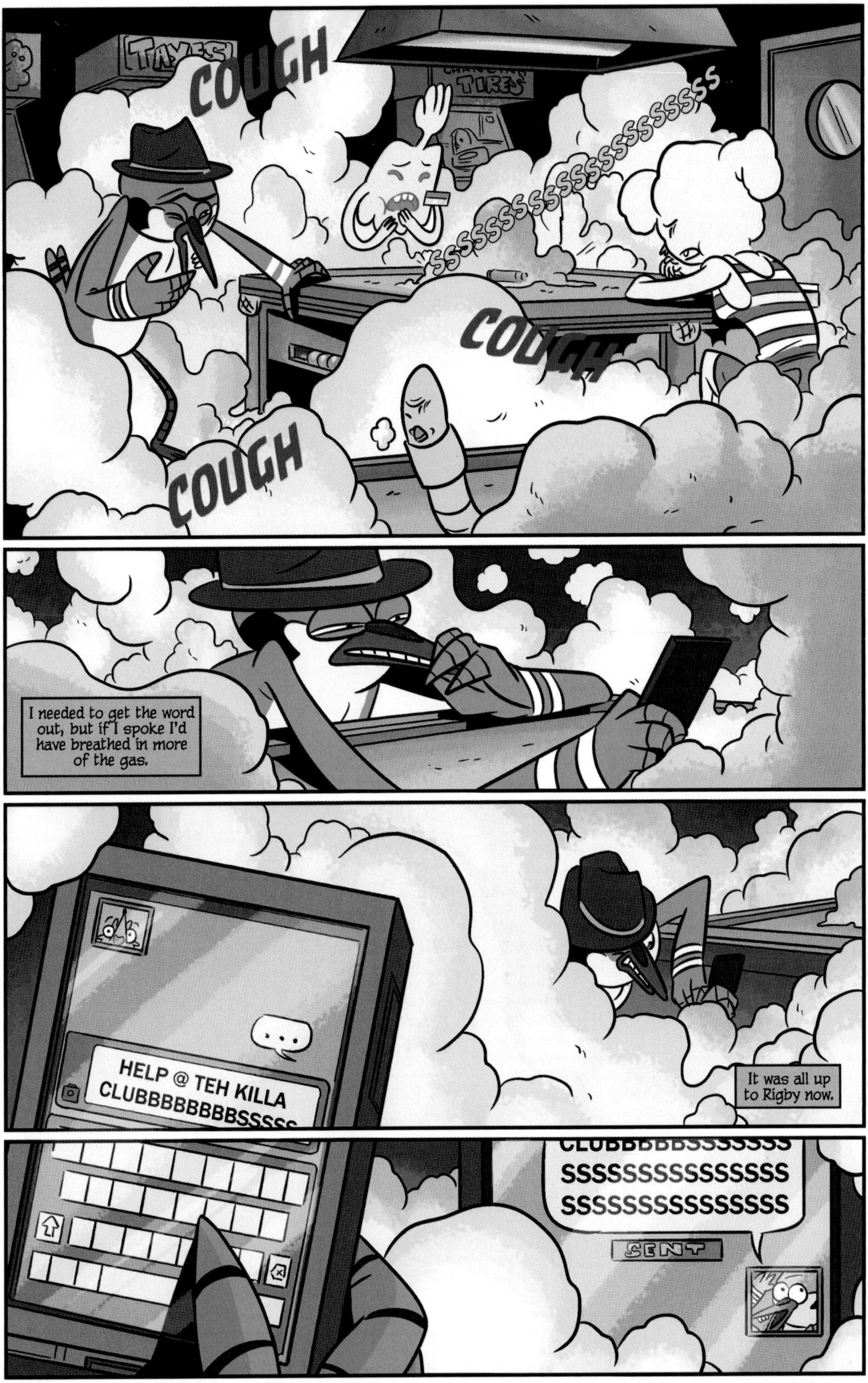
TAYES
TIRES
COUGH
SSSSSSSSSSSSSSSSSSSSSSS
COUGH
COUGH
I needed to get the word out, but if I spoke I'd have breathed in more of the gas.
HELP @ TEH KILLA CLUBBBBBBBBSSSSS
It was all up to Rigby now.
CLUBBBBBSSSSSSS SSSSSSSSSSSSSSS SSSSSSSSSSSSSSS
SENT

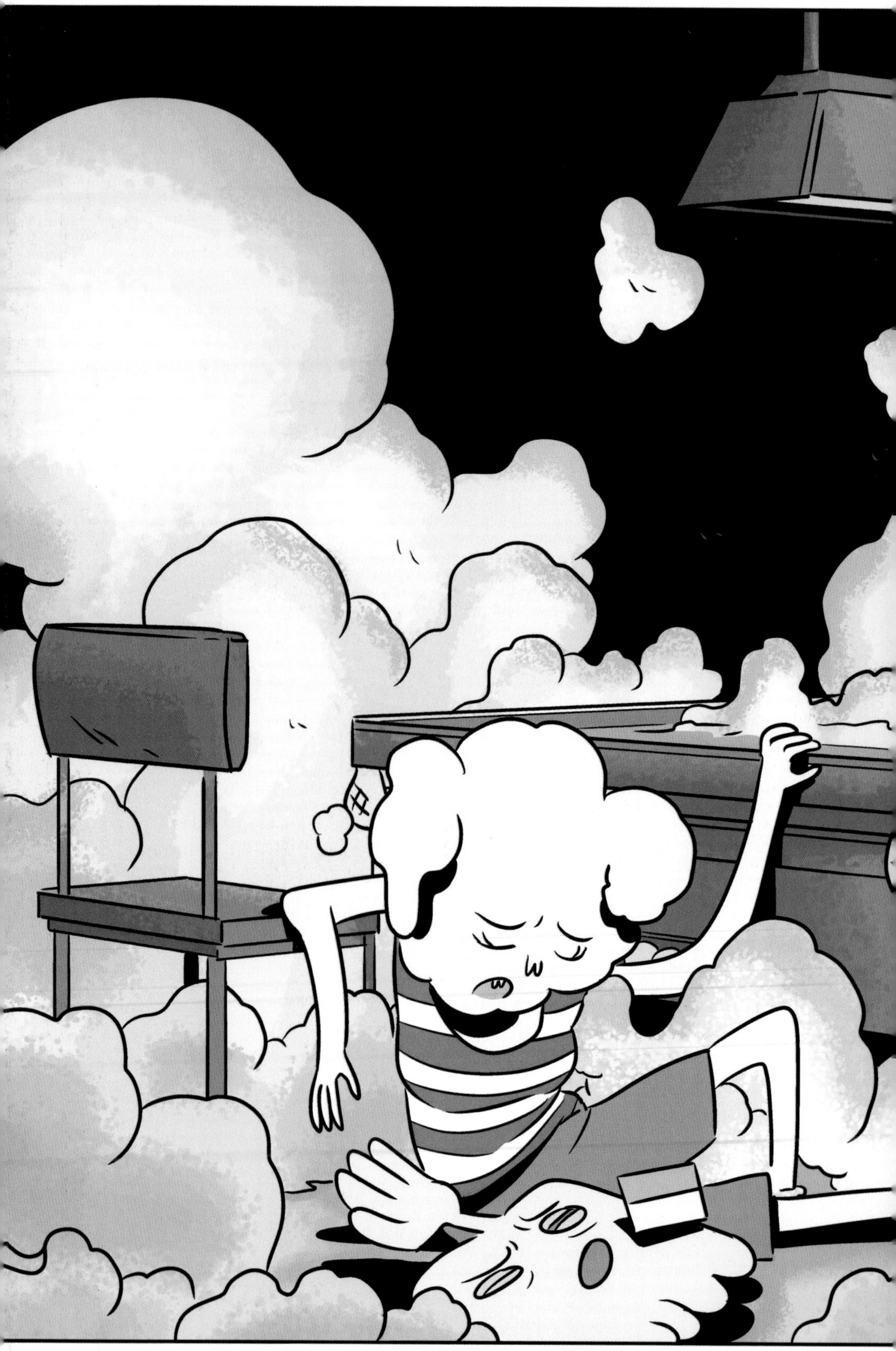

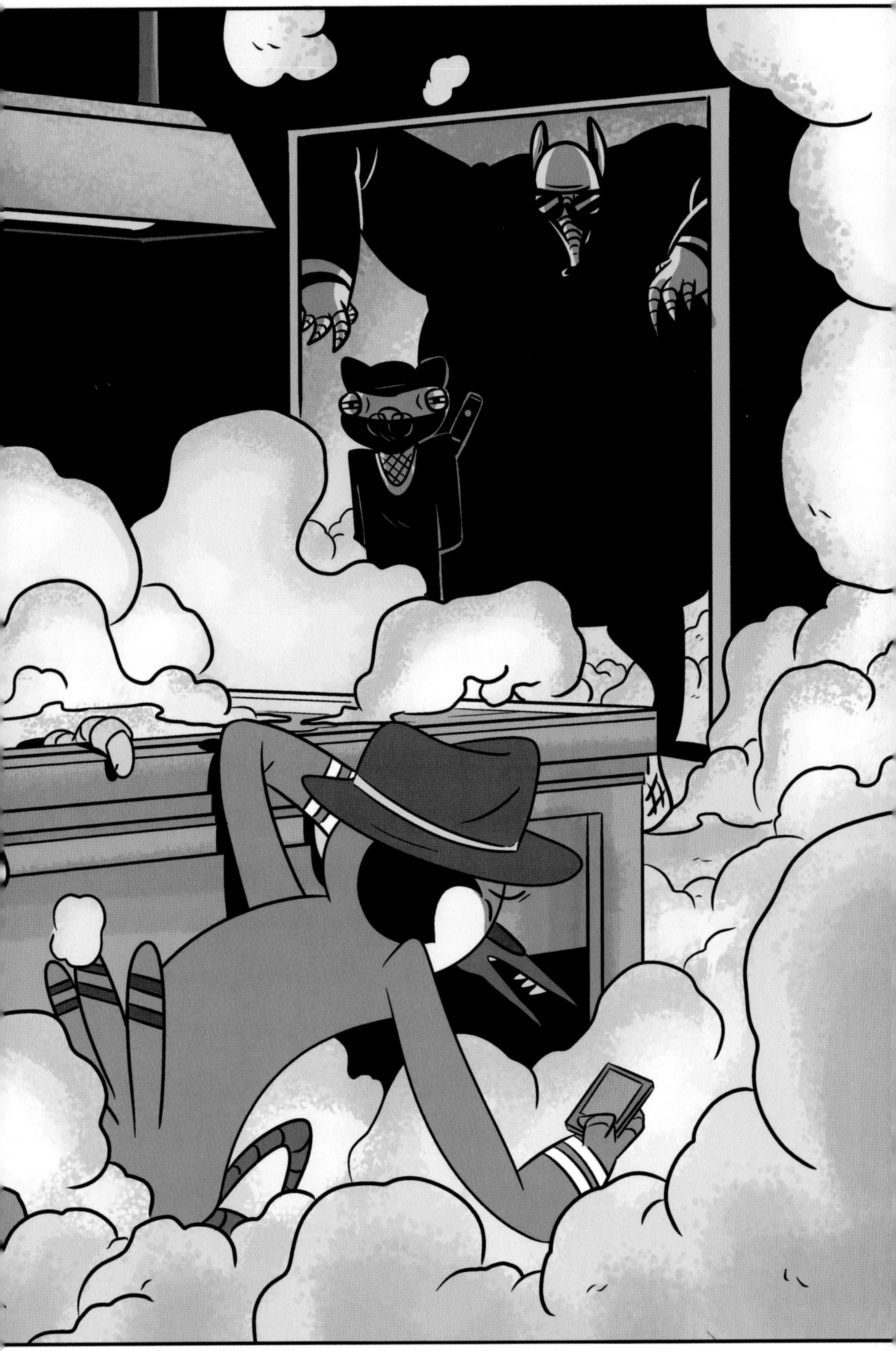

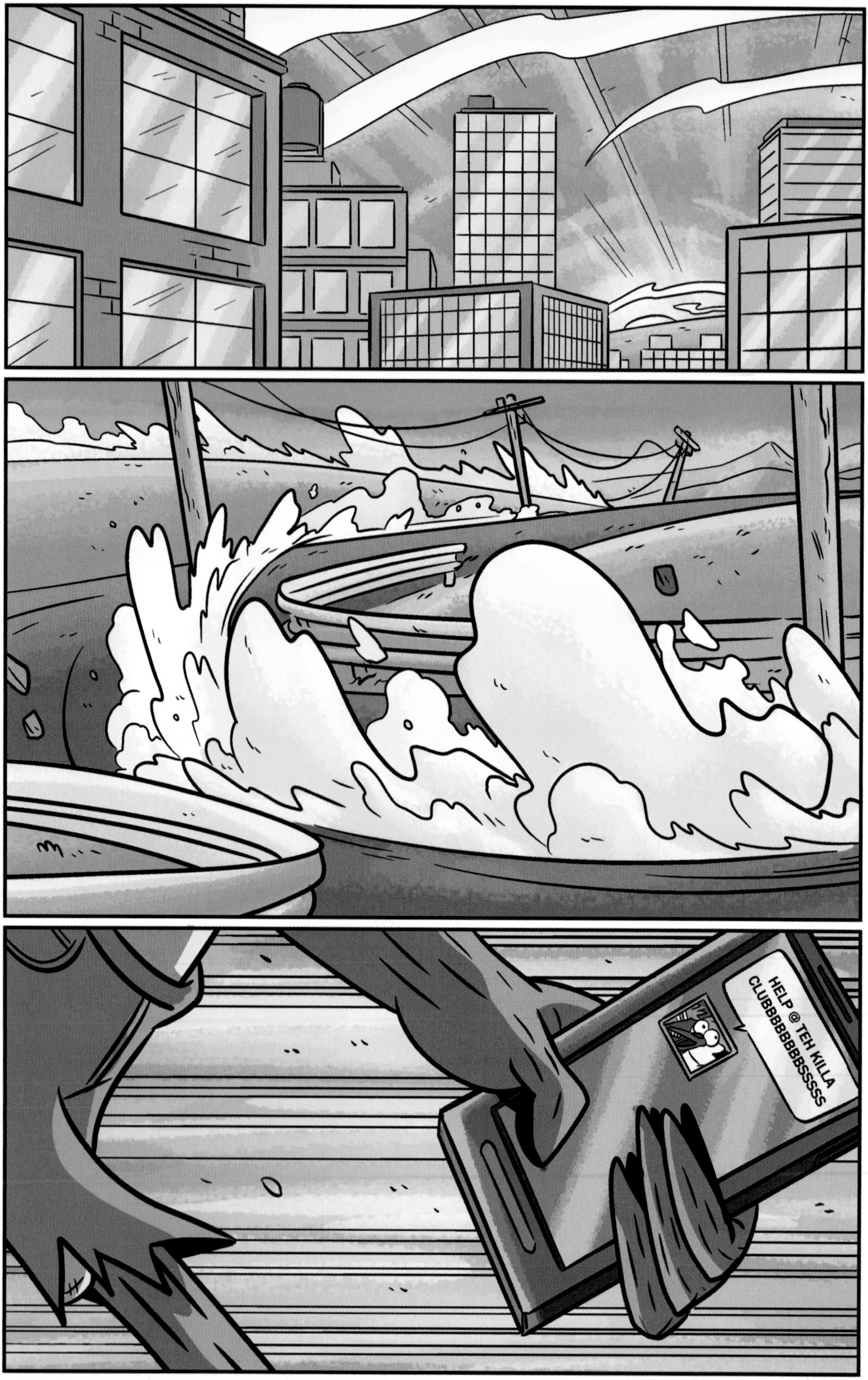
HELP @ TEH KILLA CLUBBBBBBBBSSSSS

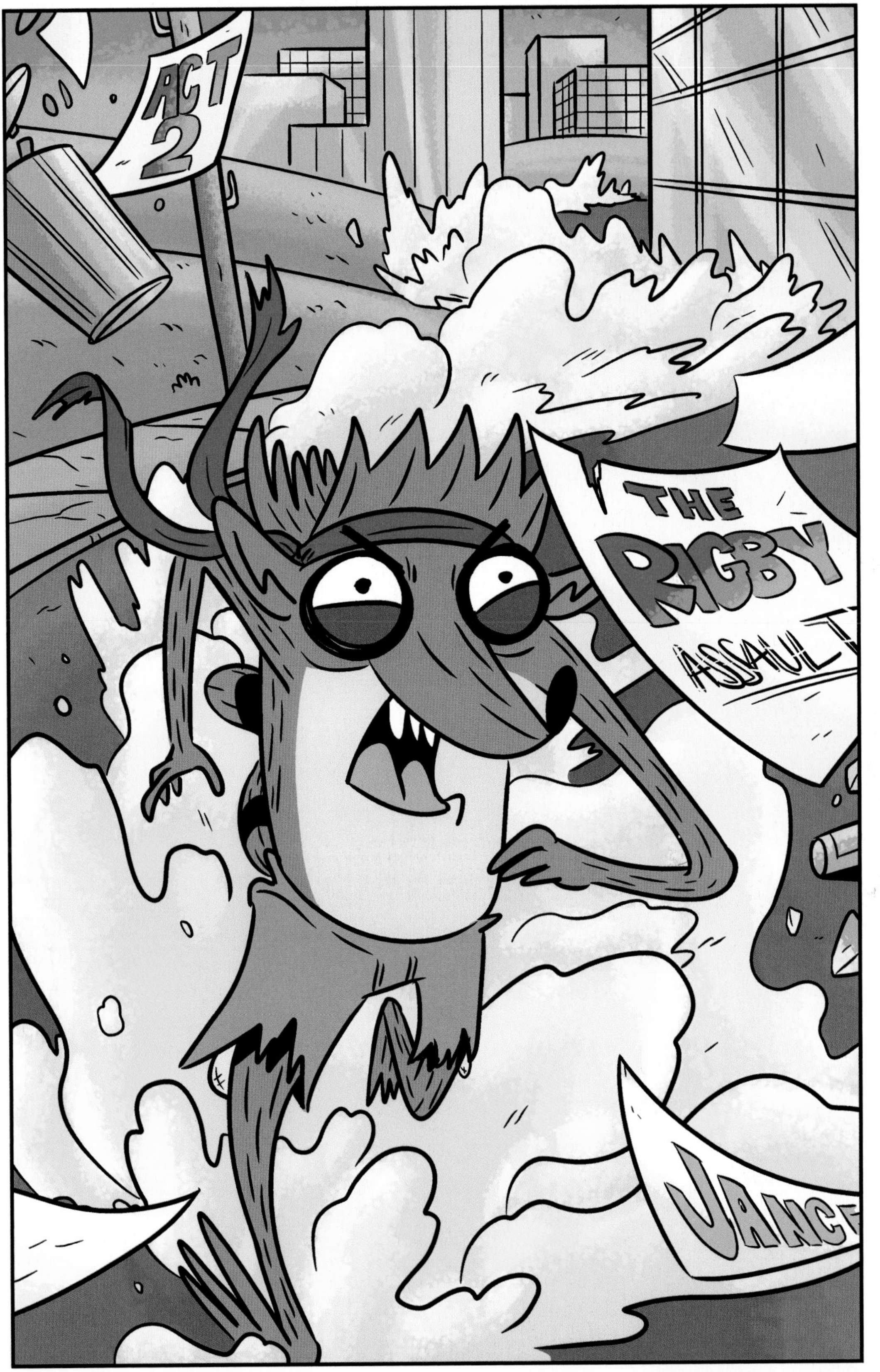
ACT 2
THE RIGBY
ASSAULT
VANCE

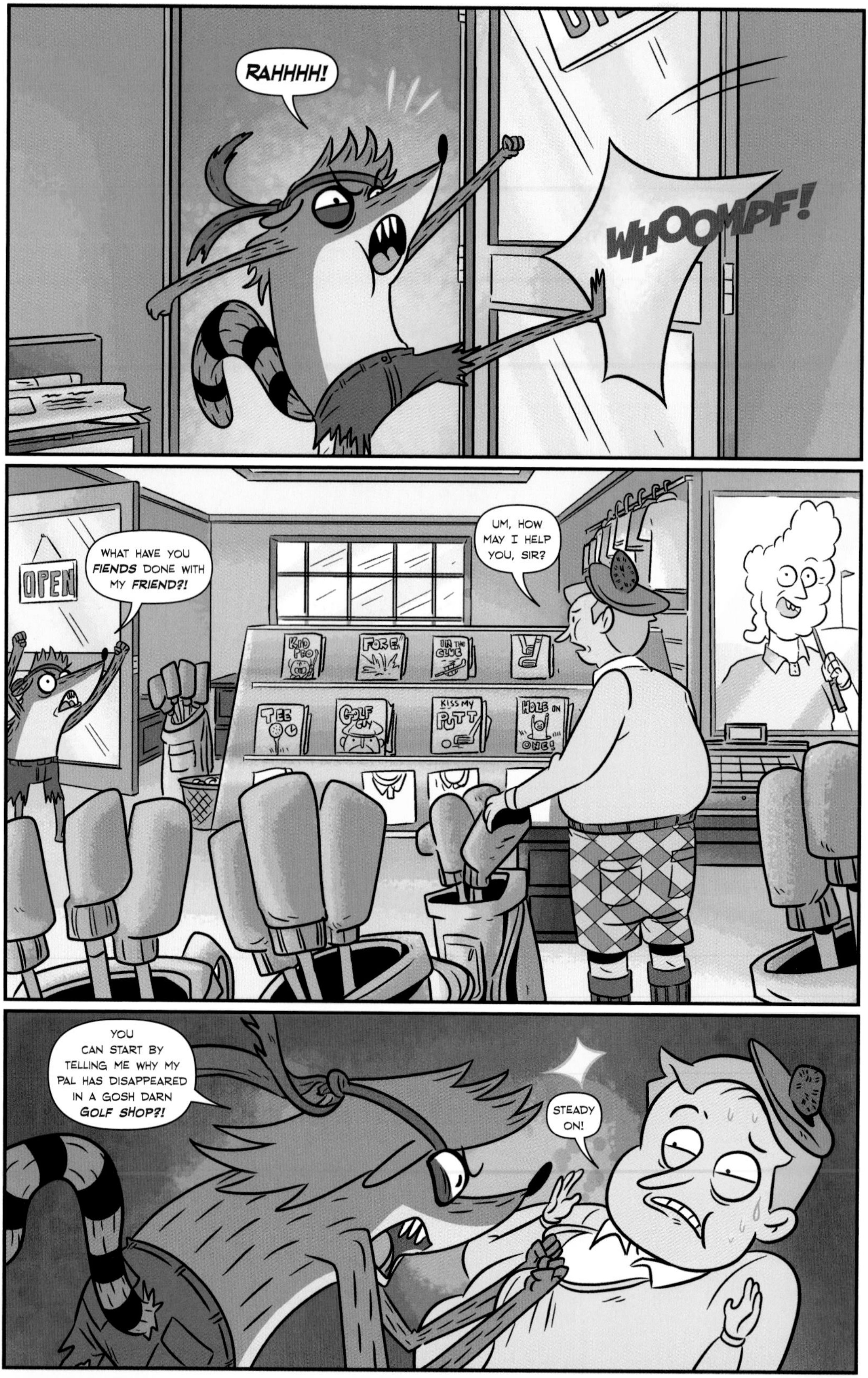
RAHHHH!
WHOOMPF!
OPEN
WHAT HAVE YOU FIENDS DONE WITH MY FRIEND?!
UM, HOW MAY I HELP YOU, SIR?
KID PRO
FORE
IN THE CLUB
TEE
GOLF GUY
KISS MY PUTT
HOLE IN ONE!
YOU CAN START BY TELLING ME WHY MY PAL HAS DISAPPEARED IN A GOSH DARN GOLF SHOP?!
STEADY ON!

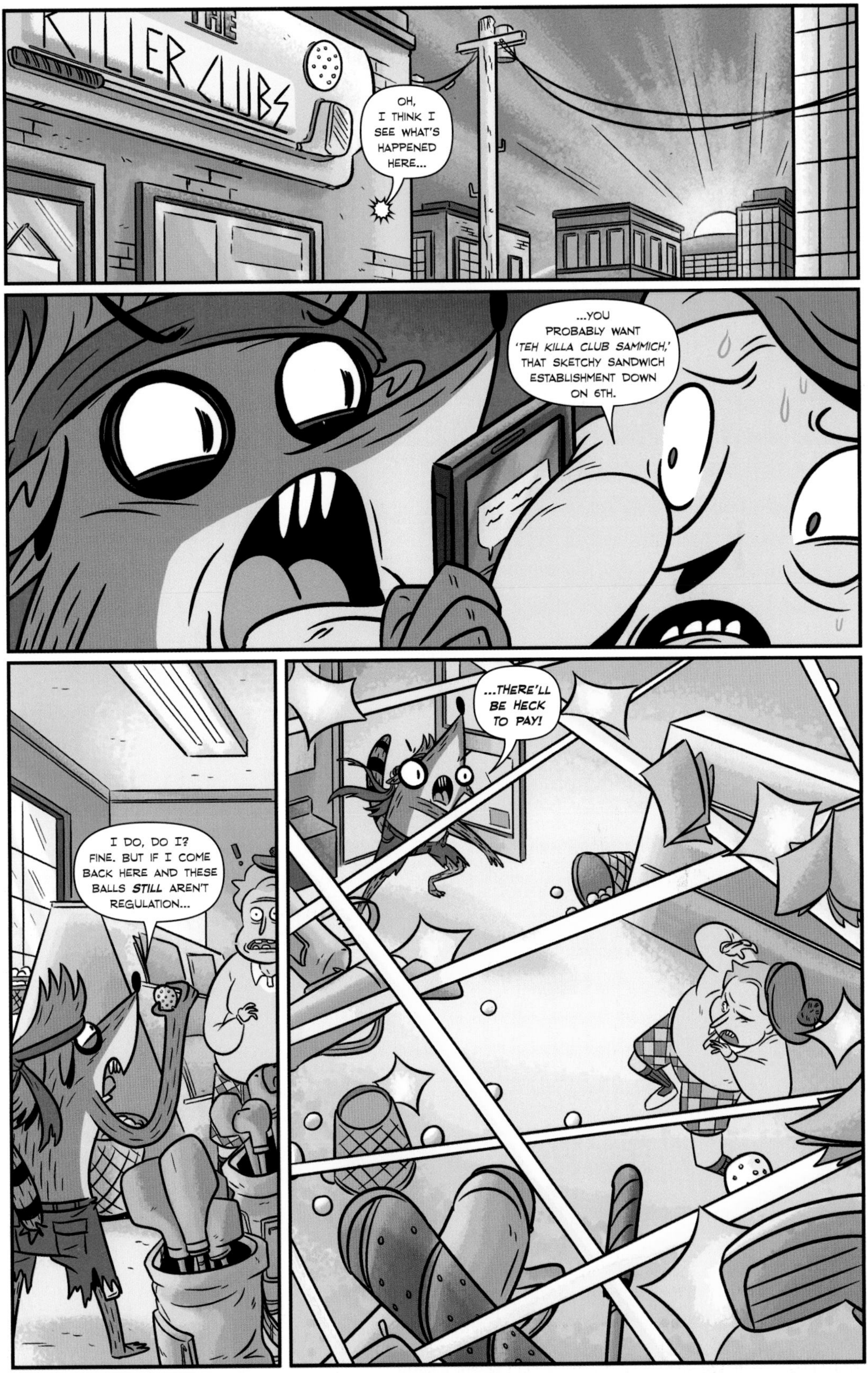
THE
KILLER CLUBS
OH, I THINK I SEE WHAT'S HAPPENED HERE...
...YOU PROBABLY WANT 'TEH KILLA CLUB SAMMICH,' THAT SKETCHY SANDWICH ESTABLISHMENT DOWN ON 6TH.
I DO, DO I? FINE. BUT IF I COME BACK HERE AND THESE BALLS STILL AREN'T REGULATION...
!
...THERE'LL BE HECK TO PAY!

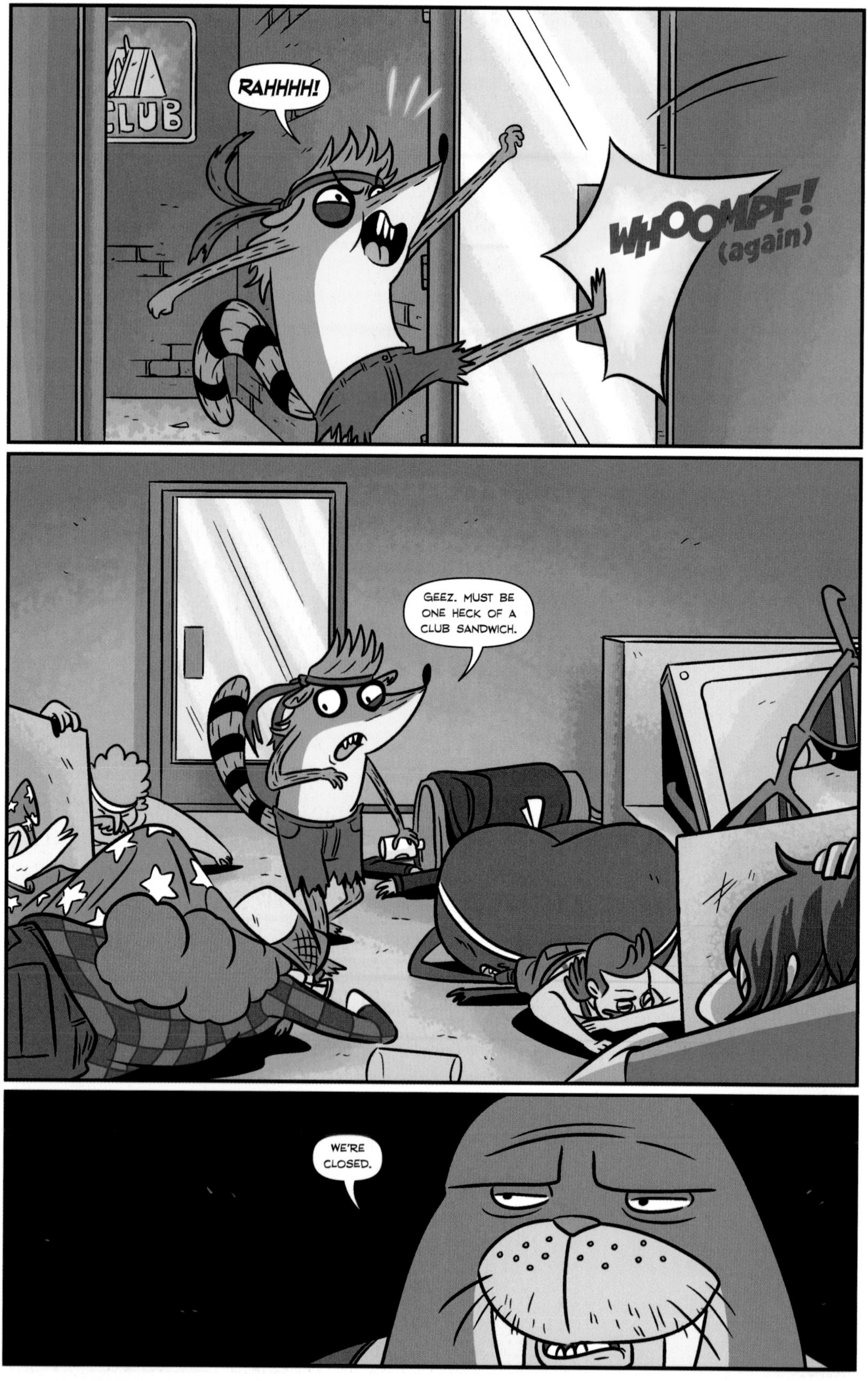
CLUB
RAHHHH!
WHOOMPF! (again)
GEEZ. MUST BE ONE HECK OF A CLUB SANDWICH.
WE'RE CLOSED.

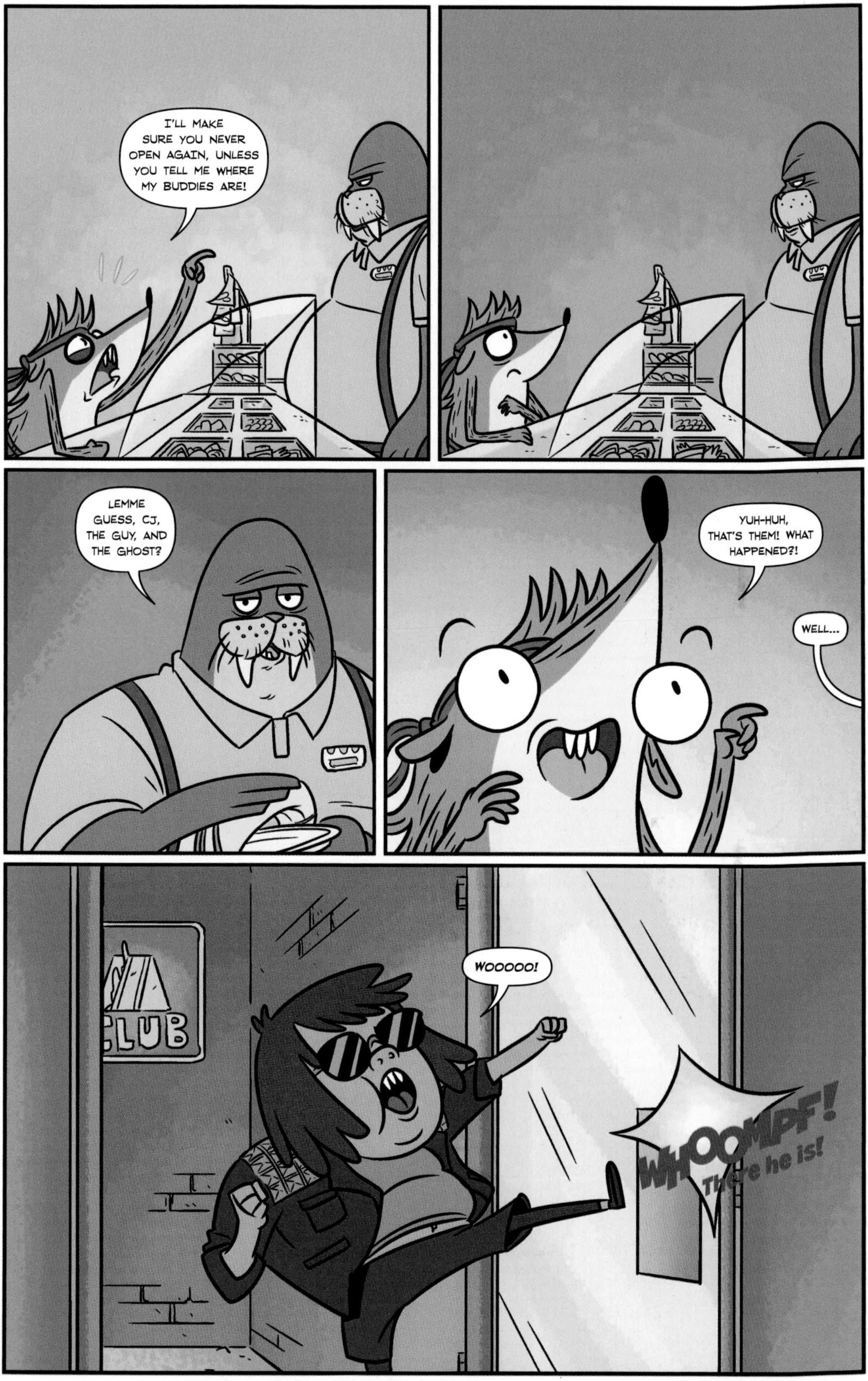
I'LL MAKE SURE YOU NEVER OPEN AGAIN, UNLESS YOU TELL ME WHERE MY BUDDIES ARE!
LEMME GUESS, CJ, THE GUY, AND THE GHOST?
YUH-HUH, THAT'S THEM! WHAT HAPPENED?!
WELL...
CLUB
WOOOOO!
WHOOOMPF!
There he is!

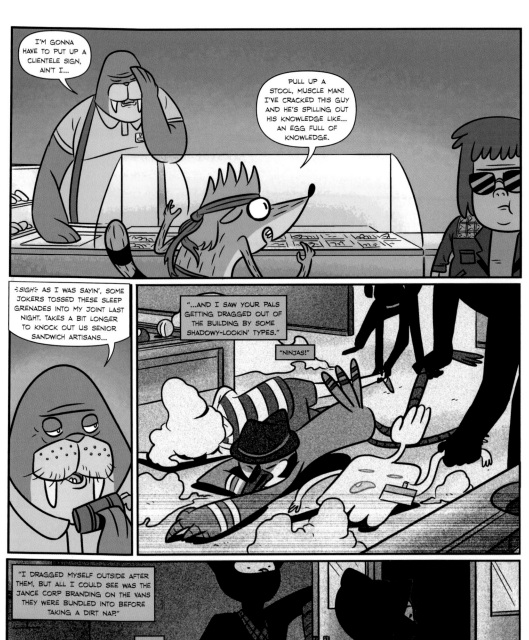

I'M GONNA HAVE TO PUT UP A CLIENTELE SIGN, AIN'T I...

PULL UP A STOOL, MUSCLE MAN! I'VE CRACKED THIS GUY AND HE'S SPILLING OUT HIS KNOWLEDGE LIKE... AN EGG FULL OF KNOWLEDGE.

÷SIGH÷ AS I WAS SAYIN', SOME JOKERS TOSSED THESE SLEEP GRENADES INTO MY JOINT LAST NIGHT. TAKES A BIT LONGER TO KNOCK OUT US SENIOR SANDWICH ARTISANS...

"...AND I SAW YOUR PALS GETTING DRAGGED OUT OF THE BUILDING BY SOME SHADOWY-LOOKIN' TYPES."

"NINJAS!"

"I DRAGGED MYSELF OUTSIDE AFTER THEM, BUT ALL I COULD SEE WAS THE JANCE CORP BRANDING ON THE VANS THEY WERE BUNDLED INTO BEFORE TAKING A DIRT NAP."

"NINJA VANS!"

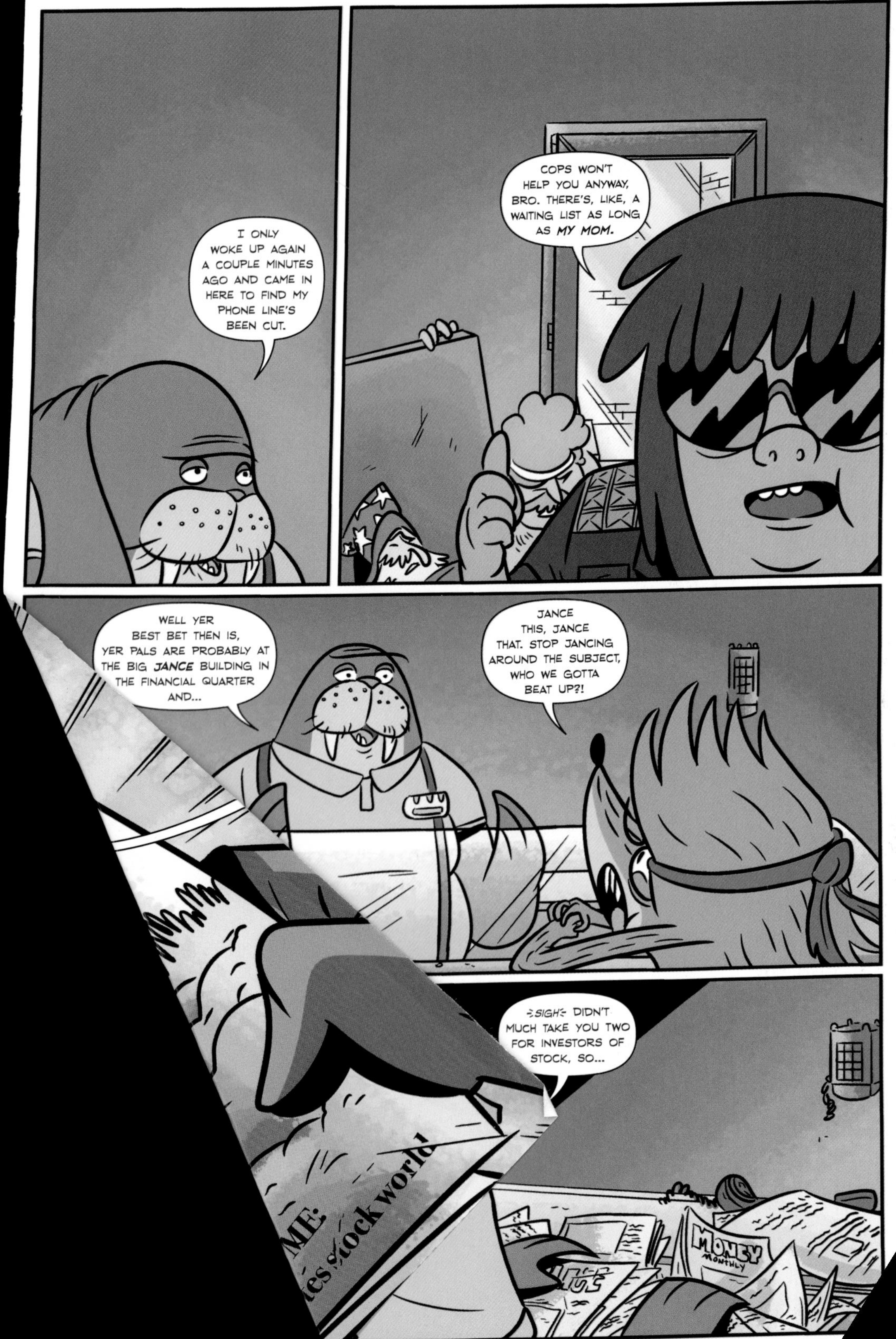
I ONLY WOKE UP AGAIN A COUPLE MINUTES AGO AND CAME IN HERE TO FIND MY PHONE LINE'S BEEN CUT.
COPS WON'T HELP YOU ANYWAY, BRO. THERE'S, LIKE, A WAITING LIST AS LONG AS MY MOM.
WELL YER BEST BET THEN IS, YER PALS ARE PROBABLY AT THE BIG JANCE BUILDING IN THE FINANCIAL QUARTER AND...
JANCE THIS, JANCE THAT. STOP JANCING AROUND THE SUBJECT, WHO WE GOTTA BEAT UP?!
-SIGH- DIDN'T MUCH TAKE YOU TWO FOR INVESTORS OF STOCK, SO...
MONEY MONTHLY

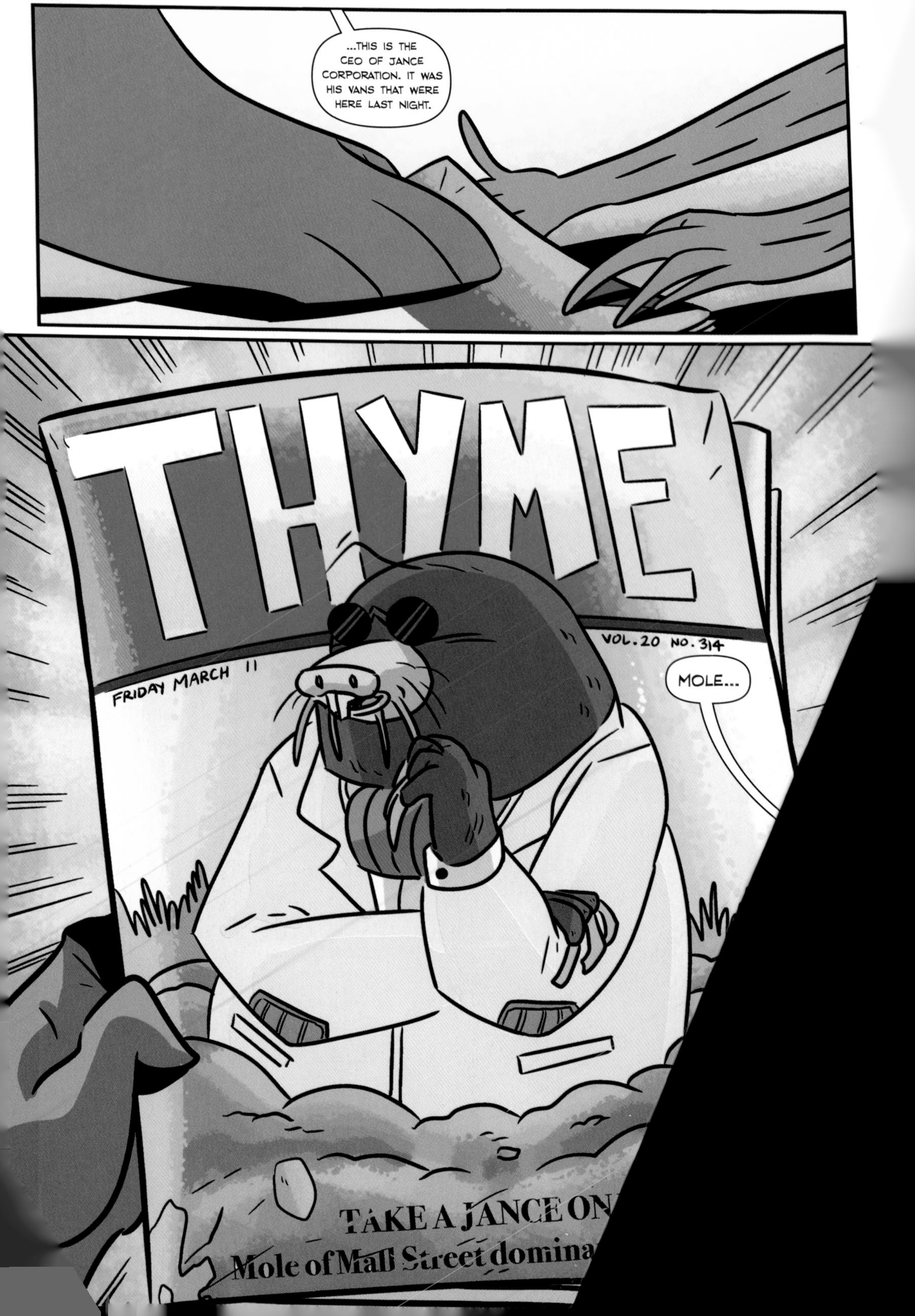

...THIS IS THE CEO OF JANCE CORPORATION. IT WAS HIS VANS THAT WERE HERE LAST NIGHT.
THYME
VOL. 20 NO. 314
FRIDAY MARCH 11
MOLE...
TAKE A JANCE ON
Mole of Mall Street

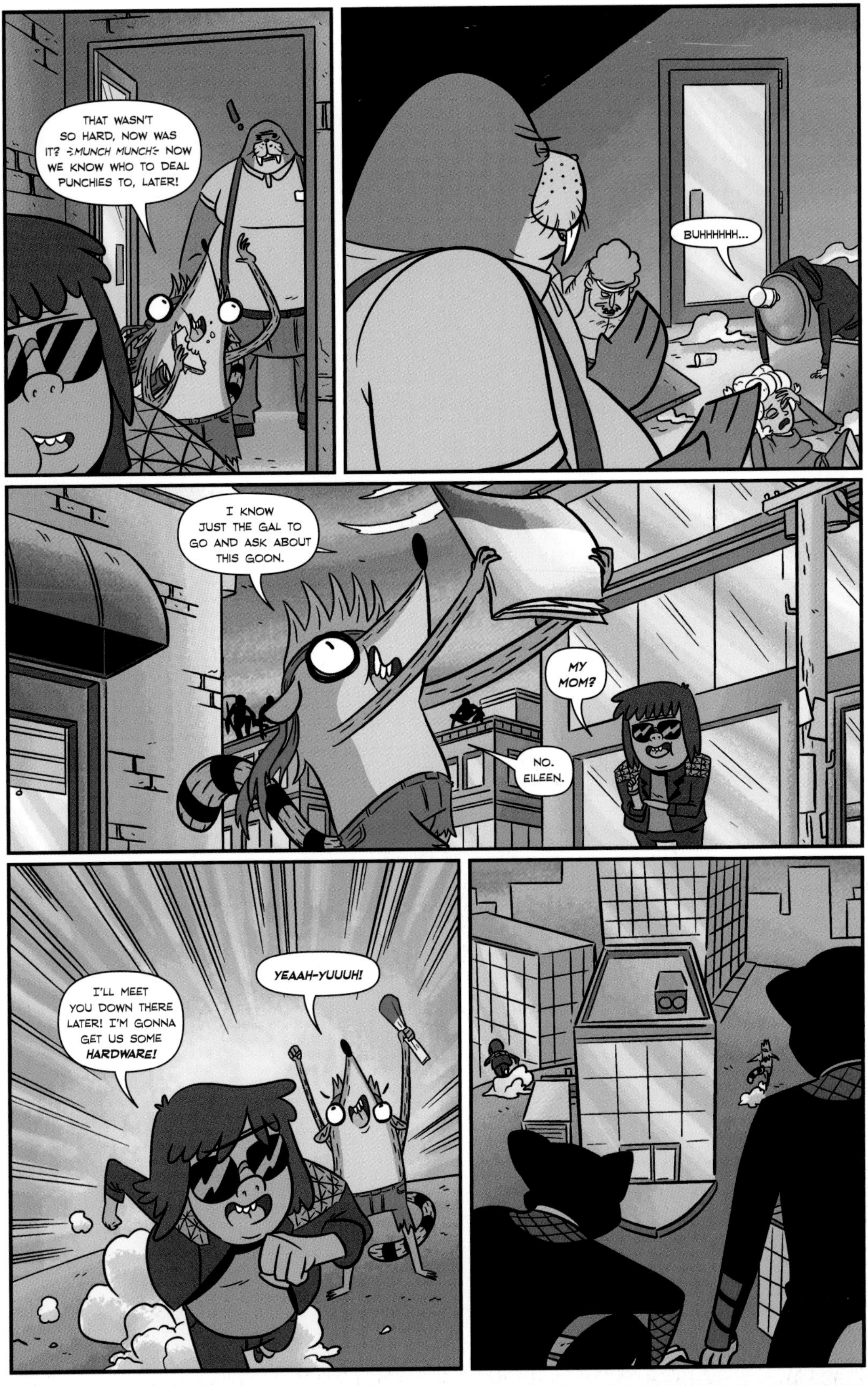
THAT WASN'T SO HARD, NOW WAS IT? ~MUNCH MUNCH~ NOW WE KNOW WHO TO DEAL PUNCHIES TO, LATER!
!
BUHHHHHH...
I KNOW JUST THE GAL TO GO AND ASK ABOUT THIS GOON.
MY MOM?
NO. EILEEN.
I'LL MEET YOU DOWN THERE LATER! I'M GONNA GET US SOME HARDWARE!
YEAAH-YUUUH!

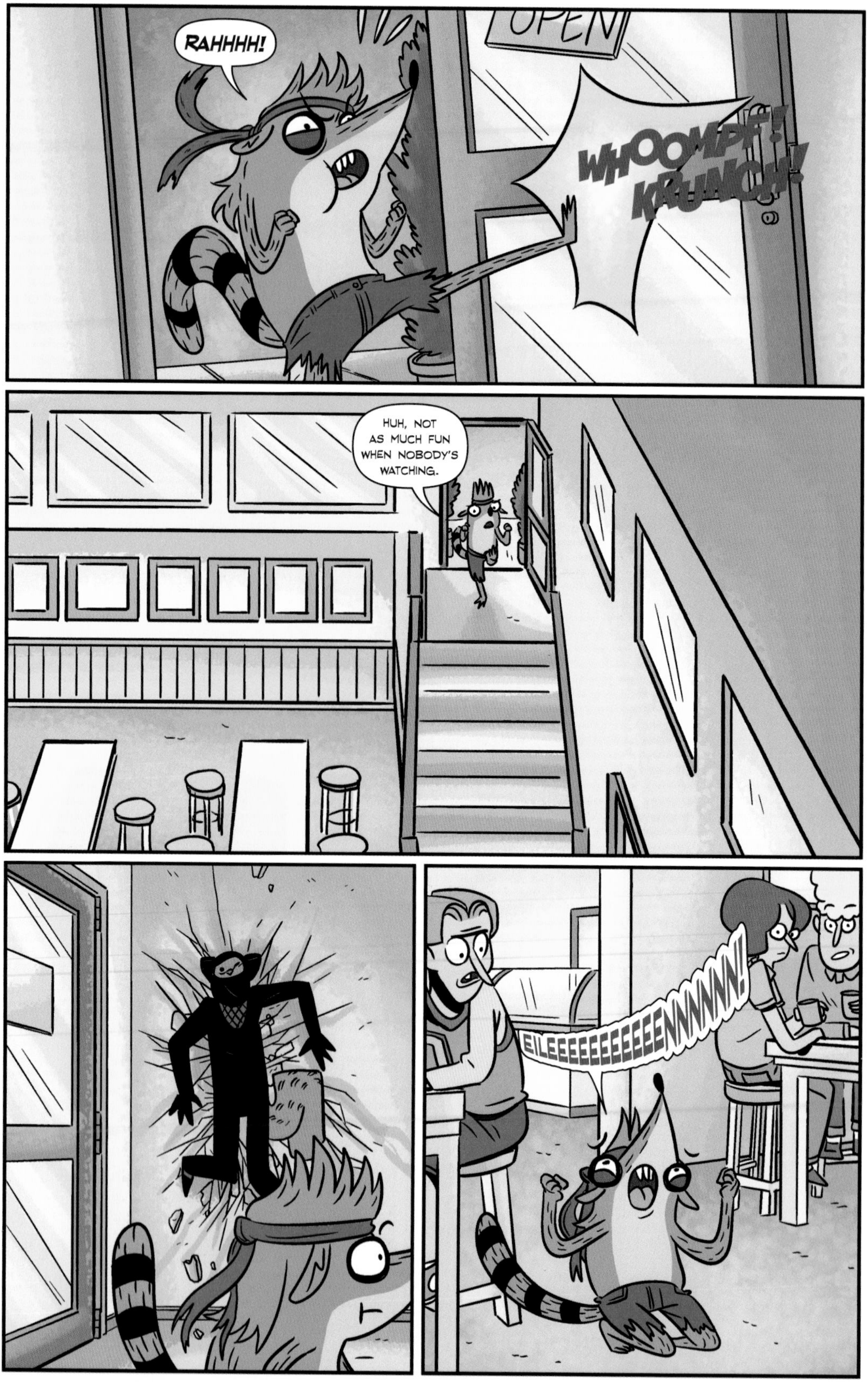
RAHHHH!
OPEN
WHOOMPF!
KRUNCH!
HUH, NOT AS MUCH FUN WHEN NOBODY'S WATCHING.
EILEEEEEEEEEEEEENNNNNN!

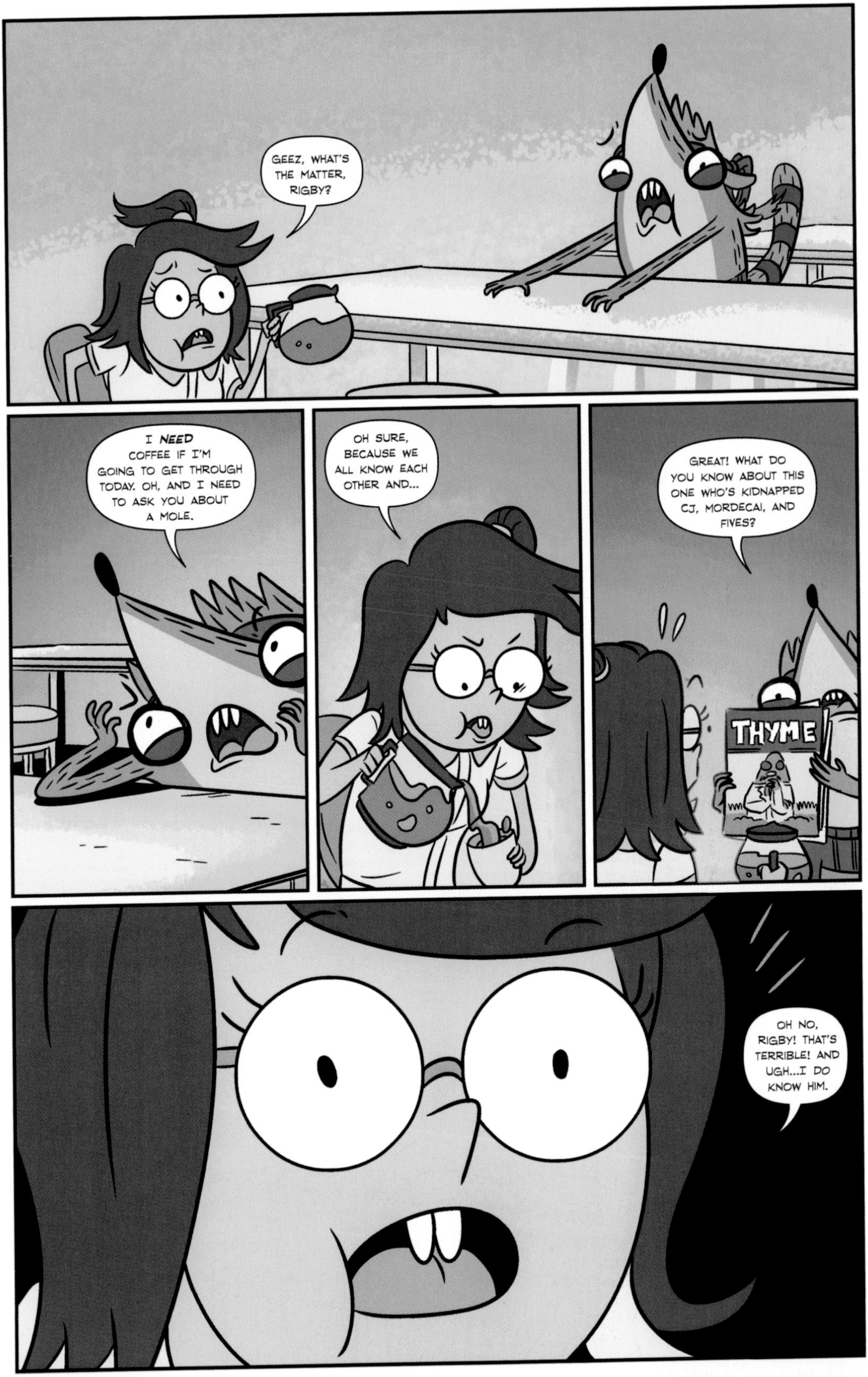
GEEZ, WHAT'S THE MATTER, RIGBY?
I **NEED** COFFEE IF I'M GOING TO GET THROUGH TODAY. OH, AND I NEED TO ASK YOU ABOUT A MOLE.
OH SURE, BECAUSE WE ALL KNOW EACH OTHER AND...
GREAT! WHAT DO YOU KNOW ABOUT THIS ONE WHO'S KIDNAPPED CJ, MORDECAI, AND FIVES?
THYME
OH NO, RIGBY! THAT'S TERRIBLE! AND UGH...I DO KNOW HIM.

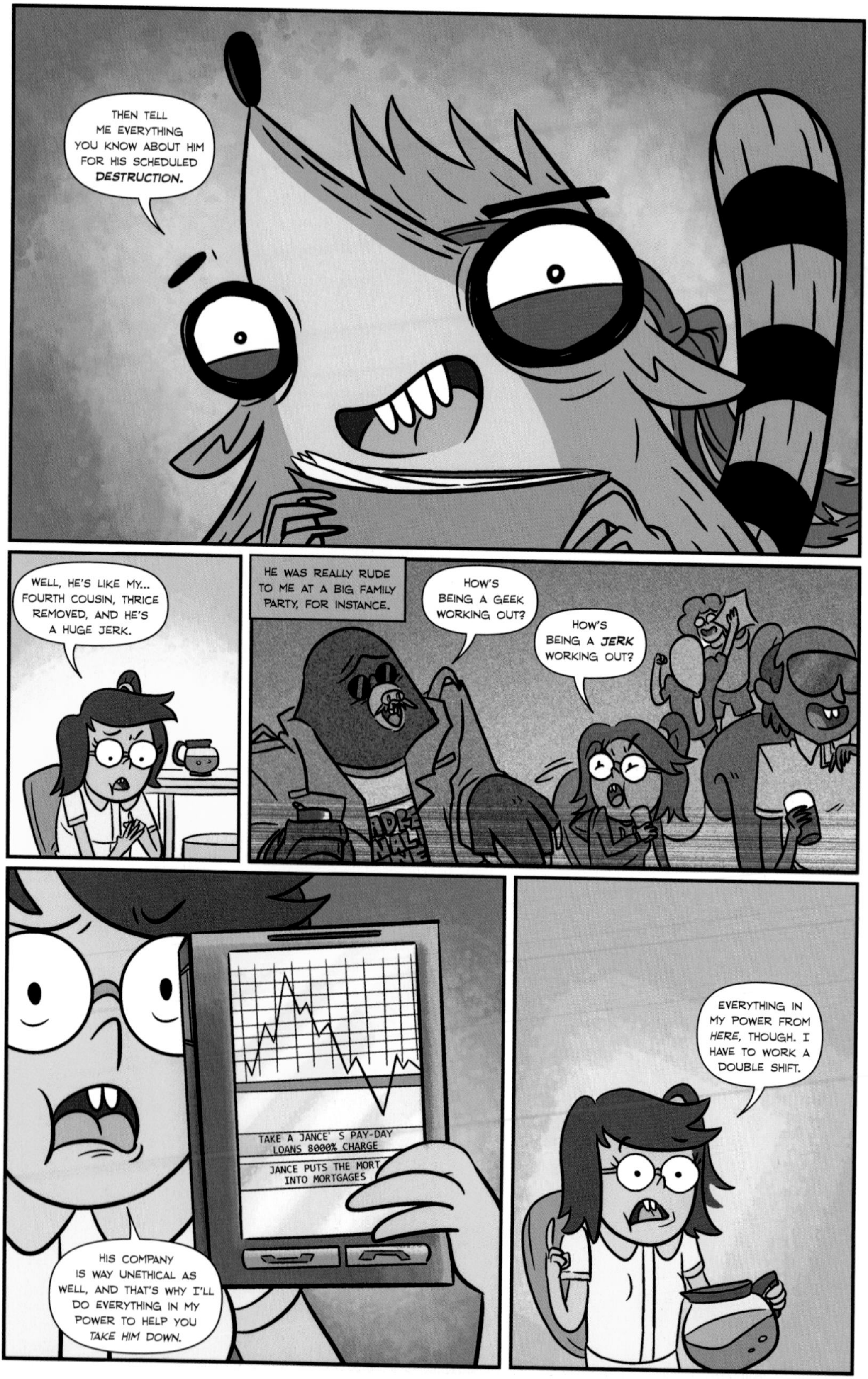
THEN TELL ME EVERYTHING YOU KNOW ABOUT HIM FOR HIS SCHEDULED *DESTRUCTION.*
WELL, HE'S LIKE MY... FOURTH COUSIN, THRICE REMOVED, AND HE'S A HUGE JERK.
HE WAS REALLY RUDE TO ME AT A BIG FAMILY PARTY, FOR INSTANCE.
HOW'S BEING A GEEK WORKING OUT?
HOW'S BEING A *JERK* WORKING OUT?
TAKE A JANCE' S PAY-DAY LOANS 8000% CHARGE
JANCE PUTS THE MORT INTO MORTGAGES
HIS COMPANY IS WAY UNETHICAL AS WELL, AND THAT'S WHY I'LL DO EVERYTHING IN MY POWER TO HELP YOU *TAKE HIM DOWN.*
EVERYTHING IN MY POWER FROM *HERE,* THOUGH. I HAVE TO WORK A DOUBLE SHIFT.

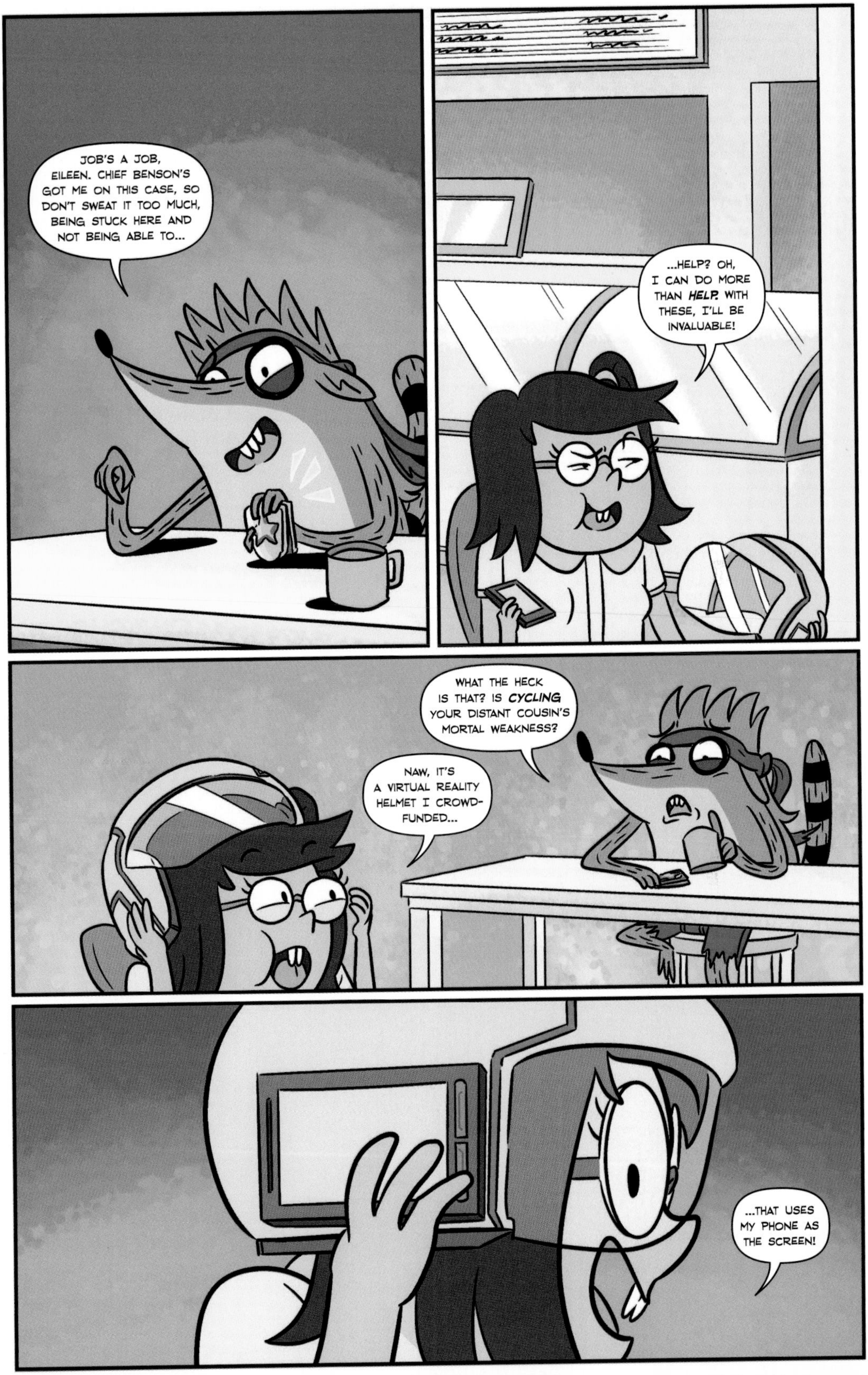
JOB'S A JOB, EILEEN. CHIEF BENSON'S GOT ME ON THIS CASE, SO DON'T SWEAT IT TOO MUCH, BEING STUCK HERE AND NOT BEING ABLE TO...
...HELP? OH, I CAN DO MORE THAN **HELP**. WITH THESE, I'LL BE INVALUABLE!
WHAT THE HECK IS THAT? IS ***CYCLING*** YOUR DISTANT COUSIN'S MORTAL WEAKNESS?
NAW, IT'S A VIRTUAL REALITY HELMET I CROWD-FUNDED...
...THAT USES MY PHONE AS THE SCREEN!

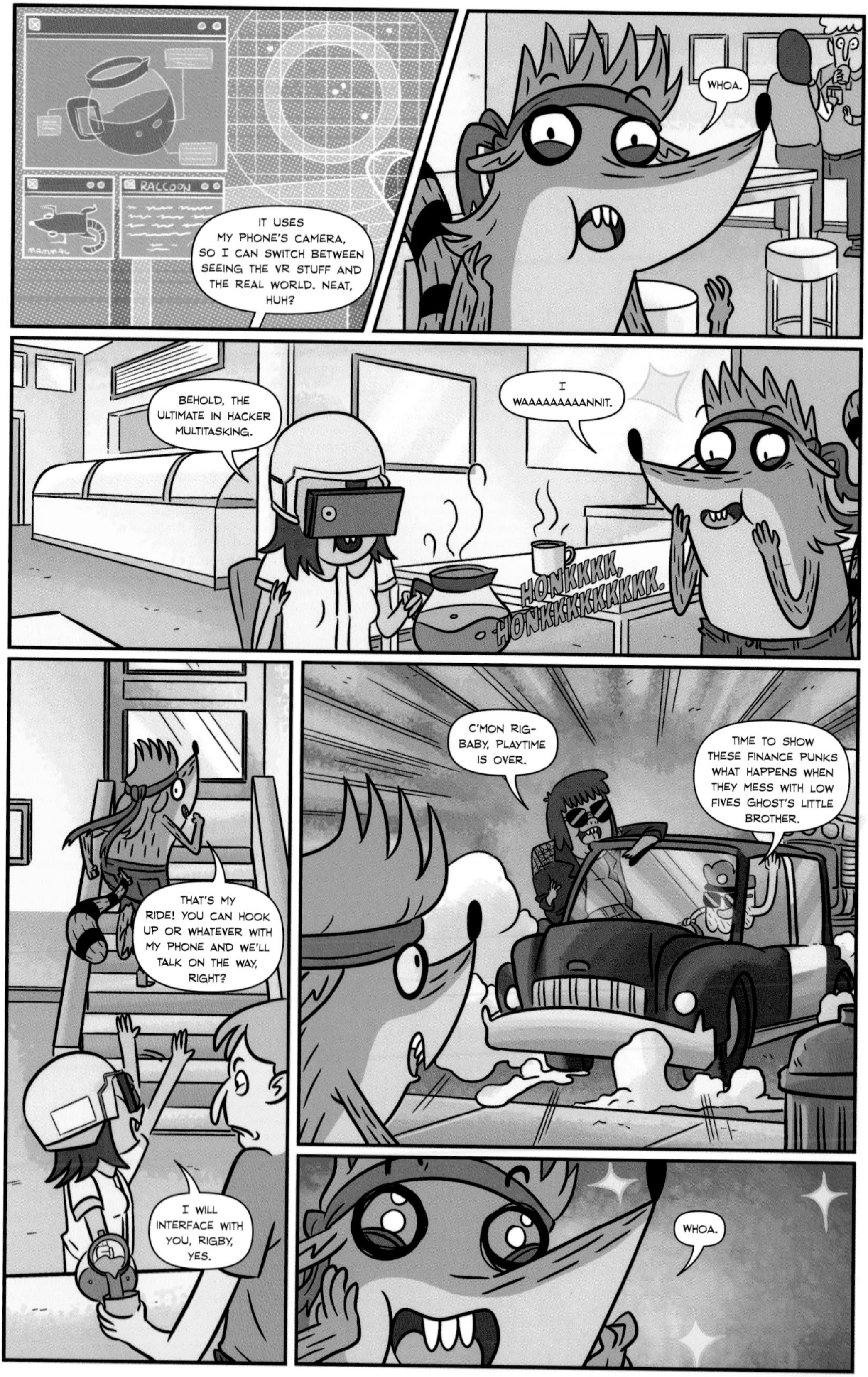
RACCOON
IT USES MY PHONE'S CAMERA, SO I CAN SWITCH BETWEEN SEEING THE VR STUFF AND THE REAL WORLD. NEAT, HUH?
WHOA.
BEHOLD, THE ULTIMATE IN HACKER MULTITASKING.
I WAAAAAAAAANNIT.
HONKKKK, HONKKKKKKKKK.
THAT'S MY RIDE! YOU CAN HOOK UP OR WHATEVER WITH MY PHONE AND WE'LL TALK ON THE WAY, RIGHT?
I WILL INTERFACE WITH YOU, RIGBY, YES.
C'MON RIG-BABY, PLAYTIME IS OVER.
TIME TO SHOW THESE FINANCE PUNKS WHAT HAPPENS WHEN THEY MESS WITH LOW FIVES GHOST'S LITTLE BROTHER.
WHOA.

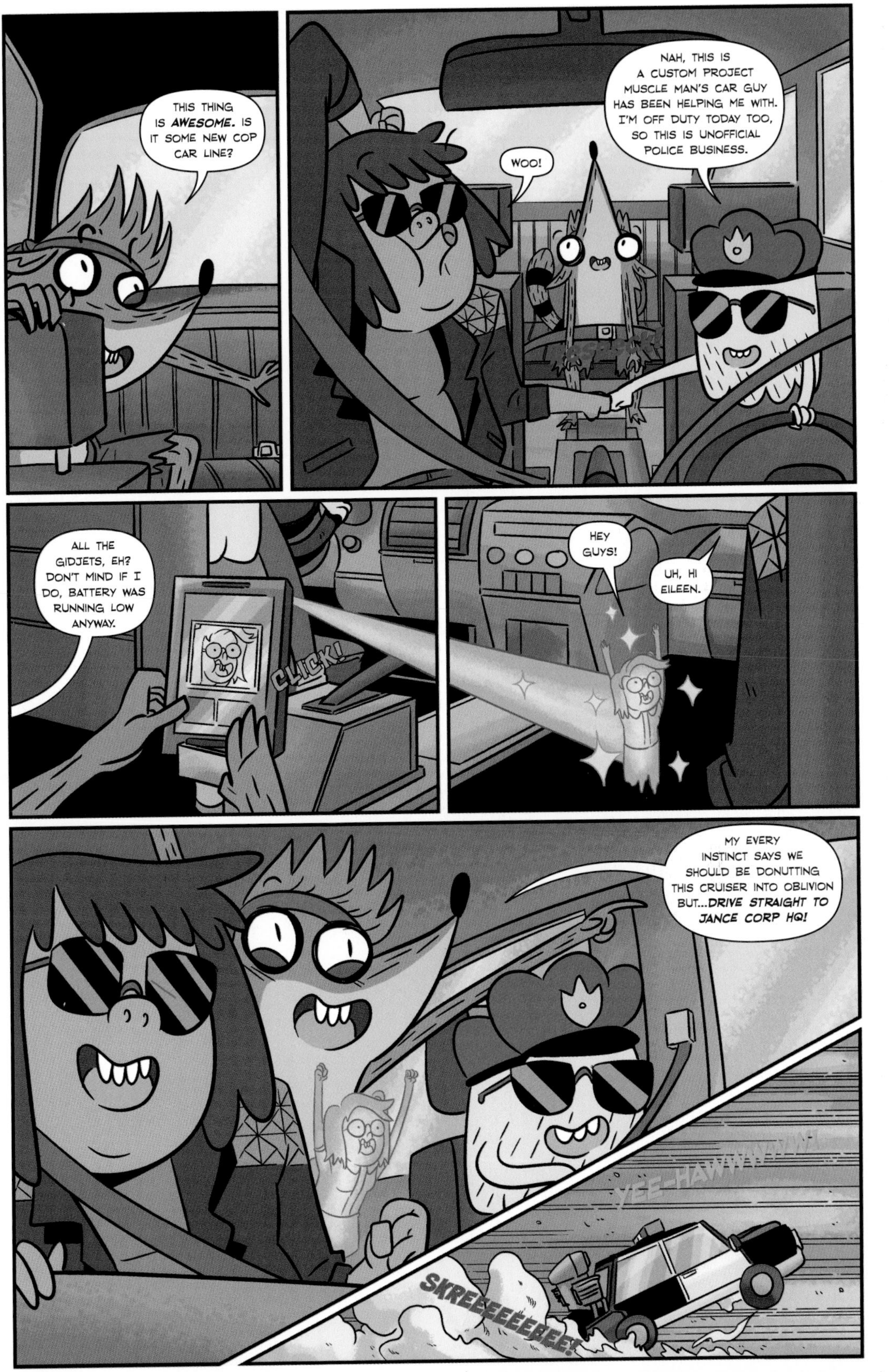

THIS THING IS **AWESOME.** IS IT SOME NEW COP CAR LINE?
WOO!
NAH, THIS IS A CUSTOM PROJECT MUSCLE MAN'S CAR GUY HAS BEEN HELPING ME WITH. I'M OFF DUTY TODAY TOO, SO THIS IS UNOFFICIAL POLICE BUSINESS.
ALL THE GIDJETS, EH? DON'T MIND IF I DO, BATTERY WAS RUNNING LOW ANYWAY.
CLICK!
HEY GUYS!
UH, HI EILEEN.
MY EVERY INSTINCT SAYS WE SHOULD BE DONUTTING THIS CRUISER INTO OBLIVION BUT...***DRIVE STRAIGHT TO JANCE CORP HQ!***
YEE-HAWWWWWW!
SKREEEEEEEEEE!

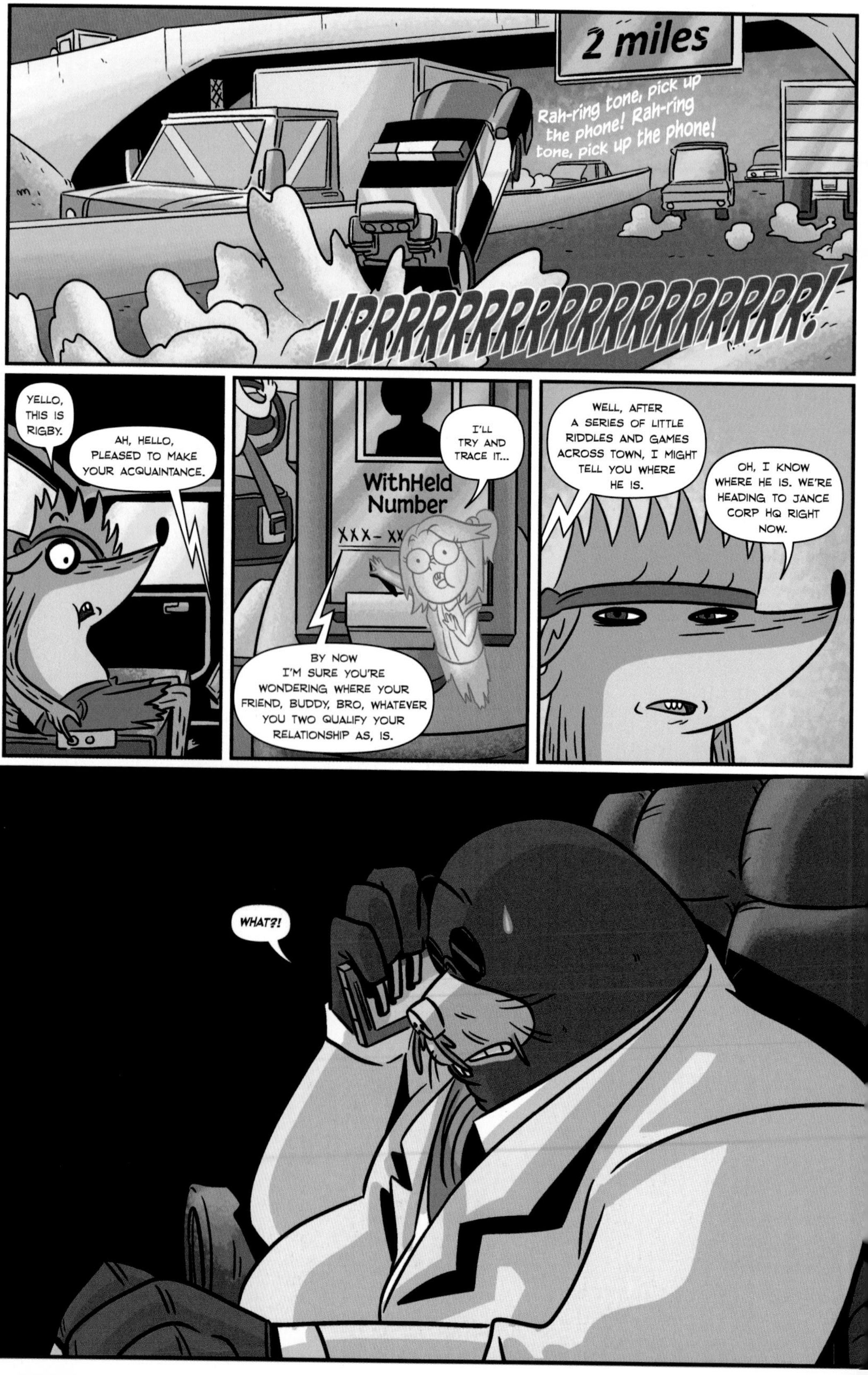
2 miles
Rah-ring tone, pick up the phone! Rah-ring tone, pick up the phone!
VRRRRRRRRRRRRRRRRRRRRR!
YELLO, THIS IS RIGBY.
AH, HELLO, PLEASED TO MAKE YOUR ACQUAINTANCE.
WithHeld Number
XXX- XX
I'LL TRY AND TRACE IT...
BY NOW I'M SURE YOU'RE WONDERING WHERE YOUR FRIEND, BUDDY, BRO, WHATEVER YOU TWO QUALIFY YOUR RELATIONSHIP AS, IS.
WELL, AFTER A SERIES OF LITTLE RIDDLES AND GAMES ACROSS TOWN, I MIGHT TELL YOU WHERE HE IS.
OH, I KNOW WHERE HE IS. WE'RE HEADING TO JANCE CORP HQ RIGHT NOW.
WHAT?!

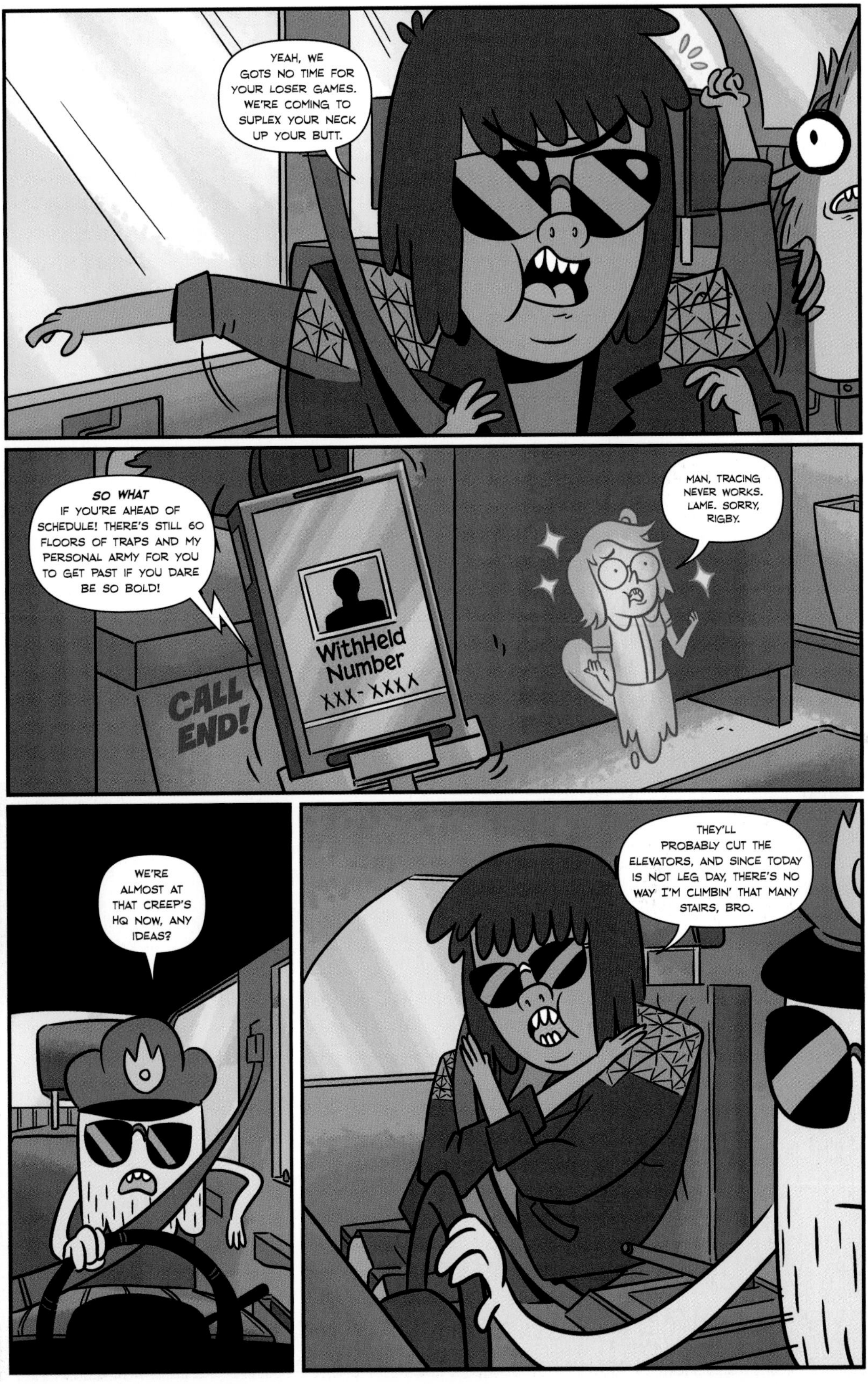
YEAH, WE GOTS NO TIME FOR YOUR LOSER GAMES. WE'RE COMING TO SUPLEX YOUR NECK UP YOUR BUTT.
SO WHAT IF YOU'RE AHEAD OF SCHEDULE! THERE'S STILL 60 FLOORS OF TRAPS AND MY PERSONAL ARMY FOR YOU TO GET PAST IF YOU DARE BE SO BOLD!
WithHeld Number
XXX-XXXX
CALL END!
MAN, TRACING NEVER WORKS. LAME. SORRY, RIGBY.
WE'RE ALMOST AT THAT CREEP'S HQ NOW, ANY IDEAS?
THEY'LL PROBABLY CUT THE ELEVATORS, AND SINCE TODAY IS NOT LEG DAY, THERE'S NO WAY I'M CLIMBIN' THAT MANY STAIRS, BRO.

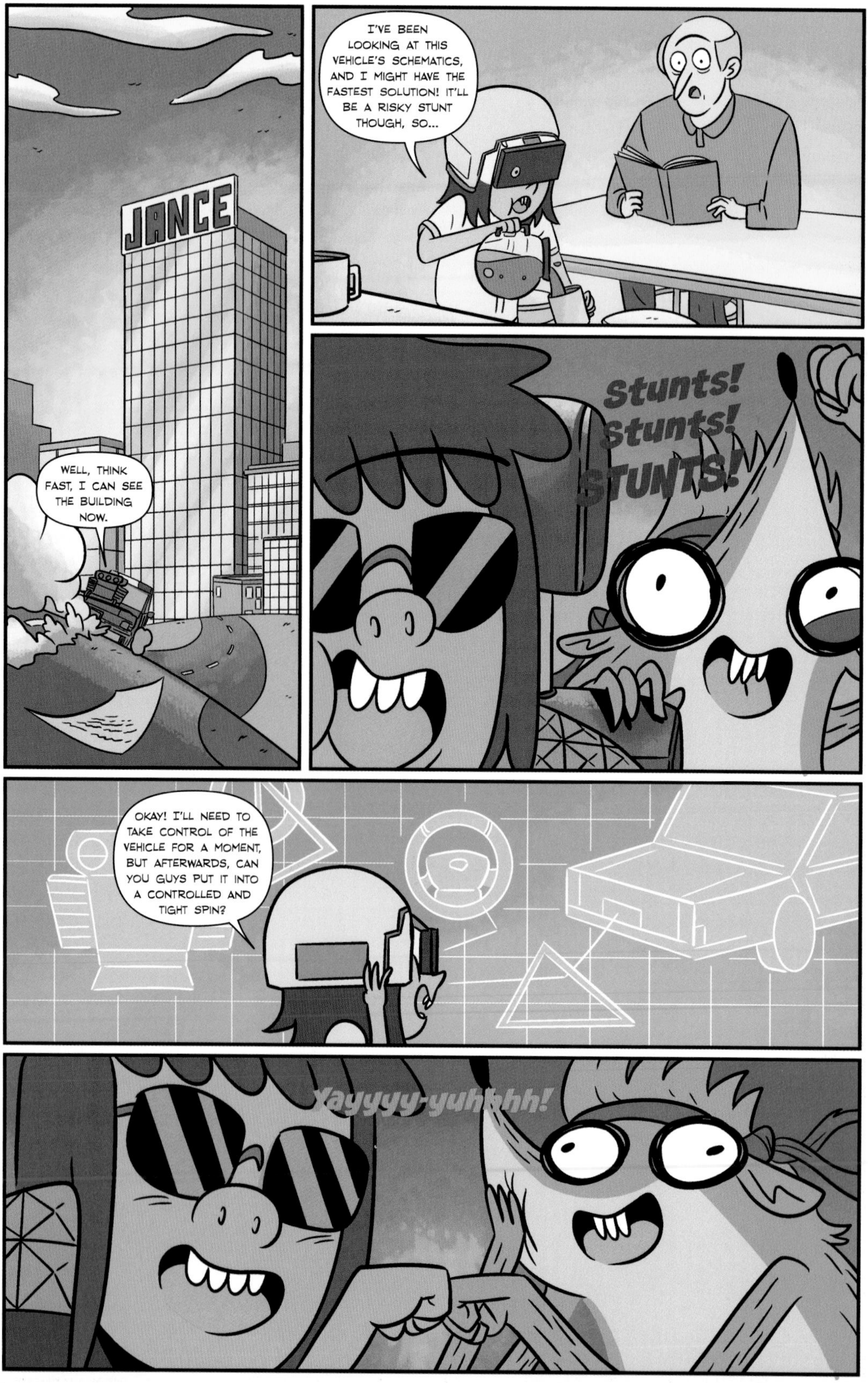
JANCE
WELL, THINK FAST, I CAN SEE THE BUILDING NOW.
I'VE BEEN LOOKING AT THIS VEHICLE'S SCHEMATICS, AND I MIGHT HAVE THE FASTEST SOLUTION! IT'LL BE A RISKY STUNT THOUGH, SO...
Stunts! Stunts! STUNTS!
OKAY! I'LL NEED TO TAKE CONTROL OF THE VEHICLE FOR A MOMENT, BUT AFTERWARDS, CAN YOU GUYS PUT IT INTO A CONTROLLED AND TIGHT SPIN?
Yayyyy-yuhhhh!

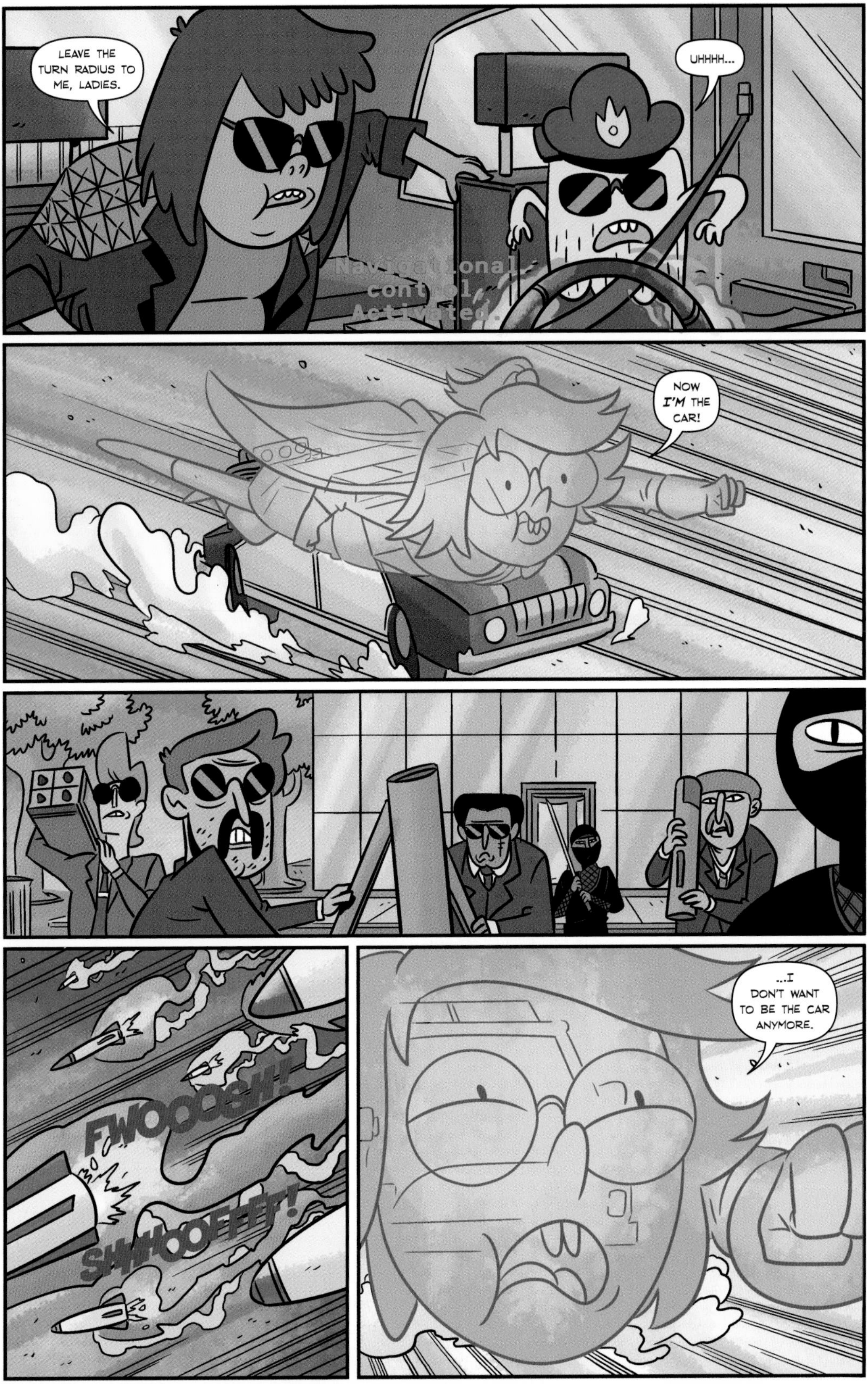
LEAVE THE TURN RADIUS TO ME, LADIES.
UHHHH...
Navigational control Activated.
NOW I'M THE CAR!
FWOOOSH!
SHHHOOFFFF!
...I DON'T WANT TO BE THE CAR ANYMORE.

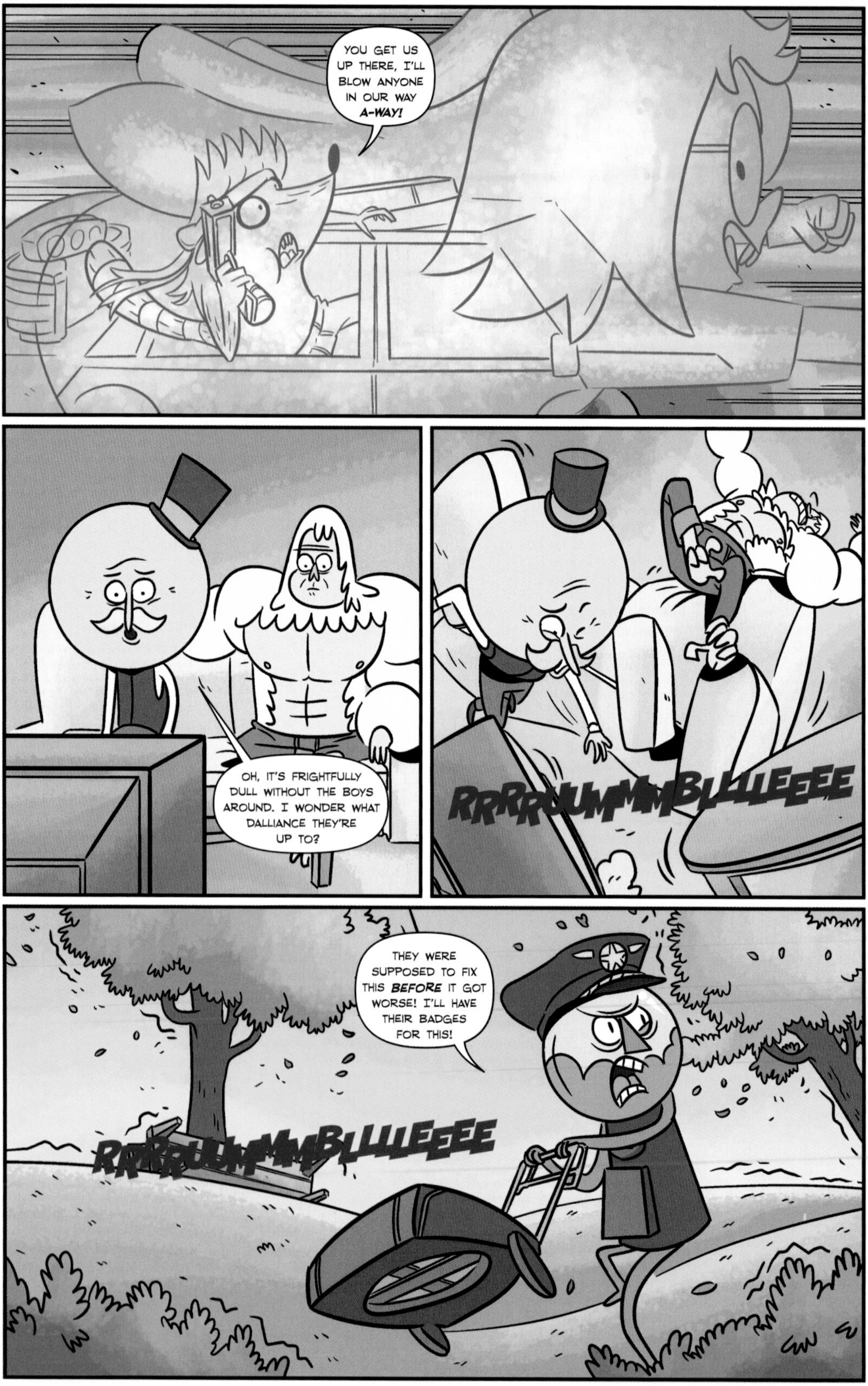
YOU GET US UP THERE, I'LL BLOW ANYONE IN OUR WAY A-WAY!
OH, IT'S FRIGHTFULLY DULL WITHOUT THE BOYS AROUND. I WONDER WHAT DALLIANCE THEY'RE UP TO?
RRRRUUMMMBLLLLEEEE
THEY WERE SUPPOSED TO FIX THIS BEFORE IT GOT WORSE! I'LL HAVE THEIR BADGES FOR THIS!
RRRRUUMMMBLLLLEEEE

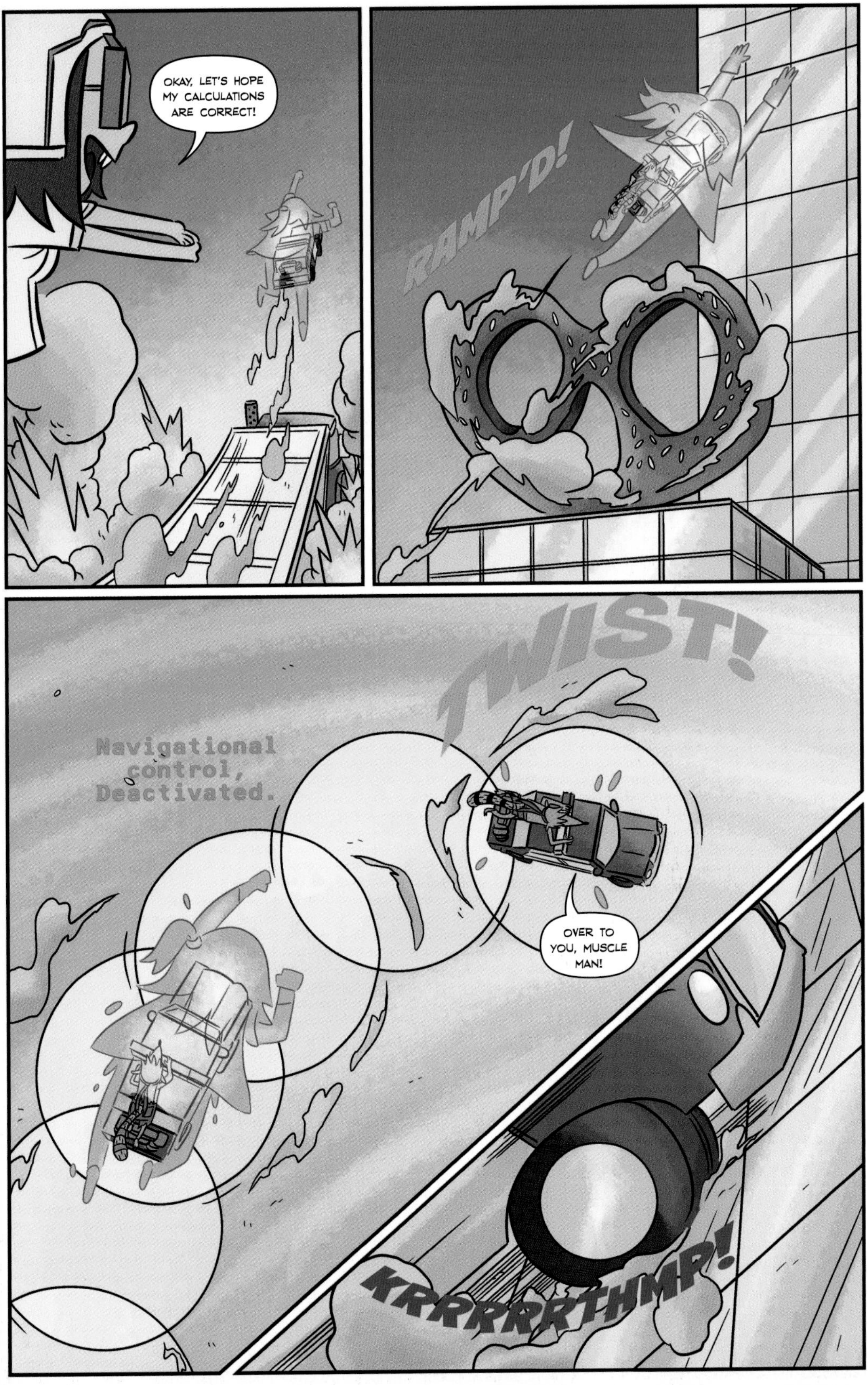
OKAY, LET'S HOPE MY CALCULATIONS ARE CORRECT!
RAMP'D!
TWIST!
Navigational control, Deactivated.
OVER TO YOU, MUSCLE MAN!
KRRRRRTHMP!

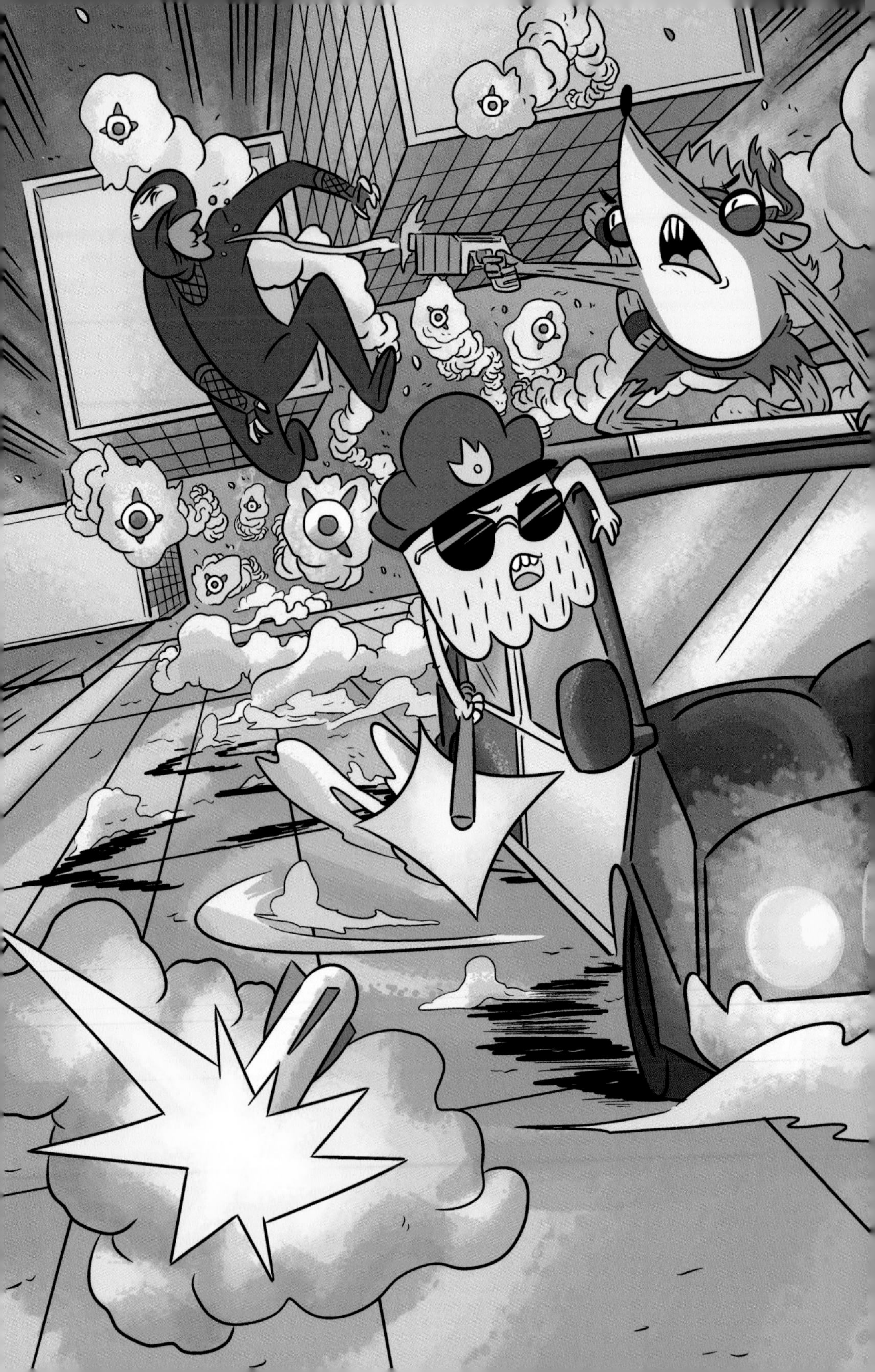

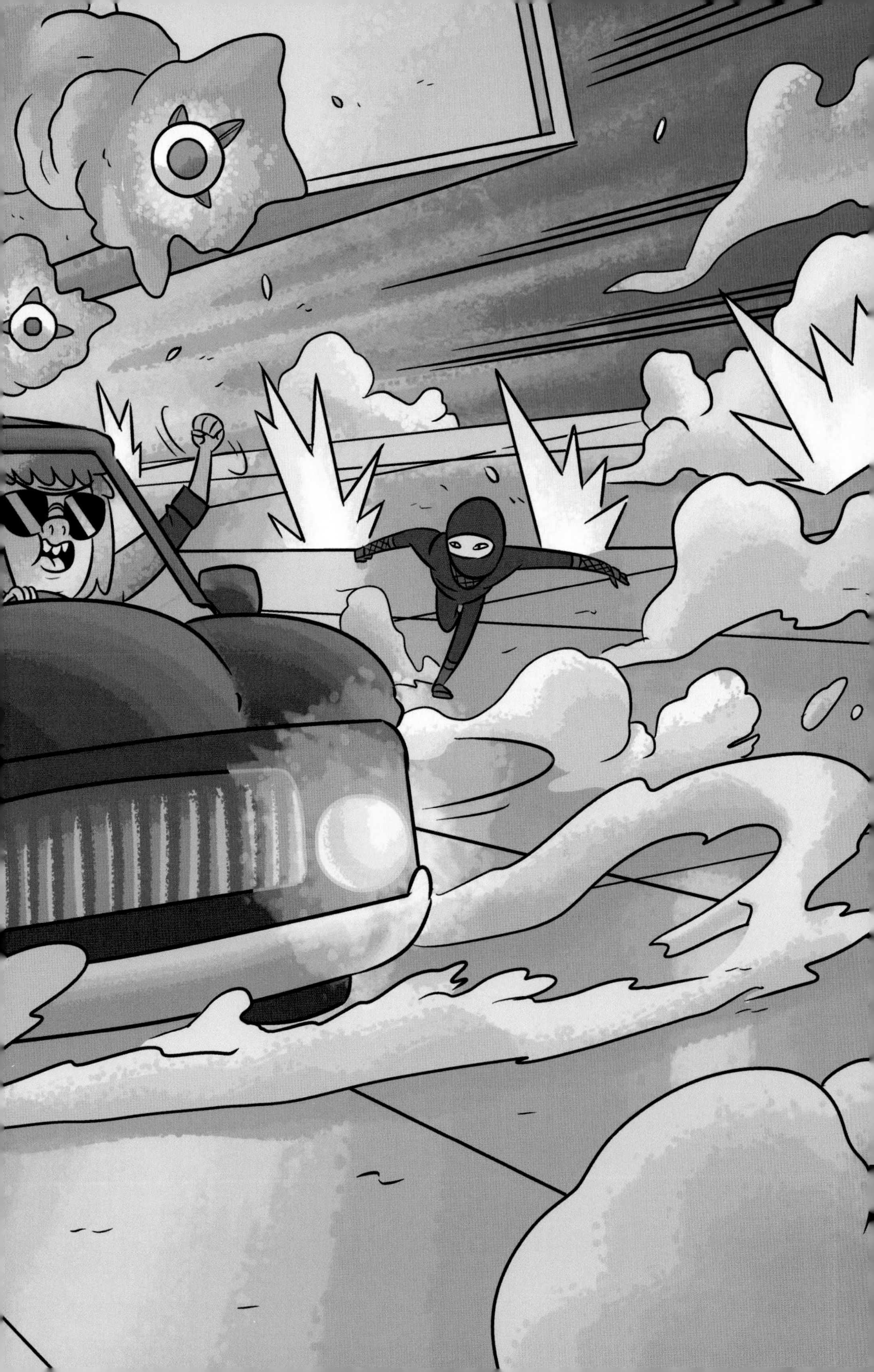

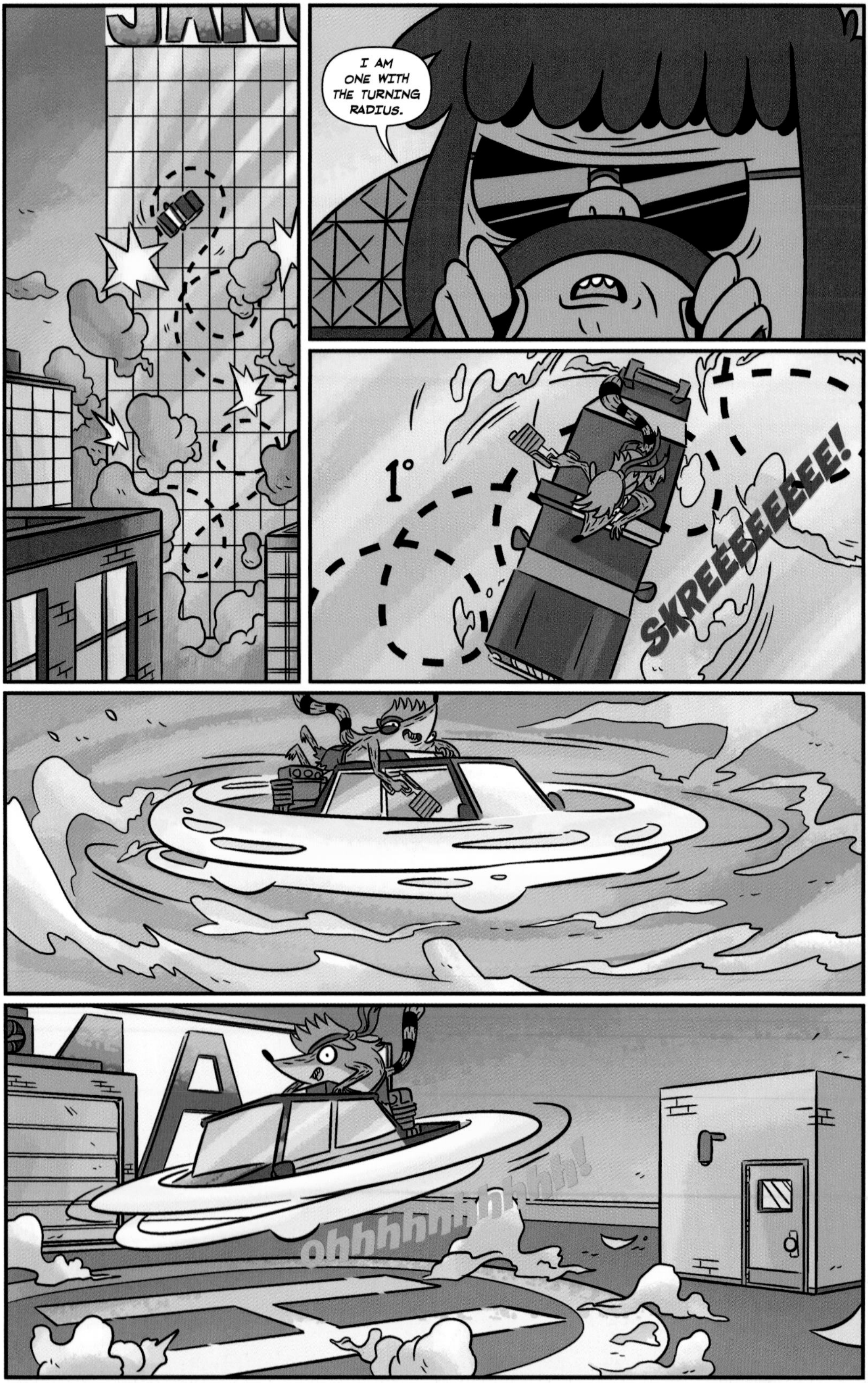
I AM ONE WITH THE TURNING RADIUS.
1°
SKREEEEEEEE!
Ohhhhhhhhhh!

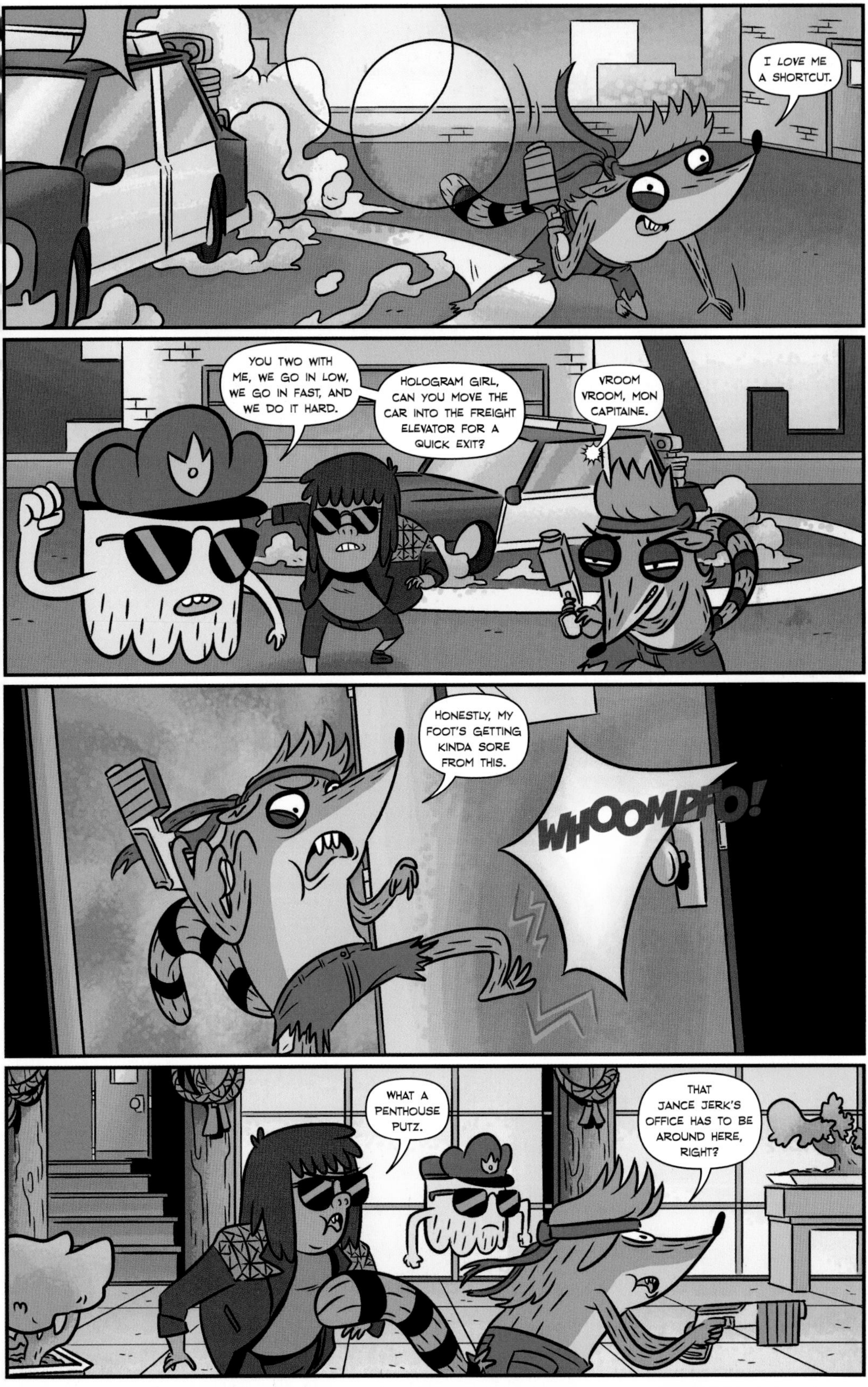
I LOVE ME A SHORTCUT.
YOU TWO WITH ME, WE GO IN LOW, WE GO IN FAST, AND WE DO IT HARD.
HOLOGRAM GIRL, CAN YOU MOVE THE CAR INTO THE FREIGHT ELEVATOR FOR A QUICK EXIT?
VROOM VROOM, MON CAPITAINE.
HONESTLY, MY FOOT'S GETTING KINDA SORE FROM THIS.
WHOOMPFO!
WHAT A PENTHOUSE PUTZ.
THAT JANCE JERK'S OFFICE HAS TO BE AROUND HERE, RIGHT?

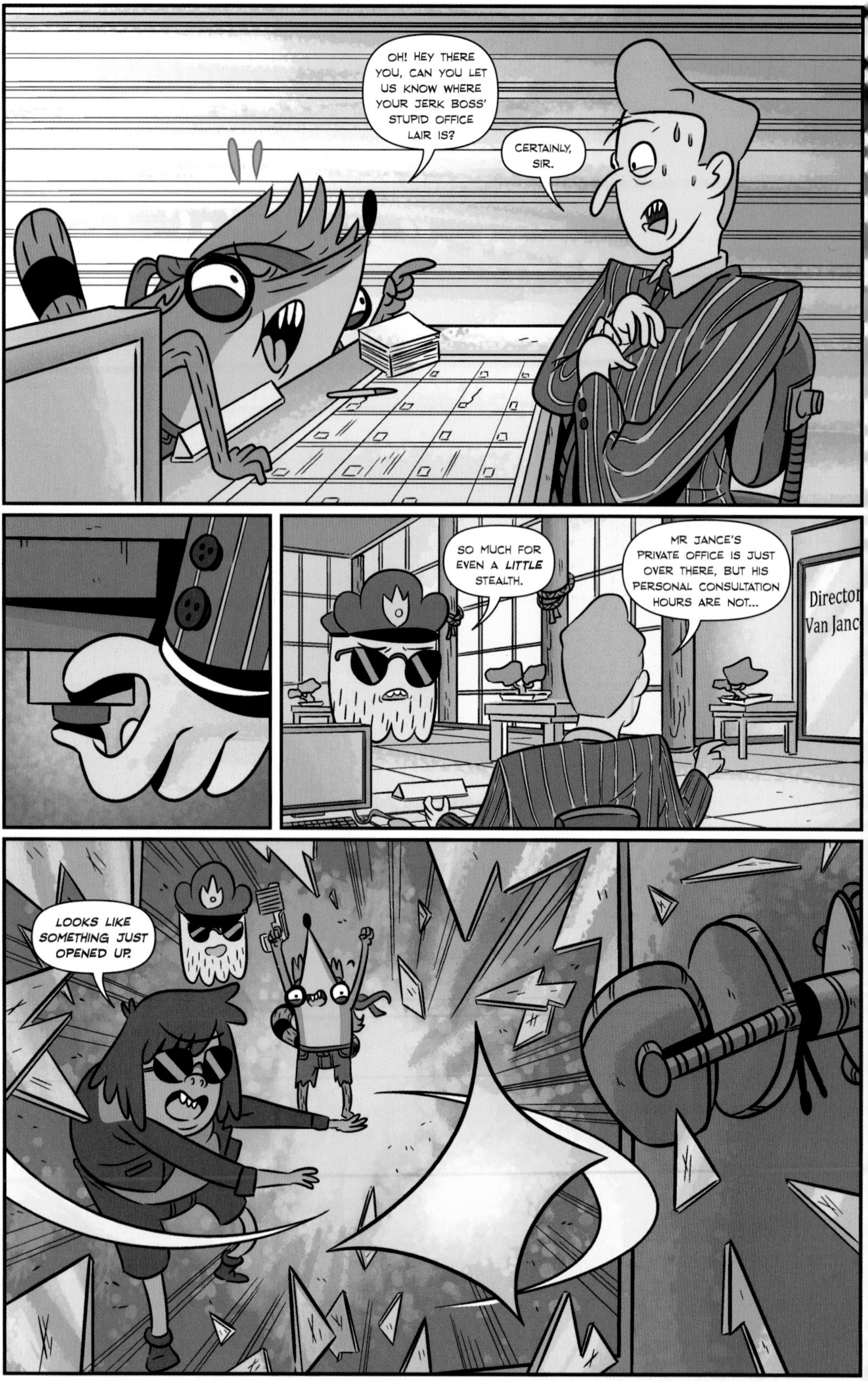
OH! HEY THERE YOU, CAN YOU LET US KNOW WHERE YOUR JERK BOSS' STUPID OFFICE LAIR IS?
CERTAINLY, SIR.
SO MUCH FOR EVEN A *LITTLE* STEALTH.
MR JANCE'S PRIVATE OFFICE IS JUST OVER THERE, BUT HIS PERSONAL CONSULTATION HOURS ARE NOT...
Director
Van Janc
LOOKS LIKE SOMETHING JUST OPENED UP.

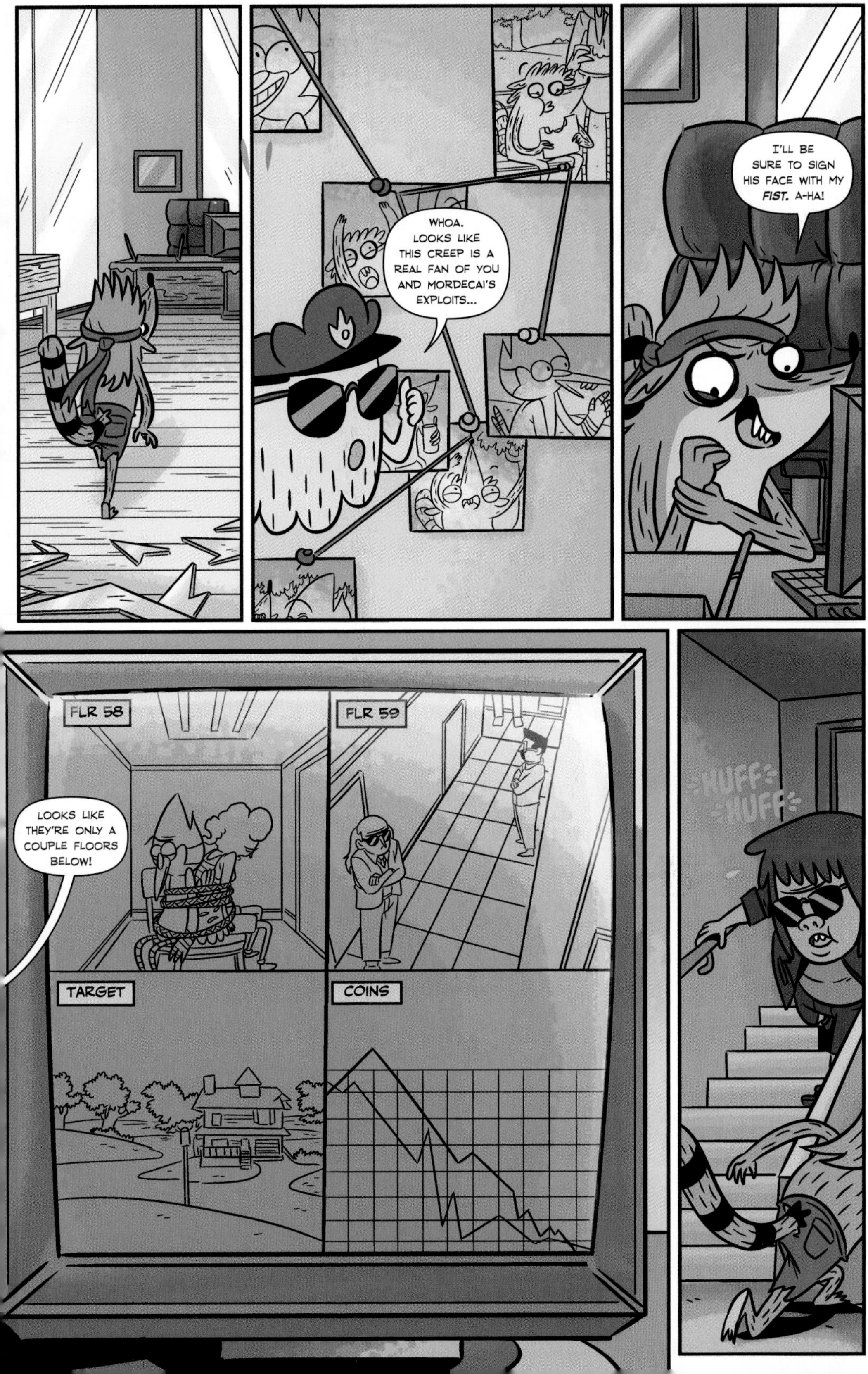
WHOA. LOOKS LIKE THIS CREEP IS A REAL FAN OF YOU AND MORDECAI'S EXPLOITS...
I'LL BE SURE TO SIGN HIS FACE WITH MY FIST. A-HA!
FLR 58
FLR 59
TARGET
COINS
LOOKS LIKE THEY'RE ONLY A COUPLE FLOORS BELOW!
HUFF HUFF

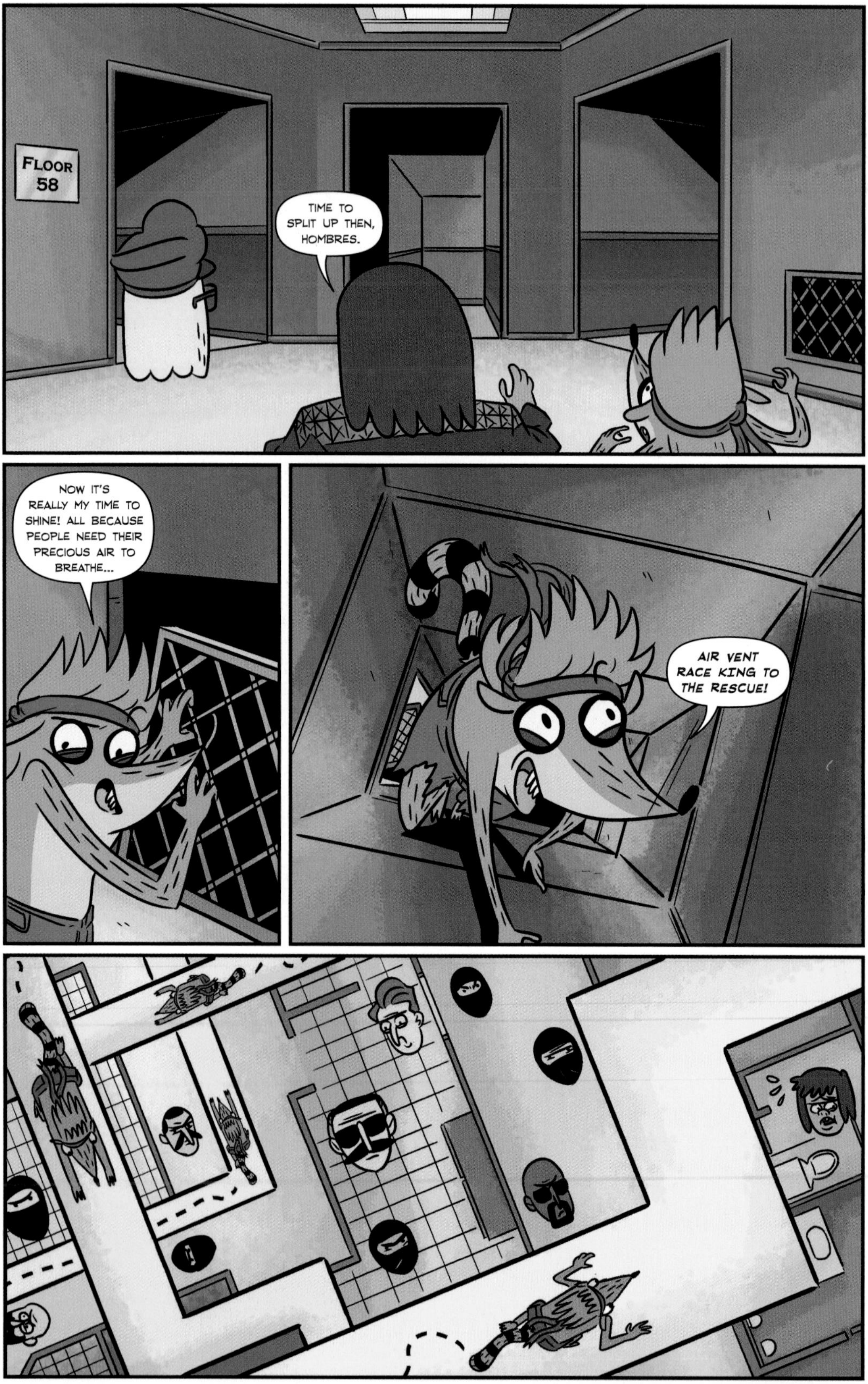
FLOOR 58
TIME TO SPLIT UP THEN, HOMBRES.
NOW IT'S REALLY MY TIME TO SHINE! ALL BECAUSE PEOPLE NEED THEIR PRECIOUS AIR TO BREATHE...
AIR VENT RACE KING TO THE RESCUE!

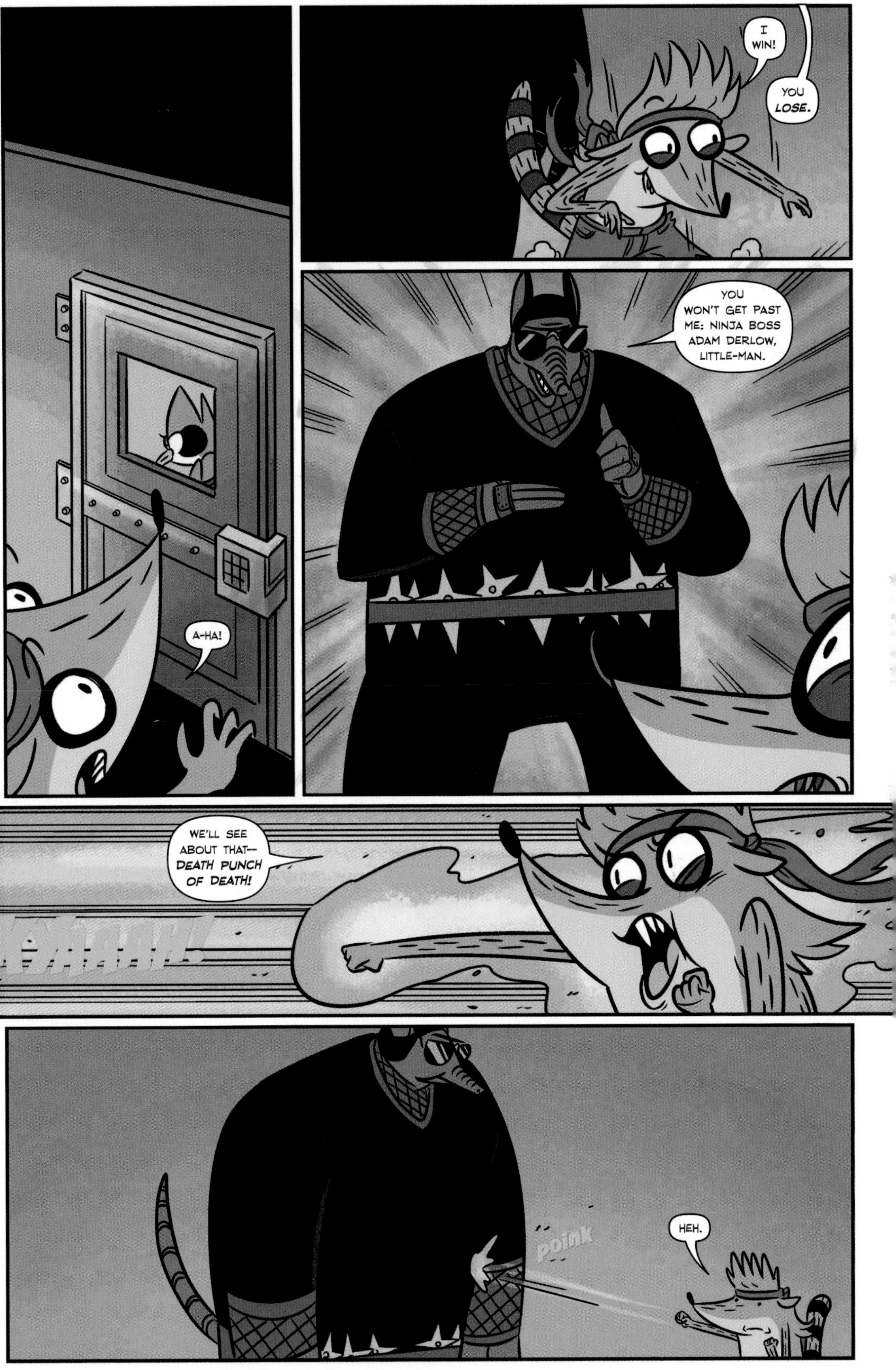
I WIN!
YOU LOSE.
A-HA!
YOU WON'T GET PAST ME: NINJA BOSS ADAM DERLOW, LITTLE-MAN.
WE'LL SEE ABOUT THAT-- DEATH PUNCH OF DEATH!
KYAAAH!
POINK
HEH.

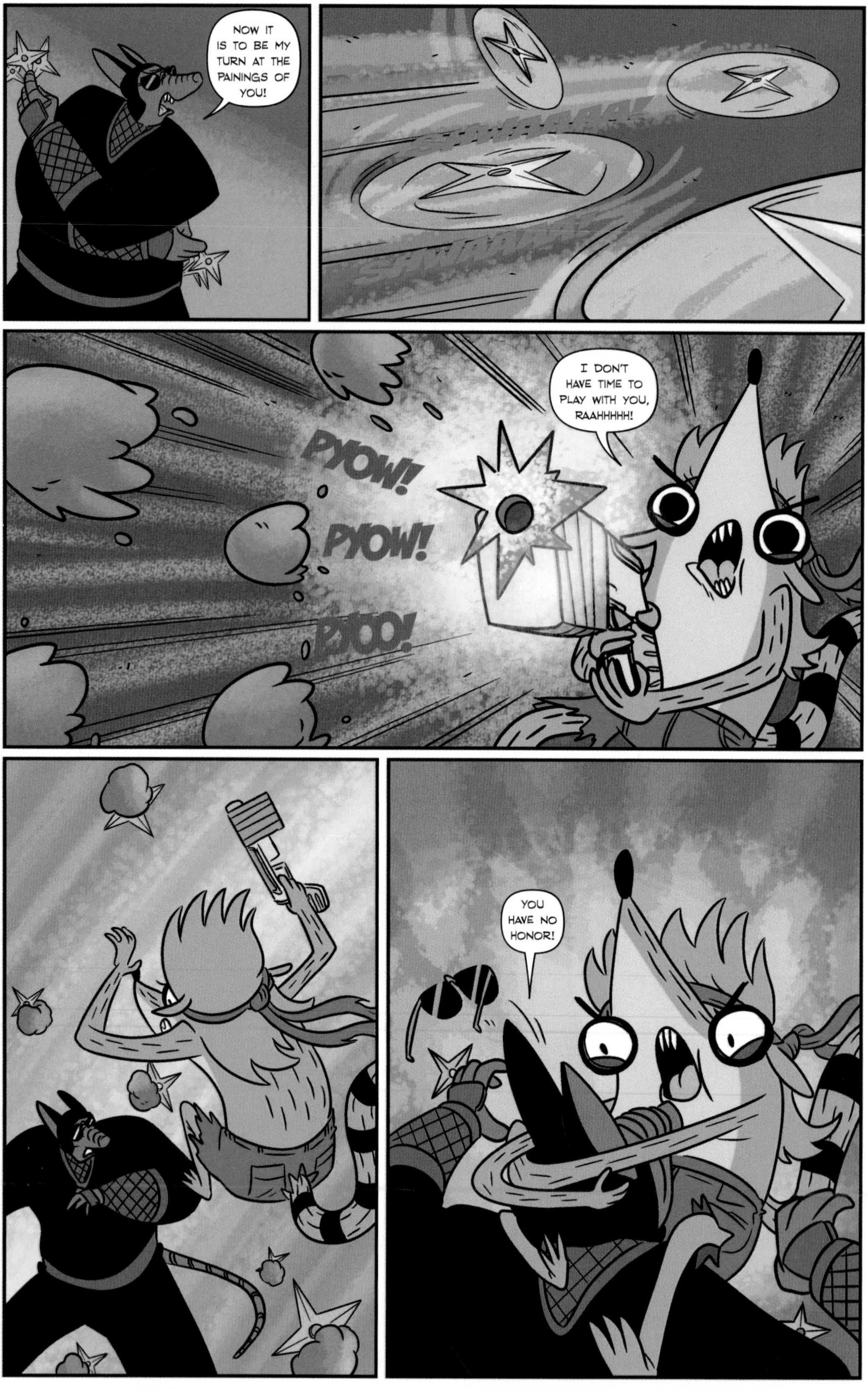
NOW IT IS TO BE MY TURN AT THE PAININGS OF YOU!
I DON'T HAVE TIME TO PLAY WITH YOU, RAAHHHHH!
PYOW!
PYOW!
PYOO!
YOU HAVE NO HONOR!

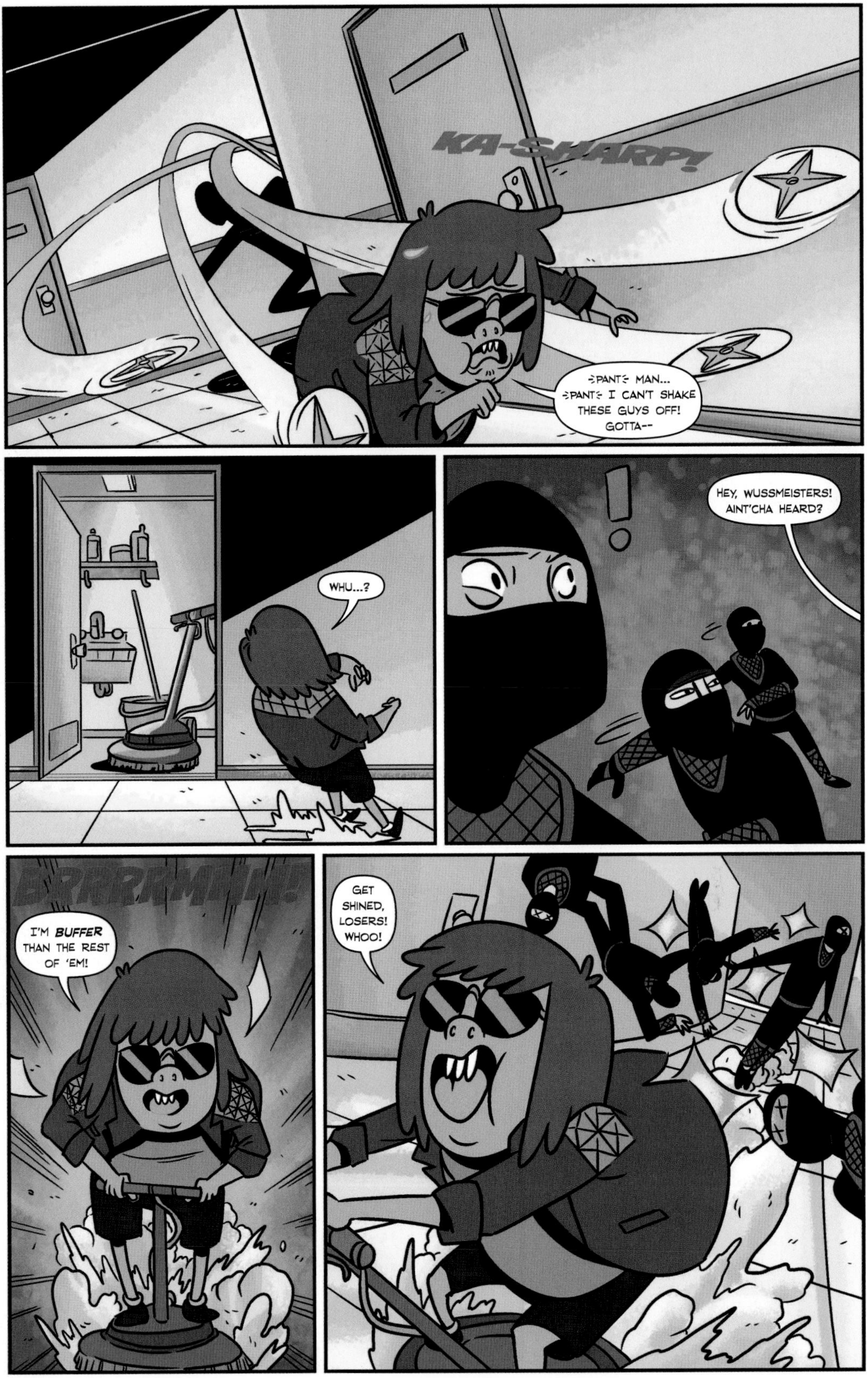

KA-SHARP!
=PANT= MAN... =PANT= I CAN'T SHAKE THESE GUYS OFF! GOTTA--
WHU...?
HEY, WUSSMEISTERS! AINT'CHA HEARD?
BRRRRMMM!
I'M BUFFER THAN THE REST OF 'EM!
GET SHINED, LOSERS! WHOO!

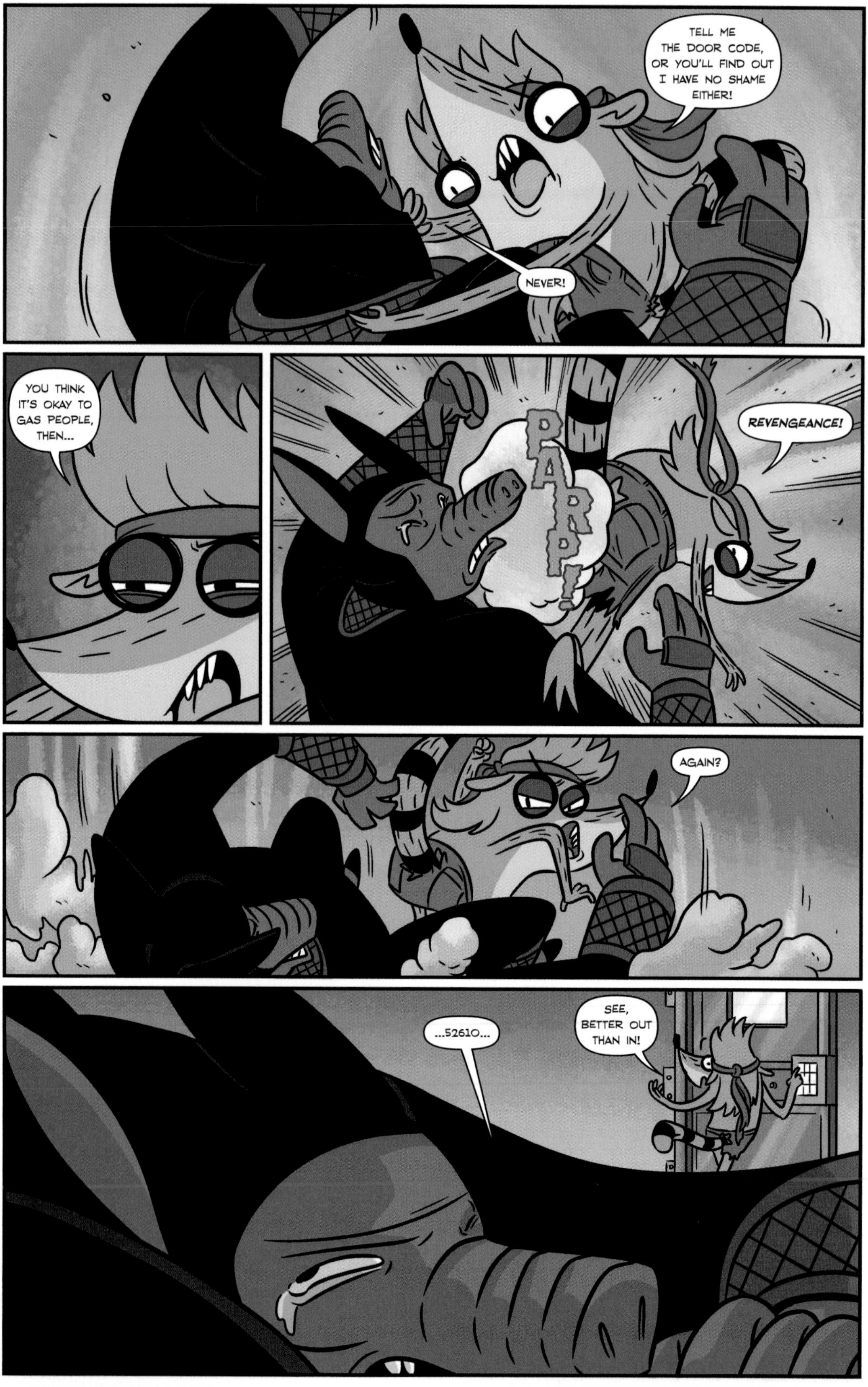
TELL ME THE DOOR CODE, OR YOU'LL FIND OUT I HAVE NO SHAME EITHER!
NEVER!
YOU THINK IT'S OKAY TO GAS PEOPLE, THEN...
PARP!
REVENGEANCE!
AGAIN?
...52610...
SEE, BETTER OUT THAN IN!

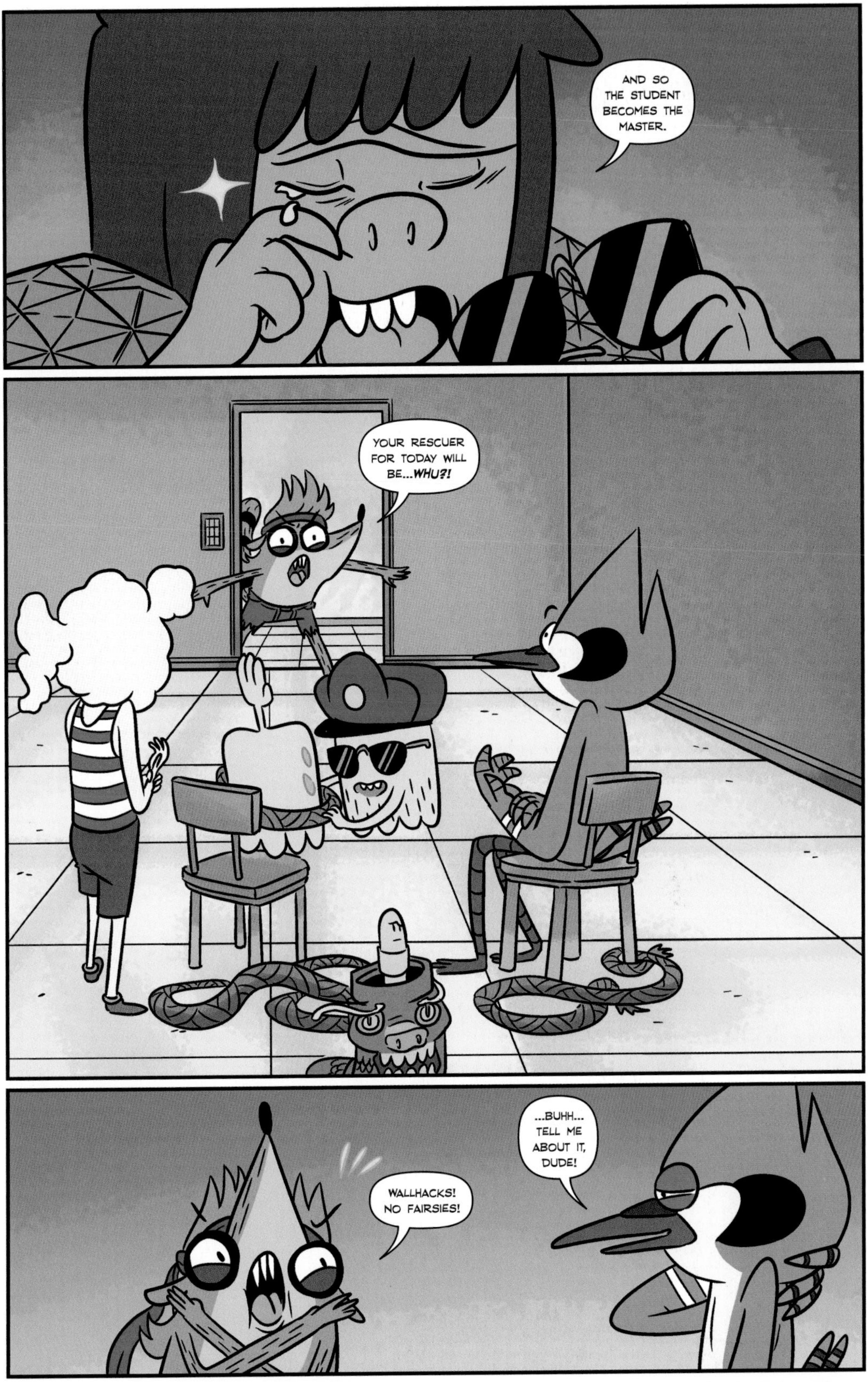
AND SO THE STUDENT BECOMES THE MASTER.
YOUR RESCUER FOR TODAY WILL BE...WHU?!
WALLHACKS! NO FAIRSIES!
...BUHH... TELL ME ABOUT IT, DUDE!

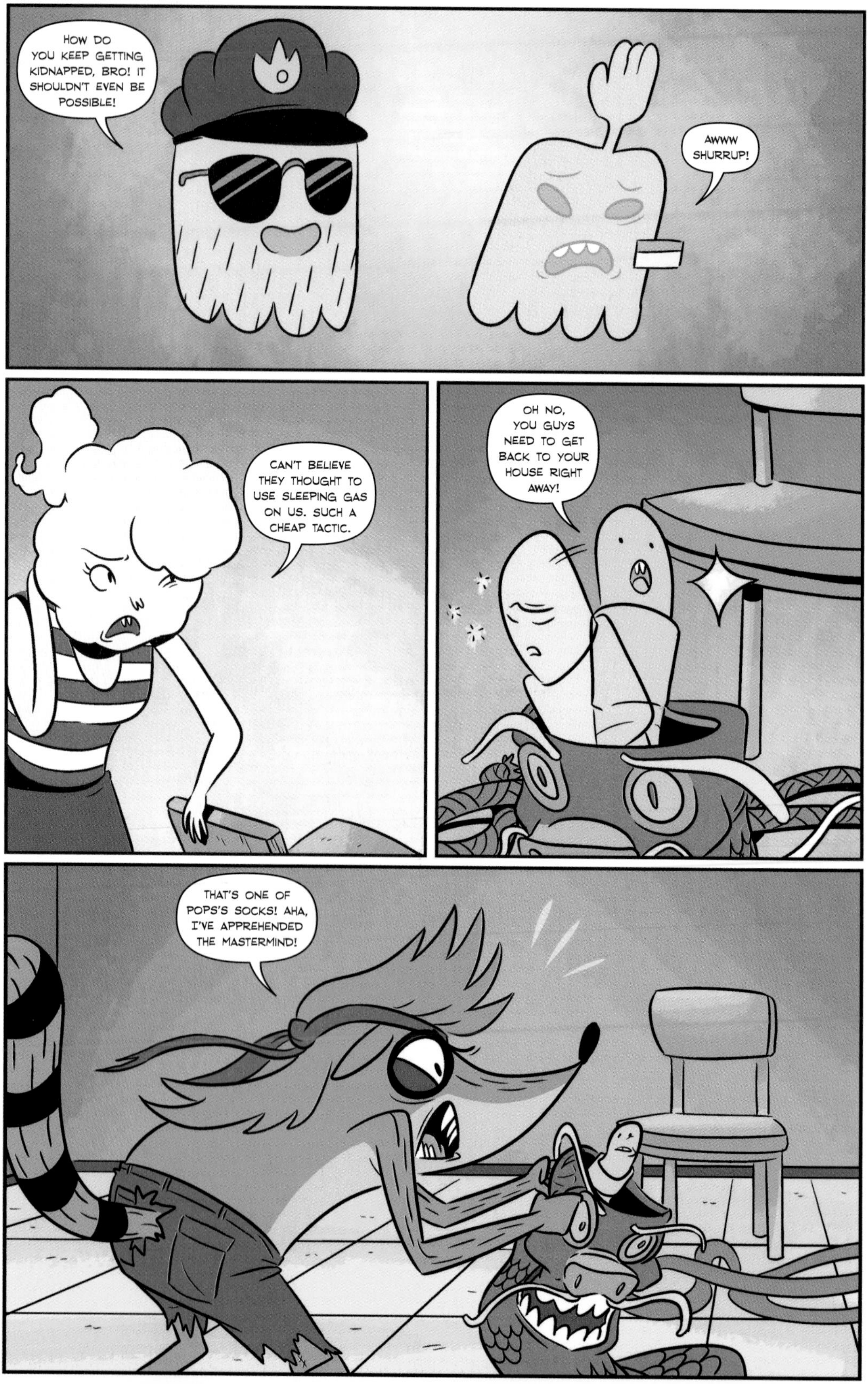
HOW DO YOU KEEP GETTING KIDNAPPED, BRO! IT SHOULDN'T EVEN BE POSSIBLE!
AWWW SHURRUP!
CAN'T BELIEVE THEY THOUGHT TO USE SLEEPING GAS ON US. SUCH A CHEAP TACTIC.
OH NO, YOU GUYS NEED TO GET BACK TO YOUR HOUSE RIGHT AWAY!
THAT'S ONE OF POPS'S SOCKS! AHA, I'VE APPREHENDED THE MASTERMIND!

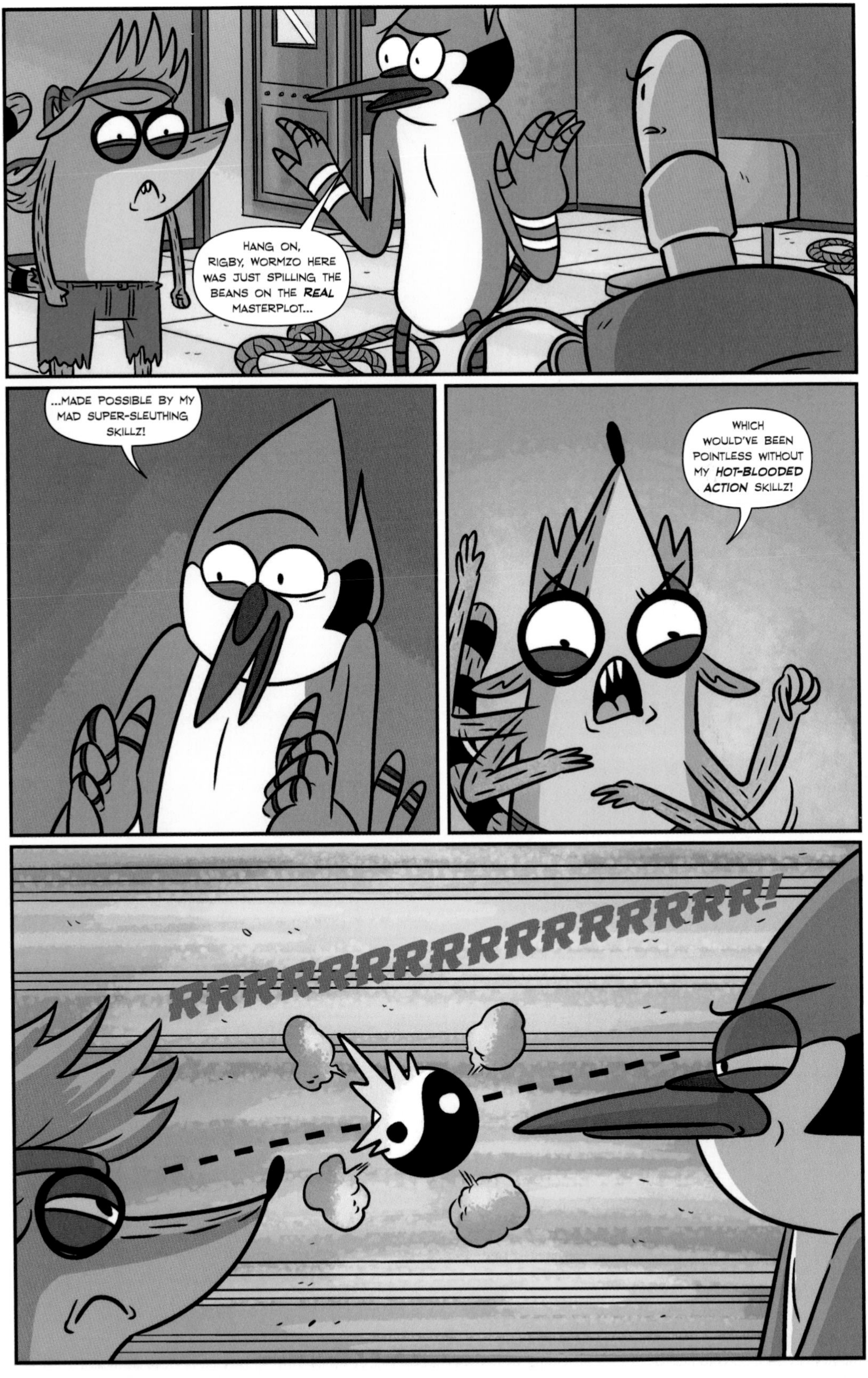
HANG ON, RIGBY, WORMZO HERE WAS JUST SPILLING THE BEANS ON THE REAL MASTERPLOT...
...MADE POSSIBLE BY MY MAD SUPER-SLEUTHING SKILLZ!
WHICH WOULD'VE BEEN POINTLESS WITHOUT MY HOT-BLOODED ACTION SKILLZ!
RRRRRRRRRRRRRRRRR!

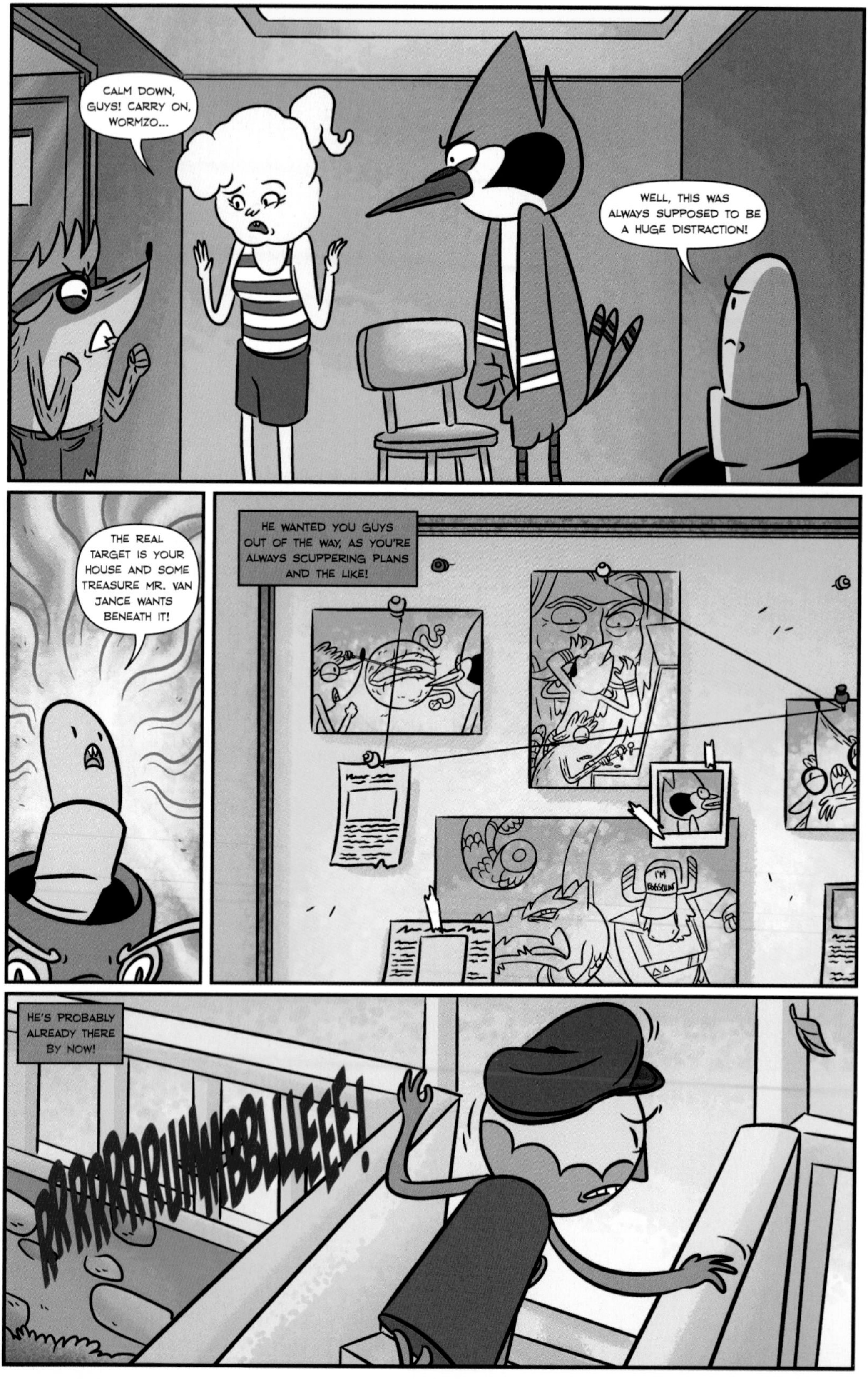
CALM DOWN, GUYS! CARRY ON, WORMZO...
WELL, THIS WAS ALWAYS SUPPOSED TO BE A HUGE DISTRACTION!
THE REAL TARGET IS YOUR HOUSE AND SOME TREASURE MR. VAN JANCE WANTS BENEATH IT!
HE WANTED YOU GUYS OUT OF THE WAY, AS YOU'RE ALWAYS SCUPPERING PLANS AND THE LIKE!
HE'S PROBABLY ALREADY THERE BY NOW!
RRRRRRUMMBBLLEEE!

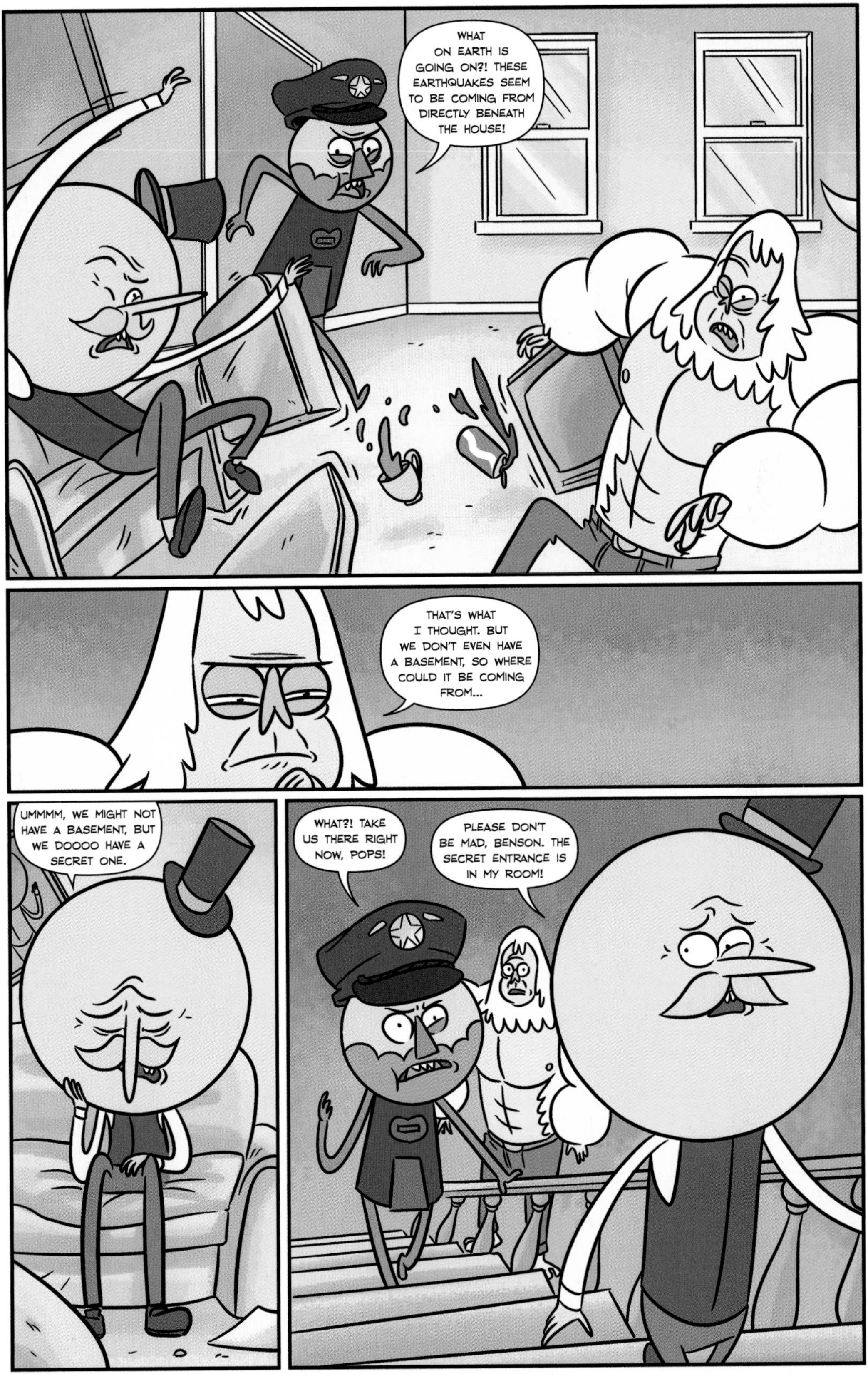
WHAT ON EARTH IS GOING ON?! THESE EARTHQUAKES SEEM TO BE COMING FROM DIRECTLY BENEATH THE HOUSE!
THAT'S WHAT I THOUGHT. BUT WE DON'T EVEN HAVE A BASEMENT, SO WHERE COULD IT BE COMING FROM...
UMMMM, WE MIGHT NOT HAVE A BASEMENT, BUT WE DOOOO HAVE A SECRET ONE.
WHAT?! TAKE US THERE RIGHT NOW, POPS!
PLEASE DON'T BE MAD, BENSON. THE SECRET ENTRANCE IS IN MY ROOM!

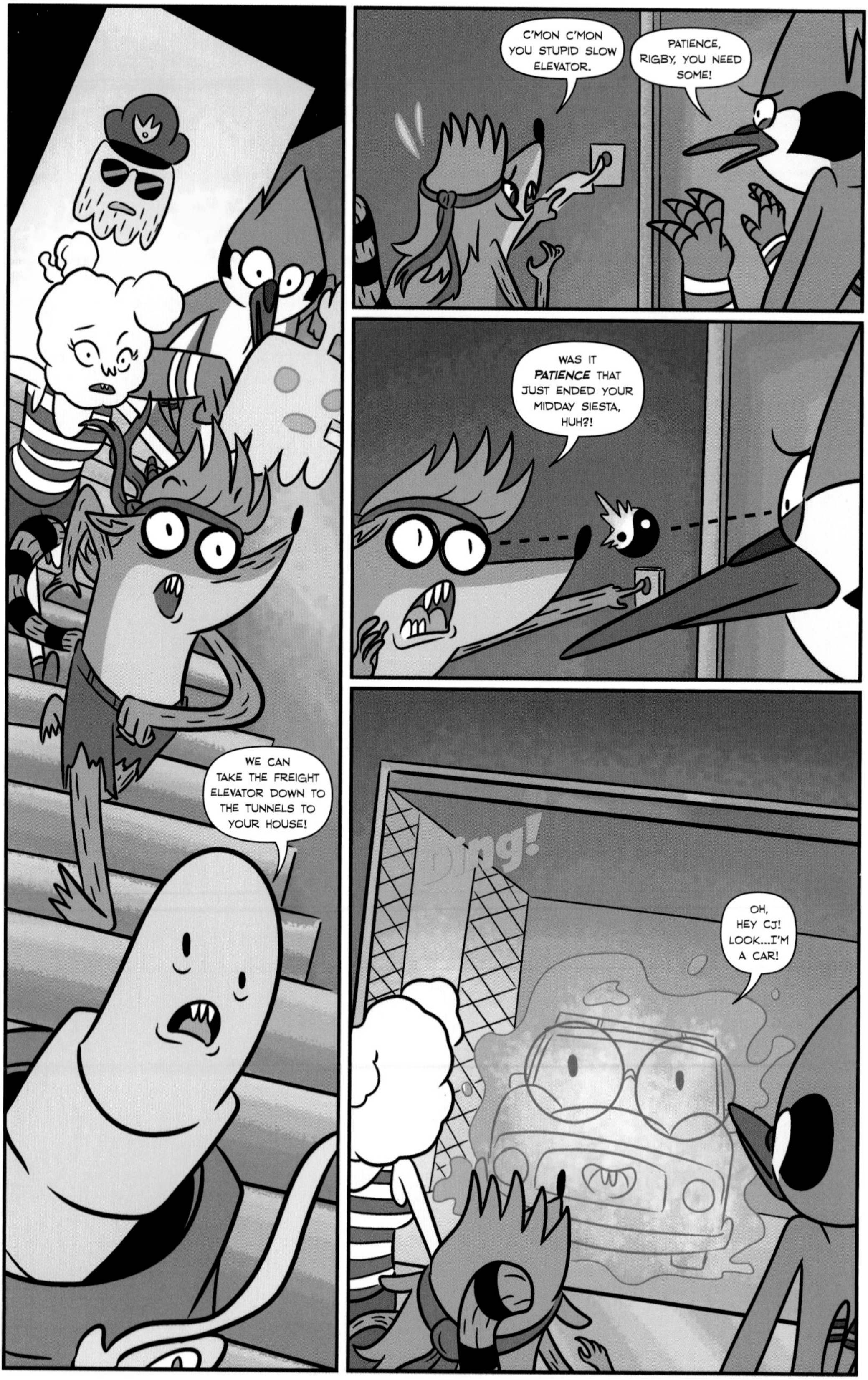
WE CAN TAKE THE FREIGHT ELEVATOR DOWN TO THE TUNNELS TO YOUR HOUSE!
C'MON C'MON YOU STUPID SLOW ELEVATOR.
PATIENCE, RIGBY, YOU NEED SOME!
WAS IT *PATIENCE* THAT JUST ENDED YOUR MIDDAY SIESTA, HUH?!
Ding!
OH, HEY CJ! LOOK...I'M A CAR!

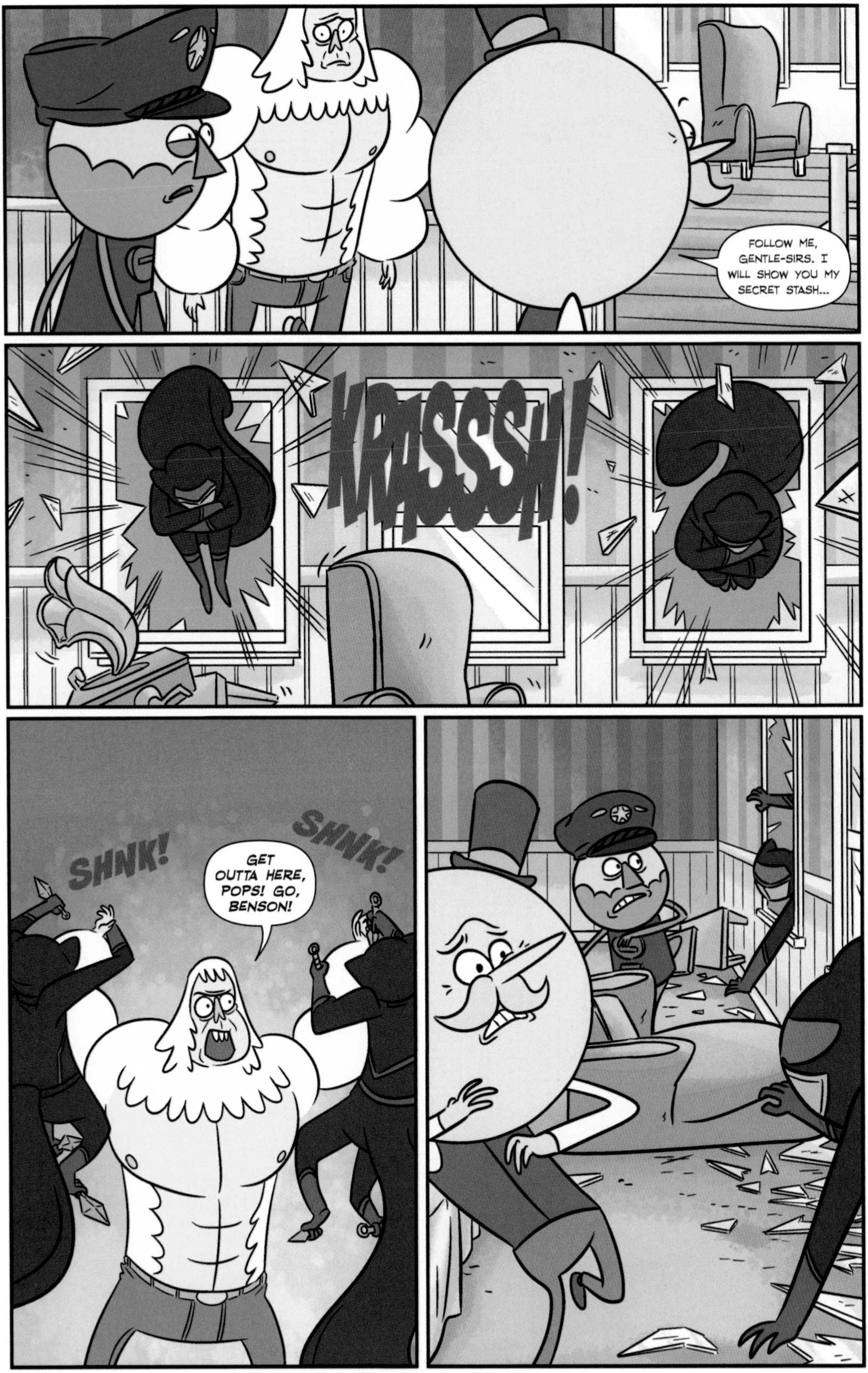
FOLLOW ME, GENTLE-SIRS. I WILL SHOW YOU MY SECRET STASH...
KRASSSH!
SHNK!
GET OUTTA HERE, POPS! GO, BENSON!
SHNK!

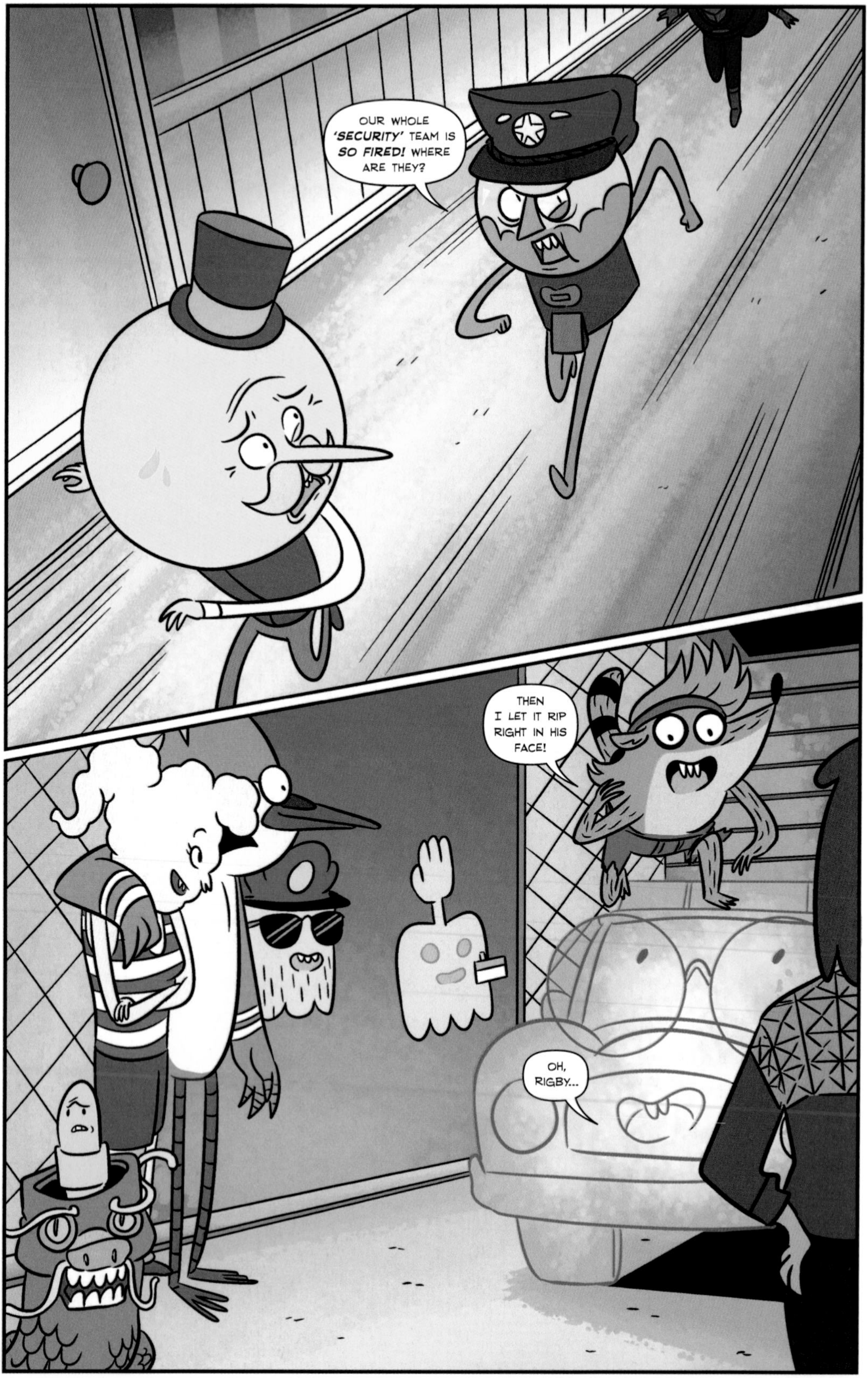
OUR WHOLE 'SECURITY' TEAM IS SO FIRED! WHERE ARE THEY?
THEN I LET IT RIP RIGHT IN HIS FACE!
OH, RIGBY...

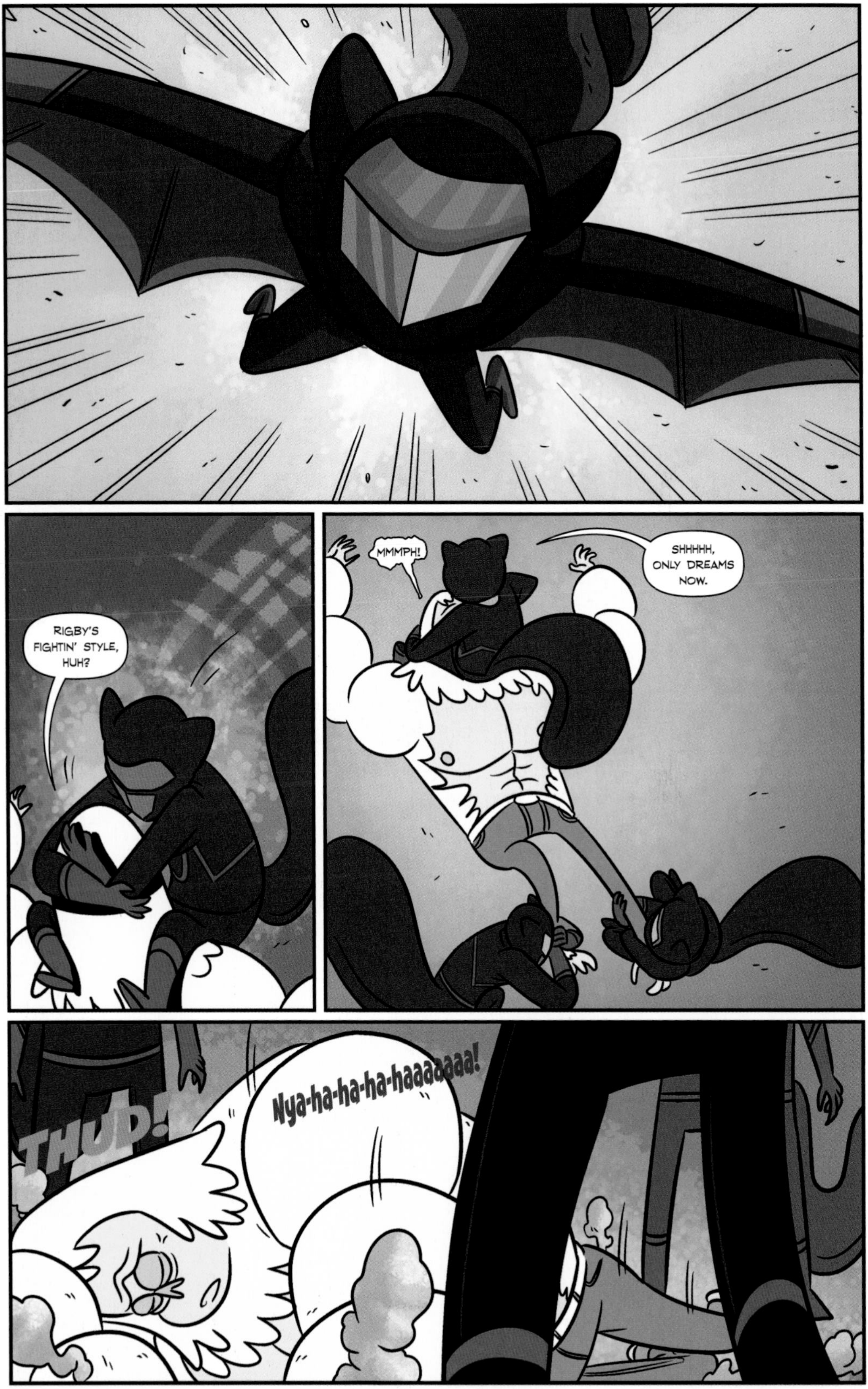
RIGBY'S FIGHTIN' STYLE, HUH?
MMMPH!
SHHHHH, ONLY DREAMS NOW.
THUD!
Nya-ha-ha-ha-haaaaaaa!

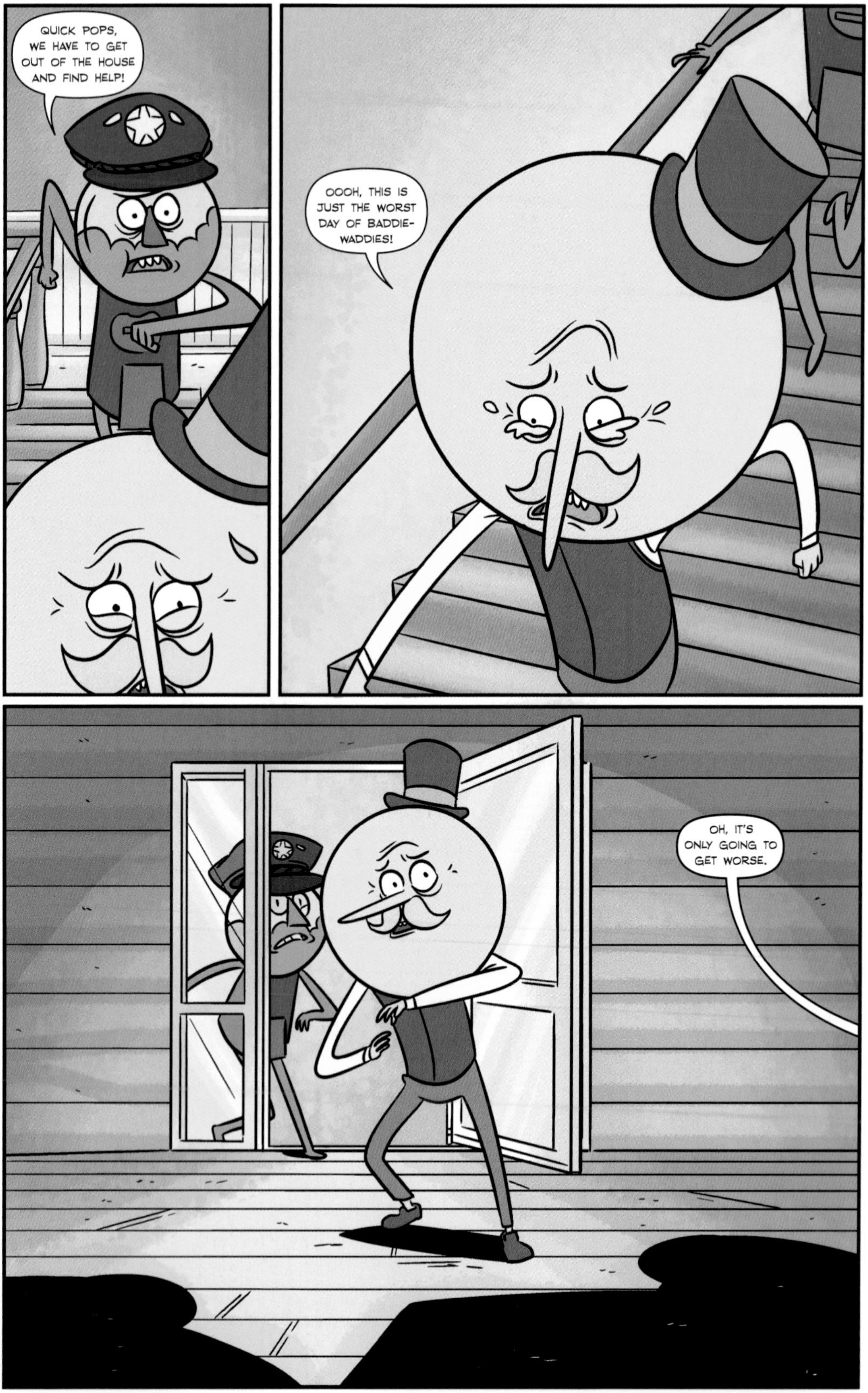
QUICK POPS, WE HAVE TO GET OUT OF THE HOUSE AND FIND HELP!
OOOH, THIS IS JUST THE WORST DAY OF BADDIE-WADDIES!
OH, IT'S ONLY GOING TO GET WORSE.

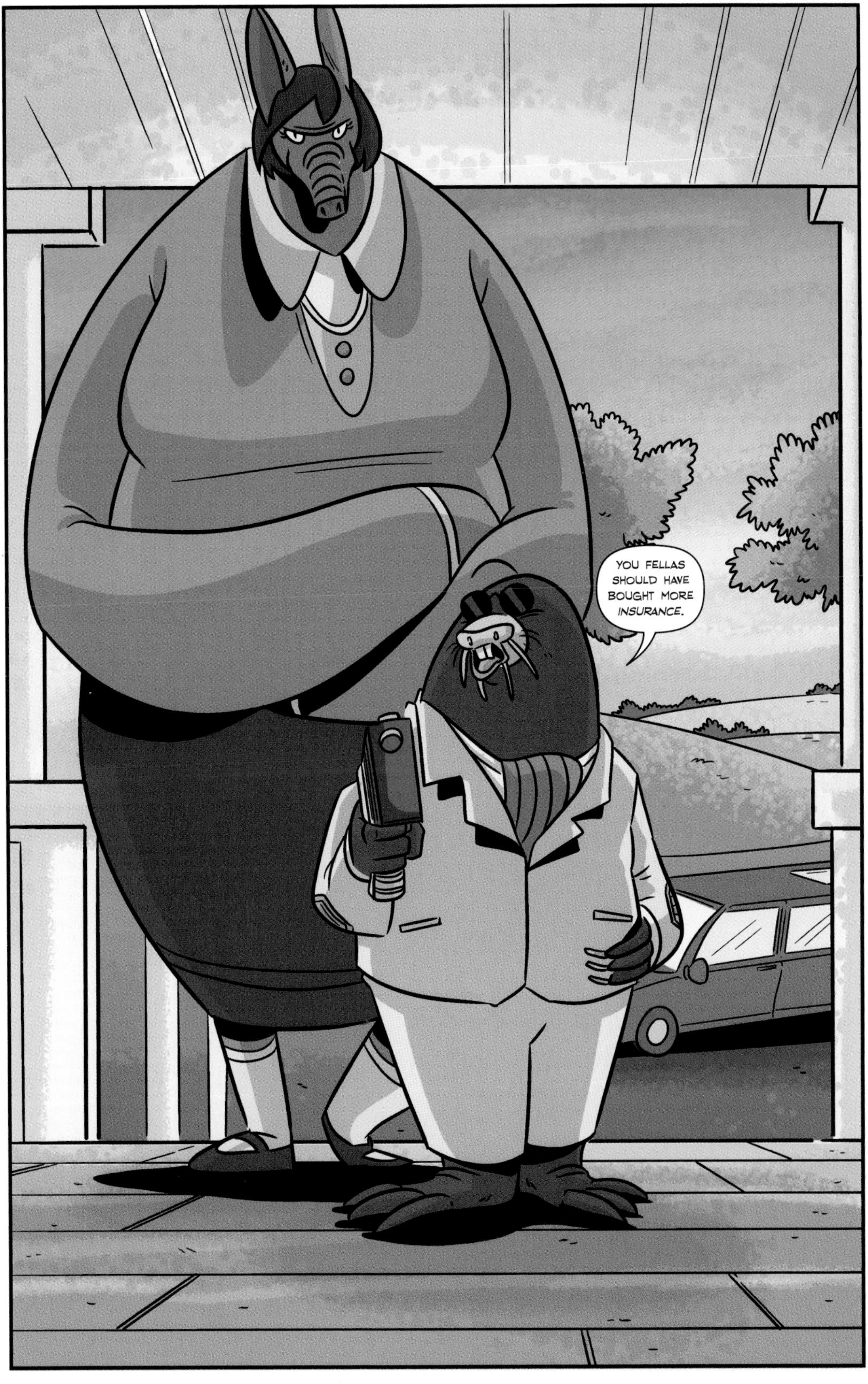
YOU FELLAS SHOULD HAVE BOUGHT MORE *INSURANCE*.

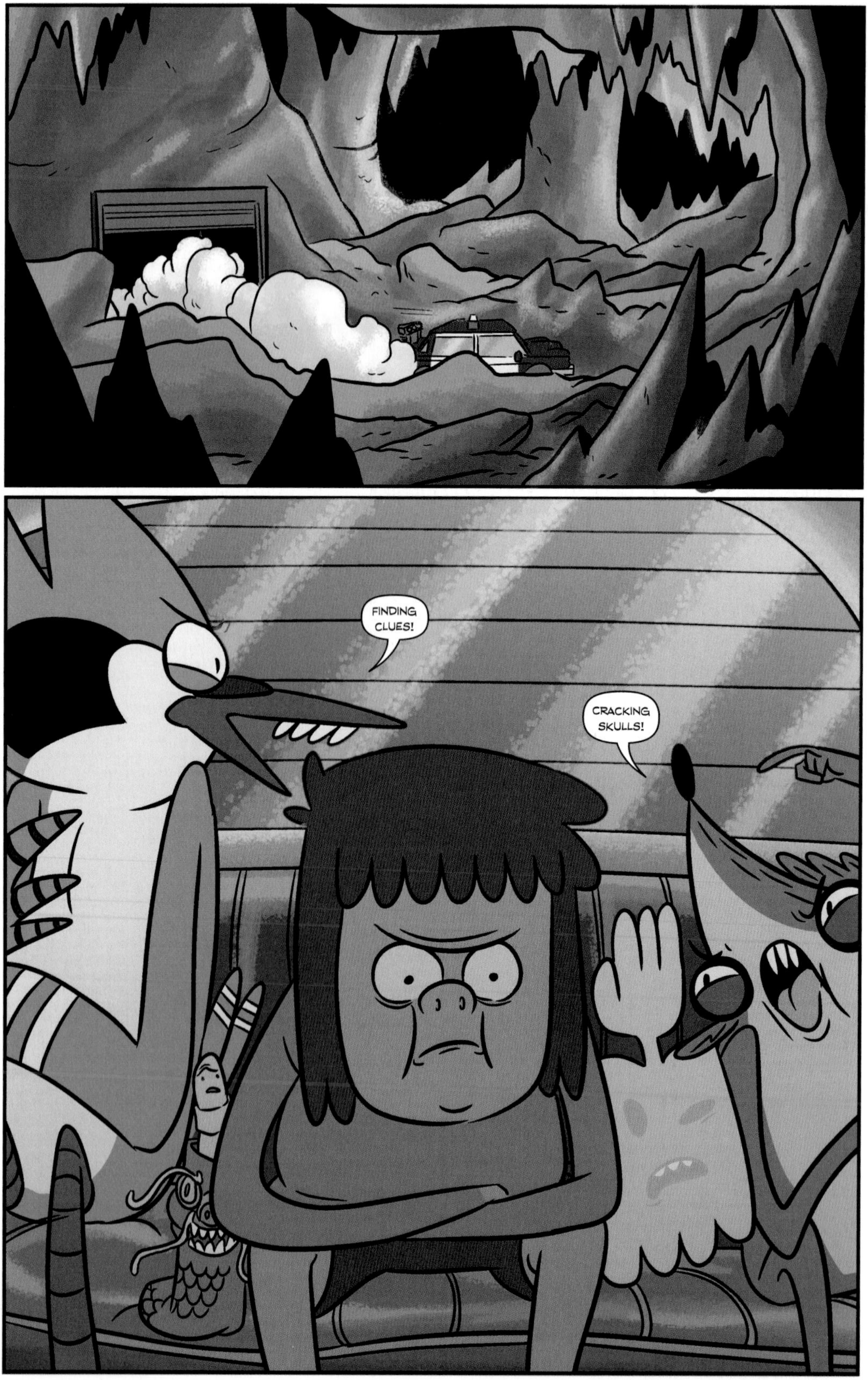
FINDING CLUES!
CRACKING SKULLS!

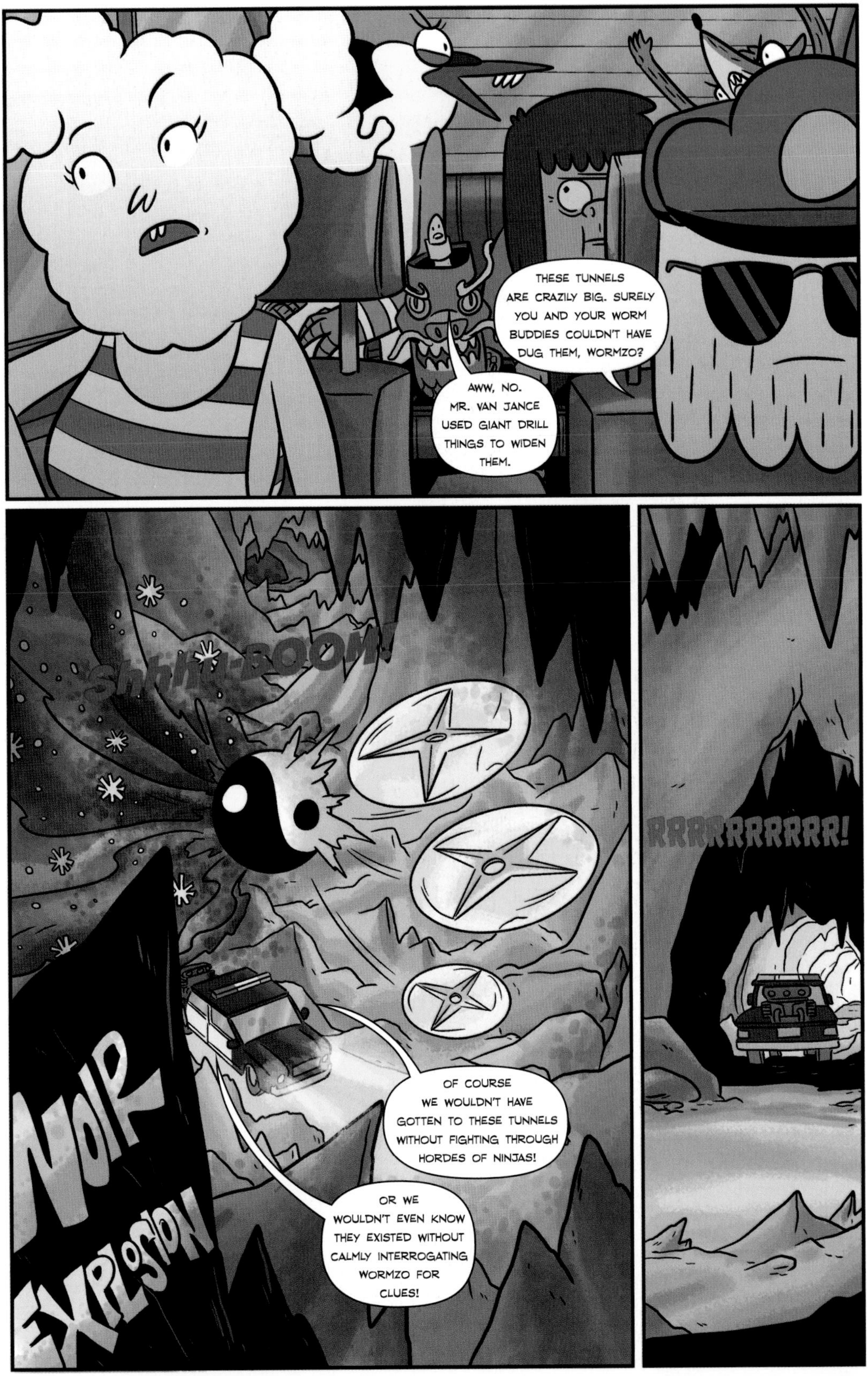
THESE TUNNELS ARE CRAZILY BIG. SURELY YOU AND YOUR WORM BUDDIES COULDN'T HAVE DUG THEM, WORMZO?
AWW, NO. MR. VAN JANCE USED GIANT DRILL THINGS TO WIDEN THEM.
Shhh-BOOM!
NOIR EXPLOSION
OF COURSE WE WOULDN'T HAVE GOTTEN TO THESE TUNNELS WITHOUT FIGHTING THROUGH HORDES OF NINJAS!
OR WE WOULDN'T EVEN KNOW THEY EXISTED WITHOUT CALMLY INTERROGATING WORMZO FOR CLUES!
RRRRRRRRRRR!

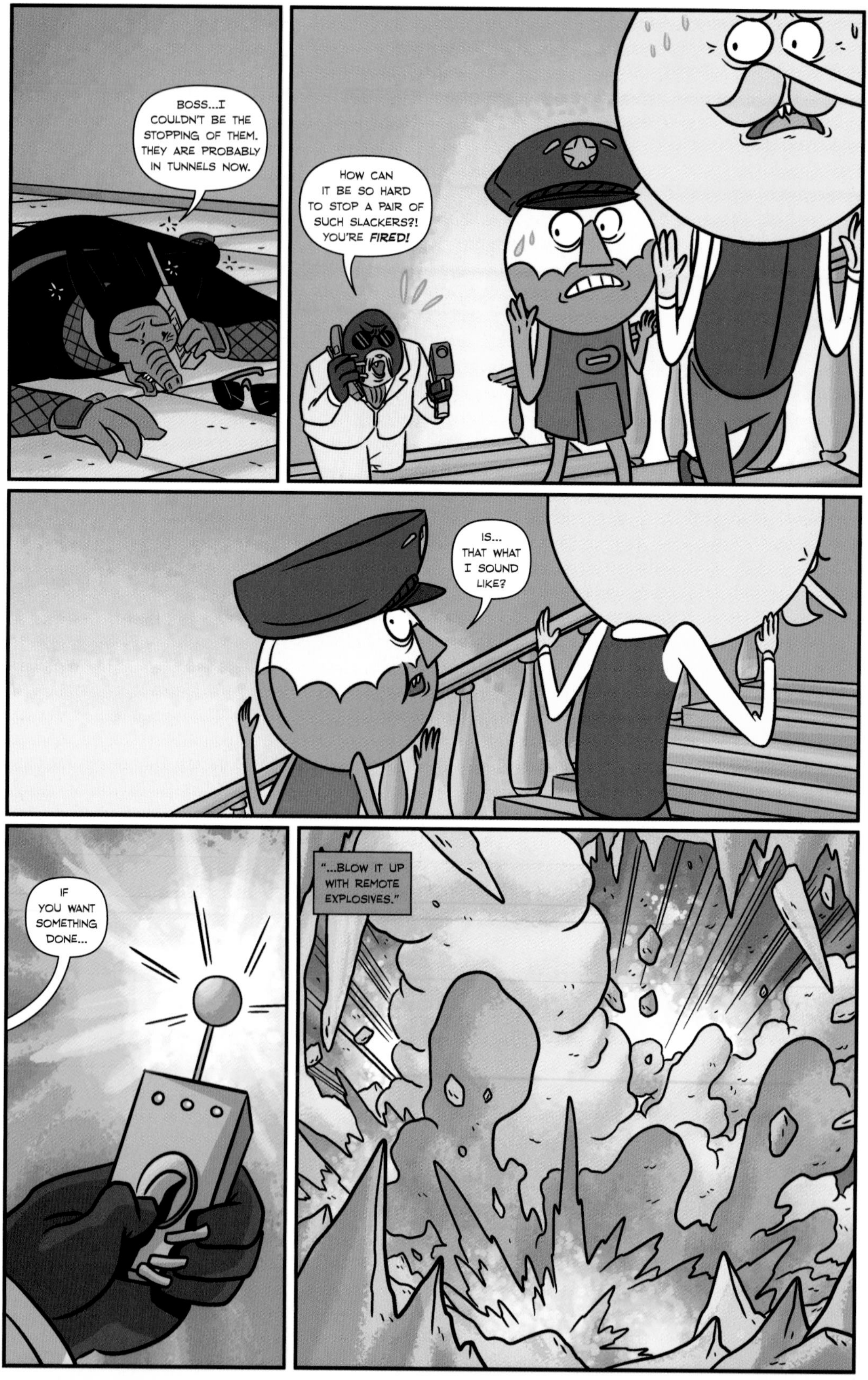
BOSS...I COULDN'T BE THE STOPPING OF THEM. THEY ARE PROBABLY IN TUNNELS NOW.
HOW CAN IT BE SO HARD TO STOP A PAIR OF SUCH SLACKERS?! YOU'RE *FIRED!*
IS... THAT WHAT I SOUND LIKE?
IF YOU WANT SOMETHING DONE...
"...BLOW IT UP WITH REMOTE EXPLOSIVES."

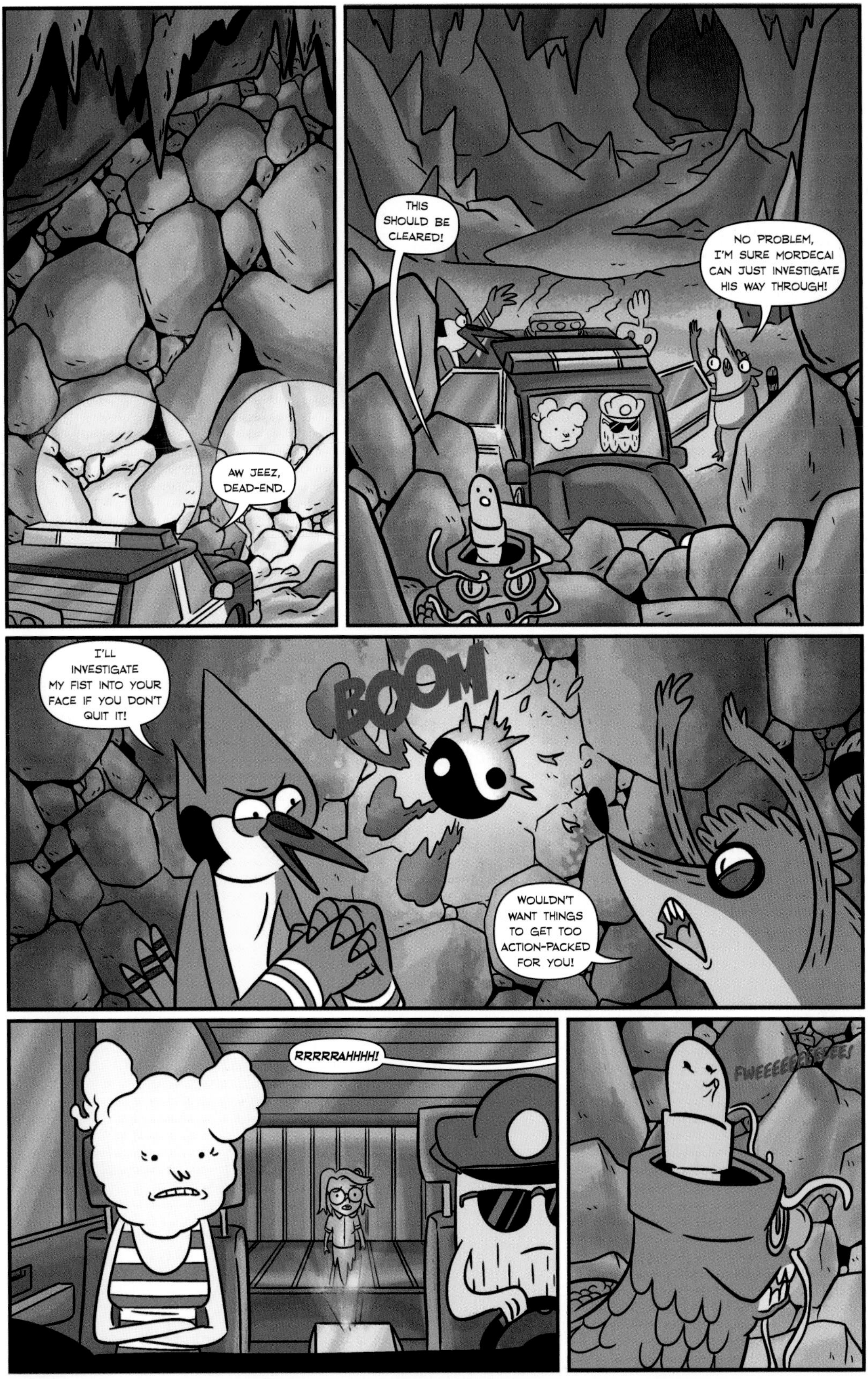
AW JEEZ, DEAD-END.
THIS SHOULD BE CLEARED!
NO PROBLEM, I'M SURE MORDECAI CAN JUST INVESTIGATE HIS WAY THROUGH!
I'LL INVESTIGATE MY FIST INTO YOUR FACE IF YOU DON'T QUIT IT!
BOOM
WOULDN'T WANT THINGS TO GET TOO ACTION-PACKED FOR YOU!
RRRRRAHHHH!
FWEEEEEEEEEEE!

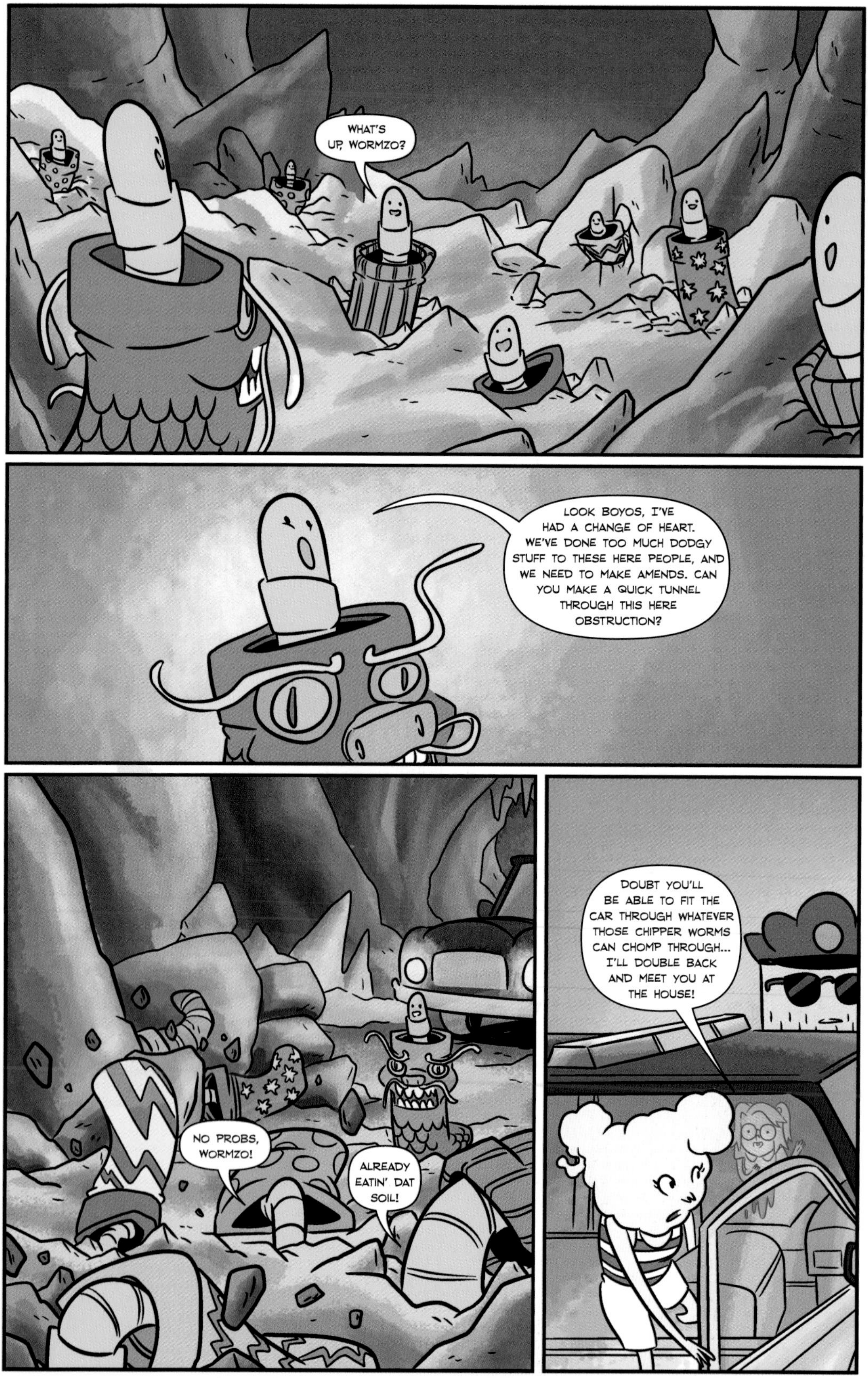
WHAT'S UP, WORMZO?
LOOK BOYOS, I'VE HAD A CHANGE OF HEART. WE'VE DONE TOO MUCH DODGY STUFF TO THESE HERE PEOPLE, AND WE NEED TO MAKE AMENDS. CAN YOU MAKE A QUICK TUNNEL THROUGH THIS HERE OBSTRUCTION?
NO PROBS, WORMZO!
ALREADY EATIN' DAT SOIL!
DOUBT YOU'LL BE ABLE TO FIT THE CAR THROUGH WHATEVER THOSE CHIPPER WORMS CAN CHOMP THROUGH... I'LL DOUBLE BACK AND MEET YOU AT THE HOUSE!

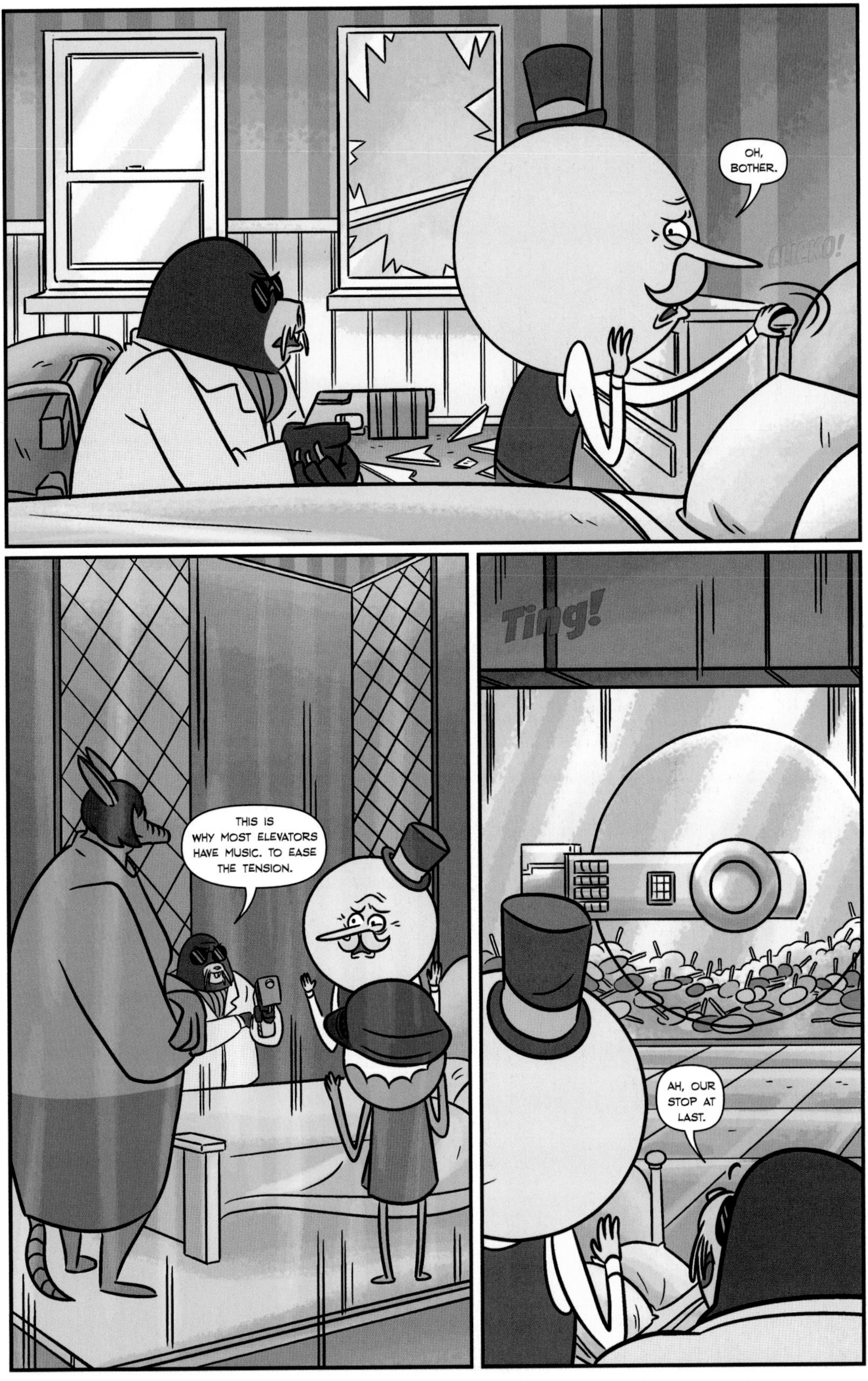
OH, BOTHER.
THIS IS WHY MOST ELEVATORS HAVE MUSIC. TO EASE THE TENSION.
Ting!
AH, OUR STOP AT LAST.

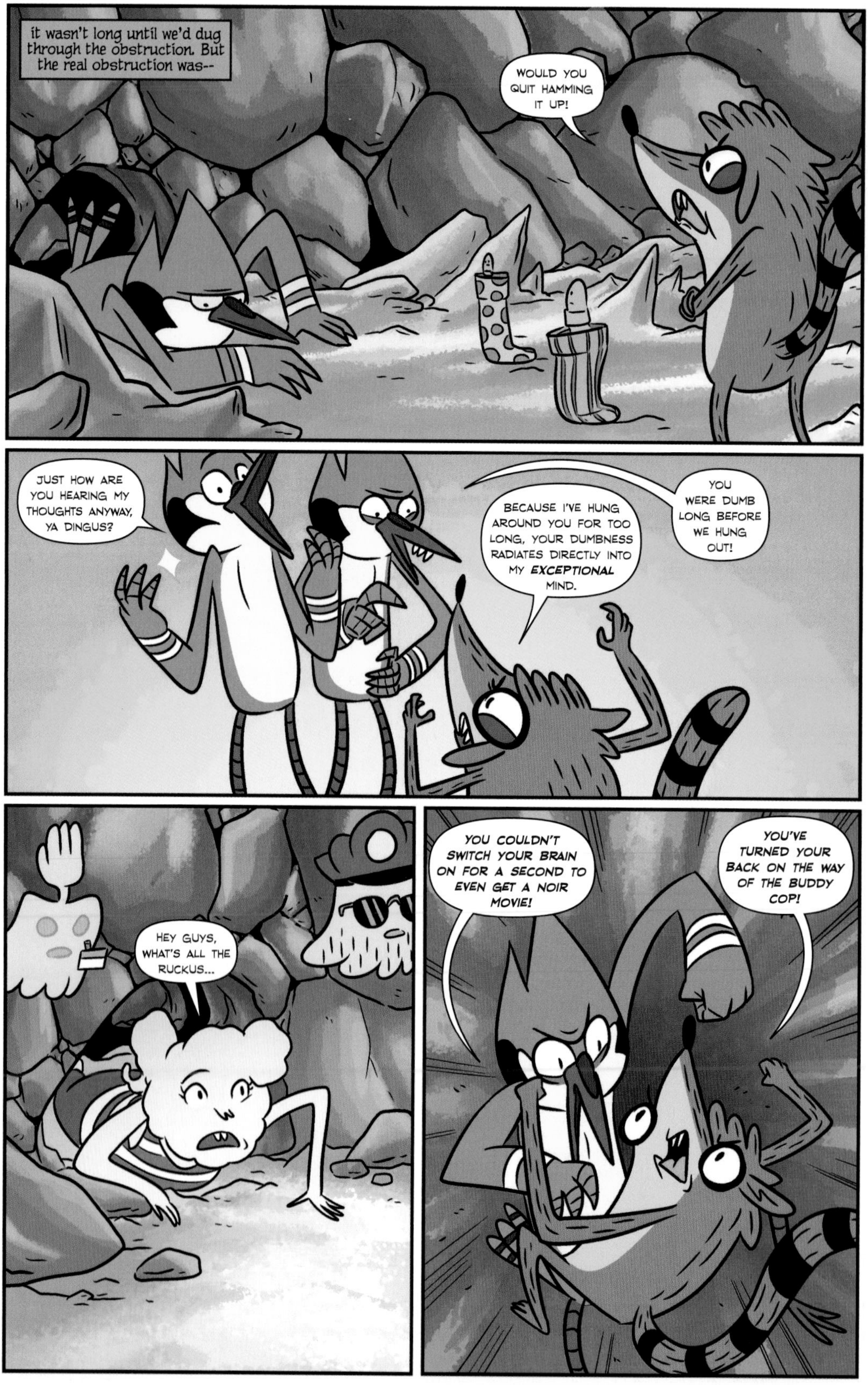
it wasn't long until we'd dug through the obstruction. But the real obstruction was--
WOULD YOU QUIT HAMMING IT UP!
JUST HOW ARE YOU HEARING MY THOUGHTS ANYWAY, YA DINGUS?
BECAUSE I'VE HUNG AROUND YOU FOR TOO LONG, YOUR DUMBNESS RADIATES DIRECTLY INTO MY *EXCEPTIONAL* MIND.
YOU WERE DUMB LONG BEFORE WE HUNG OUT!
HEY GUYS, WHAT'S ALL THE RUCKUS...
YOU COULDN'T SWITCH YOUR BRAIN ON FOR A SECOND TO EVEN GET A NOIR MOVIE!
YOU'VE TURNED YOUR BACK ON THE WAY OF THE BUDDY COP!

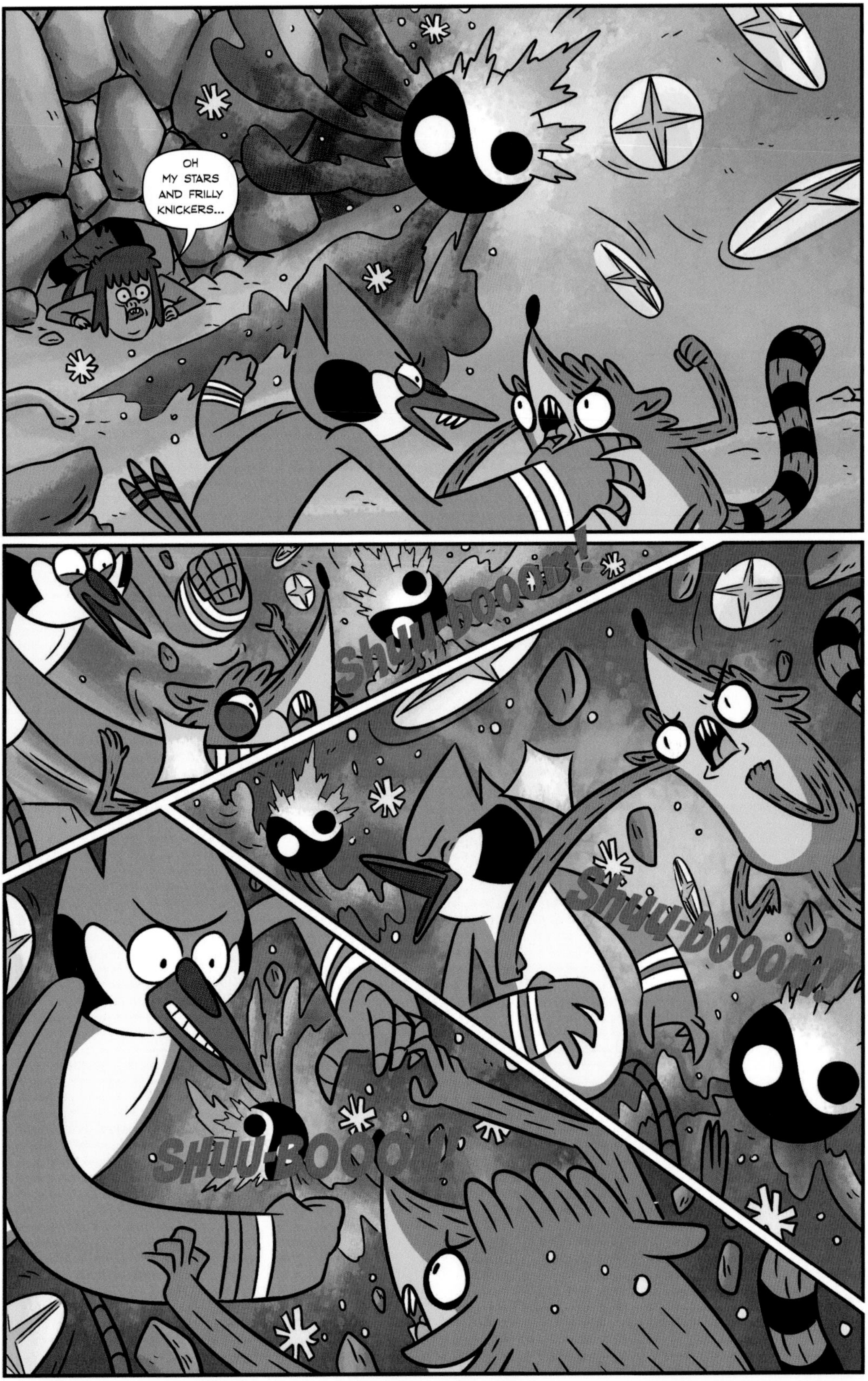
OH MY STARS AND FRILLY KNICKERS...
Shuu-booom!
Shuu-booom!
SHUU-BOOOM

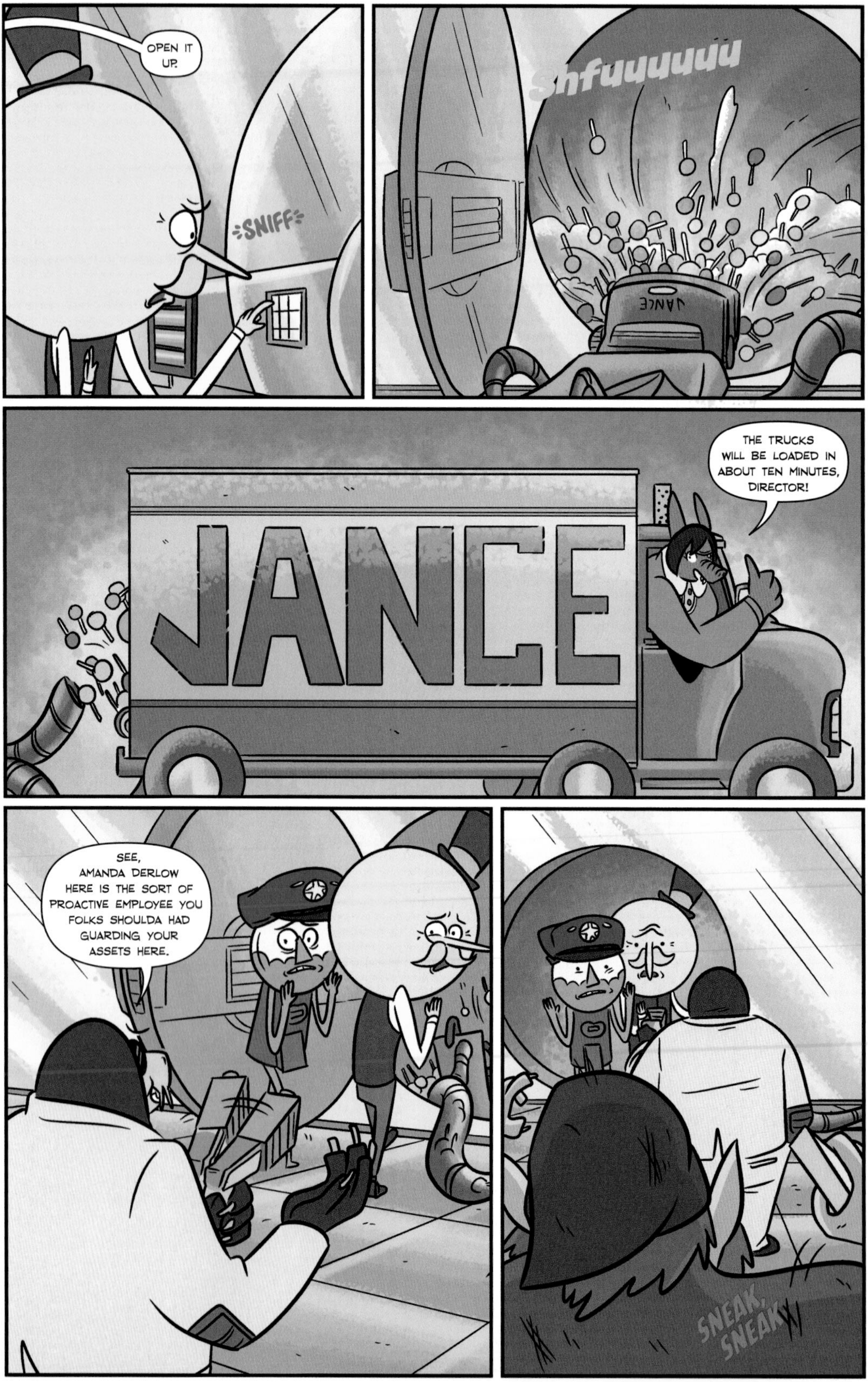

OPEN IT UP.
SNIFF
Shfuuuuuu
JANCE
JANCE
THE TRUCKS WILL BE LOADED IN ABOUT TEN MINUTES, DIRECTOR!
SEE, AMANDA DERLOW HERE IS THE SORT OF PROACTIVE EMPLOYEE YOU FOLKS SHOULDA HAD GUARDING YOUR ASSETS HERE.
SNEAK, SNEAK

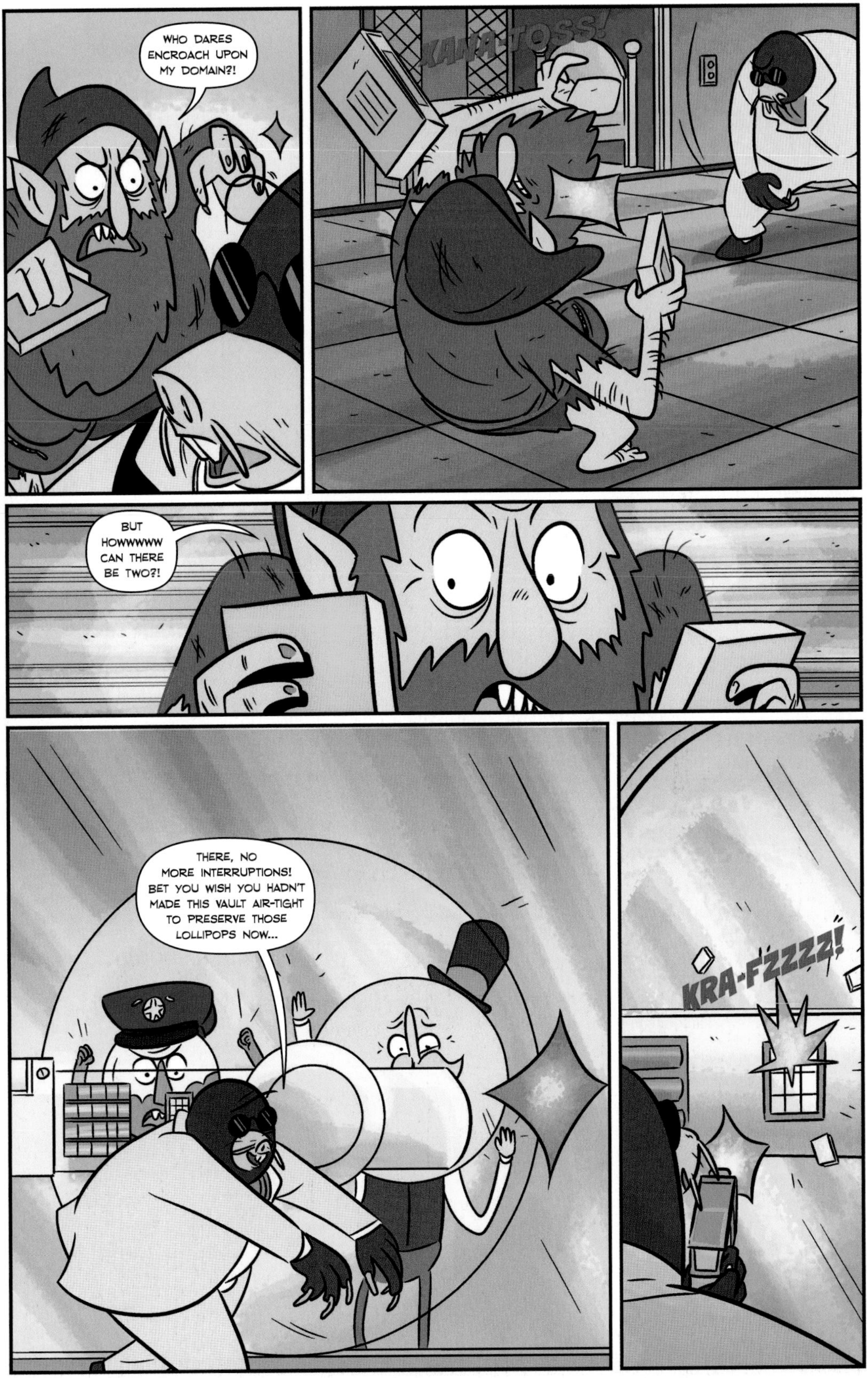
WHO DARES ENCROACH UPON MY DOMAIN?!
KANA-TOSS!
BUT HOWWWWW CAN THERE BE TWO?!
THERE, NO MORE INTERRUPTIONS! BET YOU WISH YOU HADN'T MADE THIS VAULT AIR-TIGHT TO PRESERVE THOSE LOLLIPOPS NOW...
KRA-FZZZZ!

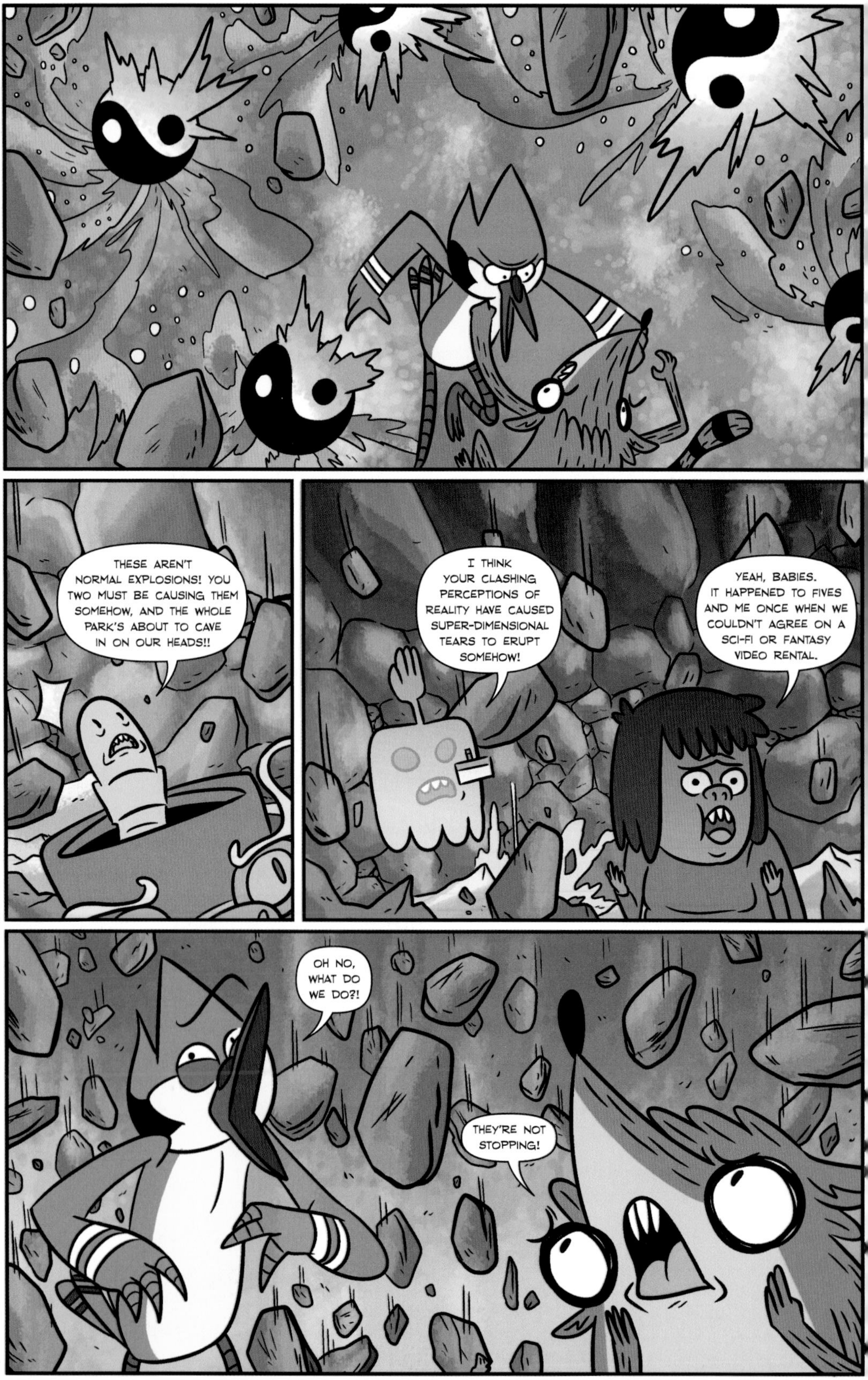
THESE AREN'T NORMAL EXPLOSIONS! YOU TWO MUST BE CAUSING THEM SOMEHOW, AND THE WHOLE PARK'S ABOUT TO CAVE IN ON OUR HEADS!!
I THINK YOUR CLASHING PERCEPTIONS OF REALITY HAVE CAUSED SUPER-DIMENSIONAL TEARS TO ERUPT SOMEHOW!
YEAH, BABIES. IT HAPPENED TO FIVES AND ME ONCE WHEN WE COULDN'T AGREE ON A SCI-FI OR FANTASY VIDEO RENTAL.
OH NO, WHAT DO WE DO?!
THEY'RE NOT STOPPING!

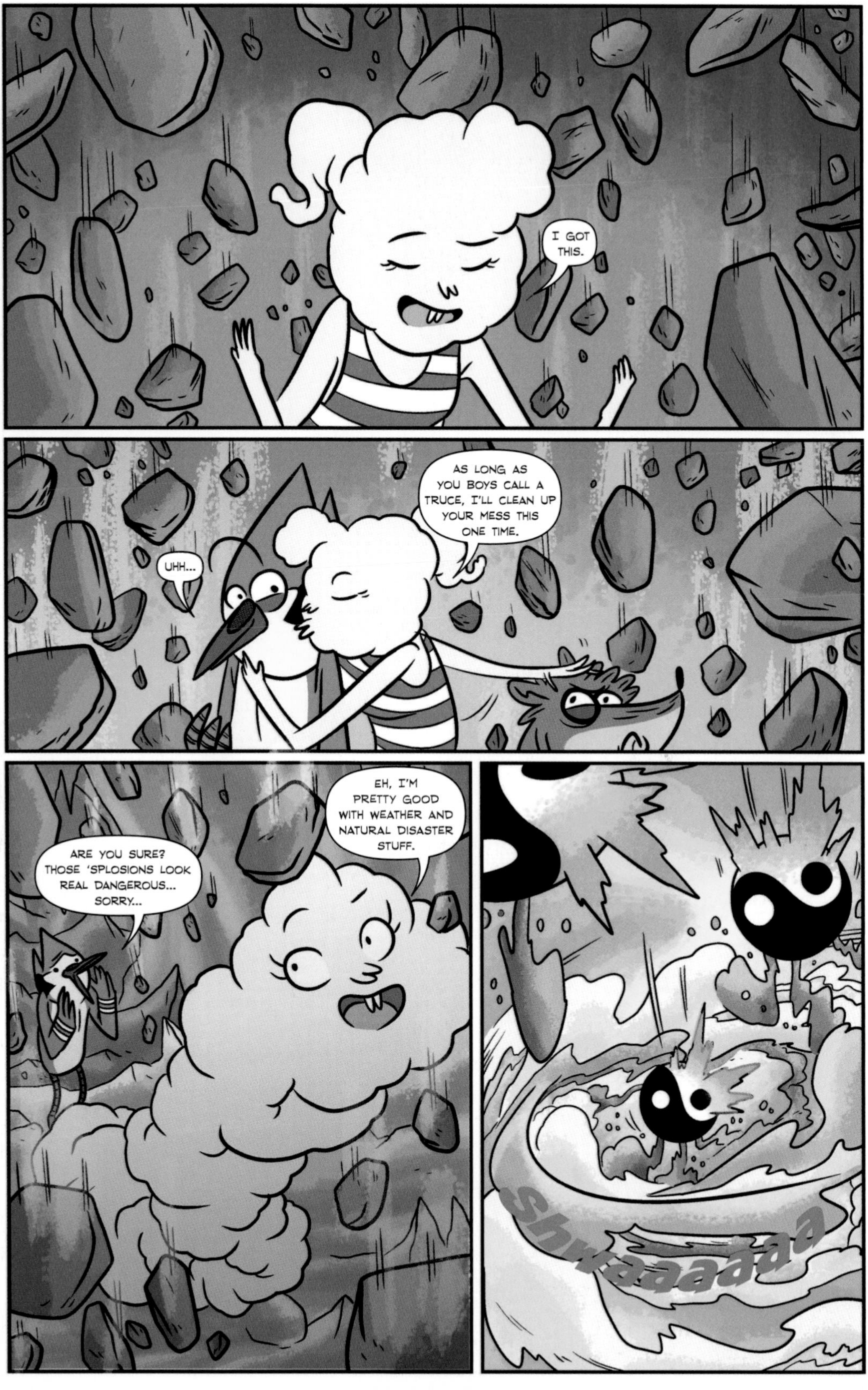
I GOT THIS.
AS LONG AS YOU BOYS CALL A TRUCE, I'LL CLEAN UP YOUR MESS THIS ONE TIME.
UHH...
EH, I'M PRETTY GOOD WITH WEATHER AND NATURAL DISASTER STUFF.
ARE YOU SURE? THOSE 'SPLOSIONS LOOK REAL DANGEROUS... SORRY...
Shwaaaaaaa

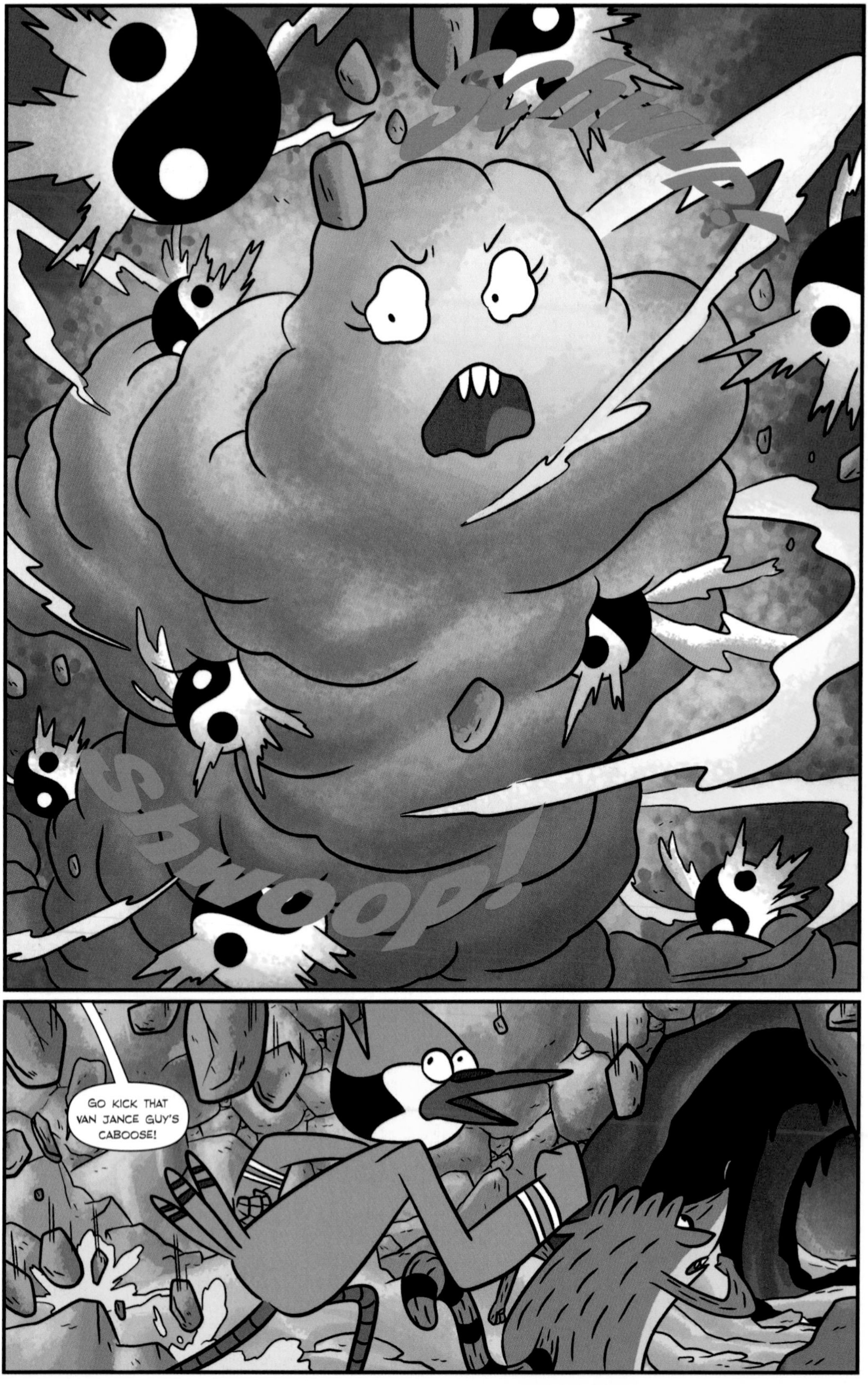
SCHWIP!
SHWOOP!
GO KICK THAT VAN JANCE GUY'S CABOOSE!

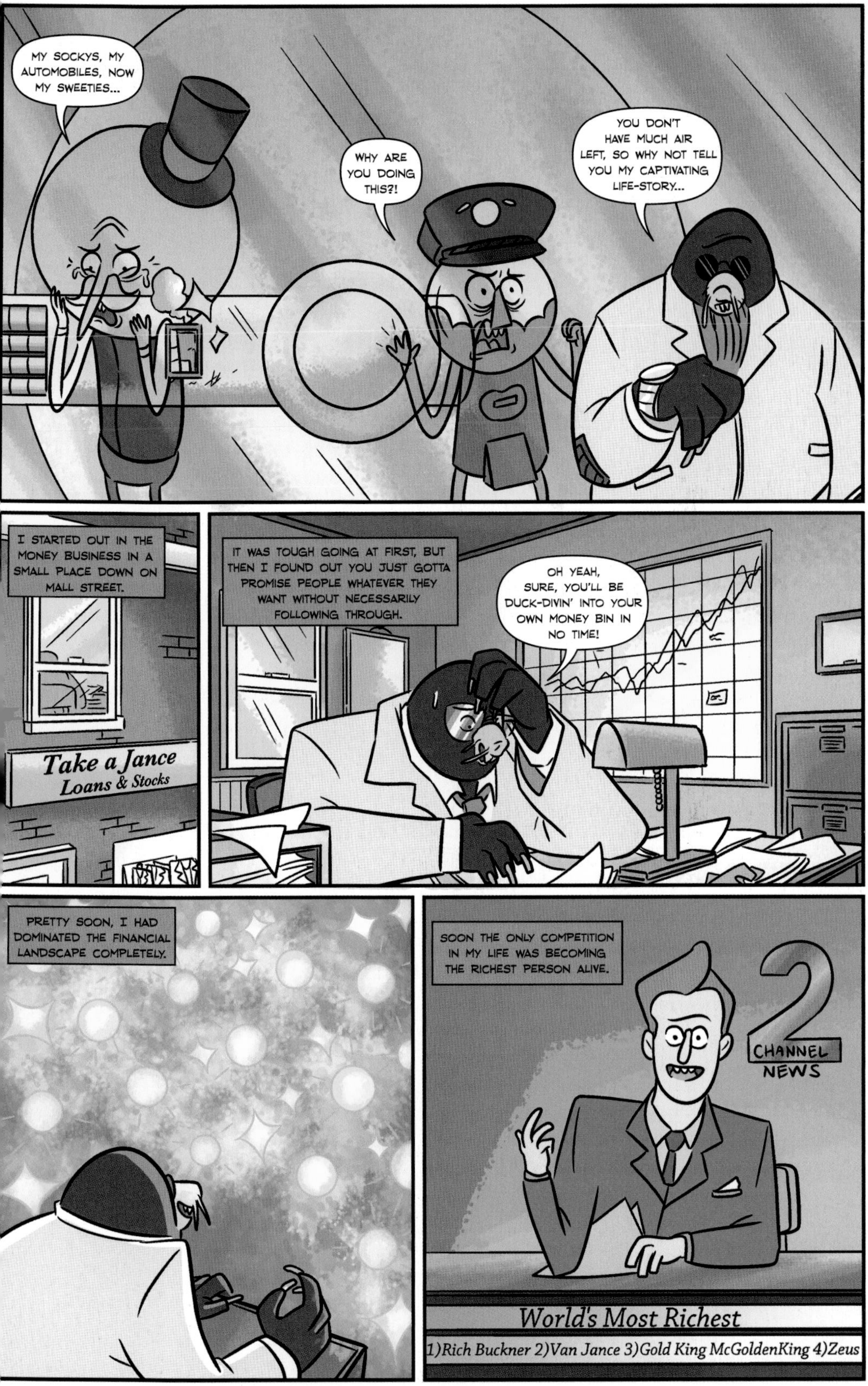
MY SOCKYS, MY AUTOMOBILES, NOW MY SWEETIES...
WHY ARE YOU DOING THIS?!
YOU DON'T HAVE MUCH AIR LEFT, SO WHY NOT TELL YOU MY CAPTIVATING LIFE-STORY...
I STARTED OUT IN THE MONEY BUSINESS IN A SMALL PLACE DOWN ON MALL STREET.
Take a Jance
Loans & Stocks
IT WAS TOUGH GOING AT FIRST, BUT THEN I FOUND OUT YOU JUST GOTTA PROMISE PEOPLE WHATEVER THEY WANT WITHOUT NECESSARILY FOLLOWING THROUGH.
OH YEAH, SURE, YOU'LL BE DUCK-DIVIN' INTO YOUR OWN MONEY BIN IN NO TIME!
PRETTY SOON, I HAD DOMINATED THE FINANCIAL LANDSCAPE COMPLETELY.
SOON THE ONLY COMPETITION IN MY LIFE WAS BECOMING THE RICHEST PERSON ALIVE.
2 CHANNEL NEWS
World's Most Richest
1)Rich Buckner 2)Van Jance 3)Gold King McGoldenKing 4)Zeus

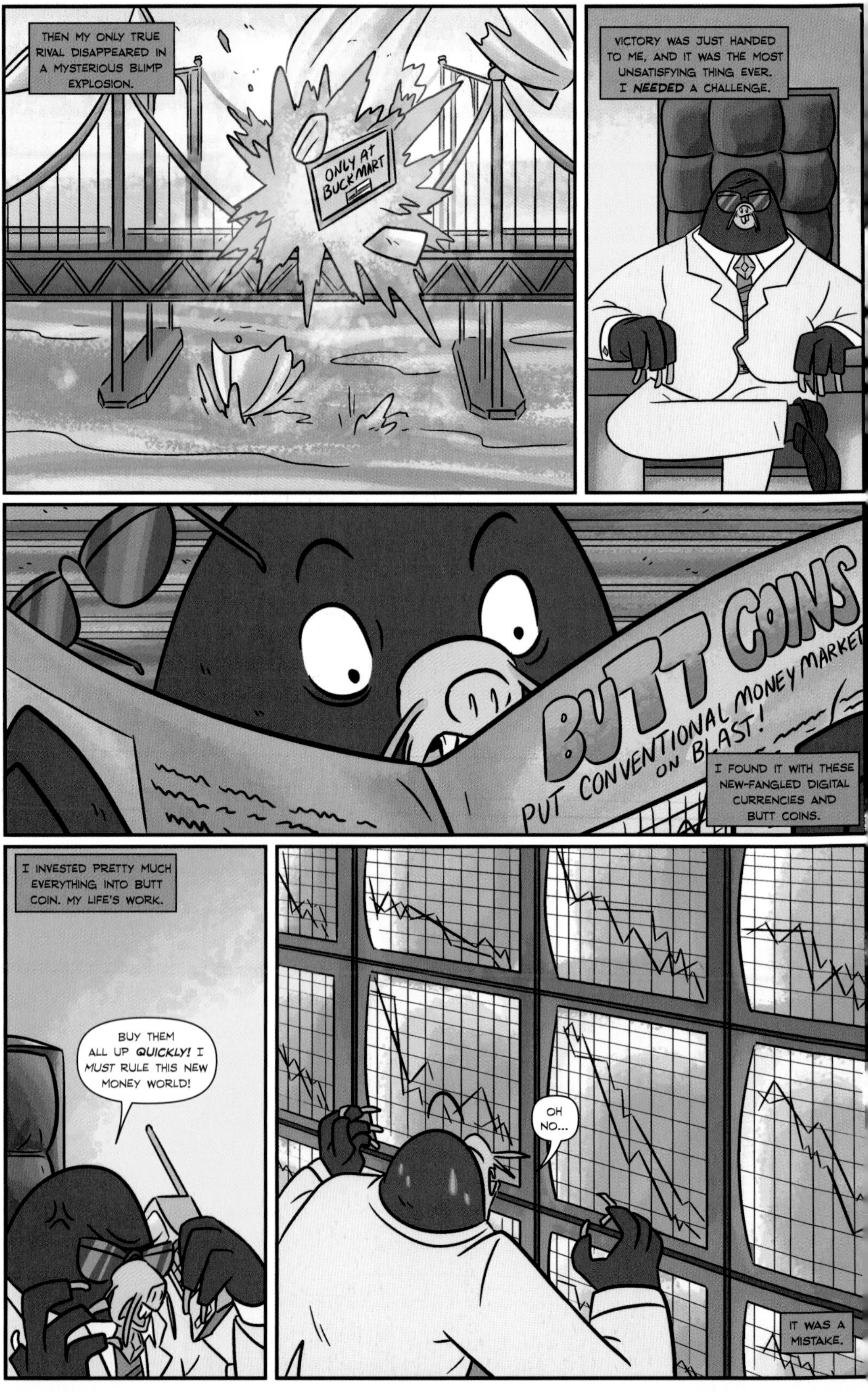
THEN MY ONLY TRUE RIVAL DISAPPEARED IN A MYSTERIOUS BLIMP EXPLOSION.
ONLY AT BUCKMART
VICTORY WAS JUST HANDED TO ME, AND IT WAS THE MOST UNSATISFYING THING EVER. I NEEDED A CHALLENGE.
BUTT COINS
PUT CONVENTIONAL MONEY MARKET ON BLAST!
I FOUND IT WITH THESE NEW-FANGLED DIGITAL CURRENCIES AND BUTT COINS.
I INVESTED PRETTY MUCH EVERYTHING INTO BUTT COIN. MY LIFE'S WORK.
BUY THEM ALL UP QUICKLY! I MUST RULE THIS NEW MONEY WORLD!
OH NO...
IT WAS A MISTAKE.

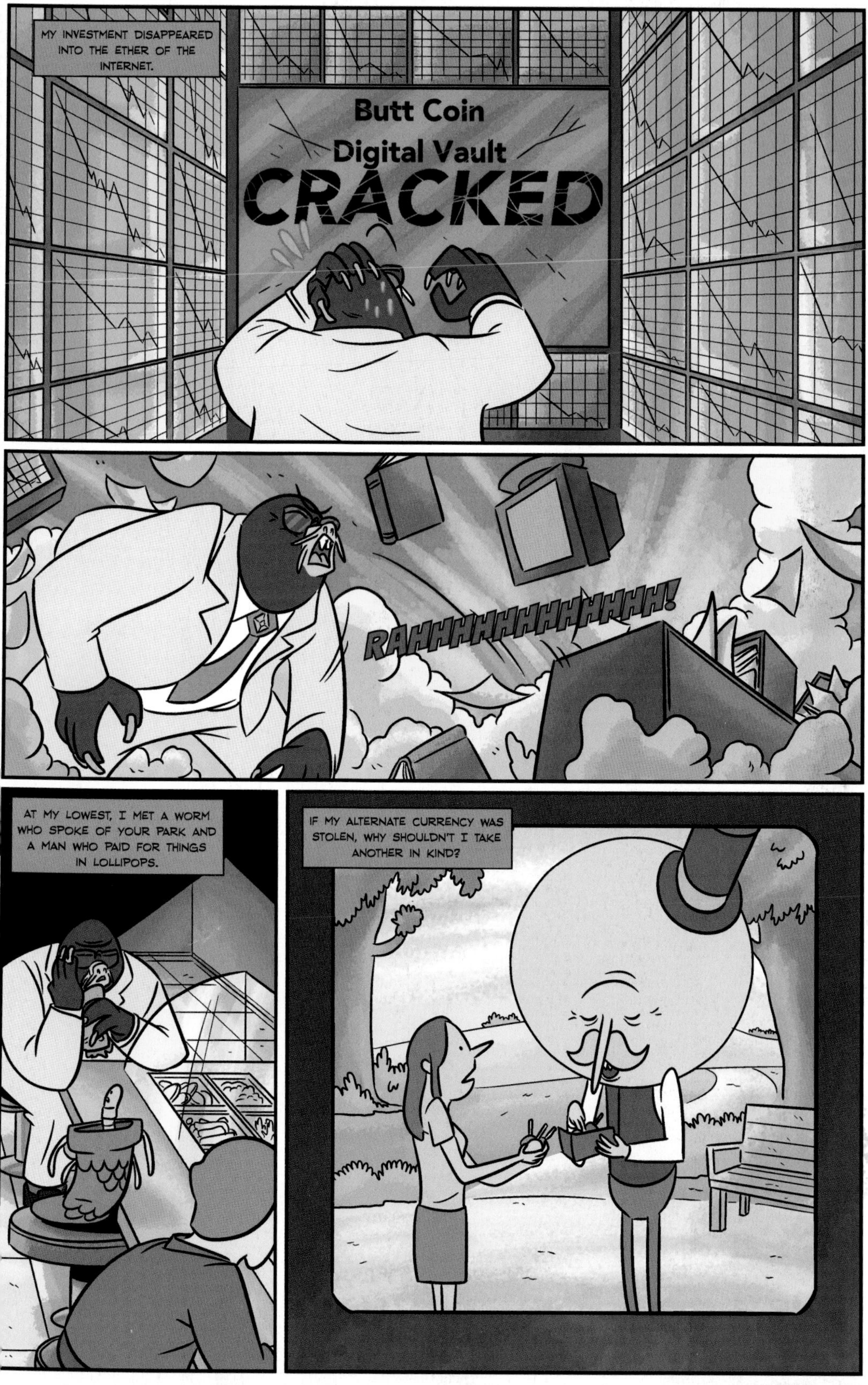
MY INVESTMENT DISAPPEARED INTO THE ETHER OF THE INTERNET.
Butt Coin
Digital Vault
CRACKED
RAHHHHHHHHHHHHH!
AT MY LOWEST, I MET A WORM WHO SPOKE OF YOUR PARK AND A MAN WHO PAID FOR THINGS IN LOLLIPOPS.
IF MY ALTERNATE CURRENCY WAS STOLEN, WHY SHOULDN'T I TAKE ANOTHER IN KIND?

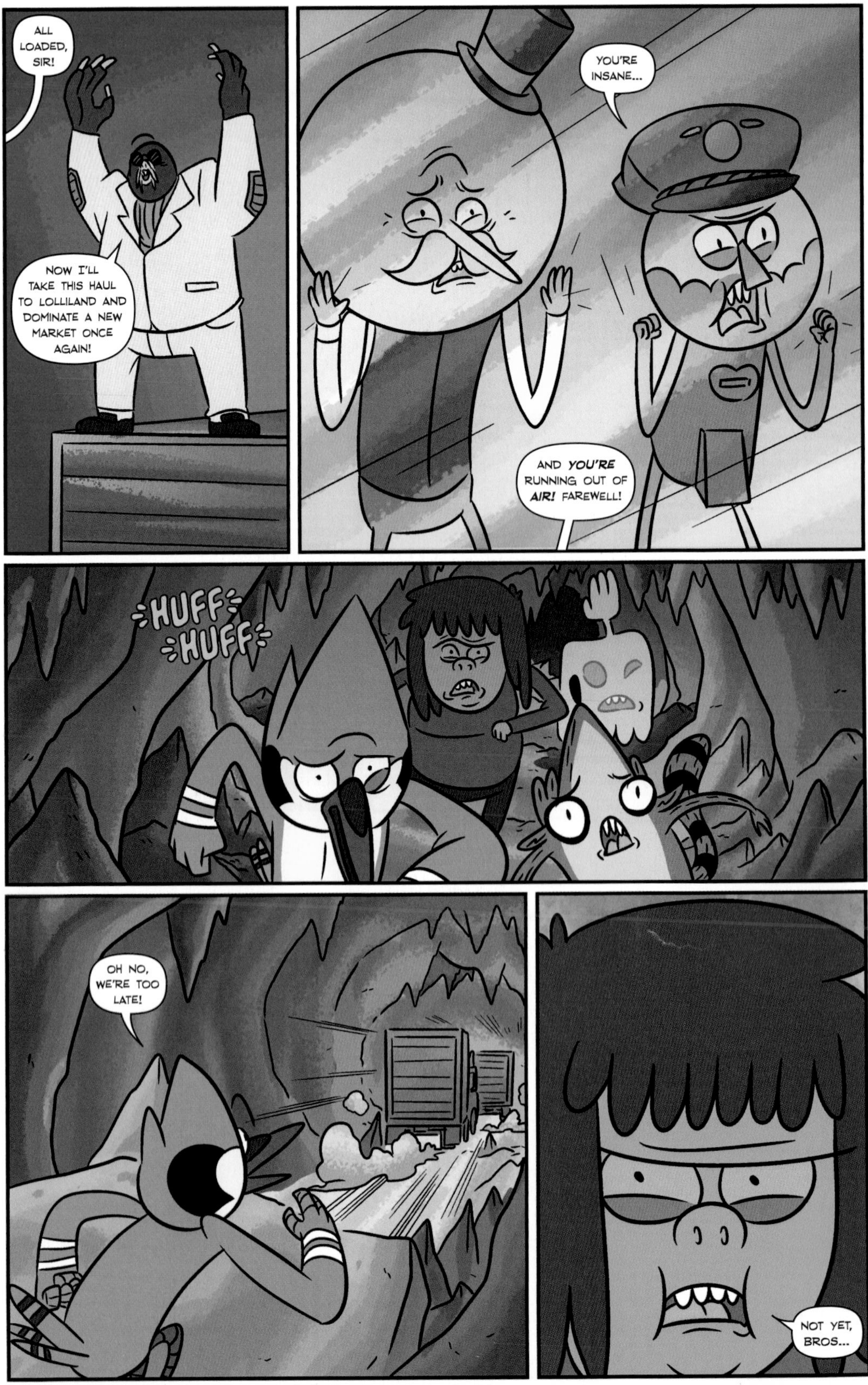
ALL LOADED, SIR!
NOW I'LL TAKE THIS HAUL TO LOLLILAND AND DOMINATE A NEW MARKET ONCE AGAIN!
YOU'RE INSANE...
AND *YOU'RE* RUNNING OUT OF *AIR!* FAREWELL!
HUFF
HUFF
OH NO, WE'RE TOO LATE!
NOT YET, BROS...

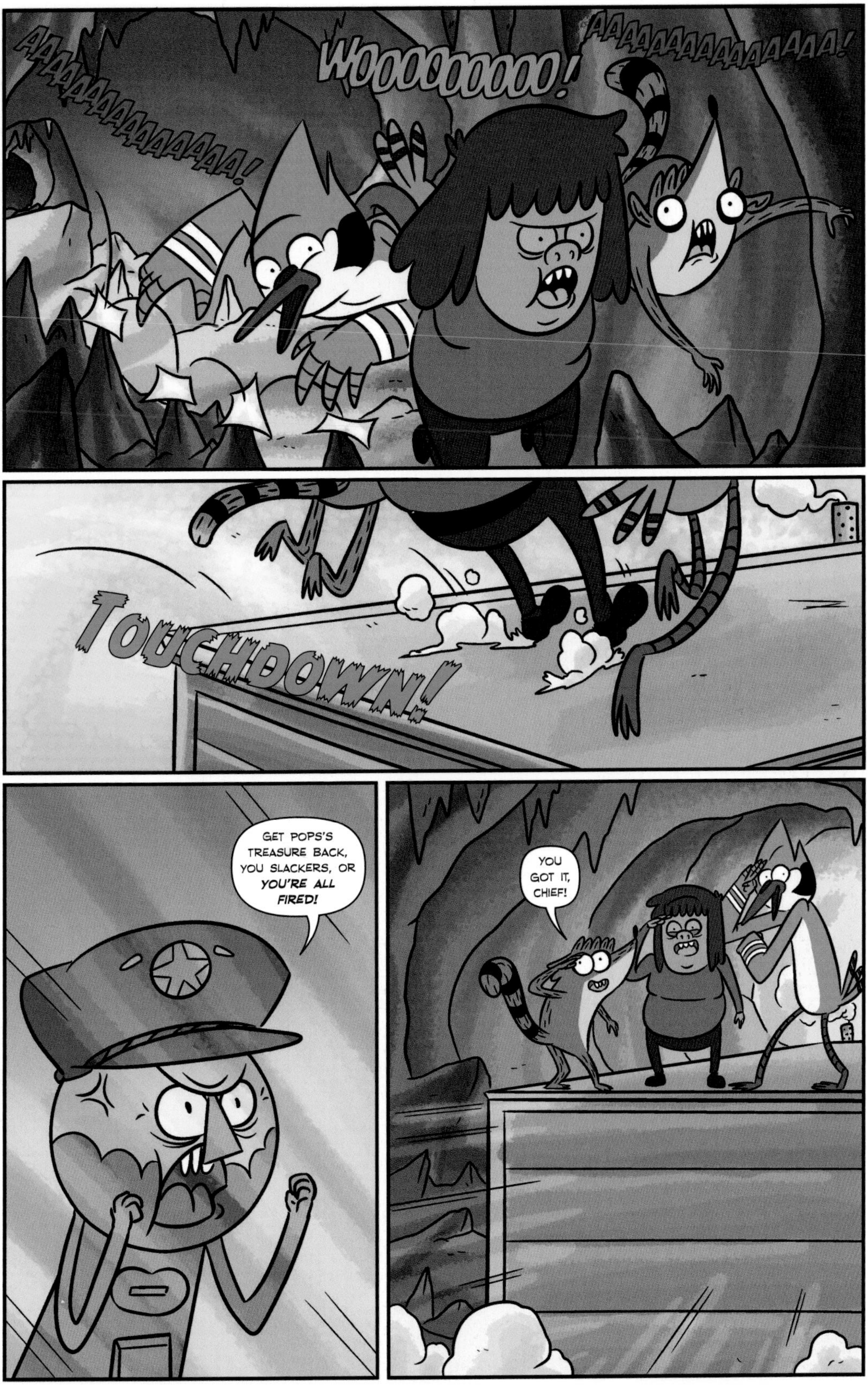
AAAAAAAAAAAAAAAAA!
WOOOOOOOOO!
AAAAAAAAAAAAAAAA!
TOUCHDOWN!
GET POPS'S TREASURE BACK, YOU SLACKERS, OR YOU'RE ALL FIRED!
YOU GOT IT, CHIEF!

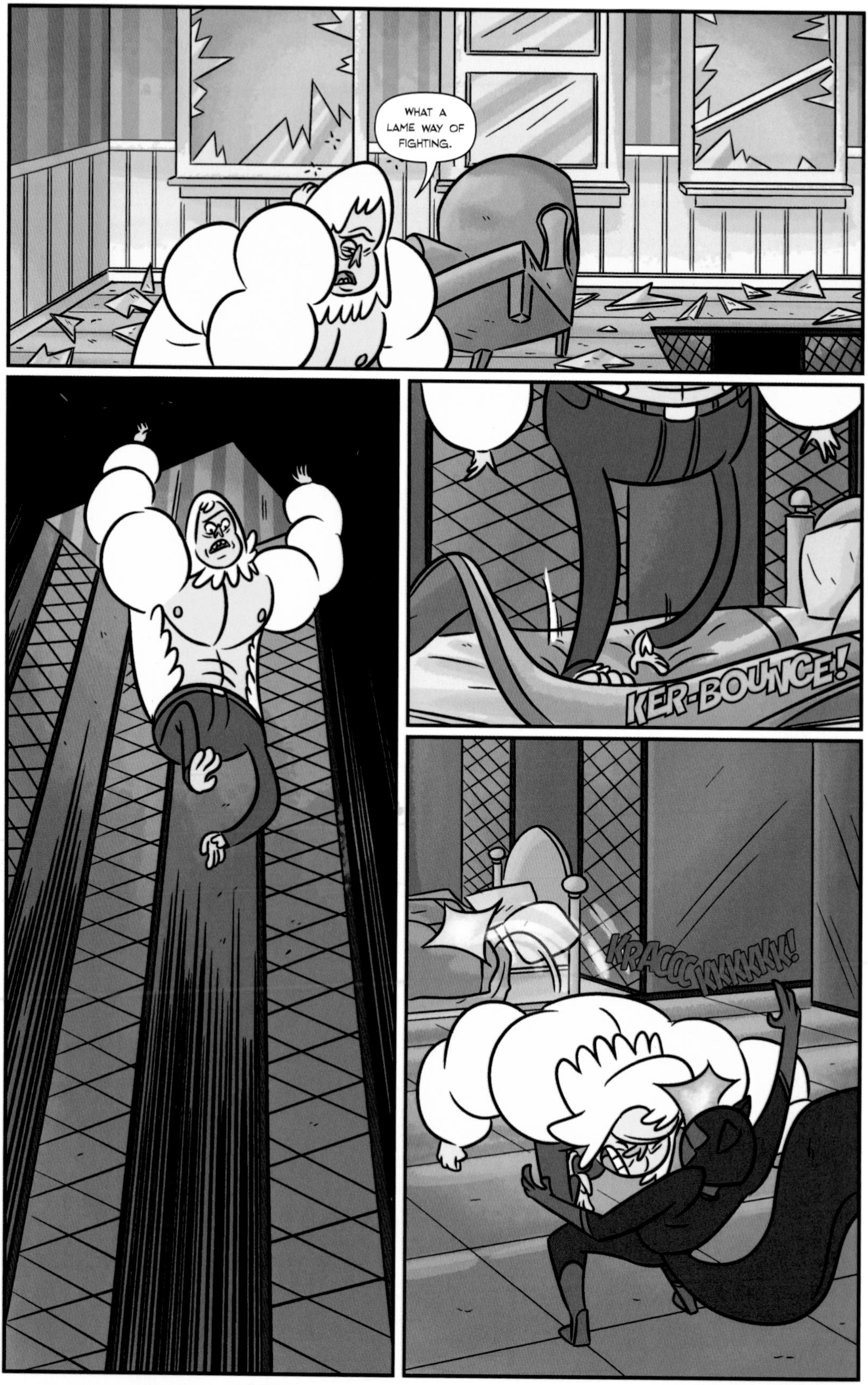
WHAT A LAME WAY OF FIGHTING.
KER-BOUNCE!
KRACCCKKKKKKK!

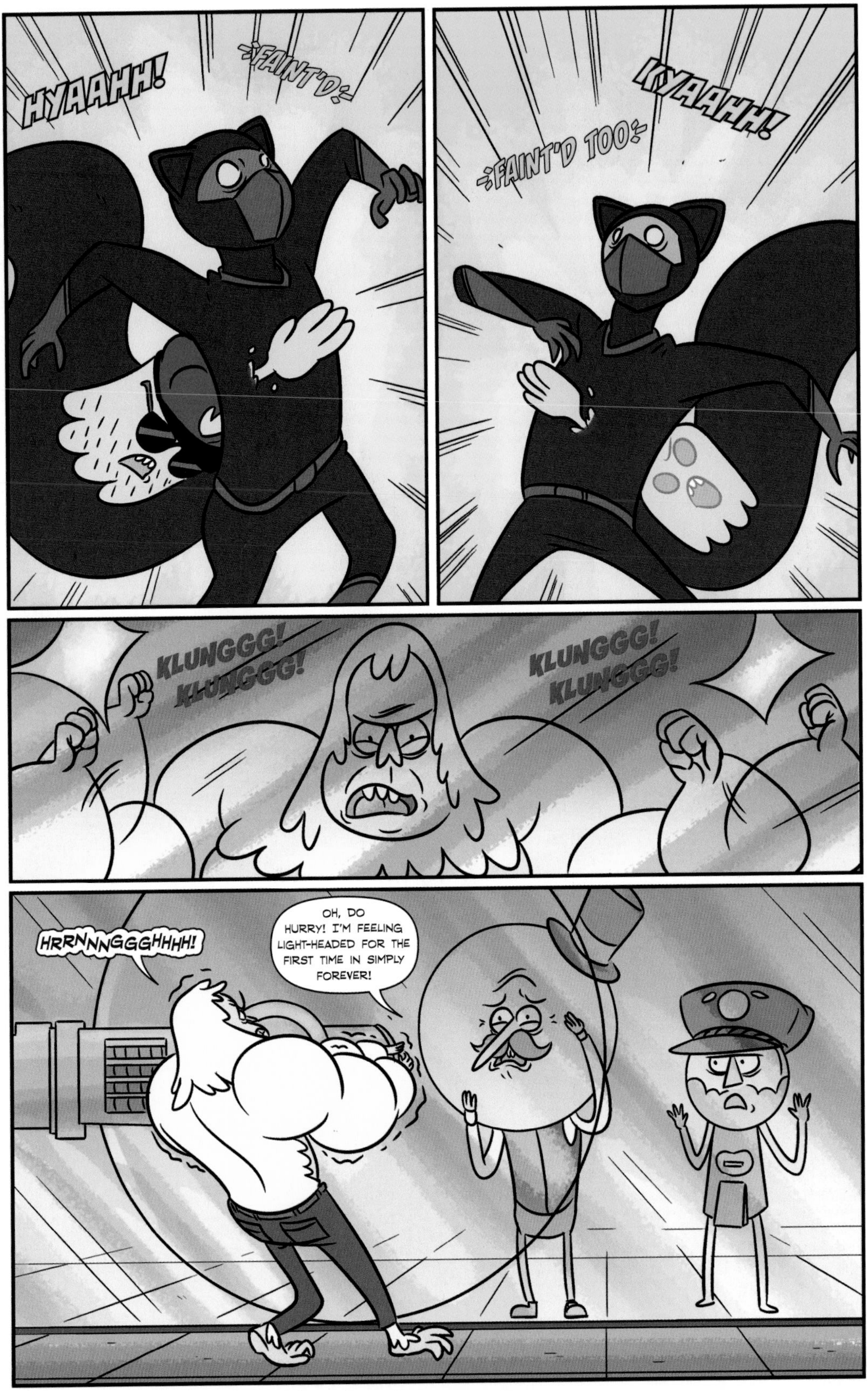
HYAAHH!
FAINT'D
KYAAHH!
FAINT'D TOO
KLUNGGG!
KLUNGGG!
KLUNGGG!
KLUNGGG!
HRRNNNGGGHHHH!
OH, DO HURRY! I'M FEELING LIGHT-HEADED FOR THE FIRST TIME IN SIMPLY FOREVER!

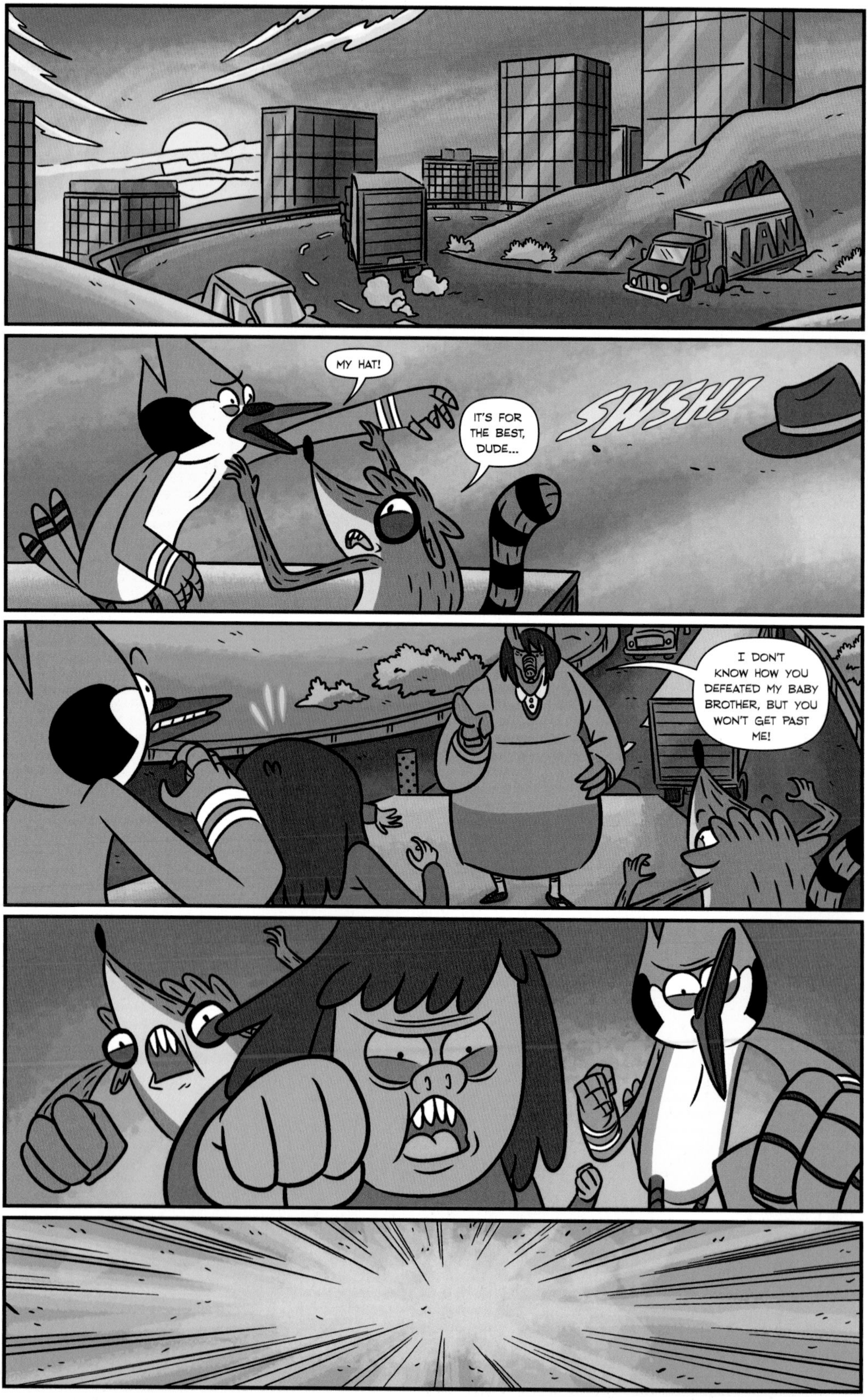
MY HAT!
IT'S FOR THE BEST, DUDE...
SWISH!
I DON'T KNOW HOW YOU DEFEATED MY BABY BROTHER, BUT YOU WON'T GET PAST ME!

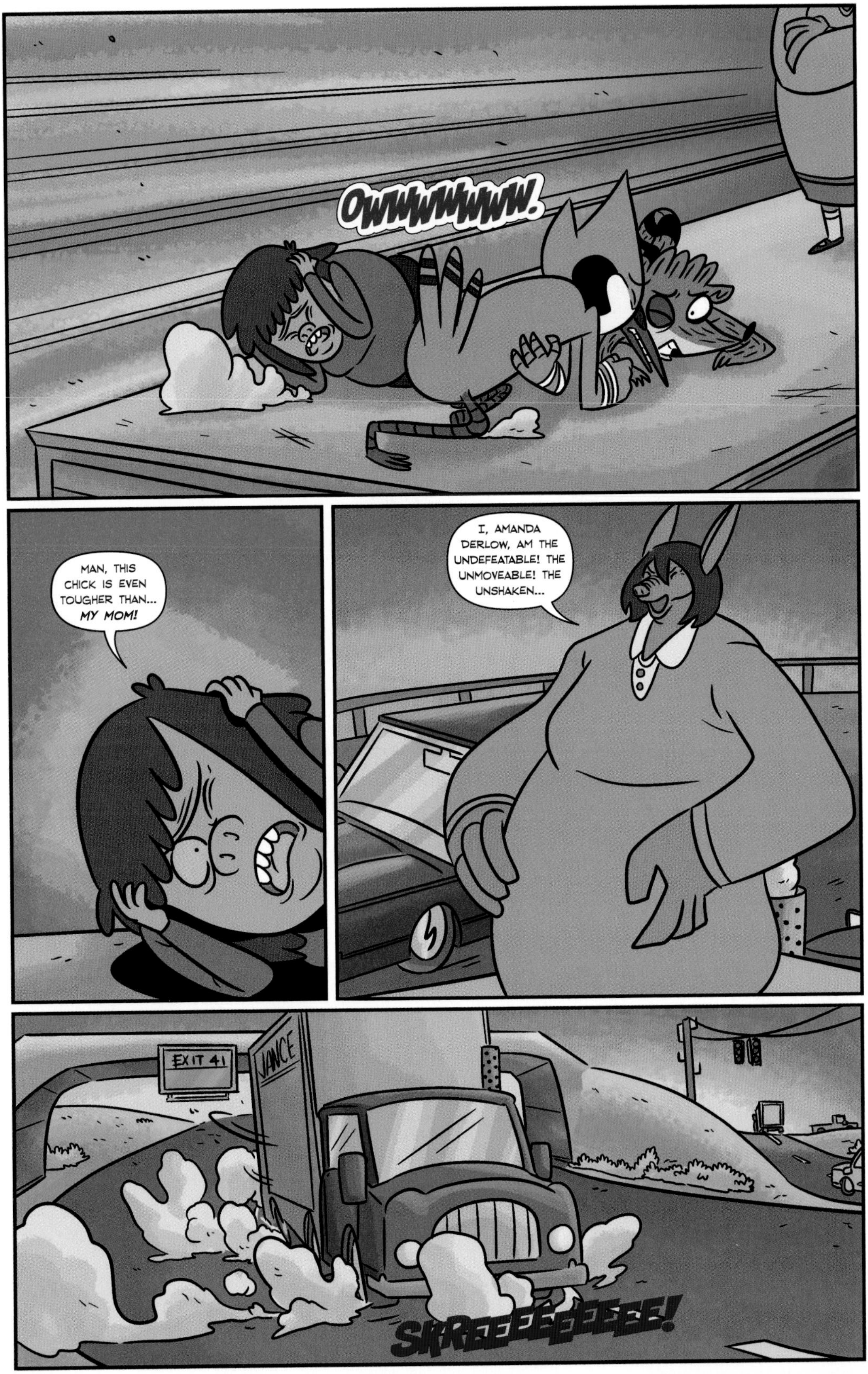
OWWWWWW!
MAN, THIS CHICK IS EVEN TOUGHER THAN... MY MOM!
I, AMANDA DERLOW, AM THE UNDEFEATABLE! THE UNMOVEABLE! THE UNSHAKEN...
EXIT 41
VANCE
SKREEEEEEEEEE!

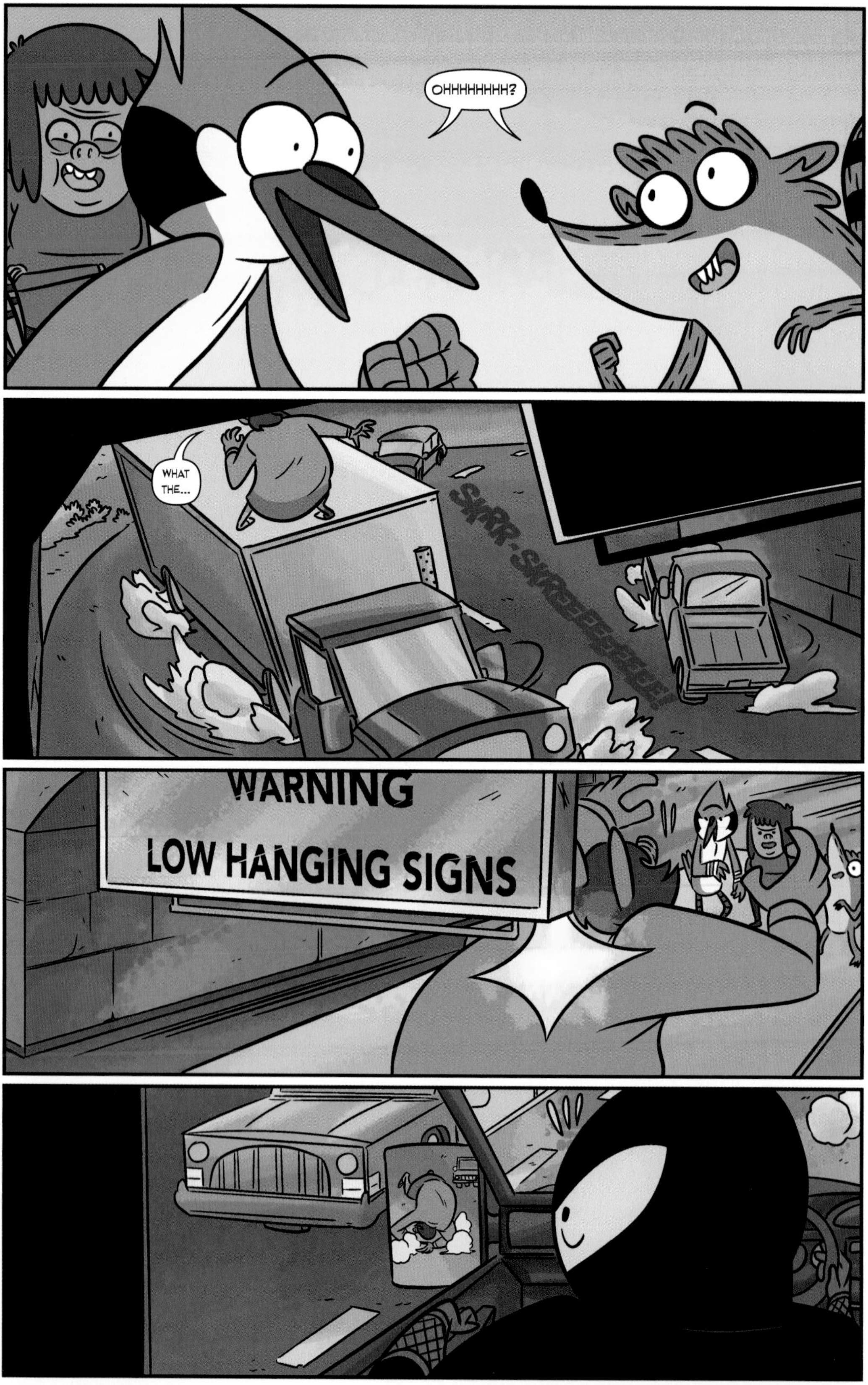
OHHHHHHHH?
WHAT THE...
SKRR-SKREEEEEEEE!!
WARNING
LOW HANGING SIGNS

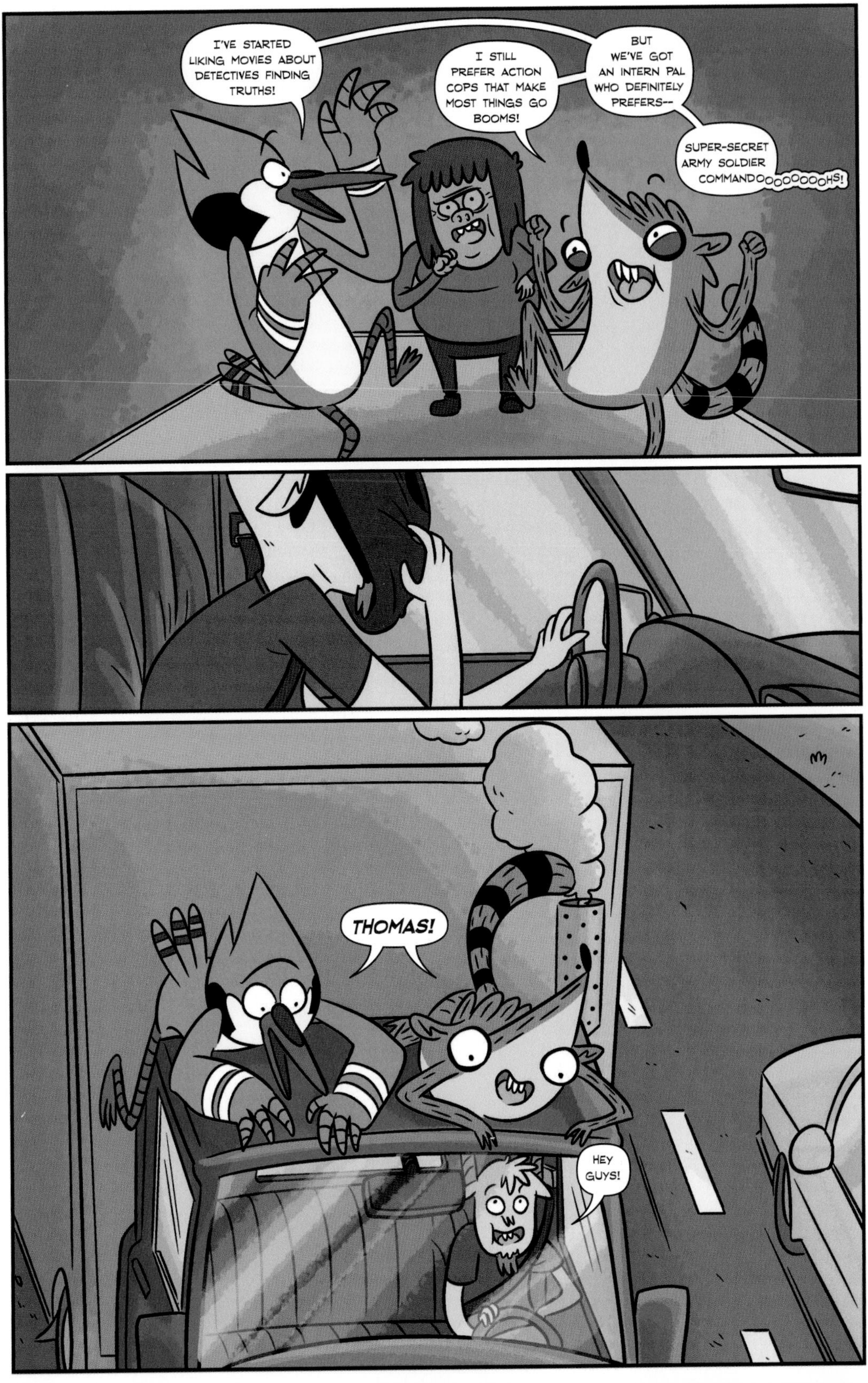
I'VE STARTED LIKING MOVIES ABOUT DETECTIVES FINDING TRUTHS!
I STILL PREFER ACTION COPS THAT MAKE MOST THINGS GO BOOMS!
BUT WE'VE GOT AN INTERN PAL WHO DEFINITELY PREFERS--
SUPER-SECRET ARMY SOLDIER COMMANDOOOOOOOOOHS!
THOMAS!
HEY GUYS!

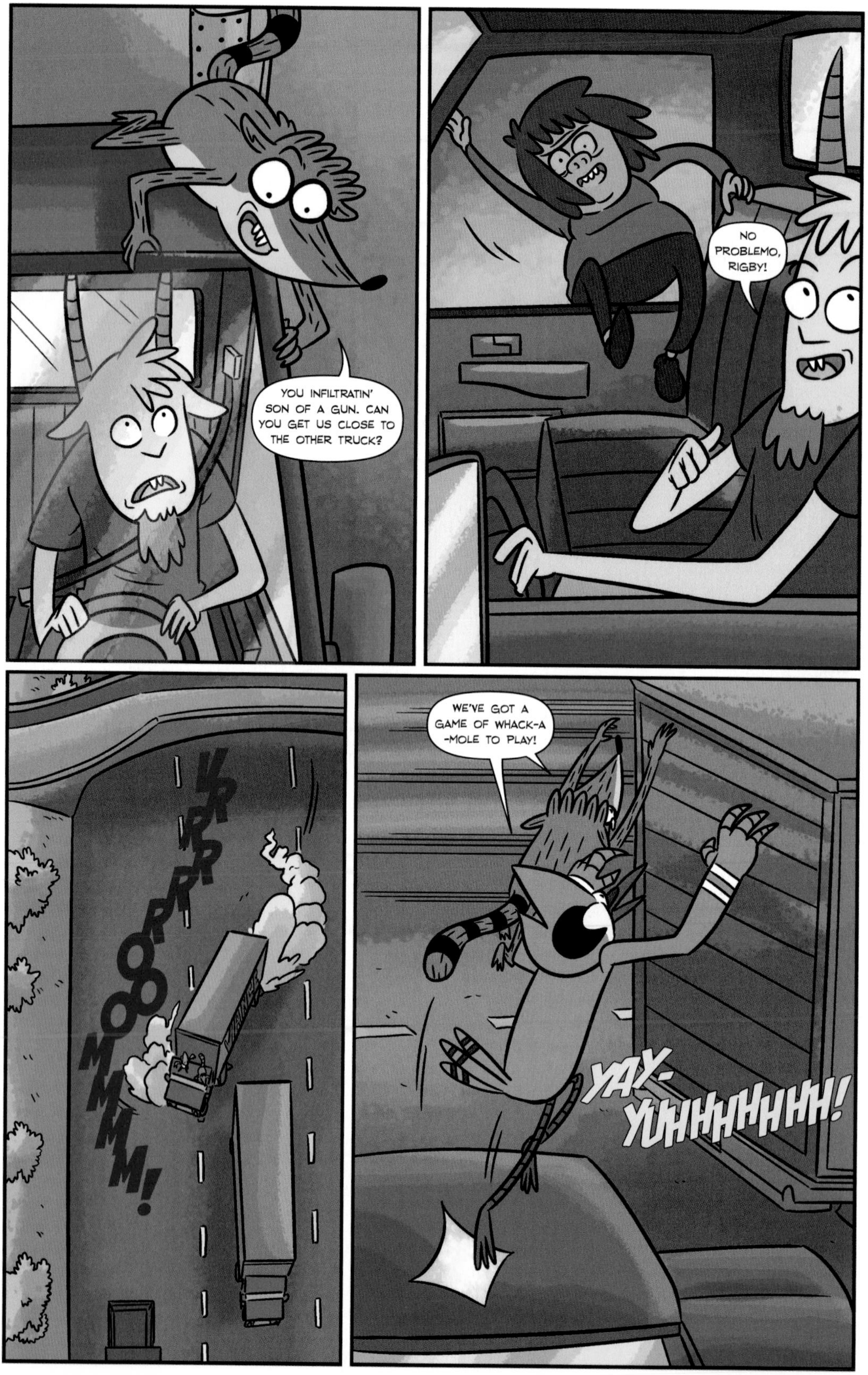
YOU INFILTRATIN' SON OF A GUN. CAN YOU GET US CLOSE TO THE OTHER TRUCK?
NO PROBLEMO, RIGBY!
VRRRRROOOOMMMMM!
WE'VE GOT A GAME OF WHACK-A-MOLE TO PLAY!
YAY-YUHHHHHHH!

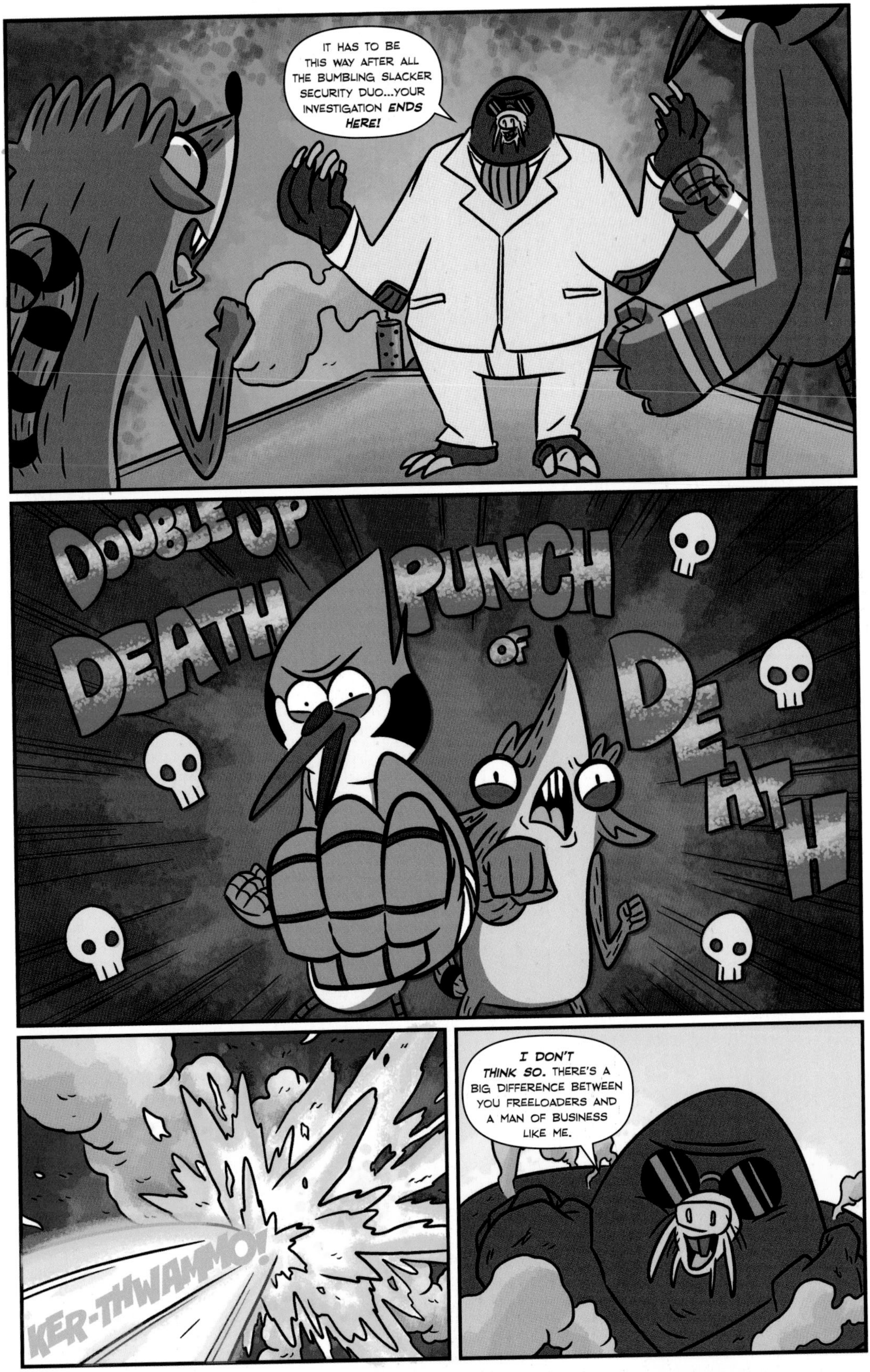

IT HAS TO BE THIS WAY AFTER ALL THE BUMBLING SLACKER SECURITY DUO...YOUR INVESTIGATION ENDS HERE!
DOUBLE-UP DEATH PUNCH OF DEATH
KER-THWAMMO!
I DON'T THINK SO. THERE'S A BIG DIFFERENCE BETWEEN YOU FREELOADERS AND A MAN OF BUSINESS LIKE ME.

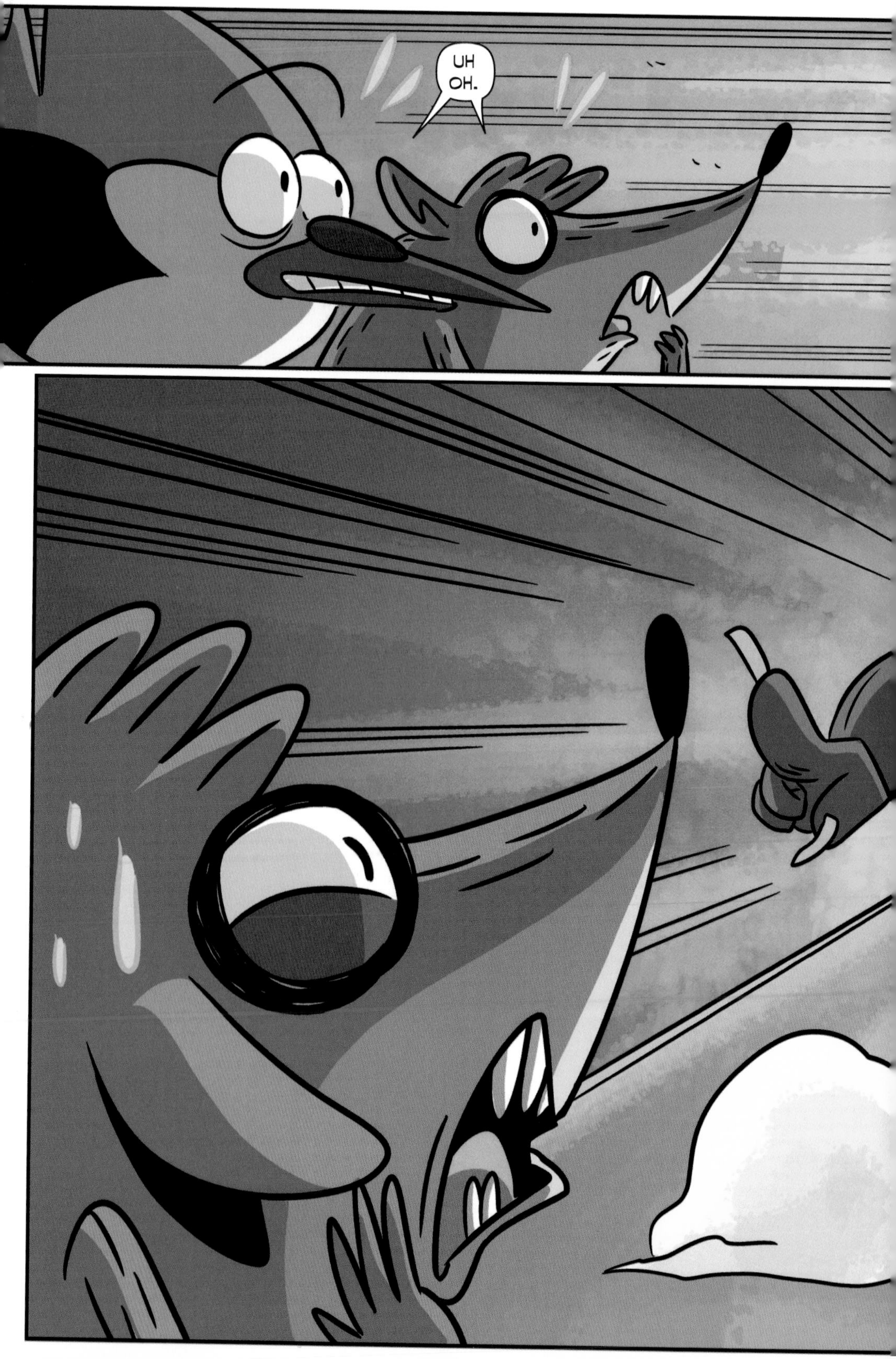
UH OH.

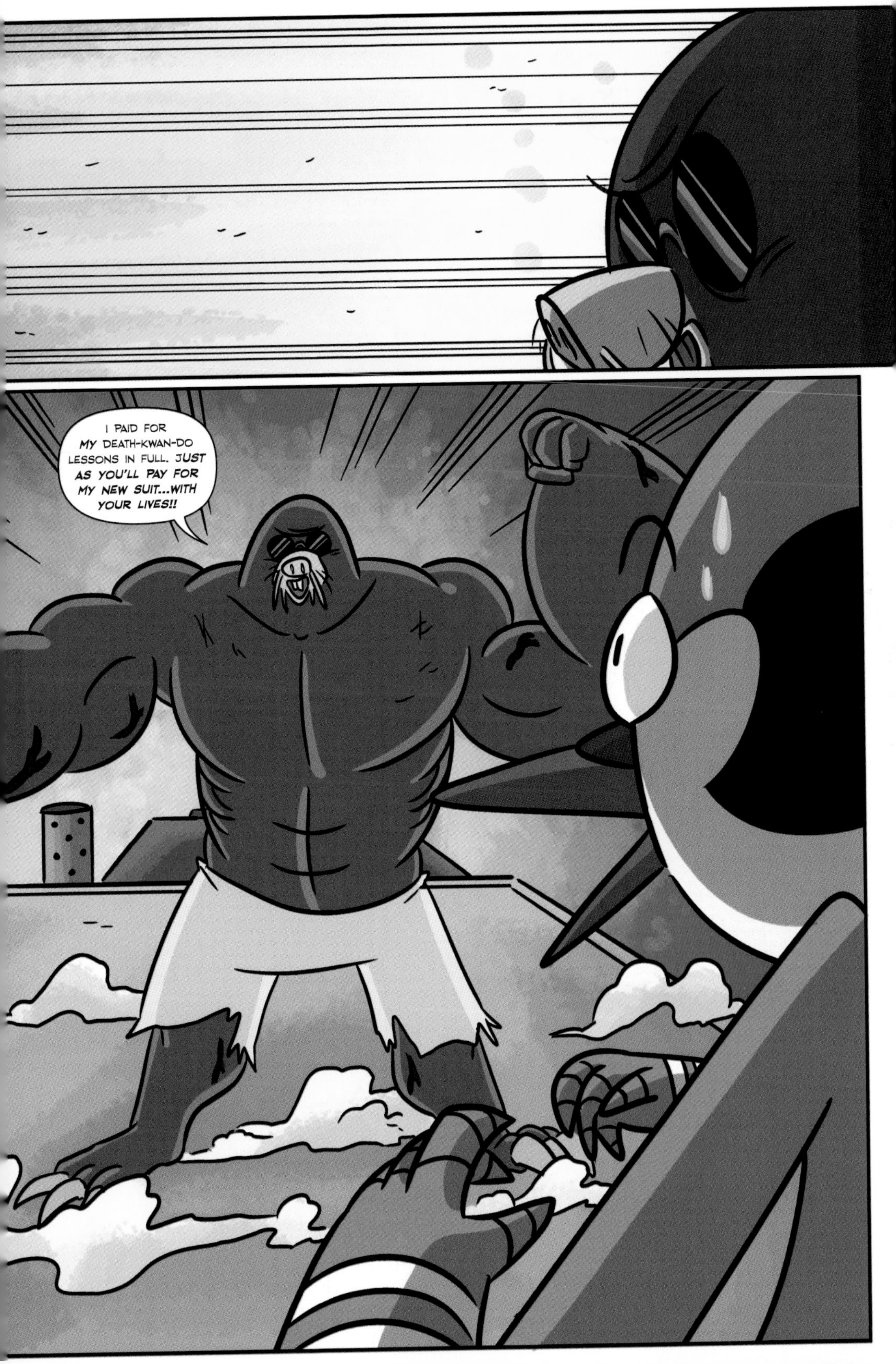
I PAID FOR MY DEATH-KWAN-DO LESSONS IN FULL. JUST AS YOU'LL PAY FOR MY NEW SUIT...WITH YOUR LIVES!!

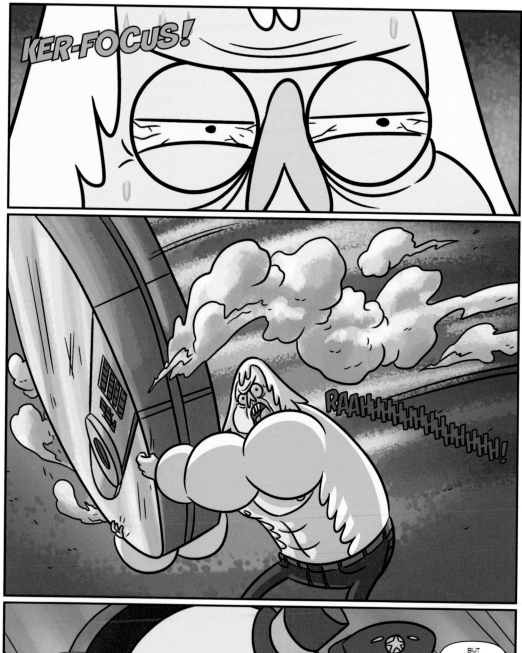

KER-FOCUS!

RAAHHHHHHHHHH!

NOW I ALSO DON'T HAVE A SECRET VAULT LEFT, EITHER...

BUT AT LEAST WE HAVE OUR LIVES, POPS.

YES, BENSON, THE GREATEST TREASURE OF ALL!

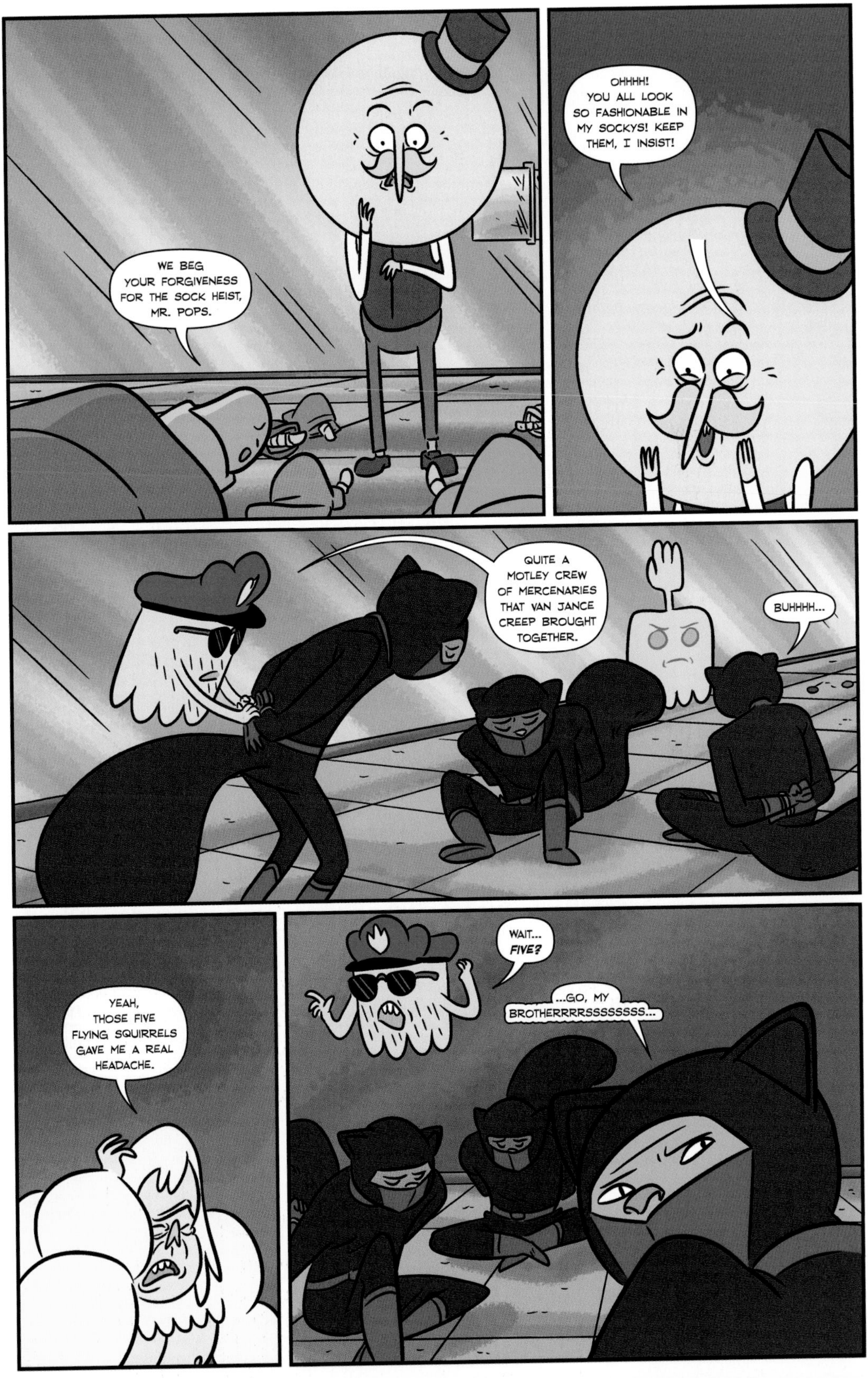
WE BEG YOUR FORGIVENESS FOR THE SOCK HEIST, MR. POPS.
OHHHH! YOU ALL LOOK SO FASHIONABLE IN MY SOCKYS! KEEP THEM, I INSIST!
QUITE A MOTLEY CREW OF MERCENARIES THAT VAN JANCE CREEP BROUGHT TOGETHER.
BUHHHH...
YEAH, THOSE FIVE FLYING SQUIRRELS GAVE ME A REAL HEADACHE.
WAIT... *FIVE?*
...GO, MY BROTHERRRRSSSSSSSS...

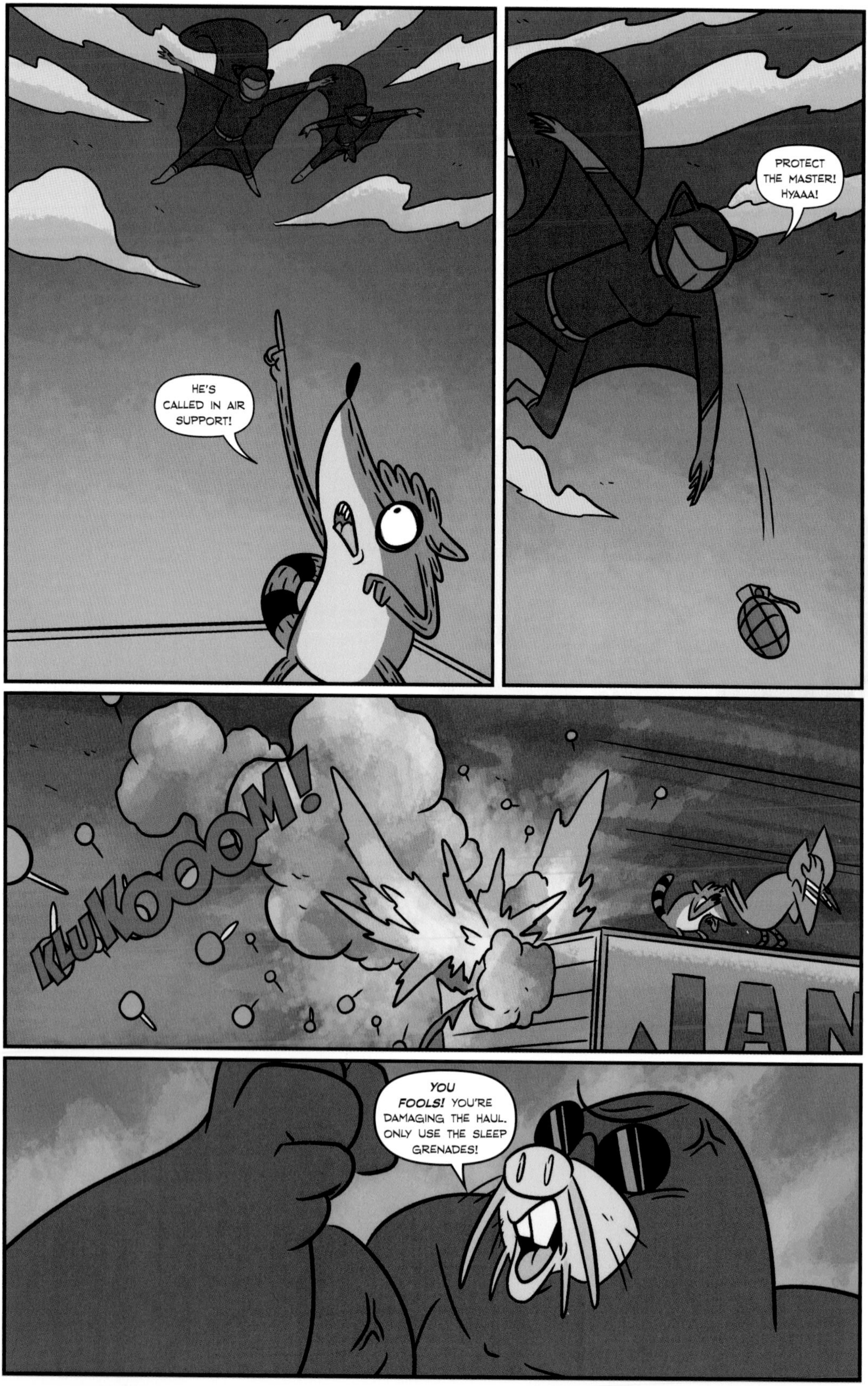
HE'S CALLED IN AIR SUPPORT!
PROTECT THE MASTER! HYAAA!
KLUKOOOM!
YOU FOOLS! YOU'RE DAMAGING THE HAUL. ONLY USE THE SLEEP GRENADES!

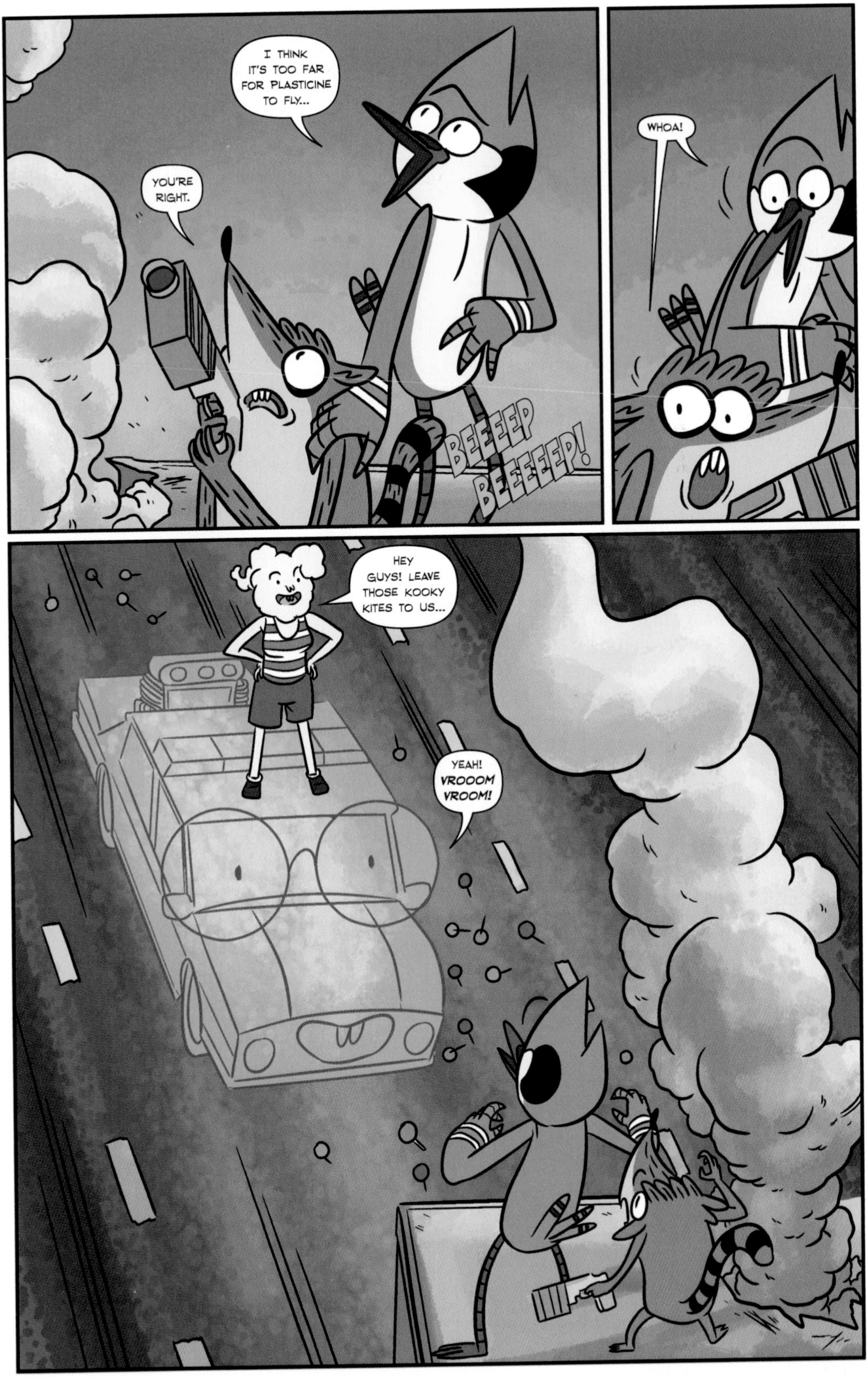
I THINK IT'S TOO FAR FOR PLASTICINE TO FLY...
YOU'RE RIGHT.
BEEEEP BEEEEEP!
WHOA!
HEY GUYS! LEAVE THOSE KOOKY KITES TO US...
YEAH! VROOOM VROOM!

...AND OUR NEW FRIENDS!

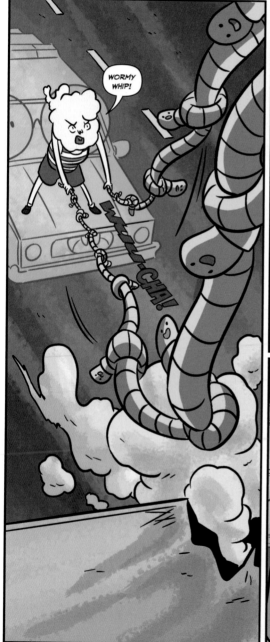

WORMY WHIP!

WHU-CHA!

ULP!

KER-SNARE!

YANKO!

TOTALLY AWESOME!

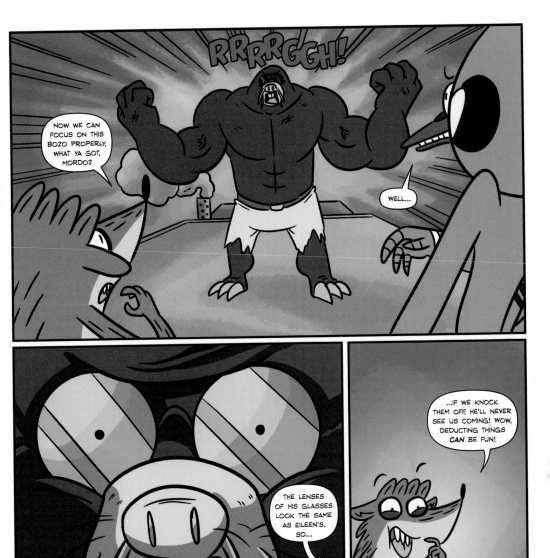

RRRRGGH!

NOW WE CAN FOCUS ON THIS BOZO PROPERLY. WHAT YA GOT, MORDO?

WELL...

THE LENSES OF HIS GLASSES LOOK THE SAME AS EILEEN'S. SO...

...IF WE KNOCK THEM OFF, HE'LL NEVER SEE US COMING! WOW, DEDUCTING THINGS *CAN* BE FUN!

BREAK TIME IS OVER! I'M GONNA SELL YOU BUMS A *TIMESHARE OF AGONY!*

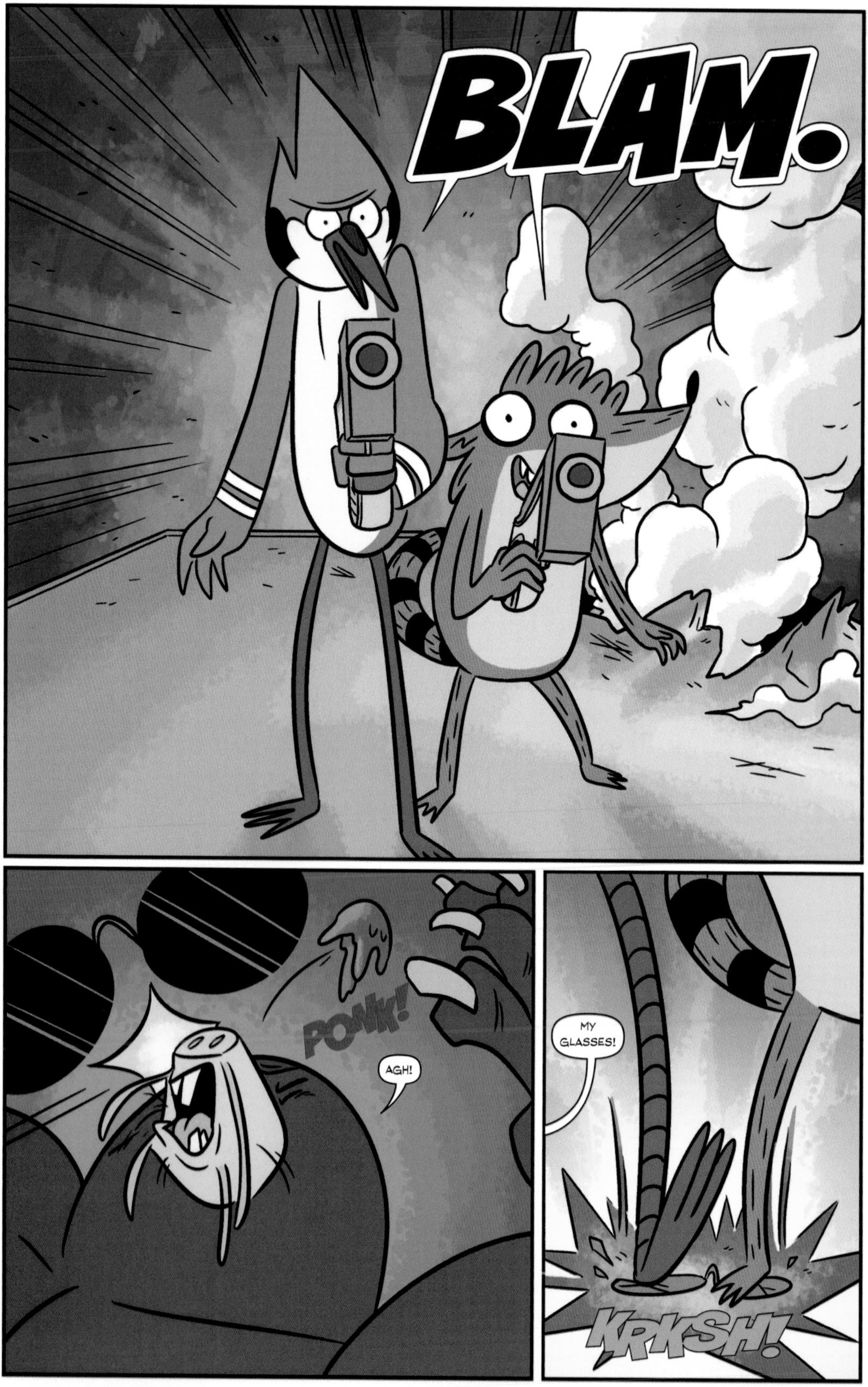
BLAM.
PONK!
AGH!
MY GLASSES!
KRKSH!

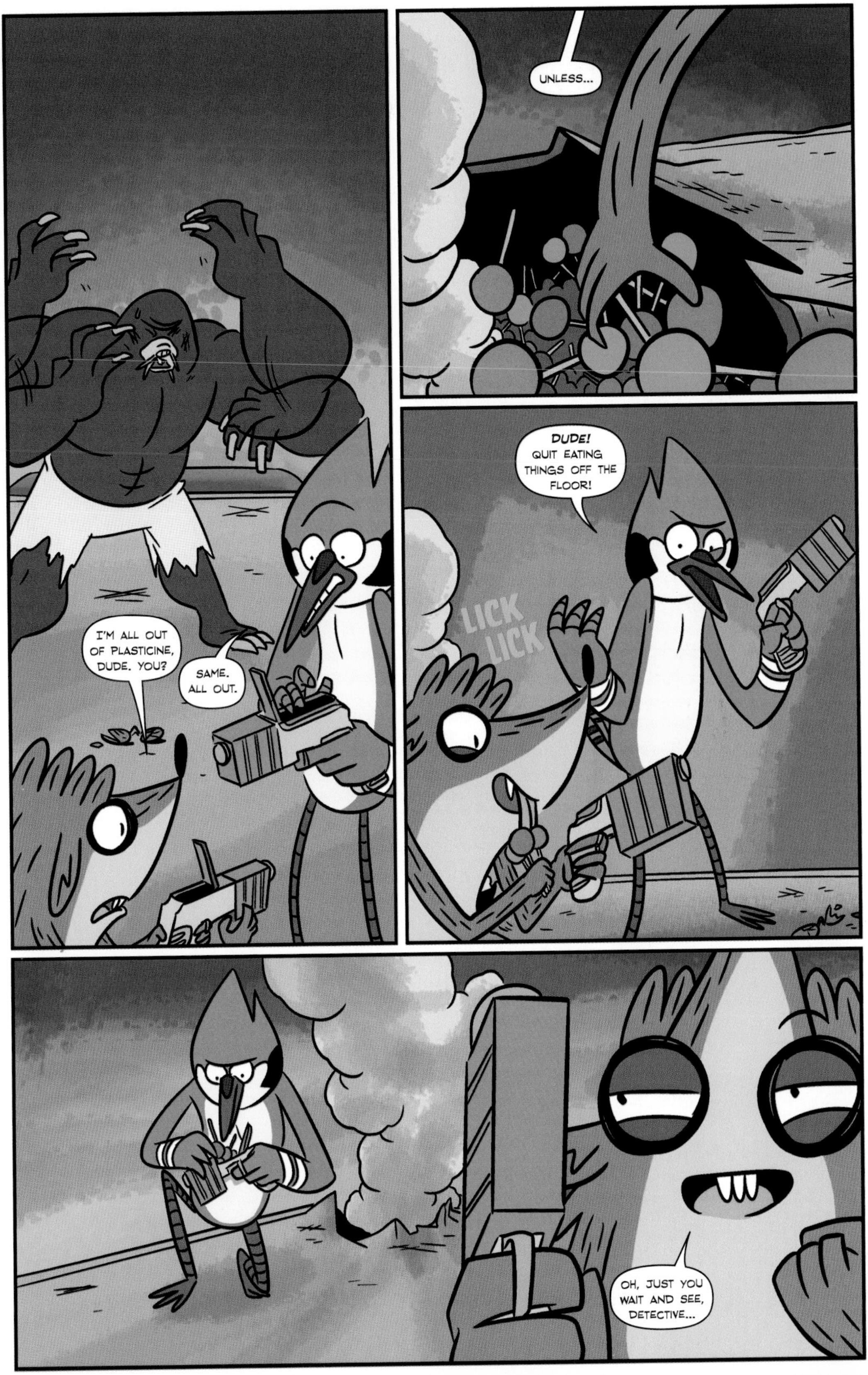
UNLESS...
I'M ALL OUT OF PLASTICINE, DUDE. YOU?
SAME. ALL OUT.
DUDE! QUIT EATING THINGS OFF THE FLOOR!
LICK LICK
OH, JUST YOU WAIT AND SEE, DETECTIVE...

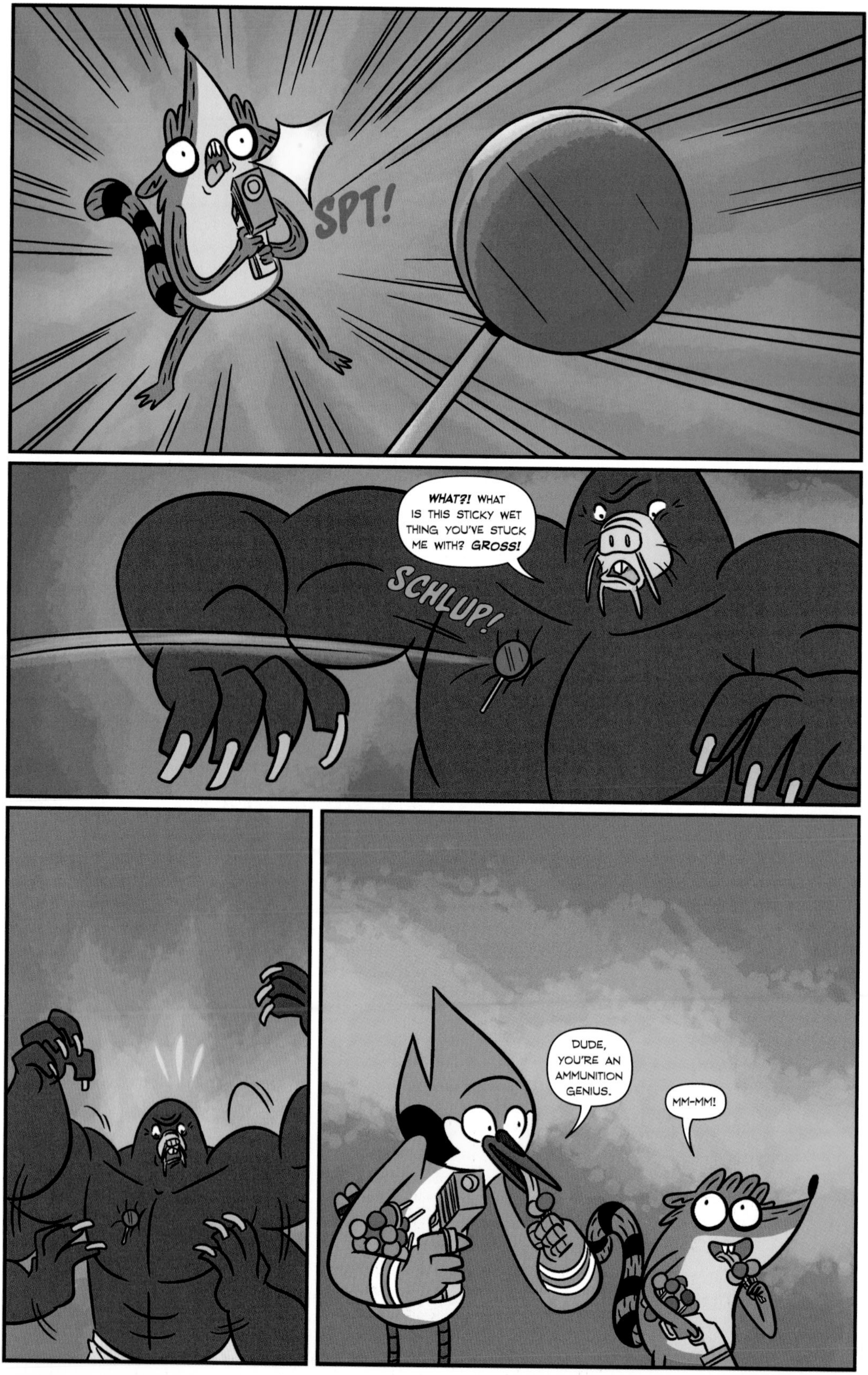
SPT!
WHAT?! WHAT IS THIS STICKY WET THING YOU'VE STUCK ME WITH? GROSS!
SCHLUP!
DUDE, YOU'RE AN AMMUNITION GENIUS.
MM-MM!

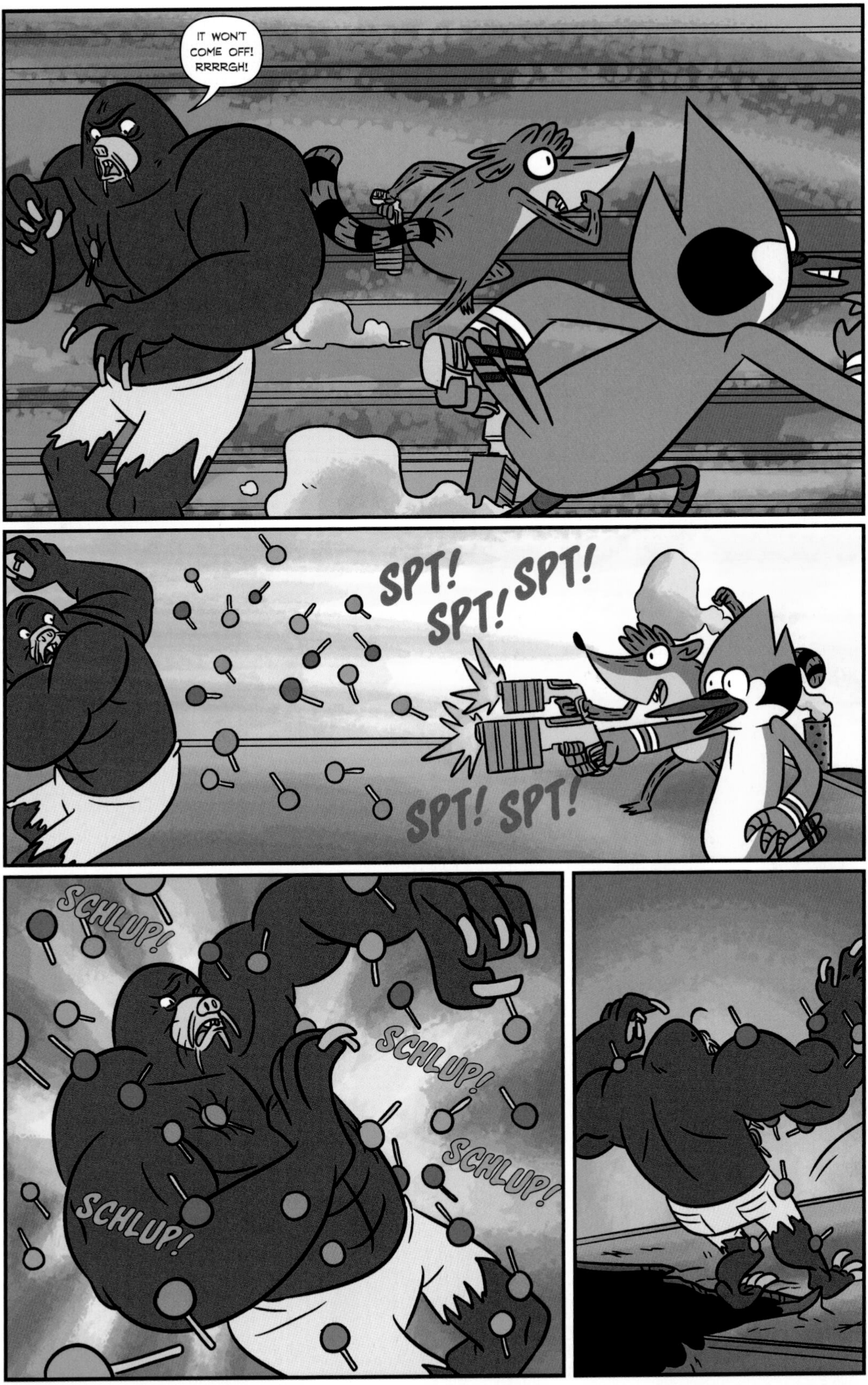
IT WON'T COME OFF! RRRRGH!
SPT!
SPT!
SPT!
SPT!
SPT!
SCHLUP!
SCHLUP!
SCHLUP!
SCHLUP!

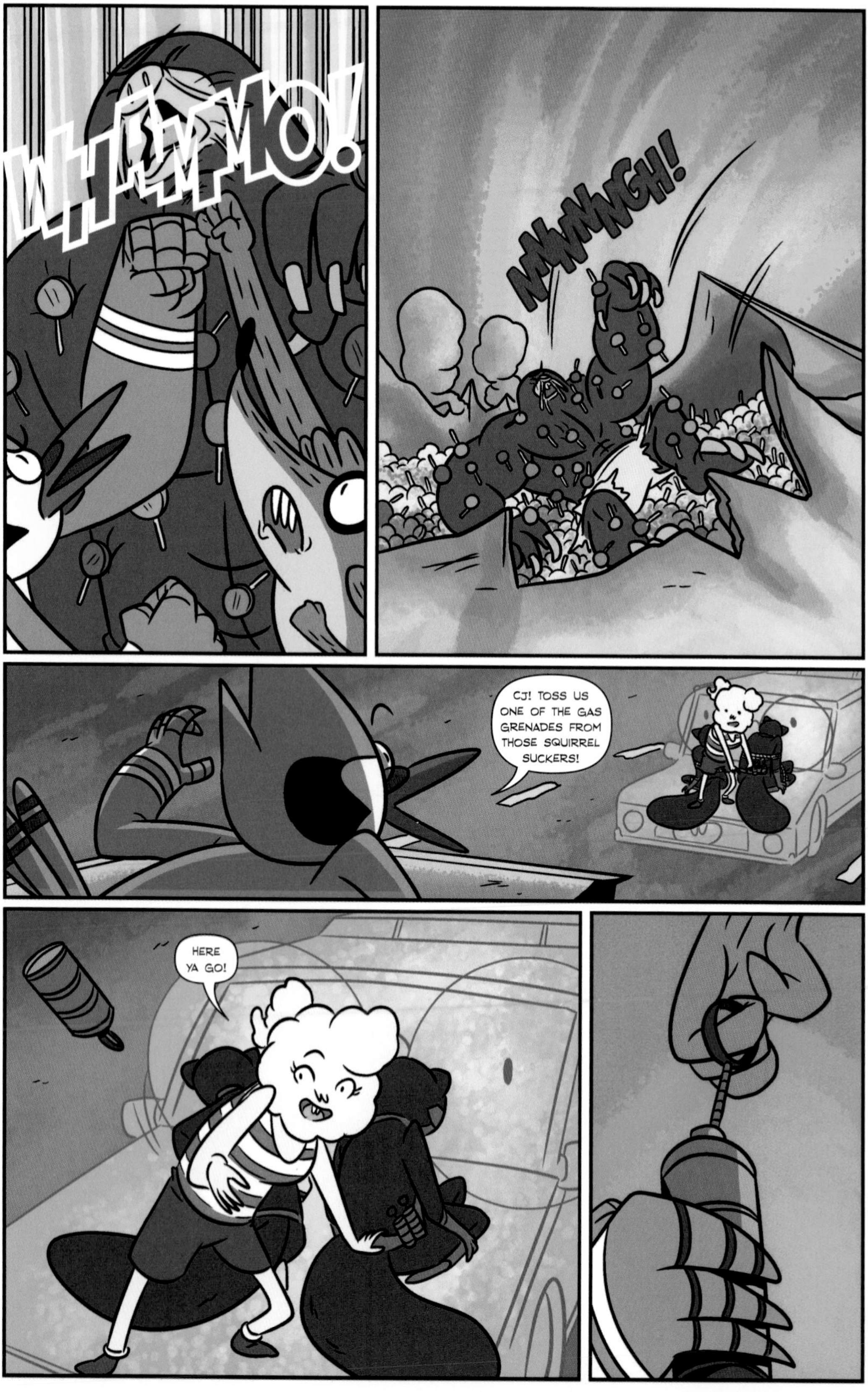
WHUMMO!
MNNNNGH!
CJ! TOSS US ONE OF THE GAS GRENADES FROM THOSE SQUIRREL SUCKERS!
HERE YA GO!

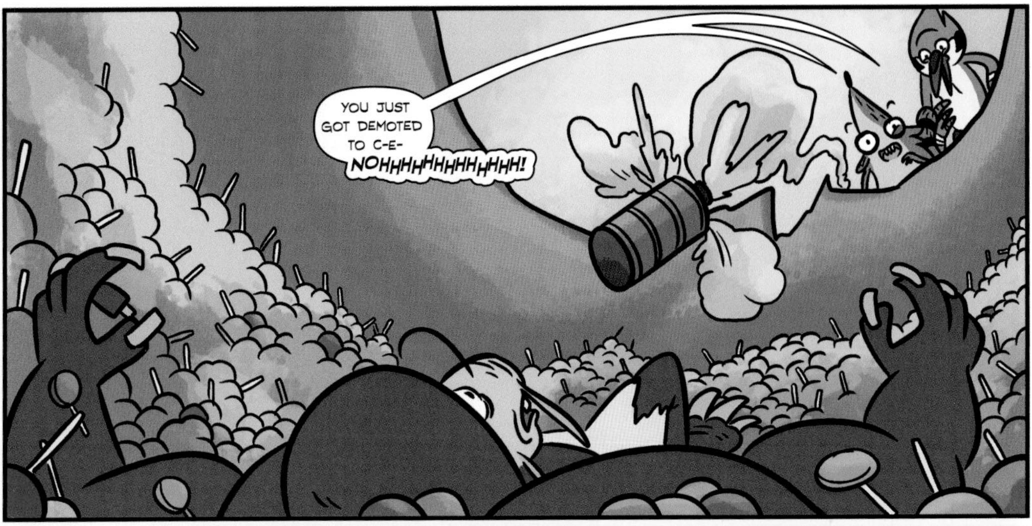
YOU JUST GOT DEMOTED TO C-E-
NOHHHHHHHHHHHHH!
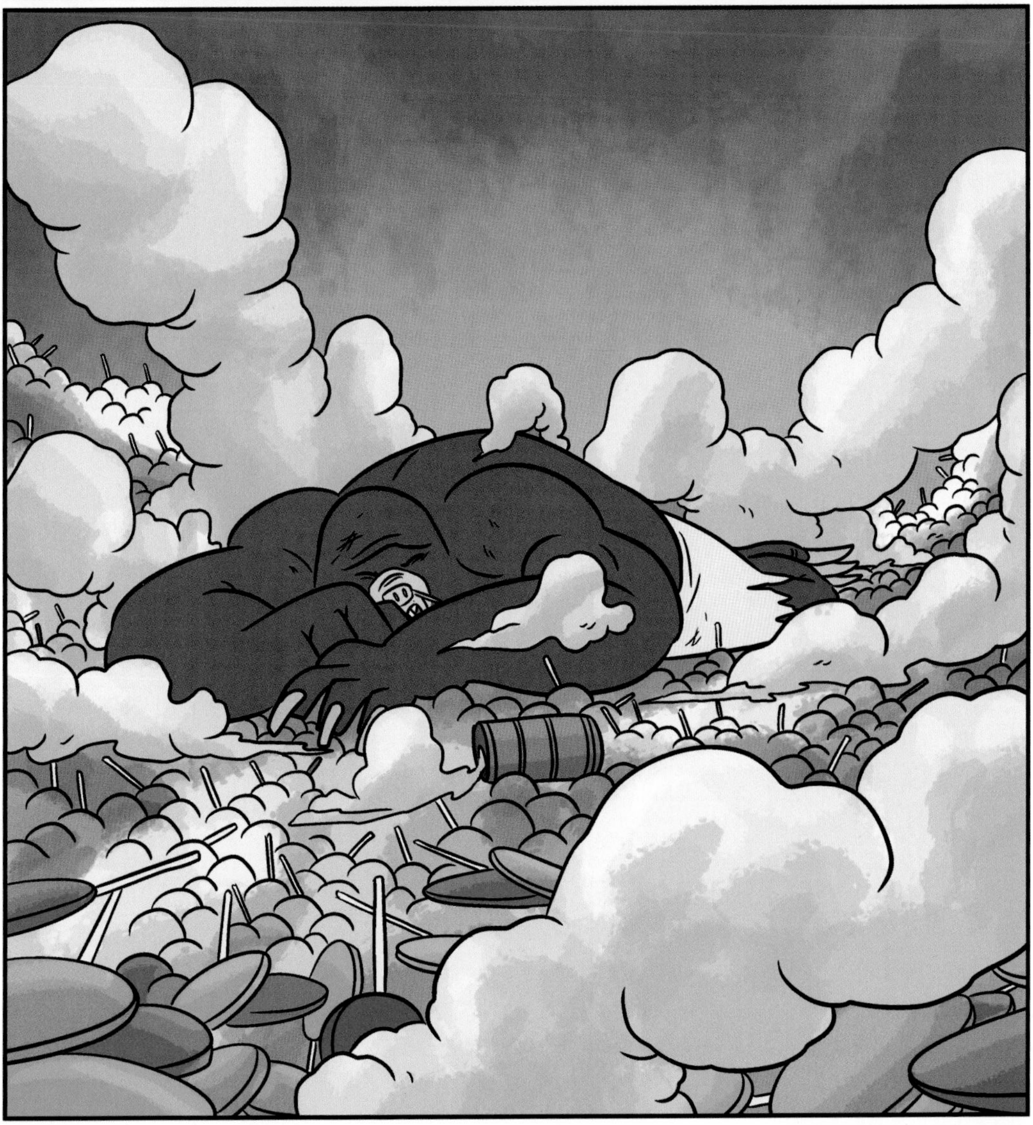

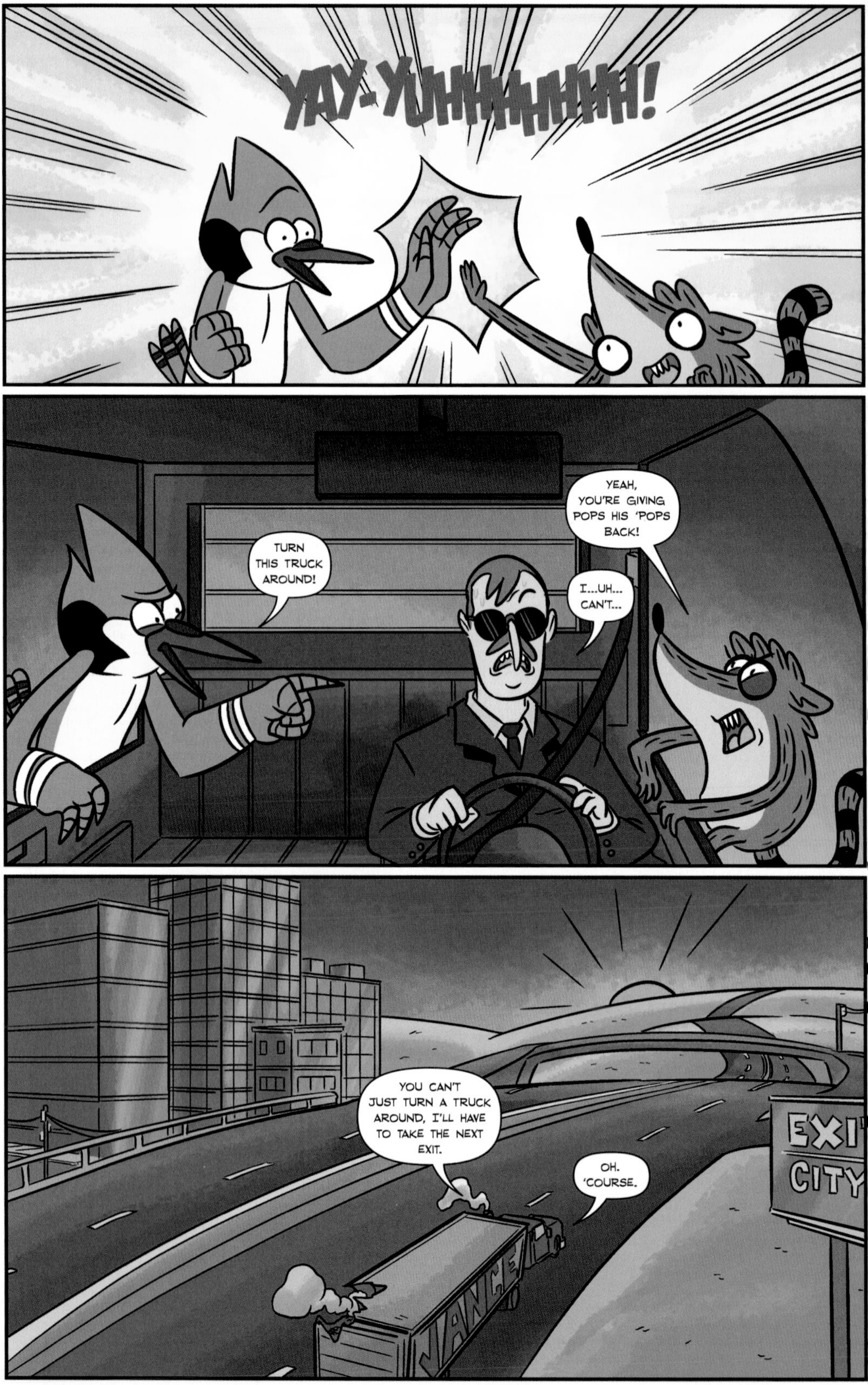
YAY-YUHHHHHHH!
TURN THIS TRUCK AROUND!
YEAH, YOU'RE GIVING POPS HIS 'POPS BACK!
I...UH... CAN'T...
YOU CAN'T JUST TURN A TRUCK AROUND, I'LL HAVE TO TAKE THE NEXT EXIT.
OH. 'COURSE.
JANCE
EXI
CITY

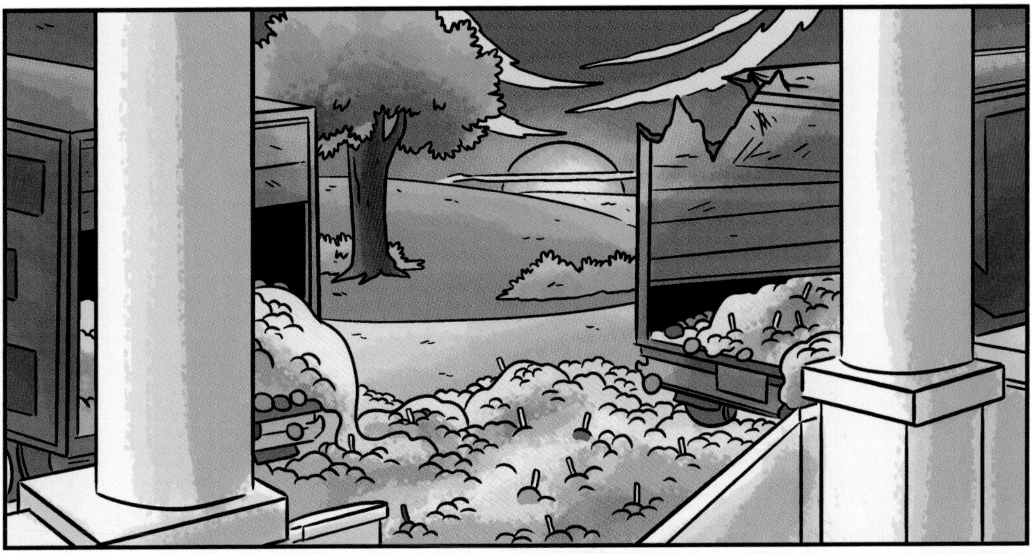

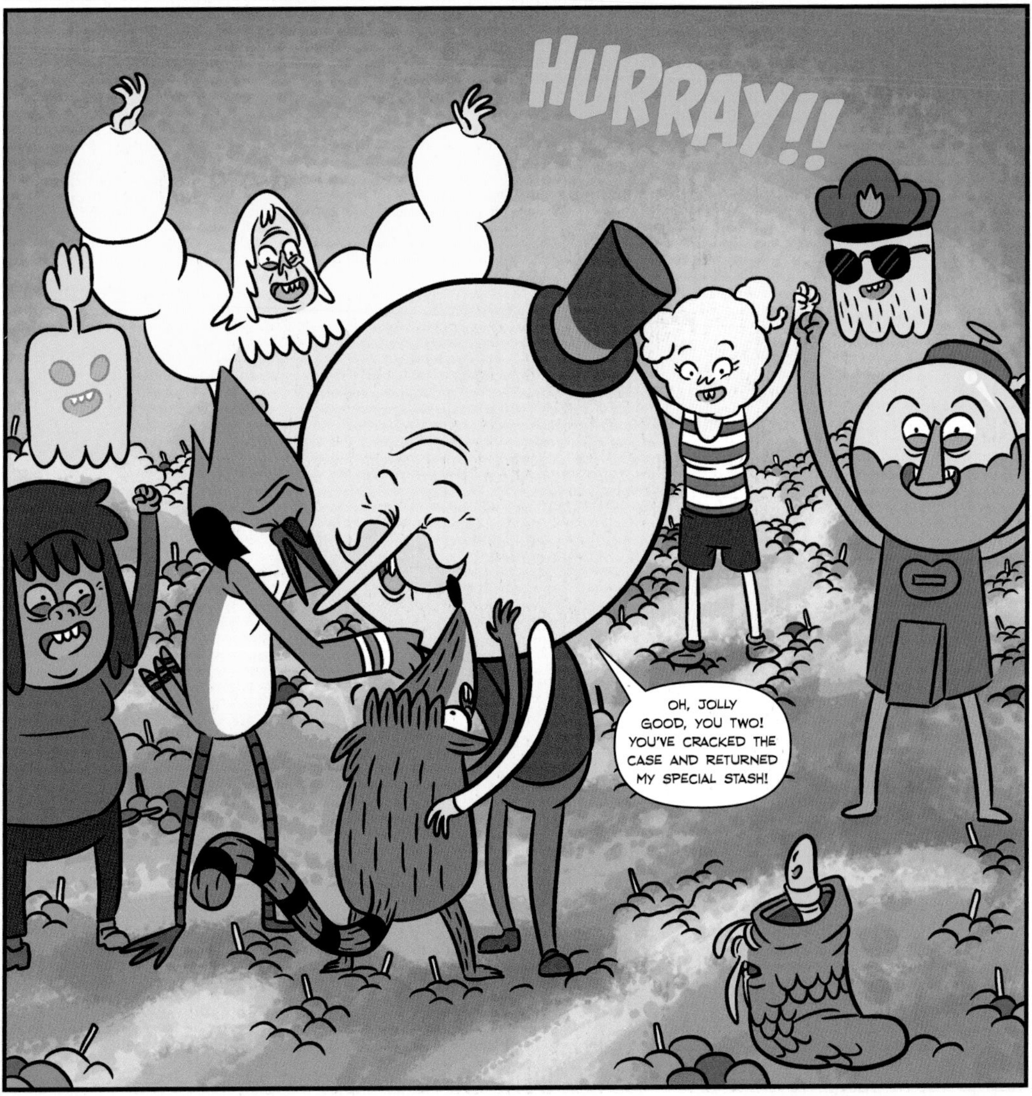
HURRAY!!
OH, JOLLY GOOD, YOU TWO! YOU'VE CRACKED THE CASE AND RETURNED MY SPECIAL STASH!

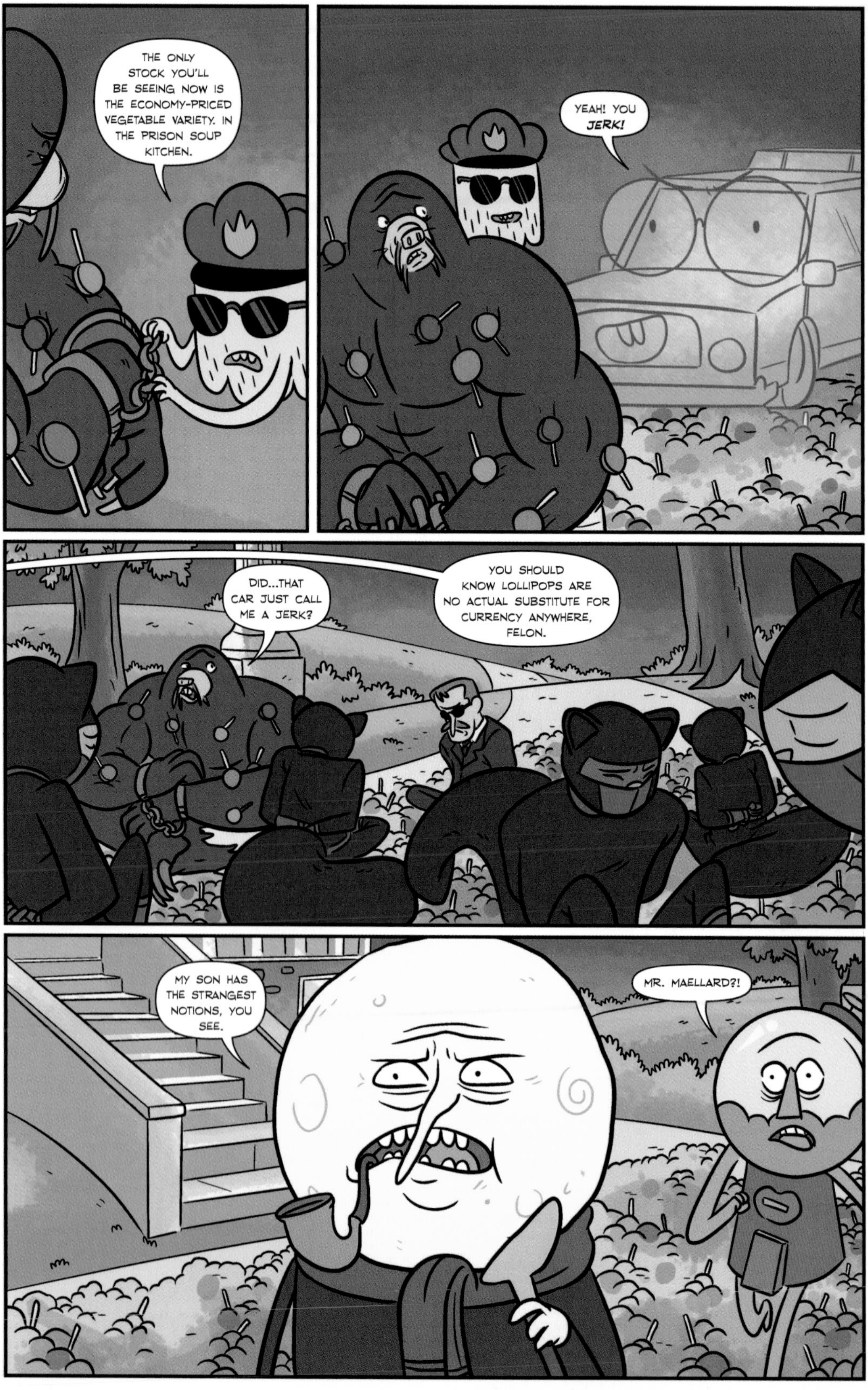
THE ONLY STOCK YOU'LL BE SEEING NOW IS THE ECONOMY-PRICED VEGETABLE VARIETY. IN THE PRISON SOUP KITCHEN.
YEAH! YOU *JERK!*
DID...THAT CAR JUST CALL ME A JERK?
YOU SHOULD KNOW LOLLIPOPS ARE NO ACTUAL SUBSTITUTE FOR CURRENCY ANYWHERE, FELON.
MY SON HAS THE STRANGEST NOTIONS, YOU SEE.
MR. MAELLARD?!

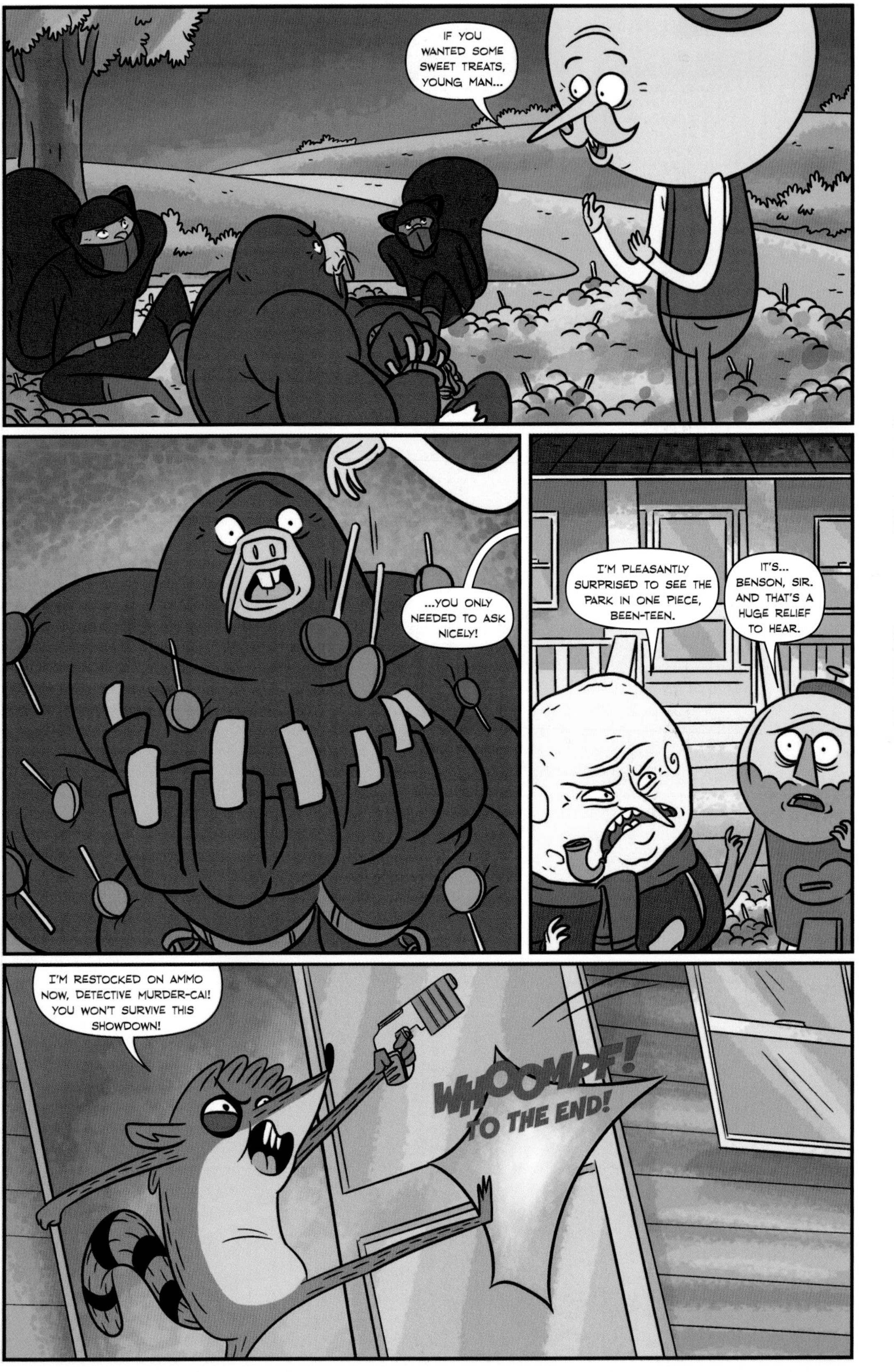
IF YOU WANTED SOME SWEET TREATS, YOUNG MAN...
...YOU ONLY NEEDED TO ASK NICELY!
I'M PLEASANTLY SURPRISED TO SEE THE PARK IN ONE PIECE, BEEN-TEEN.
IT'S... BENSON, SIR. AND THAT'S A HUGE RELIEF TO HEAR.
I'M RESTOCKED ON AMMO NOW, DETECTIVE MURDER-CAI! YOU WON'T SURVIVE THIS SHOWDOWN!
WHOOMPF!
TO THE END!

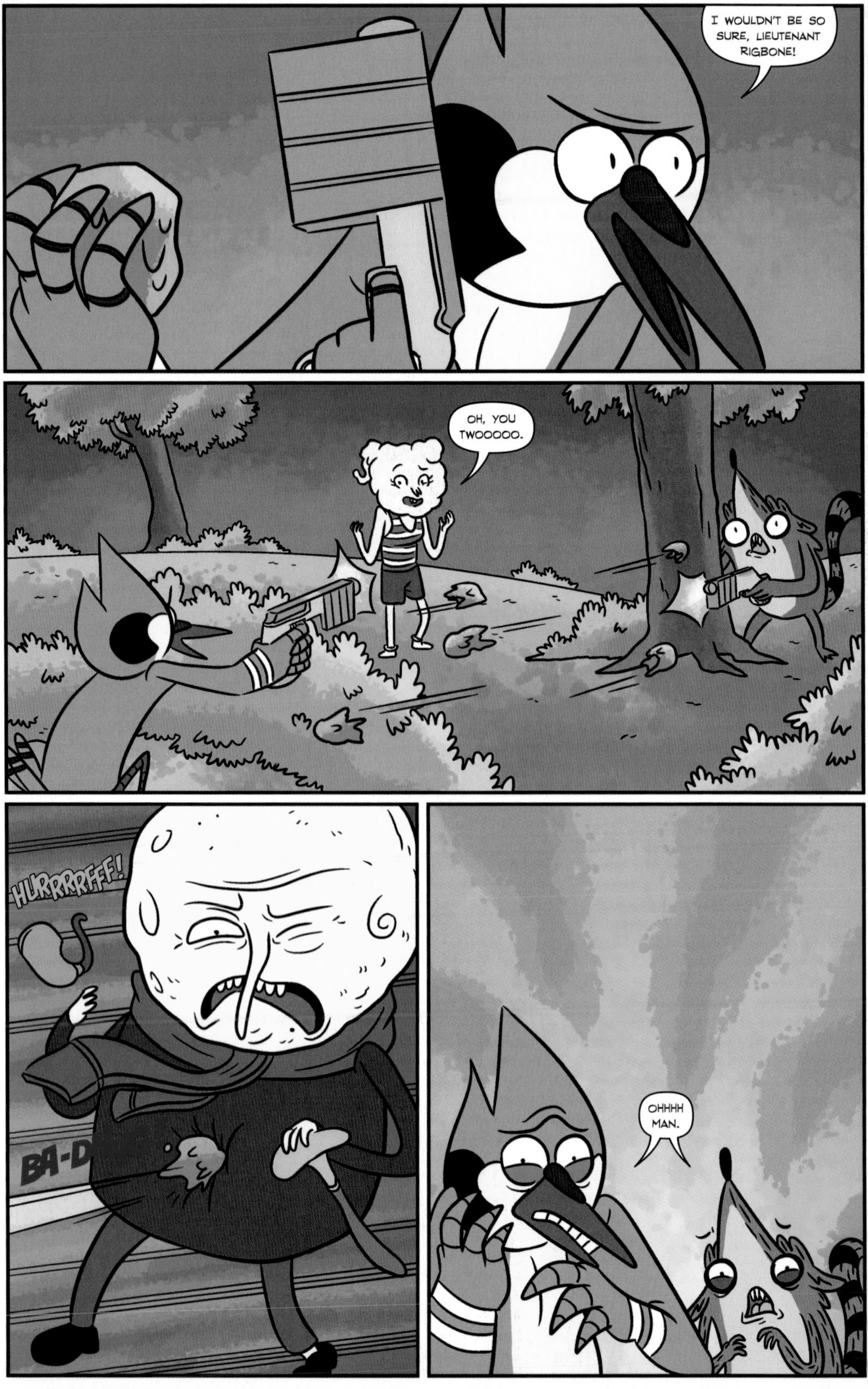
I WOULDN'T BE SO SURE, LIEUTENANT RIGBONE!
OH, YOU TWOOOOO.
HURRRRFFF!
BA-D
OHHHH MAN.

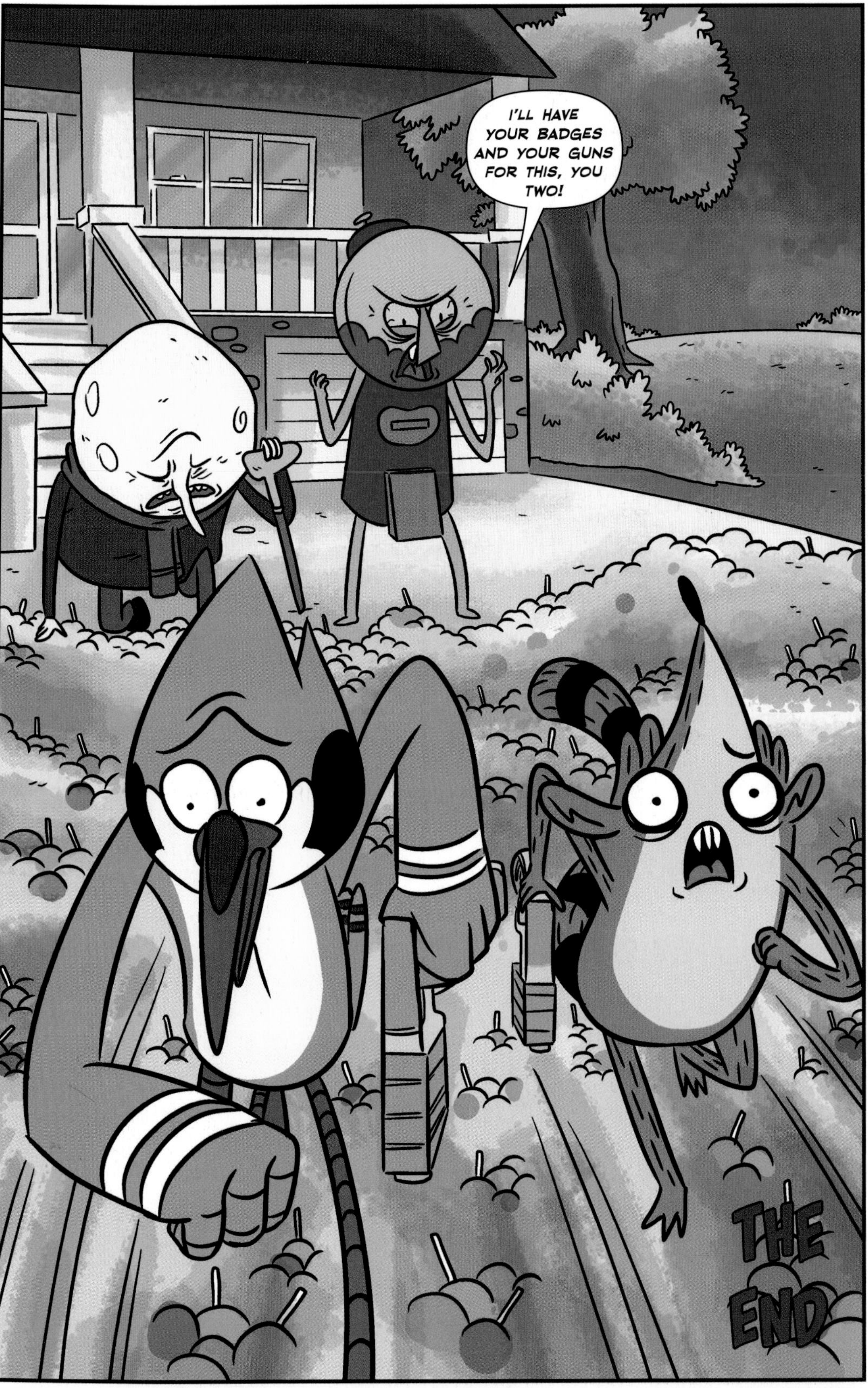
I'LL HAVE YOUR BADGES AND YOUR GUNS FOR THIS, YOU TWO!
THE END

SPRING 2016

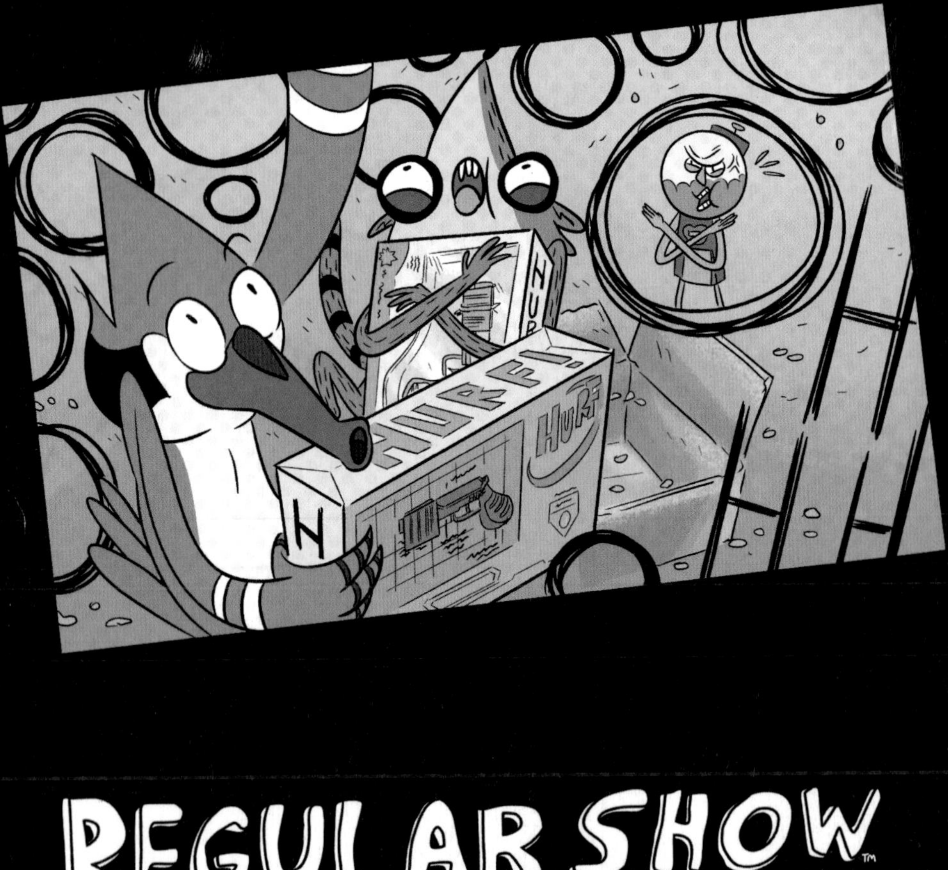

HURF!
HURF
H
HUR

REGULAR SHOW™

VOLUME 3